A KINGDOM OF IRON & WINE

THE IRONWORLD SERIES

BOOK ONE

Candace Osmond

Dedication

To my past self. The baby author.
I knew you could do it.

Acknowledgements

Thanks to those who've been reading since day one. And Corey. Thanks for sticking with me while I got it right.

Prologue

"Just like the moon, she had a side of her so dark that even the stars couldn't shine on it. So cold that even the sun wouldn't dare burn against it." - **Unknown**

I tipped my head back and closed my eyes as cool night air floated in through the open window of my stone-cased study. It caressed the back of my throat, mixed with the inhale of my cigar. And that's when I could smell her coming. Could see her in my mind for hours now. The young Summer Fae traipsing through the Dark Forest in search of me. How valiant she was to brave all that the wretched forest offered. None of it pleasant. For a Summer Fae, anyway.

But this one endured.

Children of Summer rarely ventured this far. To my fortress of stone and glass and darkness. A Dark Lord's home. But this one reeked of sunshine and desperation. She *needed* me.

The lovely creature was just a few yards away now. With a gentle squeeze of my hand, I gripped the fabric of everything around me and left the comforts of my study to appear just outside the front door. To greet her. I could smell the burn of the sun carried by whiffs of cherries from the black cherry trees that thickly lined my side of the forest.

She emerged from it, covered in dark splotches of red and purple. Only heightened by the stark, blood-red hair that hung down across the front of her torn, stained cotton dress. Her crazed eyes—like glittering emeralds—scanned and found me. And when her heaving body relaxed with relief, I realized... she was the most incredible thing I'd ever seen.

What corner of Summer did she crawl from?

"Dark Lord," she addressed, chin raised and still out of breath, but she fought to hide it.

I stuffed a casual hand inside the broad pocket of my black coat as I flicked the last of my cigar into a murky puddle. "Oden is fine." We sized one another up for a moment. She'd trespassed, and she knew it.

I watched as her wide green eyes raked over me,

scrutinizing every line. "You're not what I expected."

"Oh?" I raised a curious brow, surprised by her audacity. "And what *did* you expect? A leather-winged monster? An old crony consumed by his own darkness?"

She shook her head. I wanted to reach out and ring my finger through one of her blood-red locks that tipped the ends of her long hair. "I thought… I'd heard…." The female gestured up and down at my appearance. "I just wasn't expecting…*this*. Tall and handsome, draped in black velvet. Hair like…"

"Like what?" It'd been so long since someone stroked my ego. Was this a tactic? *She's clever, then.*

As if she could read my mind, her gaze lowered and narrowed. In an instant, she became a cunning and admirable foe. "White, like doves' wings. As if… you're trying too hard to appeal to me."

Did she know? That I could cut her half in the blink of an eye? Throw my darkness in a blade through the air and slice her in two, three, even four pieces if I wanted to. She was a trespasser. Albeit, she'd somehow survived the horrors of the Dark Forest. But I'd already let her stand in my domain longer than any other outsider ever dared. But something about this one spoke to me. Called to my darkness with questions and demands. And part of me wanted to give it to her.

So, I changed the subject.

"What brings you to this depth of hell?" I gently motioned a wave at the wall of thick trees behind her.

"My sister has caught the eye of the Summer Lord."

Kheelan. I stifled a grumble. Pompous, warmonger.

"They're to be wed within the year," she added.

"And you wish to… steal him from her?" I asked.

"No, no," she replied and sucked in a deep breath. Her scent suddenly filled with a strained sense of love. She loved her sister, but jealousy consumed her. "I wish to… find my own love."

My eyes flashed a warning. "You won't find that in my domain, dearie."

She straightened, her expression stark and cunning. Oh, she'd make a fine queen, indeed. "Won't I?"

"What is it you truly seek?" I demanded curtly. My patience was already waning.

"I need…" The Summer Fae rapidly blinked through her thoughts, then clenched both fists at her sides. "I need a love potion."

I couldn't hide my surprise. "A love potion, you say?" I turned and slowly paced in front of her. Testing how much my presence intimidated her. But she didn't so much as flinch. "And what makes you think such a thing can be done?"

She looked me firmly in the eyes and, for a split second, I saw madness there. A flicker of it. Waiting to be ignited.

"I know it can." She whipped a small knife from her belt and dragged the blade across her palm before turning it over.

My eyes widened. "What are you–"

Blood dripped to the earth at our feet. *My* earth. *My* domain.

I didn't bother hiding the annoyance in my sigh as I pinched the space between my eyes. "*Where* did you learn that?"

The female shrugged. "It doesn't matter. What *does* matter is you're now bound to me. You must bid me one request."

Curse those ancient laws. Ridiculous binds and wards created by Therians that unfortunately could be used by Fae, as well. Our world was never the same once word spread of what could be done to us. To use us. Control us. It sickened me.

"A love potion." My back teeth grit together.

She nodded with confidence. "A love potion."

I stared, unblinking. So did she. Could I use this to my advantage? She was a pretty thing, clearly a strong female. Powerful? That was yet to be determined. I kept my expression even. "I have conditions."

"Of course."

"I need to know who it's intended to be used on." A whiff of panic filled her scent, but she nodded. "And I

CANDACE OSMOND

require a bargain. To trade for the potion."

"I expected to pay," she replied coldly. "Name your price."

I clucked my tongue. "So eager to get what you want that you'd blindly enter a bargain with a Dark Lord?"

"Not blindly," she replied and returned her dagger to its hilt. "I'll hear your terms."

Her confidence was impressive. "First, I must know." I continued pacing, leaving her to fill with anticipation. "Do you seek this potion truly for love? Or for power?"

Again, her scent tinged the air with a burst of dread. But she held a lovely smile on her rounded face. "For love, of course."

"And the receiver of this potion?"

She took in a long breath. "For the king."

"The *Seelie* King?" I balked. The audacity of such a thought. An inward groan turned over in my chest. I wished I'd thought of it. "You hope to woo the High King of this world? To what end?"

Finally, she let a little of the tenor I could feel in her presence slip through, and a wicked grin tugged at the corner of her mouth. "Like I said, for love. I wish for him to fall madly in love with me so I may be his Queen, his equal."

A guffaw escaped from me. "You don't know Orion too well to believe you'd be his equal or anything close to

14

it. You'd be a trophy, at best."

"You let me handle that," she replied so coolly I almost believed perhaps she could see the future. The certainty of which she held on to this plan of hers…it was admirable.

But I was already growing tired of it. It was time to get what I wanted out of this. "Very well." I stopped pacing and tucked my hands behind my back. "I'll construct a love potion so strong Orion will grovel to his knees at first sight of you." Her answering grin was so wicked it stirred a sleepy darkness in my gut. "In exchange for your first-born daughter."

Her face paled, and she stumbled back a step. "My… *what?*"

I let my boredom show to hurry her mind along. "You heard me. A love potion in exchange for your first-born daughter."

Her gaze, laced with guilt, fell to the ground. "Why a daughter? Would any child do?"

My fingers plucked at the single button that held my black jacket closed, and I sat on a large rock. "You see, I'm in the market for a Queen myself. You may keep her, raise her, but upon her eighteenth birthday, she'll be mine."

She stared at me with pursed lips. "To what end?"

I chuckled at the use of my own words. "What was it you said? For love?"

She only hesitated a moment before offering a hand.

"Deal."

"Just like that?" I pushed to my feet. "How desperate you are for power." I closed the distance between us, let her scent envelop me. Lies, deceit, jealousy. She reeked of it all. I caressed a finger under her chin, and she lifted it to hold my stare. A formidable foe, she would become.

The Summer Fae finally let the extent of her wickedness show through and spread across her parted crimson lips. "For *love*, you mean?"

Oh, how this dance would prove worthy of my investment. "And for *love,* it shall be."

I stepped back and held out my hand. She glanced down at it and, for a fleeting moment, hesitated. Just as she moved to take it, I said, "One more condition."

She glared up at me from under her lowered brow. "The scales of this bargain are beginning to tip in your favor, Dark Lord."

"Just a simple request," I replied. "Necessary for the bargain to hold."

Her eyes darted to my still-outstretched hand. "What, then?"

"Your name."

Her fingers opened, and she reached for me with an unapologetic sneer. "Mabry."

Her soft hand slipped into mine, and I gripped it tightly, sealing the bargain in gold bands around our wrists. The tendrils of the bond crawled around our joined hands. Swirling up and around our arms until driven into both our chests with a hefty force. But it only seemed to ignite that madness I'd seen dormant in her soul only moments ago.

"Mabry Solborn."

Chapter One

Fortune favored the brave. Or something like that.

I leaned against my Vespa as I turned the acceptance letter over and over in my hands—its paper yellowed, its edges weathered from months kicking around in my jacket pocket. I'd read the words a dozen times a day, every day, all summer long.

Avery Quinn,

We're pleased to accept you into the Foundation Year at NSCAD.

The rest of the letter didn't matter. But those few words rang loudly in my mind for weeks now. I'd thought, perhaps, it would have sunk in by now. It would have felt… real. Felt…*right*.

A muffled series of annoying beeps chimed from inside my pocket, and I pulled out my phone to find a text message.

Did you tell her yet?

A wave of nausea rolled over in my gut. I sighed and quickly texted my best friend back.

No, not yet. Just about to.

I folded the letter and slipped it back into its home inside my brown leather bomber before stuffing our mail under the seat. The old, rusted lock protested as I closed and secured our mailbox—one of many cubbies in the large green metal bin. But only about half had actually been claimed in our teeny community in the middle of nowhere. My phone beeped again, and I glanced at the screen as I swung a leg over my bike.

I'll be by later to clean up the carnage.

I tapped at the buttons. *Bitch.*

It only took her a second to reply. *You love me.*

I groaned and shoved the device away before starting my bike. I got accepted to art school. My dreams were about to come true next week.

So why hadn't I told my aunt yet? Why hadn't I told her I was leaving the safe countryside she so willfully shielded me with? I'd planned on telling her all summer long but just couldn't find the words. They died in my throat. Every time. Now Summer had come and gone, and I left for the city with Julie on Monday. My phone beeped once again. But it was Aunt Tess this time.

The last time I checked, the mailbox wasn't in Russia.

Her not-so-subtle way of letting me know I was taking too long. If she got nervous when I went to get the mail, a mere five-minute drive, she'd surely lose her mind when she found out I was moving to the city in a few days. A city she fought all my life to keep me away from. I secured my helmet and sped off down the narrow dirt road that led to my aunt's cottage with a deep sigh.

I passed the half a dozen properties lining the old road, each a different variant of the next. A bungalow. A clothesline weighed down by clean sheets. A dog running around the front yard. Small farm animals in the back. Acres and acres of untouched land stretched out behind them all. A tiny, quiet piece of heaven tucked away in the country, just barely an hour outside Halifax. As beautiful and peaceful as it was to grow up in the country, it sometimes felt like a prison, especially under Tess' roof.

I loved my aunt dearly. She was good and kind. She'd given me everything I could have ever wanted. But Tess moved through life with a heavy blanket of fear draped over her back. Always seeing the potential risks in everything. And I mean *everything*.

As the last of the houses disappeared, I knew I was nearing home. Tess' stunning but modest cottage nestled in the trees. Built of rocks of every shape and color, topped with a thatched roof and wonky windows cookie-cut from the sides. It was like something out of a fairy tale.

The heavy scent of Satsuma and lilacs filled my nose as I slowed down the pebbled driveway that led to the front door. A giant, ornate thing carved of wood. Tess made her living as a landscaper, but she was something else entirely. Growing and maintaining the lush rainforest-looking property was a feat in itself, but successfully growing a Mandarin tree in Eastern Canada was like some kind of magic. She just had that green thumb with everything. I'd confidently say there was nothing Tess couldn't grow.

After fetching the mail, I left my helmet on the seat and entered the house. I could hear her in the kitchen before I could see her. The smell of breakfast and coffee saturated the air, and I willed myself to calm as I tossed the pile of sales flyers on the table.

"Anything good?" she asked. Her long blonde hair was tucked back in a single braid that hung down her back as she flipped pancakes over in a pan. She glanced at me from over her shoulder.

I smiled and sat down. "Nah, just a bunch of junk."

Her eyes darted to the table but not at the pile of mail. I noticed then a second smaller pile. I picked through the papers. Pamphlets. For online schools. My heart squeezed with panic.

"What's this?"

Tess took the pan from the stove and walked over to where I sat. She slipped a few pancakes onto an empty plate. "Just some brochures for online college classes." I gawked at her as she returned the pan to the stove and began adding more batter to it. "I thought, with September around the corner, you might want to check them out. See if any interest you. I hear there's great—"

"I'm moving to the city." The words blurted from my mouth as if with a mind of their own. Panic fettered in my chest. I stared at my aunt, who stood as still as a statue in the kitchen.

Her wild, mossy green eyes sparkled as she stared back at me. "Over my dead body."

"Tess!"

She slammed the pan on the back burner. "Avery." She leaned forward and gripped the edge of the counter. "Don't even joke about something like that."

It's not a joke," I said. "I applied to NSCAD months ago. I got my acceptance letter back in March."

"*March*?" Her face went tight. "It's August! When were you planning to tell me?"

I slunk down in my chair. "Pretty much now?"

Tess began nervously chewing at her lip as she paced

the tiny tiled space of her olive-green kitchen. "How? Why?" She stopped and looked at me. "*When*?"

I took in a deep breath. I'd been dreading this moment for so long. "Julie got into St. Mary's. It… it made me realize I don't want to stay here. In the country. I want to go to the city, with her, experience… more."

"Where is this coming from?" Tess shook her head in disbelief. "I thought I…."

My heart twinged with guilt. "Tess." I tipped my head to the side. "I love you. You've raised me all on your own when you were barely an adult yourself. We… raised each other. But twelve years of home school, living in a town with, like, three other people my age, being at least an hour away from any sign of modern life." I could feel my emotions flooding across my cheeks. "I'm afraid I'm missing out."

"But… I let you go to the city with Julie sometimes," she reasoned weakly.

Let me? I took another deep breath, this time to prevent words I knew I'd regret. "You mean those rare times I could venture to the city during the *day*, *with* her parents, and *only* for a few hours?" My aunt had no reply. "Tess, I'm not a child anymore. I—it's time for me to go."

Her face had gone expressionless. "Where will you live?"

"Julie's dad opened another coffee shop right downtown. Within walking distance to both our schools. He's letting us rent the space above it if we work a few shifts each week in the café."

She crossed her arms tightly. "What about everything else? Tuition? Books? Food?"

I took a deep breath. I'd been avoiding this conversation for months. "I received several small art scholarships that should more than cover my books and supplies. And I've saved nearly every dollar I've made in my Etsy shop over the last two years. I've done every odd job imaginable around this tiny town. Mowing lawns, painting houses, babysitting. I'm pretty much set. I…" I sucked my bottom lip inside my mouth to keep it from trembling. "You don't have to pay for anything, Tess."

My aunt's ghostly expression quickly melted into a look of concern. "Oh, Av', it's not about the money. I'd pay for whatever you truly wanted to do. I'm just…." she shook her head as she came closer and gripped the back of a chair firmly. "You're just throwing me for a loop here. This is the first I'm hearing of it. I can't believe you waited until now–" Her back went straight. "Wait. When do you go?"

I counted my heartbeats. "Monday."

Tess's big green eyes bulged from their sockets. "*Monday*?"

I stood from my chair. "I was afraid that if I told you any earlier that you'd… talk me out of it." The flicker of hurt that crossed her face made me look at the floor. "That you'd do something to stop me from going. Because, trust me," I let a shaky guffaw escape, "this wasn't an easy decision." I dared a glance upward and cringed at the wetness I saw pooling in her too-young eyes. Too young to have been weighed down with the responsibility of motherhood. "You think I want to upset you? Do you think I *want* to leave behind all this comfort? This world, the *only* world, I know?" We let a painful pause hold the moment. I took a step closer, my voice barely above a whisper. "Tess, we both know the real reason you won't–"

Her hand shot up, and tears spilled over, covering her pale cheeks. I could see the words she wanted to say but couldn't. For the same reason I couldn't. Guilt riddled me, filled every corner of my insides. And when Tess grabbed her purse from the table and stormed out the front door, I didn't even try to stop her. I stared out the wide picture window that faced the vastness outside and watched as my aunt disappeared down the gravel driveway in her old red Mustang, a thick cloud of dust billowing in her wake.

***

"Tom's making a trip into the city tomorrow if you've got anything else left to go to the apartment," Julie said as she wrangled her long golden hair into a messy knot and added another old book to her ever-growing pile. One last purchase with her employee discount, no doubt.

I'd stopped correcting her about calling her dad by his first name years ago. As much as she loved them, I knew Julie never truly considered them parents. At ten years old, they'd just adopted her too late in life. But there was mutual respect the three of them shared, and I admired it. Wished for years that Tess would show the same to me instead of coddling me like an infant.

"Yeah, I've got a couple large duffels that won't fit on my bike," I replied as I thumbed through a musty edition of Bram Stoker's Dracula. I closed the leather-bound cover and waggled it at her. "I'm getting this."

"I'll get him to swing by." She took the book and smiled as she added some notes to papers on a clipboard. When she caught me eying her inventory list, she said, "Birthday present."

A groan turned over in my throat. "I don't want to do my birthday this year."

Julie intently held my stare as she dramatically crossed something off her paper. "Funny thing about birthdays, Av', they tend to happen whether or not you want them to." She shrugged and added yet another book to her pile. "Besides, my birthday is gonna be shit, as usual. Stupid snow. We need to celebrate yours, you lucky summer child."

It was true. We were the same age, but her birthday wasn't until February, and living in the Maritimes almost always equated to some sort of blizzard.

I just chuckled quietly and let her get back to work, which involved me ruffling through well-loved texts while she added to her personal collection. The last time I'd snuck up to the city to help get the apartment ready, she'd been assembling a large bookshelf for the living room. I had no doubt Julie intended to fill it immediately.

We sat in a dank corner of the tiny used bookstore that doubled as a pawnshop. In our modest town, they use lots of businesses for multiple fronts. The burger joint was also the post office, with a tanning salon in the back.

"So…." Julie side-eyed me knowingly. Too much time had passed with me *not* mentioning Tess. "She totally freaked, didn't she?"

I stretched my legs out on the worn gray carpet where we sat between the stacks. "You guessed it."

Julie rolled her eyes. So blue they could pass as contacts. "Doesn't take a genius to guess how Tess would react to you leaving her."

"I'm not leaving her," I quickly amended. The guilt still sat heavy in my gut. "God, you make it sound like I'm running away."

"In Tess's eyes, you pretty much are." When I was too quiet for too long, Julie added a deep sigh. "Av', you're an adult now. You can make adult choices. You don't need your aunt to dictate every part of your life." I knew she was right. So why couldn't I shake this terrible grief? "I mean, unless you *want* to stay in Nowhereville and paint pictures of birds for the rest of your life."

I couldn't help but laugh. I relaxed and pressed my back against the over-filled bookshelf behind me. "So, you don't think I'm making a mistake?"

Julie gave a look that said, *for heaven's sake.* "A mistake? How is growing up and going to college a mistake? God, Av', you applied, got accepted, arranged housing, and paid for everything *yourself.* If that doesn't scream *mature and able,* then I don't know what will."

The back of my head touched a row of books. "I don't know, I just feel…."

"What?" Julie replied and began gathering up her hoard into more manageable piles. "What's really the matter?"

I thought for a moment. I didn't want to disappoint my best friend. Through everything, Julie had always been there for me. Showing me what life was like outside of Tess's reign. Not that my aunt was a horrible person, she just… cared *too* much. The paranoia with which Tess moved through life, she kept me close to it. But there was no turning back now. Julie was right. Everything was ready and waiting for us to start our new lives in the city. She'd dreamed of this moment for years. Talked about it every day. I let a smile spread across my face for her.

"Nothing. I'm just nervous, is all."

She pushed to stand up and stared down at me with

an outstretched hand. "Well, get over those nerves, sister," she replied with a cheeky grin and hauled me to my feet. "Because as of Monday, we're free."

I held on to the smile. Had to. Because inside…I was wrought with nerves. This was what I wanted. What I'd fantasized about for years. What I worked so, so hard for.

So… why couldn't I shake this feeling of dread?

***

The sun had just gone down, and I inhaled deeply the cool twilight air that floated in from the open patio door. The burr of frozen margaritas pulsing in the blender muffled the sounds of music as I prepped one of my last orders for shipping. My art wasn't spectacular, but people seemed to love my whimsical style, and the online print sales were pretty steady. Julie popped off the lid and gave a taste, frowned, and fetched the bottle of tequila to pour more into the mix.

My best friend and the stars above, having drinks and food on the patio with good music. It was shaping up to be a great night. But…Tess still hadn't returned. Nor did she answer her phone. I pushed the worry from my mind and finished wrapping the large print of gold metallic flowers in brown packing paper.

Julie skirted around the rustic dining table that divided

the open space and handed me one of the margaritas she held. "Etsy shop still going strong?"

I sighed happily and smoothed the shipping label sticker over the top corner. "Yeah, surprisingly."

"Surprisingly?" she mock-scoffed. "Av', you're talented as hell. Embrace it."

I took a long sip with the straw and cringed through the cold sensation that stuck in my throat. "Paintings of pixies and flowers isn't exactly what I want to be known for."

Julie shrugged and plucked a piece of cheese off a snack tray. "What *do* you want to be known for, then?"

I thought for a moment. I loved my art, my style. I'd curated it and honed it over the years, and now I was known online as the whimsical artist. I'd worked hard to build my platform, promote my little shop. And people genuinely seemed to love my stuff. But...I wanted more. I wanted to see other artists, work with them. Immerse myself in a world of different perspectives and talent.

"I want...." I took a deep breath. "I want to own a gallery someday. Where I can surround myself with all kinds of art."

Julie beamed proudly with a straw in her mouth.

Just then, the front door swung open, and Tess strolled in with a large bag in hand. My heart sped up as I caught her tired stare. What had she been doing all day? When my aunt hung her coat on the rack and headed over to where we stood, Julie cleared her throat loudly.

"Oh, look," she said over-enthusiastically and threw me a wink as she turned toward the patio doors. "Stars."

When my best friend disappeared outside, I turned to Tess, who stood near the old floor model stereo system we'd salvaged from a yard sale years ago. She turned the music down to a comfortable tempo. I didn't want to be the first to speak, but her silence was scratching at my nerves.

"Where have you been all day?" I asked.

She still didn't answer, and I watched as my aunt walked over and fetched the shopping bag she'd entered with and set it on the table.

I took a deep breath. "Tess, I just wanted to say I'm sorry—"

"Don't," she spoke. She stared at me for a long moment before heaving a defeated sigh. "Look, I know I haven't exactly handled what happened to your parents... well." Her throat bobbed with a nervous swallow.

We hardly ever spoke of them. It was too hard for her. And me, well... I never knew them. A random stranger with a gun and a plan made sure of that. It was their unfair deaths that had kept me tucked tightly under Tess's wing. My mother was her only sister, her only family. As much as Julie and I made fun of her overprotective ways... we both knew why Tess did it.

"It… changed me. In one fell swoop, I'd lost my everything and with it… a whole world. And then parenthood was thrust upon me." Her hand flung up to stop the protest that already filled my mouth. "A responsibility I was more than happy to take on. But I had absolutely no idea what I was doing." She rubbed her hands over her tired face. "I guess what I'm trying to say is… you're my everything, Avery. And maybe I held on a bit too tight."

"A bit?" I edged jokingly.

Tess shot me a look that said, *don't push it, I'm trying here*. "I spent the day with Mr. Ryan. I went to the city, he showed me where you guys will be living. I drove up and down the area, checked out your school." When I gave a puzzled look, she continued. "I just had to see it all, visualize where you'd be living."

Something like hope blossomed in my chest, and a smile forced its way across my face. "So, does that mean you're cool with it?"

"Cool with the focus of my life moving to a dangerous city where I can't protect her anymore?" she threw the sarcastic reply at me. "No, not really." Tess shook her head and glanced at the bag on the table. "But you're not a kid anymore. You're an adult. A woman. And I can't keep you close with promises of cupcakes and cozy blankets." Her pale, slender hands reached inside the bag and hauled out a large, unmarked brown box. She pushed it toward me and motioned for me to open it. "Happy birthday."

Emotions bubbled up, overwhelming me. I'd expected so many outcomes from today. For Tess to demand I stay home, do online school. I even entertained the possibility that she might insist on moving in with us. That was the best-case scenario in my mind all day. I'd combed over all sorts of options all day long.

But I never expected this.

My fingertips pried at the neatly tucked flaps on the box and opened the lid to find a beautiful deep brown leather bag nestled in green paper. My eyes tingled from the wetness that suddenly pooled there. I couldn't stop staring. The antiqued brass fixings, the hand-stitched seams. I traced my fingers over the two letters branded on the front. *AQ*.

"It's a travel bag," Tess said from over my shoulder. "For artists."

"Tess…." My throat refused to release the words. My aunt wasn't a rich woman by any means. We'd always had everything we needed to be comfortable and happy. But nothing more. The bag… it must have cost her a fortune.

Her hand gently wrapped over the back of mine, and I looked into her glistening green eyes. Almost as green as the tissue paper that held my new bag. "So, you can bring your art supplies back and forth." She fixed her stare, but I could see the grin she hid. "For when you come home every weekend."

"*Every* weekend?" I balked.

Tess let out a laugh. "Fine, every second weekend."

"Once a month," I reasoned.

She paused, making a show of considering it, then gave me a side glance. "Deal."

And in that moment, I knew… something had changed between us. An untying of sorts. A loosening of some knot.

Things would never be the same.

Julie appeared from the patio, an empty glass in hand. Her cheeks were already flushed. "You hens done pecking, or can I join the party?"

Tess pulled us both close and, with a hand on either of our shoulders, she pressed her lips together before saying, "You two take care of each other, okay? Be one another's person. You two have a bond that's so rare. You have no idea. Don't let it go."

"Geez, Tess," Julie scoffed drastically. "We're going to college, not heading off to war."

My aunt let out a laugh, and I saw her visibly relax. She motioned to Julie's empty glass. "Is there one of those for me?"

"Of course!" Julie spun around, the hem of her over-sized white t-shirt flapping outward, and fetched the pitcher and another glass before filling all three of them.

We clinked our frozen drinks together, and I knew that was the end of it. No more worry. No more doubts. Everything was going according to plan, and, in a matter of days, I'd be starting my new life in the city. The three of us drank together on the ground-level patio that looked out over Tess's magnificent backyard.

With twilight long gone, the night sky covered us in a blanket of navy silk, speckled with endless stars. In the never-ending thick of trees and bushes, solar-powered twinkle lights came to life and illuminated the lush garden that wove in and out and around everything. Stones, statues, lawn gnomes, birdbaths. You name it. Tess's garden had it.

When the chill of late-night began to creep in, Tess wrapped herself in a wool throw blanket and stood up on wobbly feet. "Well, ladies, I bid you goodnight." A slight hiccup burped from her throat. "I'm all margarita-d out."

"Night, Tess," I called as she slipped inside the patio door.

Julie and I leaned back on the oversized rattan chair, wide enough for two, and sipped on the last of our once-frozen drinks. Low music notes played from my phone on the coffee table at our feet and danced in the air. The moon, a massive silver medallion in the sky, shone down on us so brightly we hardly needed the torch lamps that burned on either end of the patio.

Julie mindlessly picked at the rips in her jeans as she

stared out at the vastness of Tess's garden with a strange and distant look. "God, it's something fit for a fantasy, isn't it?"

I stared admiringly with her. "Yeah, it's definitely something. I'm just glad she had a hobby to focus on besides me."

Julie chuckled quietly and leaned back. "Yeah, can you imagine if Tess didn't have gardening as a release? I'd be saving you from some high-up tower deep in the woods right about now."

"No handsome prince?" I kidded.

"You don't need a prince, Av'." She rolled her neck to the side and turned her gaze to me. Her head rested up against the back of the chair. In the moonlight, she was even more beautiful than during the day. Her creamy skin seemed to absorb it; her long yellow hair sparkled with it. "Neither of us do. We're going to be queens of our own lives. Starting on Monday."

I shoved at her with a laugh. "Always with the dramatic."

Julie stood up, wavered for a moment while she found her legs through the weight of tequila that filled her, and offered me a hand. "Let's walk."

We strolled through the garden, smelling flowers, guessing the names of one's we'd never bothered to learn over the years. We'd always just made-up silly terms for them, different ones each time we walked through. Piddly wagons and trunk flutes.

When Julie plunked down on the edge of a large stone fountain that Tess had salvaged from an old property she'd helped restore, I sat down next to her and stretched my legs out before crossing my ankles. My hands gripped the coarse edge, keeping me from toppling backward. Too much tequila.

"Care for one more drink?" Julie asked and pulled a bottle of red wine from somewhere. *Had she been carrying that the whole time?* The bottle was made of a deep red glass, and etched vines covered its surface. She waggled it cheekily. "Happy birthday."

"Where did you get that?"

"I've been brewing a batch of wine all summer," she replied and gnawed the cork out with her teeth. She spat it across the grass. "I think I finally got it right. This is the first good bottle, so I saved it for today."

She took a long glug before handing the bottle to me. I stared down at the open neck, admired the hand-blown work of it, and wondered where the hell Julie got it. But then again, my best friend was sometimes an enigma. She spent more and more time in the city the older we got. Her parents weren't strict like Tess, and Julie had the freedom to come and go as she pleased. She'd always come home and regale me with tales of her visits, the people she'd meet, the food she'd try. Parties. Dates. Everything I missed out on for the last eighteen years.

Never again.

Surprised by its light weight, I took the bottle and gripped the long neck as I put the mouth to my lips. I chugged back a good mouthful and let out a satisfied groan when I finally handed it back. The wine was intense, but the aftertaste was something else entirely. Warm, spicy. Like sunshine sliding down the back of my throat.

I stared upward and admired the stars. Neither of us spoke. It was a comfortable silence we often hung out in. I'd no idea how much time had passed while we sat there on the edge of the sleeping fountain, drinking Julie's wine sip for sip. My veins hummed, and I relished every second.

Finally, she let loose a long, quiet sigh. "You ever just *know* something–" she shrugged and set the bottle down on the grass between us. "Like, not in your mind, but with some other part of your body?" She peered up at the midnight sky with me. "I know I'm meant for something more than what this tiny town can give me. And I'm going to find it."

My cheeks burned with a radiant glow of wine and tequila and happiness. But, deep in my gut, something soured. Jealousy. The look in Julie's eye, the certainty she held so close. I wanted that. I wanted so badly to be as sure of something as she was about her future.

I picked up the bottle and set it back down when I realized

it was empty. "I'm not sure if I'm cut out for the city life. I want to be, though."

Julie smiled and slipped her palm across my back with an assuring touch. "You'll be just fine. I promise. We've got a whole new world awaiting us, Av'."

My eyes locked on hers and the insides of my head swarmed in circles. I took a few deep breaths to steady myself, but nothing was stopping the wave of a drunken stupor that threatened to wash over me. I blinked away the blur that filled my vision and, in the distance, saw the out-line of a jagged-topped building appear over the horizon, and a strange, winged shadow flew over it. *A castle?* No. It couldn't be. I shook my head and rubbed at my eyes. When I opened them and looked at my best friend, I gasped. Julie sparkled as if covered in stardust, her platinum hair gleaming like white silk in the moonlight. But it was her features that startled me. Sharp and angular, exaggerated and out of proportion. Darkness closed in from the edges of my vision.

I was passing out.

The black curtain closed in just as the sound of Julie's concerned voice drifted away, and I felt the water in the fountain splashing across my back. But rather than touch the bottom… I kept falling. Backward. Downward. Spiraling through dark waters as my numb limbs drifted outward from my body.

Mumbled voices touched my ears, and I struggled to hear what they were saying. So many of them, tiny, musical whispers. I couldn't tell if they came from my own mind or from somewhere else. Suddenly, my lungs burned, and my eyes flew open in panic.

I was drowning.

But the voices became more apparent, and I could hear them now. The words they whispered to one another as if I couldn't hear them. As if I weren't there at all.

That's her!

There she is!

Where has she been? Are you sure it's the one?

Look at the hair.

Red as blood.

It's the one we've been searching for.

Poor thing. Has no idea what's in store for her. The queen will tear her into ribbons.

As my lungs strained in my chest, I gave a few weak attempts to kick my way to the surface, but I was too weak. Too weighed down by wine and tequila. Tiny lights appeared around the edges of my blurred vision. Brightening and forming a moving mass. Like a swarm of fireflies. They grew and grew until the light became too much. I shielded my eyes from the blinding light and waited as the last of my breaths pushed from my chest.

But one more voice seeped into my ears. Darker,

deeper, and more sinister than all the rest.

Death awaits her.

Chapter Two

The morning sun filled the living room where I slept. I cracked one eye open, watching the dust floating in the air. It almost looked like tiny fairies. Too delicate to touch. I focused on it for a while, wondering if I was dying. This was a hangover from hell.

When the burn of mid-morning filtered in across the living room and formed a stifling layer of sweat on my face, I gave up trying to stay asleep. The confines of a hangover from hell enveloped me, refusing to let me lift my head from the sequined pillow below my face. As I attempted to roll over, I fought against the wave of nausea that sprang to life in my stomach and nearly fell off the couch. I struggled into a sitting position and strained to look over at Julie's body slung across the round wicker chair on the other side of the room. Her green eyes were rimmed with pink as she blinked at me. She looked as bad as I felt.

A moan scratched in my throat as I rubbed my face, sore from the sequined imprints across my cheek. The sounds of clanking pans came from the kitchen and the high-pitched chime of dishes clinking on the marble countertop.

I cringed and curled forward on my lap. "Jesus, Tess. Could you *be* any louder?"

The low chuckle that came from behind told me the noise was intentional.

My fingers reached for a tepid glass of water that was left on the coffee table all night, and I chugged it back. I waited a moment for my stomach to settle before I set it down again.

"I'm never drinking again," I grumbled hoarsely to Julie.

Her answering moan told me she agreed. She slowly adjusted into a sitting position. "I might have to adjust the recipe on the next batch."

"Or just drink less," I replied.

Behind us, the sounds of chair legs screeching over the tile floor brought my shoulders to my ears. "Breakfast is ready," Tess announced in a cheeky tone.

Julie and I shuffled across the living room and plunked down in chairs on opposite ends of the table. Tess sat between us and glanced back and forth with a grin as she stuffed scrambled eggs in her mouth.

"When do you two leave for the city?" Tess asked and stirred sugar into her coffee. "Is there anything I can help with?"

I took a few cautious sips of coffee. "The plan is to head up tomorrow, Monday. Orientations are on Wednesday, and actual classes start the following week." I picked at a plain piece of toast. "But I have a few paintings I'd like to bring if you could take those in the Mustang. Not sure how well they'd travel strapped to the back of my Vespa."

"I'm leaving later today with Tom, so I'll already be there waiting," Julie added.

Tess nodded thoughtfully. "I've got a few things to do today, but I'm all yours tomorrow."

"Thanks, Tess," I said with a weak smile. I felt like death. My hair hung long and matted around my face and, when I attempted to wrangle it into a bun, I realized it was slightly damp at the roots. My mind stilled, and flashes of last night flickered across my vision. The tequila. The wine. The fountain. The strange nightmare that had followed well into the night. "Did I... fall in the fountain last night?"

They both laughed, and Julie filled her plate with eggs and bacon. How could she eat? I could hardly stand to smell it. She gave me a taunting look when I stifled a gag. "Yeah, you drunken fool. I had to haul your heavy ass back up to the house." She waved a piece of bacon in my face before stuffing it in her mouth. "Best to lay off this stuff anyway."

I kicked her chair. She threw another piece of bacon at me, and I gagged again.

"That's it," I said and stood up. My head spun. "I'm going back to bed."

Their laughter followed me all the way to my room, where I shut the door and collapsed in the nest of blankets atop my comfy bed. Within minutes, I let the lure of sleep take me away, but somewhere in the back of my mind… or perhaps a dawdling lost memory… a voice whispered in my ear, but I was too far gone to let it linger. The two words barely registered before I drifted off.

He's coming.

✻✻✻

I'd slept the day away. But I couldn't feel guilty for wasting the last few hours I had at home because Tess had been absent the whole day. The sun had long dipped below the horizon, and I sat in the backyard, surrounded by twinkle lights and summer torches that lined the gardens.

I perched on a low stool, earbuds in, paintbrush in

hand, as I filled the canvas with images that busied my mind from the intense dreams that overran my mind. That was usually how my inspiration came to me. An over-active imagination mixed with vivid dreams of creatures and adventures into other worlds.

I stopped for a moment to take in the collage of random things that spewed from my brush and covered the canvas before me. A bright horizon, sharp-pointed tips of a castle cutting the sky, a shadowed set of wings stretched in the distance. The chill of the night gently blew against my exposed arms, and I set my brush down. I wouldn't finish the piece, but I had to get the images out of my head before leaving for the city. One last painting in the best studio in the world. Tess's garden. It had served me well over the years. Set fire to my imagination and inspired me to paint pictures of elves, fairies, and other mythical creatures.

I removed my earbuds, and the sound of the world around me sharpened with the silence of the garden. Something rustled in the bushes behind me, and I spun around with a gasp that stuck in my throat. I scanned the darkness, squinting to see between the shadowed lines of branches and trellises covered in vines. My heart pounded in my chest, beating a pulse all the way up to my ears.

Nothing was there.

But I couldn't shake the unnerving feeling of being watched, so I began packing up my supplies, my fingers trembling. A few brushes fell to the ground. I spotted a large, strangely shaped shadow stretching and moving across the grass as I bent to pick them up. Slowly, but enough to distinguish between the sway of trees and... whatever it was moving toward me. I shot a glance upward to the skies, but they were empty. Nothing above was causing the ground to cover in shadow like this.

A tiny blue light flickered in the bush like a single firefly. So quick, I nearly missed it. I stared and stared, trying to catch another glimpse. More rustling, louder this time, perked my ears, and I dropped everything to run for the patio door.

A low, eerie whisper crept through the air, too quiet and muffled to make out the words. With every hasty step, I felt a coldness looming over my back, eyes watching, fingers reaching. I didn't dare turn to look until I got to the sliding door and slipped inside. When I slammed it shut and set the latch, my heaving breath fogged the glass as I peered outside.

Again, nothing was there.

The shadow was gone. A sort of lightness fell over the garden once more. *What the hell was that?* Between the drunken hallucinations in the fountain and the vivid nightmares I'd had while sleeping off my hangover, I was beginning to think I was scaring myself out of leaving. But I couldn't have imagined what had just happened.

Was I losing my mind?

✳✳✳

Sleep came easier than I'd hoped. Only seconds after I crawled into bed later that night, I found myself deep in a dream. But it only took a few breaths to realize…it wasn't a dream at all. It was another nightmare. Darkness surrounded me. My bare feet dug into the wet, cold earth beneath me as I ran through a thick forest of deadened, leafless trees.

Long, wiry branches whipped at my skin as I broke through them, unbothered by the gashes on my legs and arms. Drops of blood created a path in my wake, leading my pursuer right to me. No matter where I went, no matter how fast I ran, they'd find me. The dense shadow bit at my heels, reaching for my back, grabbing for my fingers.

My hair snagged in a bramble and tugged me to a stop. Frantically, I ripped the locks free just as the ominous presence rushed up to me like a surging wave. Invisible, but there. I knew it was there. Could feel its icy breath on my cheek. I took off running again, clumsily stumbling over tree roots and fallen debris. Fighting my way through the never-ending forest. With every step that pounded into the earth, I could hear the whisper. The voice taunting me like a pulse.

She's coming. She's coming. She's coming.

The sound drummed in my chest, growing louder and more profound the closer it got. But I could see a hint of light in the distance, through the mess of twisted black branches. I quickened my steps and willed my legs to move faster, stretch further. Just as I broke through and emerged into the blazing sun, the voice screamed at me, *she's here*!

As I fell to the ground, my body flailed awake in my bed. In the darkness of my bedroom, I sat upright and hugged my knees close as I worked to settle my breathing and calm my frantic heart.

It was just a dream. It was just a dream.

But, after a few minutes, my fingertips were still numb, and I struggled to take a single deep breath. I hadn't had a nightmare like that since I was a kid. When Tess would let me crawl into bed with her in the middle of the night without question because she knew. She'd wrap me in her arms, under the warmth of her blankets, and soothe me back to sleep.

I peeled back the comforter and swung my legs off the bed. I was a grown woman, but part of me craved that distant comfort, the one from my childhood. Maybe it was because I was leaving tomorrow, or perhaps I'd taken on Tess's same paranoia about the world and manifested these nightmares myself.

Whatever the case, I crept through the dim, sleepy cottage and peeked inside my aunt's bedroom. She was sound asleep, and I immediately felt guilty for even thinking of it. But the nightmare still lingered on my skin, and I couldn't face my own bedroom alone.

As quietly as I could, I slipped inside Tess's room and eased myself into the empty space near the edge of the bed. When the mattress sagged with my weight, she rolled over.

"Avery?" she croaked.

"Sorry," I whispered. "I… I couldn't sleep."

She lifted the blankets without a second thought, creating an opening for me. I laid down and nestled my back against her as she wrapped the blanket tightly around me. Her warmth seeped into my skin, soothing me. Reminding me of how safe I was there. In my aunt's cozy home away from the world. I took a deep breath. It must have all been nerves.

"What's wrong, Avery?" Tess whispered.

I wanted to assure her everything was fine, but Tess always knew. Could always tell. "Do…do you think I'm making a mistake?"

"A mistake would be getting bangs," she replied tiredly and tightened her arm around me. "You're just growing up. It's natural to be nervous about the unknown. Of changes, huge ones like you're about to make tomorrow." When I didn't reply, she added, "Are you having second thoughts?"

"I don't know," I told her honestly. "I mean, I don't

have to go to college, I guess. My Etsy shop is taking off. I could build on that. Expand. Make a career of it."

Tess sat upright, and I half-turned to look at her behind me. "Where is this coming from? Isn't this…I thought this was what you wanted."

I chewed at my lip. "Yeah, but what is it you want? I can't just leave you out here all by yourself."

In the cut of moonlight that slipped in through the curtains, I saw her smile. "It doesn't matter what I want anymore, Avery. I can't protect you from the world forever. I know I didn't really let you stretch those wings growing up, but it's because I had no idea what I was doing. I was the same age you are now when…."

I swallowed dryly. "When my parents died?"

Tess nodded and tears formed in her eyes. "I just wanted to shield you from anything that could hurt you. I just wanted you to… be happy."

"And I was–I *am*," I assured her.

She smiled warmly as she moved some straggly hair from my face and cupped her hand over my cheek. "The city can be dangerous. We both know that. And what happened to your parents that night… it doesn't mean… the city *can* be scary, yes. But it can also be freeing. You've got Julie. You've already impressively taken care of every single thing without my help. You'll be fine." I took a deep breath and nodded against her hand. "But you have to call me every night."

"Tess!"

"Okay, okay." She laughed tiredly and flung the blanket over both of us as she cuddled into my back for sleep. "Every second night."

Chapter Three

The blistering summer sun was high in the sky when Tess and I headed for the city. She was in her convertible, me on my Vespa. We packed the last of my things in the backseat of her car while I trailed behind. The sounds of the radio blared from Tess's dashboard speakers, creating a soundtrack for us to drive to.

I hated riding in vehicles. I always got car sick. Every damn time. Tess had made a deal with a neighbor one year when I was barely fourteen. I'd worked in his little roadside corner store all summer, serving passing tourists and fleeting locals. Day in and day out. It was a glorified candy store with bins of five-cent candies and freezers of homemade ice cream sold by the scoop. It was one of the best jobs I'd ever had, and I got a bike out of it. Not only a bike… *freedom*. Freedom from taking the bus or driving in cars wherever I went. Salvation from swirling nausea and daily vomiting of chronic motion sickness.

As the faint shapes of houses–sub-divisions–came into view, I knew we were close, and I cursed myself for not cleaning my goggles before we left. My brown leather gloves crunched around the handlebars as I turned to follow Tess around an exit. We entered through Hammonds Plains and made our way through Bedford. *The scenic route*, Tess always called it. She loved to see architecture. The parks. The beautiful landscaping brightened every crook and corner. The closer we got to downtown Halifax, the faster my heart beat. This was it. The last drive I'll make to the city as a country girl. I was a city woman now. As corny as it sounded in my mind, it felt…nice. Hope filled my chest in a dizzy twirl, and my wind-beaten lips slightly cracked as I smiled.

I thought about the few trips Julie and I spent time here. With her parents. How many afternoons I'd snuck off with Julie without them. How many trips I'd made to Halifax for art shows and exhibits with Tess.

Now it was my home.

We were nearing downtown. I could see the bustling waterfront in the distance. I followed Tess's car up and down a few narrow streets—the ancient, historic downtown never made sense to me, but there was beauty in it. The random streets, the stunning architecture, the art. Live acoustic music along the boardwalk. As nervous as I was, I knew… this was where I belonged.

I pulled up to the one parking spot Julie and I shared across from the coffee shop. It banked the edge of a vast field of grass. A thick forest on one side, flower arrangements, and benches along the other. I smiled as I saw myself sitting there with my sketch pad in hand.

I removed my helmet and goggles. Tess was still looking for parking. Probably the biggest downfall of city life. Parking was a privilege you had to fight for. I stepped off my bike and leaned against it. Let the warmth of the motor seep into my chilled legs. I couldn't stop staring at the park. I'd never seen it at night, with streetlights and solar bulbs trailing whimsical designs all over the place.

Something moved in the distance through a patch of light. Shadow to shadow. I blinked and tried to follow the slight flicker of darkness that fleeted across the park lawn before me. My heart sprung into a panic, and I froze. Unable to move, unable to blink.

And that's when I heard it again. The voice. The whispers. Just like in the fountain, in the garden, and in my dreams ever since. This time, the tone felt more sinister as it vibrated in my chest with a deep purr. The shadowed being slinked across the grass, making its way toward me like a sheet of black silk, its voice in the breeze. Behind it, a tiny blue light, a spec, formed in the dense bushes of young trees. It floated around like a firefly, and I heard the voice again. Clearer.

Avery…

My stomach clenched. It knew my name now.

A hand clasped around my shoulder, and I let out a stark yelp as I nearly knocked over my bike.

"Avery!" Julie said, her face alight with joy. She'd been looking forward to this night for so long. "I called out to you from across the street like ten times. You okay?"

I took a deep breath and steadied myself. I am *not* losing my mind. "Yeah, I'm good. Just a long drive."

"Come on." She waved for me to follow as she turned toward the coffee shop. "Tess is waiting inside."

I glanced up at the mint green sign above the door and front windows. The Chocolate Kettle. The menu offered every kind of tea imaginable. Plus, all sorts of coffees and lattes and cappuccinos. But the baked goods were the best part. Baked in-house, and as simple as a few muffins and bagels, some cookies and pastries, but almost everything was chocolate. Chocolate of all sorts.

They purposely mismatched the tables to give the place a boho vibe inside. Deep wood tones. Woven fabrics of jewel tones hung around windows. A few rustic chessboards sat about for people to play, and nineties Alanis cooed in the background. An old metal spiral staircase led to our apartment above. But there was also a private entrance at the back of the building. This was the fifth Chocolate Kettle location Julie's dad had opened in Nova Scotia, and he apparently had plans to expand outside the province next year. Julie never really let on, but I could tell she was proud.

Tess stood near the front counter with three lidded coffee-to-go cups stacked under her chin. She walked toward us, and I took a long stride and relieved her of two cups. I handed one to Julie.

"Hey, Julie!" the male barista behind the counter greeted with an eager smile. His wide, up-swept eyes practically sparkled at her.

She soaked it up and tucked her hair behind her ear with a grin. "Hey! I didn't know you were working tonight."

"Yeah, just got here," the guy replied. He hadn't taken his eyes off her since we walked in.

I bit back a chuckle and nudged her arm. "Oh, uh, guys, this is Tomas. The new evening manager for the café." Julie motioned to Tess and me. "And Tomas, this is my best friend Av' and her aunt Tess."

"Aunt?" His dark eyebrows raised under the bit of floppy black hair that dangled across his forehead. "You're not a student?"

Tess rolled her eyes. But I knew she loved the compliment.

"Nope, just this one." She pointed a thumb at me.

Tomas adjusted his black apron. "Avery, right?" He held out a hand.

I shook it with a nod. "The one and only."

He had a charming laugh. "I feel like I already know you," he said. "Julie talks about you all the time."

"Well, that's unfortunate," I kidded. "Are you going to school?"

Tomas wiped down the counter in front of him and smiled at the patrons enjoying their coffees. "Media Arts at NSCAD."

"No way," I replied. "I'm doing my Foundation year."

"Cool," he said. "I finished mine last year. You'll love it there."

Some customers came in, and we waved to Tomas as we took our seats near the front window. It felt good knowing that there'd be a somewhat familiar face at my school. I took a sip of my coffee as Tess pulled out two small pink boxes, gift wrapped with tiny bows. She handed one to each of us.

"A house-warming slash starting school gift from me," Tess said.

I moaned. "You didn't have to–"

"Open it."

I looked at Julie, and she gave a shrug as she lifted the lid of hers. It was a bracelet. I opened my lid to find the same thing; beautiful woven leather straps held beads of earthy green placed every few inches along the length.

"Those beads are made of pressed thyme," Tess said. "It's supposed to be good for protection."

Julie already had hers on, and she admired it in the dim lamplight that hung over the table. "Thanks, Tess! I've been looking for something just like this."

I ignored Julie's overt enthusiasm and hugged my aunt. "Thanks."

When I pulled away, she thrust two more things at us. Mace bottles.

"Tess!"

"Take them," she insisted. She held them out until we each wrapped our hands around them. She pulled us both close. "Never walk alone in the forest or the parks, do you hear me?"

The light mood darkened, and I nodded solemnly. Julie did too. We all knew how my parents died. Murdered in the park during the night. Right here, right downtown. Tess was with them, and she barely got away from the attackers with infant me in her arms.

I took the mace from her and stuffed it in my shoulder bag. "Thanks for everything. I mean it."

After Tess headed home, Julie and I grabbed the few things from my bike and headed for the private entrance meant for us. Julie twisted the key in the lock and pushed open the heavy front door. We stepped inside, and I set down my things to take it all in.

The space was meant for storage, but Julie's dad had converted it into an apartment for us. A small kitchenette lined a back wall, a bathroom next to it, and it faced the rest of the open apartment. A round, second-hand dining table anchored the space, with a comfy living room on the other side. On the back wall, there were three mismatched doors. My room, Julie's, and a tinier, spare bedroom we planned to use for storage.

A modest balcony jutted off the living room, barely big enough for a couple of chairs and a folding end table. It was no castle, but Julie had given it as much character as possible. Plants of all kinds littered the entire apartment.

Ivies draped over the windows and doors, some of my paintings hung on the walls, the old sofa we'd found at a yard sale was cleaned up and covered in mountains of throw pillows that spilled onto the floor. An enormous basket of fruit sat on the table and a card balanced on top. Julie grabbed it and flipped it open with a smile.

"Your parents?" I asked and fetched my bags from the porch.

Her pale cheeks flushed, and she tucked the note in her pocket. "Tomas."

I shot her a devious grin. "And? When were you going to tell me about him?"

Julie shrugged and helped me with my things. "Nothing to tell. Dad hired him at the beginning of the summer to train the new staff before the opening. I came in a few times to learn and help." When she saw the look on my face, she rolled her eyes. "He's… nice."

"Nice?"

"I'm not looking to start anything right now," she replied. "I have… other things to focus on."

"Sure, sure," I said mockingly and brought all my stuff into my room.

One wall of white painted brick held my bed, an end table, a small armchair. An old white dresser on the other side. A large window divided the space, the old-fashioned kind that moaned on its rusty slides when I lifted it open.

The view of the park was spectacular. The room wasn't much, but it was all mine, and a sense of satisfaction sat heavy in my gut. I set my things down and removed my jacket before heading back out to the apartment.

Julie stood near the balcony door with a bottle of wine in her hand. Same as the one we drank on my birthday. She waggled it and nudged her head toward the door. "Care for a celebratory drink?"

"What are we celebrating?"

The old metal screen door creaked as she shoved it open. "Our freedom."

Always with the dramatic. I chuckled and shook my

head. "Fine. But just one. I don't want to end up falling off the balcony or something."

We sat in the folding chairs and looked out over the city. Our city.

"Yeah, apparently, the first bottle of any batch is a bit strong," she said as she poured us two cups of her spicy wine. "Did you have crazy dreams that night?" If she noticed the way my face paled, she said nothing. "Reminds me of that time we drank the absinthe I'd snuck back from my senior trip to Quebec."

I remembered that trip. Not going on it, of course. But I remembered being so jealous of Julie and missing her like crazy while she was gone. Being home-schooled, I'd missed out on all the fun high school events and trips like that. Senior trips, high school guys, dating, clubs, sports teams. But now I was starting new, an adult who could decide the path her life could take. Would take. I never wanted to miss another thing.

We clinked our glasses together and sipped gently as the sounds of the city played for us. Cars and people. Music from the downtown streets was nothing more than rows of Irish pubs.

"This is it, Av'," Julie said with a sense of finality. She took a deep breath and closed her eyes as her head tipped back. When she opened them, she turned to look at me. "This is how it starts."

"What does?" I took another sip of wine. The burn on my throat was oddly comforting. Despite being so strong, the wine was delicious, like a basket of fruit chased with hot sauce.

"Life," she replied. "*Our* life." She topped up her glass. "I've been dreaming of this moment for years."

I couldn't help but think of that lingering nagging feeling in the back of my mind. I wanted to be as confident of everything as Julie seemed to be. But the vivid nightmares of the last few days haunted my thoughts. And as much as I fought to push them away, they were there. Taunting, making me question my own sanity. Was I just scaring myself out of settling here?

Julie must have read my face. She leaned forward in her chair. "Look, I know this is hard for you. You have no idea how much it means to me that you're here, too. I can't imagine doing this without you."

I gave her a reassuring smile. "I'm totally fine, Jules. You just know how I am. Fear of the unknown and all that." Her expression said, *you think*? "I mean, you at least would come in and hang out here all the time. You know people."

She had a knowing look on her face. "You will, too. In no time." She set her glass down and leaned over to fetch a bag I hadn't noticed was sitting on the floor between us. She pulled out a slender rectangle wrapped in brown paper and handed it to me.

"What's this?" I asked and took it in my hands.

She beamed. "Belated birthday gift."

I peeled back the carefully wrapped paper to reveal a pallet of paints. But not just any paints. I stared down at the rows of colors, unlike anything I'd ever seen before. Purple that shimmered in the light and changed to green. Gold so faceted it looked like actual gold dust. My eyes brimmed with tears, and warmth rushed up through my body at the gift.

"Where on earth did you get this?" I asked, my voice cracking with emotion.

"I had them made." She seemed unbothered by it, as it were no big deal. But I knew these must have cost a small fortune.

I tipped my head to the side. "Julie–"

"Don't. I wanted to. You're such a good friend to me, Av'. You deserve the world. We both do." She stopped to take a sip of wine. "I think the city will be good for you."

I drank a mouthful and let it heat my belly. Maybe she was right. About everything. Perhaps this was the beginning. I could already feel the weight of worry melting away as I let myself relax.

A blank canvas.

***

Wednesday came fast, and with it, Orientation Day at my school. Julie walked with me to the historic brick building that housed the infamous NSCAD and hovered outside the front doors while I grabbed two coffees from a rolling coffee cart. The vendor was young and looked like he was still recovering from a weekend on the town. Which he probably was. Halifax was an artsy city but also known for its university life. St. Mary's, Dalhousie, NSCAD, and a plethora of community colleges. Downtown comprised three kinds of people: bustling business types, tourists, and university students.

I handed Julie a coffee. "Aren't you going to be late?"

She shook her head, unable to look at me as she focused on people passing by. "My orientation doesn't start for another half an hour."

I sipped my too-hot coffee and seethed as it burned my tongue. "Sure you're not here to glimpse a particular hottie barista?

She gave me a playful shove. "Bitch." I laughed and watched her step down onto the street, and she turned to me before crossing. "I'll see you later."

I waved her off before heading inside the large double glass doors. When they closed behind me, all sounds of the city cut off, and I was suddenly immersed by all there was to look at. The school side that faced the street outside was made almost entirely of arched windows, which let a ton of natural light fill the creative spaces. Walls of rough stone painted white in some places, left untouched in others.

A front desk sat in the middle of the entryway with a busy receptionist behind it with a tight look on her face as she managed an endless stream of incoming calls. I'd no idea where I was supposed to go, but I didn't want to bother her, so I wandered. Smells of paints and clay and other mediums filled my nose, and I inhaled deeply. Students and faculty busied about, headed for their tasks for the day.

I pulled out my welcome package and rifled through the papers until I found the campus map. Just when I thought I turned down the correct hallway, I stopped and groaned at the rows of black unmarked doors. How did anyone get around here?

"Lost already?" spoke a familiar voice, and I turned to find Tomas. His dark brown hair was swept back neatly, and he wore a casual outfit of jeans and a white t-shirt.

I blew out a breath and held up the map. "This is useless."

"Come on." He laughed. An oddly comforting sound. Like holding a warm cup of tea. "You were headed in the right direction. Orientations for Foundation year students are usually right down here. They just haven't marked any of the doors yet."

I followed him to the end of the hall, where a set of double doors waited. I could see why Julie liked him. Tomas was sweet and kind and comforting just to be around. He exuded a calm presence. When he stopped and peeked in through the small window, he looked at me with a nod.

"Here you go."

"Thanks," I replied and stuffed my map back in my bag. "Hey. Uh, what are you doing tonight?" He gave me a curious look. "I don't know how appropriate this is, considering you're kind of my boss, but do you want to hang with Julie and me? If you're free? Just hordes of junk food and terrible movies." I shrugged. "Probably some drinks."

Tomas thought for a moment. "I'm working tonight. At my parent's Korean restaurant in Dartmouth. But maybe another time?"

Julie would probably kill me. "Deal."

He left me to head off to his class, and I entered through one of the swinging doors to find a packed room. Orientation had already begun, and all heads turned to gawk at me. Embarrassment flooded my cheeks. The prof at the front paid me no attention as I lowered my head and found an empty seat near the back. But immediately regretted it when I caught the death glare from the girl I sat next to.

She wore a permanent scowl on her stunningly perfect face. Framed by long braids, entwined with gold threads, each one flawless. Her features, deep and sharp against the dark tones of her skin, made her terrifying and lovely at the same time. If I were to put her on canvas, I'd call the painting *Nightshade*.

I stammered over my words as I whispered, "Sorry, is this seat taken?"

She just continued to glare at me as if she were willing me with her thoughts to leave. I cringed and cowered away from her as I bent to fetch my bag from the floor. "Cool, I get it. I'll find another seat." As I stood to move, my back hunched over as to not alert the speaker that I was interrupting yet again, my flimsy paper coffee cup squeezed in my hand, and the top popped off. Hot coffee spilled all over her lap, and she leaped to her feet with a pissed-off groan.

"Oh, my god!" My loud reply alerted the entire room, and sounds of annoyance bounced off my back. "I'm so sorry–" I tried to wipe at her black dress and fishnet leggings, but she just huffed in anger and swatted my hand away.

"Don't fucking touch me," she seethed and threw a conscious glare around the room behind me. She narrowed her piercing black eyes at me before spinning in a huff and stormed out of the room.

I stood there, breathless and frozen. *What the hell just happened?*

"Is everything alright back there?" the prof at the front

called out impatiently.

I turned around, my face surely as red as the brick that made up the surrounding walls. "Uh, yes. Everything's fine." I quickly slipped into a chair. "Sorry for interrupting."

The speaker picked up where they left off, and I sat there, thankful I was in the back where no one could see the beads of sweat that broke out on my face and the breaths that heaved from my chest as I willed my heart to calm the hell down.

My first day wasn't off to a great start.

Chapter Four

The following week went by in a blur of disjoint- ed and awkward moments. Moments of me desperately trying to adjust to my new life. On the second day of classes, my bike wouldn't start, and it was raining, so I'd braved the metro bus. It was only a ten-minute ride, but it was enough to turn my stomach upside down. I'd been sitting in class all of five minutes before I bolted to the bathroom. Not before I accidentally knocked some books off the edge of the angry girl's desk. The death stare she'd given me as she slowly bent to pick them up was enough to give me nightmares.

But I'd already had plenty of those.

I spent my days failing to fit into my new life. I spent my nights tossing and turning in a pool of sweat as I fought off a cavalcade of nightmarish hallucinations. Nothing cohesive. Just a mess of flashes and images that seared into my mind by the time the morning sun broke across my bedroom.

The dark membrane of a bat-like wing as moonlight shined through the leathery skin. Eyes so completely black they seemed to ooze tar from their sockets. Winged creatures circling the jagged tops of a dark castle in the far distance. My arm, outstretched, long black claws gripping and puncturing my skin. But the blood that dripped from the wounds wasn't red.

It was as black as night.

Every morning, I'd awake with a start and hold the scream in my chest. I didn't want Julie to know. Didn't want her to see how horribly I was adjusting to our new life. She seemed so happy, so... comfortable. Her classes were off to a great start. She'd come home each day and regale me in details of what she did, what she learned, who she met. I didn't want her to feel guilty for it. But makeup could cover only so much, and the puffy bags that were forming under my eyes were taking on a lovely, bruised tone.

Friday finally rolled around, and I slogged home from classes with a weight on my chest. Glad to be done with it and away from it all. But dreading the downtime where my nightmares could catch up with me.

I collapsed on the sofa, jacket, boots, and all, and let an exhausted moan erupt from me.

"Rough week?" Julie asked from the kitchen. She poured herself some wine before grabbing another glass from the cupboard.

"You could say that." I pushed myself into a half-sitting position.

"That chick still giving you trouble?"

I toed off my boots beneath the coffee table and twisted my long red hair into a messy bun at the top of my head. "She's not really doing anything at all. She just... stares at me. Gives me these looks as if she's ready to rip my throat out with her teeth or something."

Julie skirted around the sofa and set down a glass of wine in front of me. I took it and twisted it slowly between my fingers.

"What did you do to piss her off so much?"

I shrugged. "Nothing. Well, I mean, I accidentally spilled my coffee on her during orientation." Julie laughed and sipped from her glass. "But it can't be that. Not now, not... *still*. Plus, it's not just me. She treats everyone like that. Even the prof." I blinked. "God, I don't even know her name yet. She rarely speaks in class."

Julie leaned back in the chair as she balanced her sock feet on the edge of the wooden coffee table that sat between us. I could smell something hearty–our dinner–cooking in the oven. "Well, sounds like she's just a good ol' fashioned bitch. If you'd gone to high school with me, you'd know the type." Julie raised her glass and took another sip. "Welcome to the real world, Av'. Bitches be everywhere."

I sank into the couch with a groan. Julie pushed a piece of paper across the table with her toe.

"What's that?" I asked.

Her sky-blue eyes sparkled with mischief. "There's a gallery looking for an intern. Someone to do menial tasks. Probably just cleaning, but it's an in."

I sat up and plucked the folded paper from the table. "What do you mean?"

"A job, Av'," she replied. "Something for your resume. Something to give you that leg up over the rest of your class."

I opened the flyer and stared at the words without registering them. "Isn't that a bit premature?"

Julie shrugged and leaned forward. "I'm already on a waitlist for a temp job at the library."

I didn't bother reading it and set it on the cushion next to me with a deep sigh. "It's the first week, Jules. I think I'm at maximum capacity for overwhelming things."

She looked at me with a grin. "Just read it. Look at what gallery it is."

Too tired to argue with her, I took the paper and opened

it again, taking in words this time. My eyes widened, and I could see Julie grinning from the corner of my one eye. "Gallery Danes?"

"You're welcome."

Gallery Danes had always been my favorite in the city. I read the words out loud in hopes they would sink in. "Gallery Danes is looking for a student or temp to work one day a week in the gallery. Duties include sweeping, mopping, organizing stock, window cleaning, accepting deliveries, etc. All interested applicants are to fill out the form on our website. Position to be filled by the end of the month."

"You should do it," Julie encouraged. "Apply."

I stared unblinking at the paper. I'd never get this job. Not over the more qualified people who no doubt already applied. Not over the many art students that went to my school. But I wondered then if Julie was starting to catch on to my misery, and this was some attempt to cheer me up. I managed a smile for her as I folded the paper and tucked it away in my pocket.

"Sure, I'll think about it."

She hopped to her feet. "We need to do something." She threw back the last of her wine and set down her glass. "Something to celebrate surviving our first full week in the city."

"Like what?"

Her response was a wicked grin.

***

A few hours later, under a blanket of night sky and city lights, we stood in a long line of university students eager to let loose. The music inside the club pounded against the wall we all leaned against. And the bass vibrated beneath my feet.

The line moved forward, and I took a step closer. Julie bounced on her toes with excitement. Her long legs hung from the short black halter dress she wore, and I shivered just looking at her bare arms.

September in Halifax wasn't exactly warm, and I tugged at the hem of my long sleeve red shirt while regretting the black leather pants she'd insisted I wear. The top half of my body was cold, while the bottom half was literally sweating under the unforgiving fabric. At least I'd worn comfortable footwear, my burgundy Doc Martens.

The line moved again, and Julie and I were finally at the front. The beefy bouncer that handled the door held it open as he sized us up.

"IDs," he grunted.

I shot Julie a look that said, *I thought this club never checked IDs?* A fact she'd assured me before we left the apartment. She kept her expression aloof as she swung her long blonde waves over her shoulder. Her fingers slid over the back of his massive hand, and she blinked coyly up at him.

"I'm afraid we didn't bring them with us," she practically cooed.

The man's thick brows pinched together as he stared down at her. He opened his mouth to no doubt turn us away, but Julie leaned forward and whispered something in his ear. When she pulled away, her pale face beaming with a grin, the bouncer looked between the two of us and gave a curt nod as he took one step to the side.

He held the door open for us, and I gave Julie a quick questioning look. I waited for her to enter first and then followed hesitantly behind. As I passed the bouncer, I dared look up at his scrutinizing expression, and, for a split second, something flashed in his eyes. A rainbow of color that made him look unnatural. Unnerving. When he blinked, the colors disappeared, and I stamped into the dark noise of the club. Either he had some crazy contacts, or exhaustion was wearing on me.

"What did you say to him?" I shouted into Julie's ear.

She threw me a grin over her shoulder. "I told him to find me for a dance on his break."

"That's it?"

Her response was a cheeky shrug, and she tugged me further into the club. I wasn't prepared for what I found inside the building. What I'd assumed was a typical nightclub was actually an old four-story building converted into four different clubs. All accessible from inside. A series of staircases took us from one level to the next, each one offering a unique atmosphere.

On the lower level, a fast-paced dance party, complete with shot girls wandering the floors. The next, a fancier, more subdued area full of classy tables littered with wine glasses and cocktails. The bartenders wore bow ties. The top floor was more my style, with a quieter atmosphere and a live band playing on a small floor-level stage. But Julie came to dance, and dance is what we did.

We plunged into the night with drinks and laughter. We danced to every song. When we needed a break, we'd head upstairs and sit in a booth while we sipped beers and listened to whatever folk band played. At some point, plates of food appeared in the crowd, balanced on expert hands, and we snagged some nachos.

After a couple of hours, the throbbing in my ears matched the pulsing in the soles of my feet. I desperately needed to sit. The half a dozen drinks Julie fed me swirled in my head, and I wiped my slick forehead as I leaned against a tall metal stool.

"Bathroom?" Julie fought to say over the pounding music.

I shook my head. "I just need some air!"

She scanned around as she danced in place. "I'll go with you! Just wait for me to use the bathroom!"

I nodded and followed her as she took me by the hand and led us through the congestion of dancing bodies. But my head swam even more, and I desperately needed air before I passed out. I squeezed her hand, and when she glanced over her shoulder and mouthed the word *outside* as I gave a show of fanning myself.

Julie chuckled and held up a finger to tell me she'd meet me out there in a minute, and I took a deep breath as I made a beeline for the exit. I threw myself against the heavy metal door and fumbled out onto the sidewalk, where the cool night air immediately soothed me. I balanced myself as I leaned forward and braced my hands on my bent knees, and heaved the fresh air in and out of me. Desperate to purge nausea from my body.

Next to me, a plume of cigarette smoke billowed around a small group of smokers, and I moved further down the sidewalk until I reached the mouth of a dark, narrow alley that divided the club from the next building.

My head stopped spinning, and I could finally stand straight. I leaned against the rough stone exterior as I waited for Julie, my skin still thrumming with vibrations of music and dance and drink. She was right. Despite inevitable nausea from being in close quarters, I needed this. I needed to get out of my own head for a moment and let loose.

When the smokers had gone back inside, I shoved

off the wall to move closer to the club entrance so Julie would see me, but a rustling from the alleyway caught my attention. Shadows moved in the darkness as I peered inside the narrow opening.

Heaps of garbage and boxes were piled in the far corners, but I couldn't see anything that moved. I stood there and stared for a moment, willing my eyes to adjust, scanning for…anything. I heard it when a black garbage bag toppled over, and a few stray cans rolled to the ground. The voice. The whisper that haunted my dreams.

Avery…

I froze.

"Who's there?" I called into the darkness. "Who's… following me?"

When nothing responded, nothing moved, I dared take a step closer. Curiosity overpowered my fear and sense of self-perseverance. I was tired of this. Either something *was* following me, or I was indeed losing my mind.

I stepped further into the alley, convinced it was probably just a stray cat and I just desperately needed sleep. I toed the toppled garbage bag, flipped it around with my shoe until something scurried out from beneath it. I let out a shriek.

A rat.

But beyond that, beneath piles of crumpled garbage, that same blue light I'd seen before. But it was a small fissure in the stone, glowing and emanating an almost blinding light. It changed when I blinked, and a small ball of light appeared. Like a single Christmas tree light, only this time it grew and grew, expanded until I had no choice but to shield my eyes. Something flew around my head, tangling in my hair, and I swatted at whatever it was. A bird, a bat. I'd no idea. The shadows of the alley spun around me; my vision burned with glowing blue lines of light.

I stumbled backward as I struggled to exit the alleyway, and two arms caught me before I met the concrete sidewalk. The blue light was gone, and the alley was shrouded in darkness once again. I turned, expecting to find Julie, but found myself face to face with a man. A strange man with long, straggly black hair that partially covered his worn but strangely handsome face.

He towered over as he glared down at me with a scrutinizing expression. His large brown eyes widened, almost in recognition. But I'd never seen him before in my life, which only meant… it wasn't recognition I saw. It was something else. I struggled in his hold, and he gripped my arms tightly as he pulled me hard up against his leather jacket. He reeked of cigarettes and something like black cherries.

"Well, well, well." His raspy smoker's voice made me shudder. "What do we have here?"

I writhed against his tight grip. "Let me go."

The guy pulled me close, and I could have sworn he… *smelled* me. "This is an interesting turn of events."

For once, my pathetic stomach was my saving grace. Nausea took root once again, and I couldn't stop my stomach from heaving even if I wanted to. I puked all over his leather jacket and then his combat boots. The booze went sour in my mouth.

The guy instinctively shoved me away, and I fumbled back a step just as Julie appeared from behind. "Avery!" She came to a stop by my side and pushed at the guy's shoulder. "Get away from her, you creep!"

He held up both hands. "Hey, I'm the victim here." He motioned to the vomit that ran down his front. "Maybe you should tell your girl not to wander in dark alleys alone. Especially around here."

Julie smoothed the hair away from my sweaty face. Her eyes were crazed and worried. "Av', you okay?"

I nodded. When we both looked back, the guy was gone.

"Christ, Avery," Julie chastised. "The *alley*? What were you thinking?"

"Just getting some air," I replied. Then I remembered. The blue light. I wiped my face with the back of my hand and spun around to peer down into the narrow darkness. "Where did it go…"

"What? The guy?" Julie asked. "He's gone."

"No." I shook my head as the rapid events of the last few minutes fought to settle in my mind. "No, there was…" Was what? A fairy? A stalker lightning bug? I took a deep breath, and the remnants of vomit burned in my throat. "I think I need sleep."

Julie flung an arm around my shoulders and turned us in the direction of the apartment. "Come on then. I think that's enough fun for one night. Let's go home."

Breaths came easier with the more distance we put between the club and us, but I couldn't shake the feeling of someone–*something*–following, lingering in the shadows. Watching the whole way back.

Waiting.

***

Moonlight filtered through the leathery veil of a batwing, revealing the dark membranes. Balls of light exploded in the distance. Shaking the Earth. Like war sounds. My head seemed to float, only tethered by its attachment to my body. *A dream. This was a dream.* No… I glanced down at my bare arm, overturned to expose the tender flesh of its underside. A long gash slowly ripped down the length of it.

A nightmare.

Long, crooked black fingers wrapped my arm, squeezing

and coaxing the blood from the wound. Only… what oozed from the slice was black as night and thick like tar, just like before. The hand that gripped me–the body it belonged to existing outside the confines of my nightmare–tightened its grip until the blackness inched up my arm, covering every inch of skin until it reached my shoulder. Then my neck.

It crawled over my jaw and pried open my lips. I fought against it, but it was no use. My mouth gaped, and the darkness spilled inside, filling me. A gurgled scream erupted from my chest, and I fell backward into the void of nothingness. The only sound to be heard was that of a low cackle. Deep and menacing.

The sound of my phone ripped me from the nightmare. The early morning sun filtered through my white curtains, and I let a few deep breaths of air cleanse the tendrils of the horrid dream from my lungs. My phone continued to ring, and I reached over to swipe it from the little nightstand that held a mess of books and dirty dishes.

I tapped the green button and held it to my ear with a shaky hand. "Hello?"

"May I speak to Avery Quinn, please?" a female voice responded.

I sat upright. "This is she."

"Good morning, Avery," they replied. "I'm calling on behalf of Gallery Danes regarding the temp position. Would six o'clock this evening work for you?"

Bewildered, I glanced around my room. Then flexed my hand in front of me, ensuring myself this was real. I wasn't still in a dream. "I'm sorry… uh, what's this about?"

A slight sigh came through the line. "The temp position available at Gallery Danes. We're conducting interviews this evening. I called the number you provided on the application."

"I… I didn't apply–"

"Avery Quinn. Foundation year at NSCAD. I have your application right here. Sent in yesterday," they said with a clip of annoyance.

I rubbed at my tired face. What was happening? Then it hit me. I flung the blankets off and stood from the bed. "Yes. Oh, yes. Sorry," I feigned a laugh. "Mornings. Yes, six o'clock works perfectly. I'll be there."

"Excellent," the woman replied evenly. "Bring your portfolio. Celadine will see you then."

Celadine. Kell-ah-deen. I rolled the word over in my mind. Such a unique name.

I let her hang up first before I set the phone down and stormed out to the apartment. I grabbed a pillow from the couch as I stomped over to Julie's bedroom and swung the door open. She was asleep, but her eyes peeked out from under drowsy lids as I hurled the pillow at her.

She bolted awake. "What the hell?"

"Guess who just called me for an interview?" I stood

and crossed my arms.

Julie blinked the sleep away and yawned over a grin.

My eyes bulged. "You *applied* for me?"

"You wouldn't have done it otherwise!" she countered. "And I know it would have killed you to see someone else get the job."

I spun on my heel and stormed away with a groan.

"You're welcome!" she called after me, her laugh trailing behind.

She was right. I just wished she'd told me. With everything that's been happening… I didn't need any more surprises in my life. I'd forgotten all about the job opening, but at least I had the whole day to prepare.

As six o'clock neared, I pulled into the gallery parking lot and turned off my bike. As I removed my helmet and stared up at the looming building with a smile, I couldn't tuck away. I loved this gallery. Tess had brought me here so many times over the years, even dared to sign me up for a weekly kid's art class when I was seven. It was the first time I'd been around so many kids my age in the same room. It had been the best six weeks of my young life. Even though it made her nervous to be in the city, she'd brought me in every Saturday, and I always walked away so sure of what I'd wanted in life.

This. I'd wanted this. And still did.

With a deep breath, I headed for the grand entrance, a

set of black double doors nestled in the face of the massive alabaster building. Its old gothic design was just one of many sights to behold in the city. Halifax was well known for its boastful historic architecture. Gothic revival, Victorian, Georgian. Restored brick exteriors, mismatched yet cohesive, littered the streets as intricately carved gargoyles and other creatures watched over everything from ledges and pointed tips that cut the sky.

Gallery Danes was no exception. A stark white gem in the center of it all. The plaster exterior seemed to soak up the sunlight as two large columns held up a beautifully carved awning that shadowed the two black entrance doors. I gripped the brass handles and tugged them open, immediately met with the familiar scents of paints and ink and damp concrete.

I strolled over to the front desk, a semi-circle in the middle of the front space, topped with white marble to match the sprawling floors. A receptionist sat behind it. She spotted me and smiled as she clicked the Bluetooth device in her ear.

"Hi," I greeted as I approached the desk. "Avery Quinn. I'm here for the temp interview?"

"Excellent," she replied, and I immediately recognized her voice from the phone call earlier. She pointed to the left, where a small group of people waited in rows of black leather chairs. "Have a seat with the others, and I'll let Mrs.

Danes know you're here."

The phone rang, stealing her attention away, so I just nodded in thanks and strolled over to the waiting area. I spotted a few familiar faces. People from my school. Some from my class, others I'd just passed in the halls. Older, more experienced. Definitely more qualified for this job than I was.

There were only a few empty seats, all surrounding one person. A girl. And, as I made my way through the dozen or so applicants, I realized why these seats were empty.

They circled the angry chick from class.

Her silky black hair was done in a million tight braids she piled loosely atop her head, and her lips were coated in a matte black lipstick, only slightly darker than her skin, that added to her intimidating beauty.

I stopped in my tracks as her black eyes peered up at me with a look that said, *Do it. Sit here. I dare you.* I chewed at the inside of my lip as I contemplated my options. I could stand against a wall and wait. Or I could take a seat next to her and brace against whatever spite she threw my way.

Whispers rose from the others, undoubtedly gossiping about the scary bitch that sat off to the side by herself. And, at that moment, I realized something. She was just a girl. Like me. An art student. She wasn't some terrifying monster. She wasn't going to bite.

And I would not let her intimidate me.

I marched over to where she sat and took a seat right next to her with a brazen smile. I ignored the resounding gasps that piped up from the others and plucked a magazine from a little side table. I mindlessly flipped through the pages, unable to read any of the words. The weight of her stare pressed in on me. I could practically feel her discontent pulsing in the slight stretch of air that hovered between us.

Some time passed. Three applicants went into an office when called and emerged after only a few minutes each. Their faces alight and beaming, as if they'd just seen their favorite celebrity. I'd never actually met or even seen the gallerist, Mrs. Danes. I was curious now but couldn't bring myself to focus on anything else aside from the tangible anger that radiated from the left.

I closed the magazine and turned toward her. "Look, I get it, but if you're still angry about the coffee–"

"What the hell are you rambling about?" The whites of her eyes grew, contrasting beautifully against her dark skin. Almost hypnotizingly so.

I struggled to find words. "The, uh, the coffee I spilled on you during orientation."

She just rolled her eyes and angled her legs away from me as she crossed one over the other. "That's the least of my worries."

What was her deal? "Well, regardless, I'm sorry."

She pretended to pick at her perfectly manicured black nails. Matte, like her lips. "Just stay out of my way."

A rush of embarrassment flooded my cheeks. "I... I didn't know I was–"

The office door swung open again, and the woman called out a name. "Maxine Carmichael?"

The girl seething in unwarranted anger rose from her seat and smoothed out her silky black romper. Jeez, she was like a dark goddess. Everything about her was perfect, not a hair or pore out of place. She headed toward the woman in wait, not bothering to throw me a second glance as she disappeared behind the door with a leather portfolio tucked under her arm.

I let out a long, hot breath that I hadn't realized was burning in my chest and glanced around. My eyes caught the gaze of one of the other applicants, a girl I recognized from the halls at school. I tipped my chin, keeping her attention, and leaned closer.

"Who is that chick?" I asked her. "The one that just went in?"

Her eyes widened. "You don't know?" I shook my head, and she sighed. "That explains a lot. That's Maxine Carmichael. Local artist and a total bitch. Fucking talent-ed as hell, though. I'm not even sure what she's doing at NSCAD. She doesn't need it."

I wanted to ask more, but the guy next to her began

speaking, and the girl turned to engage with her friends. I sat back and pulled out my phone. I punched Maxine Carmichael into Google. Her website was the first in the search results, followed by endless local news articles featuring her art. I scanned unblinking at the dark wonder of Maxine's work. While mine could be considered magical, colorful, and whimsical, Maxine's was dark, tortured, and... violent. Blood and charred footprints, broken bones, and blackened forests. A quick look around her website proved she had preferred mediums—charcoal and sculpting.

The office door swung open and ripped me from the obsessive haze. Maxine strutted out, no sign of a smile, but she wore a sense of smugness as she stomped right by me, her chin held high. As she passed, she glanced down and flashed me a look that said *good luck*. But not the wishful kind, more of a... *good luck doing better than me*.

"Avery Quinn?" the woman called as she checked the clipboard in her hands.

Suddenly wrought with nerves, I stood and made my way over to the door. She motioned with her arm and ushered me inside. The door closed behind me, and I turned to find an office so unlike the pristine neatness of the gallery.

Heaps of books laid about, threatening to topple over at the slightest touch. The walls were littered with frames showcasing beautiful sketches of landscapes—mountains, meadows, the sea. Shelves sagged under the weight of more books, broken up by haphazardly placed trinkets. And, in the center of it all, a desk.

A woman sat behind it, waiting patiently for me to acknowledge her. But I had no words to offer, only the look of utter surprise. Mrs. Danes was unlike anything I was expecting. All day, I'd dreamed up the image of a sweet older woman, dressed in beige pantsuits with hair neatly tucked back in a bun, maybe a pair of glasses balancing on her nose.

But I stood and stared back at a stunning woman. I struggled to believe she was much older than Aunt Tess. Her exposed arms displayed tattoos that covered nearly every inch of the palest skin I'd ever seen. Dark eyeshadow rimmed violet eyes—no doubt contacts—behind a pair of oversized cat-eye glasses. Her hair was a heap and tangle of dreads and braids she kept swooshed atop her head, and I immediately knew why Maxine had changed her own hairstyle today.

"Avery Quinn, I presume?"

I shook away the daze. "Yes, yes, that's me." I lunged forward, a little too eager, and offered a hand to shake. She happily accepted it, and I marveled at the soft coolness of her skin. Like a doctor's touch. "Thank you for seeing me today, Mrs. Danes."

She let out a puff of air and waved me off. "Oh, god, please, call me Celadine. I'm not old enough to be a Mrs. yet."

Words. Why couldn't I find them? My mouth gaped soundlessly as I continued to stare at the eclectic beauty before me. My hands sweat, and I fumbled with the leather portfolio in my grip. Celadine grinned and motioned to the chair across from her desk.

"Please, have a seat."

I plunked down in the plushy chair and waited for her prompt to start the interview, but she only eyed me curiously, her chin resting on her delicate and tattooed hands.

"Have we met before?" she asked.

"What?"

She leaned back in her chair. "You look familiar. Surely we've met somewhere. A showing?"

My cheeks warmed. "Uh, no. I would definitely remember meeting someone like you."

I regretted the words immediately, but Celadine only chuckled under her breath as she shifted in her seat and picked up a piece of paper. She pushed her glasses further up her nose and read.

"Avery Quinn. Foundation year at NSCAD." She set the paper down and eyed me. "Are you enjoying your classes?"

"Yes, very much so," I told her. My clammy fingers gripped my portfolio tightly. Why was I so nervous?

"Have you chosen your preferred field to focus on yet?"

Finally, a topic I could talk about for days. Somewhere,

deep down in my gut, stirred a bit of confidence. "I want to experiment with as many mediums as I can while doing my first year, but I have been focusing on watercolors, oil paints, and sketching for most of my life." I swallowed dryly. "But I hope to move into Fine Arts, eventually. Get my Bachelor's."

One of her dark eyebrows arched. "And where do you see yourself in, say, ten years?"

"Well," I cleared my throat and avoided her direct gaze. "One day, I'd like to be where you're sitting, actually. I want to run my own gallery."

She stared at me for a moment, a little too long for comfort. What was she thinking? Did I look like a little fool to her? This was an interview for a temp job to clean the gallery, and here I was spewing off dreams of grandeur.

Celadine held out her hand, palm up. "Let's see your work."

I stomped down the self-consciousness that bubbled up and leaned forward to place my portfolio in her hands. She flipped through its laminated pages, examining each one with an unreadable expression behind those cat-eye glasses. Finally, she handed it back to me.

"Avery, tell me why you think you deserve this position over the many others who applied."

Her statement caught me off-guard. She didn't even

comment on my work. My mind raced for a reply, but all that came out was, "I don't." Celadine tilted her head. "Any of those applicants would be a great choice, I'm sure. There's a lot of talent out there, people who would love to work here."

Again, she let a long and empty pause hold the space between us as she eyed me curiously.

"The job is a paid temp position," she finally spoke and began ruffling through the mess of papers on her desk. "It's just minimum wage, but you'll learn a lot here, even though it's just one day a week. Saturdays. But I might get you to come in on the occasional Sunday, too." She stopped and glanced at me from over the rim of her glasses. "Are you cool with that?"

My entire body hummed with excitement and disbelief. "Yes, I can definitely do that."

"Excellent," Celadine replied and nodded at a particular piece of paper she'd been looking for. She handed it to me. "Fill this out with your tax and payment info and give it to Helen at the front desk. You can start tomorrow if you like. Just for an hour. Pop in and learn the ropes."

I shook my head. "Wait. I have the job?"

"Yes," Celadine assured. "That is if you want it."

My cheeks went tight with a smile. "I do. Yes, I absolutely do. Thank you *so* much." I chewed at my lip. "But, what about the others?"

She chuckled. "I'll let them down easily."

Celadine stood and came around the desk to open the door for me. I stood from my seat and tucked my portfolio under one arm while I shook her chilly hand with the other.

"Thank you," I told her, and she just nodded once. Just as I passed through the doorway, I turned. "Oh, I just wanted to say how much I loved the Mitchell Showcase you did last year. The nighttime theme, it was breathtaking."

Celadine gave me a satisfied look. One that spoke more than a thankful response. "I think you're going to like it here, Avery."

I knew I would. This was my dream job. But I left the gallery with my stomach in knots because I also knew that Maxine Carmichael was my competition, and she didn't strike me as the type to lie down easily. Or at all.

Chapter Five

I slowly fell into a comfortable routine. My nerves seemed to settle, and the nightmares kept at bay. The days turned into a couple of weeks, and I woke each day eager and ready. I learned my way around the labyrinth that was my school. Classes were something I looked forward to; being immersed in a world of everything I loved.

However, sitting in the same room with Maxine each day was no picnic. I'd said nothing about my new job except to Julie, Tomas, and Tess. And I knew the exact day Maxine figured out she didn't get it. The class had ended. Everyone began filing out of the room and dispersed into the halls outside. Maxine's phone rang, and she stopped to answer it as I'd bent to tie my sneaker, and I'd overheard her already angry tone drop to a low bellow of annoyance.

"Then who got it?" she'd seethed into the phone. "That's fucking bullshit. Do I need to get my mother–*Just tell me.*" Her wide eyes flashed to me from across the hall, and a shiver ran down my spine. She'd said nothing, just tossed her phone in her bag and spun on her heel before leaving the building. I'd heard the front entrance door slam from where I stood, frozen on the second floor.

She hadn't said a word to me since. Didn't stop her from giving me a death stare every chance she could, though. Or a hip check in the hall. Or slamming doors in my face as we moved from studio to studio for different classes.

But, as much as I'd wanted the gallery job, the wrath of Maxine was making me question it. Especially after I realized that being a weekend temp at an art gallery literally meant *janitor*. Two weekends in a row now, I'd hopped on my bike and drove to work, where I spent my time cleaning up after the kids' art classes, mopping floors, dusting displays, and refilling the stock room. I'd yet to even cross paths with Celadine, let alone learn anything of value about my chosen career.

On the third Saturday, at the end of my shift, the sun tucked itself behind the horizon and a deep orange hue filtered in through the windows that lined the front of the gallery. I meandered in the space near the front where the kids had finished their art class, taking my time cleaning up the mess as Helen packed up her things for the day. I wanted to wait around, wanted to see if I could at least catch a quick exchange with my boss. Remind her that I worked here, and I could do much more than grunt work.

I wanted to *learn*.

As if Helen could read my mind, she piped up, "If you were hoping to get a job here so you could work with Mrs. Danes, it'll never happen."

My cheeks filled with heat as I slowly collected some brushes. "Does she not work in the gallery or something? I never see her."

Helen shoved her arms through the sleeves of a flowery trench coat. Careful not to knock a single perfect chestnut hair out of place. Helen seemed like a plain Jane professional against Celadine's colorful appearance. "She works nights, mostly. But she's a very private person and works alone." I watched her walk over to me as she dangled a set of keys in her hand. "So, I'd drop any notion you might have about working with her. We've had many temps over the years. None have stuck around, especially after they realized how inaccessible she is."

"Oh." I couldn't hide the disappointment in my voice even if I tried.

Helen gave me a pitiful smile and handed me the keys.

"I've got to go. I can't stay late today. It's my nephew's birthday."

"You want me to lock up?"

Helen shrugged. "I don't see why not. You still have work to do. Plus, the showroom is where the valuables are, and it's already locked." She pointed at the exit. "Bolt the handles and enter the key code *one seven five five two* after you've left the building. Otherwise, you'll be locked inside."

I stuffed the keyring in my pocket. "I can do that."

Helen said her goodbyes and headed out to her car in the parking lot. I watched her through the massive picture window that overlooked the front exterior before turning back to the mess left behind by the kids. Canvas and paints, and supplies littered the space. Tiny fingerprints coated the chairs and even the floor. Good thing we gave them water-based paints. Regardless, I'd still be there a while.

I wrangled my long crimson hair into a messy bun and set my phone down with a playlist of my favorite music filling the air as I worked. Wiping and tidying, and returning supplies to the storeroom. I held a still-wet canvas in each hand when I turned and accidentally knocked over a cup of black paint. Unable to catch it with my arms already full, I just watched and cringed as it smashed to the floor and splattered all over a drop cloth.

"Shit," I muttered and set the canvases off to the side.

I thanked the heavens that most of it seemed to land

on the drop cloth, but an image revealed itself as I tucked the corners in to contain the mess. A memory. Pulled from the string of nightmares that had plagued me during my first week in the city. I bent and, with a finger, smeared the blackness around, adding to the image. Finishing it. The way I remembered it. Until I recognized the shape of a bat-like wing stretched across the cloth. I put my weight on my legs as I tucked them underneath me and let myself get lost in the creation.

The hard and fast tempo of The Distillers played while I worked. Spreading and adding more paint, using all ten fingers as I filled the cloth with a collage of things; leafless trees, crooked branches, the blackness that had oozed from a gash on my arm–it wound around each shape, tethering them all together like a string of lights.

Then, lastly, a pair of horrifying eyes, so dark and deep and sinister, just staring back at me from the floor as I stood to take in the mess of art that just spewed from my fingers. I took a deep breath as if it cleansed me to have purged it physically.

It was… beautiful. In a strange and unnerving way. So unlike anything I usually painted. It reminded me of the striking work I'd seen on Maxine's website.

"It's a lovely piece," spoke someone from behind. I spun with a startle. I hadn't even heard the doors open. She stood there as if she'd always been hovering behind me. A navy silken kimono flowed to the floor, scarcely covering the skin-tight black jumper she wore underneath. She left her long braids and dreads down but half-tucked back at the nape of her neck.

"Celadine," I said with a breath. I followed her gaze to the mess on the floor and was suddenly awash with embarrassment. "Oh, sorry! I'll clean this up—"

"No need to apologize for making art in an art studio," she said and waved it off. "That's what the space is meant for, is it not?"

A tingle brushed my cheeks. "I suppose it is."

Celadine tucked her tattooed hands behind her back as she studied the piece on the floor with a closer look. I held onto a breath as if it were a pillow. Waiting for her to speak, to say anything about it. Finally, she straightened and gave me a smile.

"I'm sorry for not being around during your first few weeks here at the gallery. My brother is in town, and I'm dealing with some… pressing matters."

Disappointment fluttered in my gut. But I stomped it down. "Oh, no, that's totally fine. I don't expect… " I sighed. "I… don't know what I expected, actually." Before she could comment, I added, "Is everything okay? With your brother?"

Her violet eyes flashed and then fell to the art on the floor again. "Yes. He's a rep for the gallery. He travels all over, meets with clients. Artists. Makes deals overseas." She heaved a sigh. "But he's still my little brother and annoys me so."

I loosened a chuckle. "I can relate. I'm an only child, but my best friend Julie… she's like a sister." I thought of how I'd landed the interview. "Annoying at times. *A lot* of times."

Celadine's face beamed with a genuine look of admiration. But it quickly changed back to something a little more unreadable. She pointed at the cloth on the floor. "What's the subject?"

I stared down at it with her. A coldness filled my chest. "What haunts my dreams."

The dark eyes drew me in again, urging me to pull the memory of the nightmares to the front of my mind. I shook it off and looked at my boss, whose striking stare raked me over. She tilted her head.

"Where did you say you came from again?"

Confused, I said, "I was raised by my aunt in the country. Out past Elmdale."

"And your parents?"

I chewed at my lip. "They, uh, they… died. A long time ago." To lighten the mood, I chortled. "I know. I'm a tragic YA heroine."

Her body relaxed and leaned toward me. "I'm so very sorry. Do you remember them?"

"No," I said and shook my head. "I was never given that luxury. They died when I was a baby. Um... " I bit back tears. I wasn't sure why they tickled my eyes; I never really cried for them before. "They were killed. Shot. Here in the city."

She didn't reply, and an awkward silence hung in the air. The only sound was music still playing from the tiny speaker on my phone.

Unable to stand the quiet, I began collecting more supplies. Fighting to ignore the way she lingered. Staring. Watching. Did she know how unsettling her presence was? Did she look at everyone like that? I took a tub of dirty brushes over to a large marble sink and began cleaning them. I could feel her stare at my back. I dared a glance over my shoulder and met her curious gaze as we exchanged an awkward smile.

"You know," Celadine finally spoke. Her voice was like a cold purr. I shut off the tap, and half turned to face her. "I'm thinking about taking on an apprentice." Hope blossomed in my chest as she sauntered around the mess and came toward me. "Someone to teach about the gallery, about art dealing." Her sharp black eyebrows raised in wait. "I'd love for it to be you if you're interested."

"Me?"

"If you're up for the task," she replied with a grin.

I turned fully, watery paint dripping from my fingertips.

"I am, yes, absolutely."

"It's a lot to take on," she added with a faint warning.

I nodded quickly. "Okay."

"Are you able, with school?"

"Yes."

"Other commitments?"

My stomach clenched with anticipation. "I just have two obligatory evening shifts at a coffee shop each week."

"I only work nights," she replied warily.

I nodded, my mind racing over my schedule and how I could make this work. "That's fine. My shifts are only a couple of hours. They end at nine. I could come by after that."

She crossed her arms. "It'll be nearly every night."

I shrugged, trying to show it was no big deal. "I'm a night owl."

Her purple eyes widened with satisfaction behind her large cat-eye frames, and she smiled as she held out a hand. "Then it's a deal." I stared at her fingers, covered in tattoos and chunky rings. This was it. This was what I'd been waiting for. I took her hand; cool and soft, just like before. Celadine's grip firmed with a shake. "Apprentice."

"I wish you could come home this weekend," Tess pleaded on the other end of the call. I sat on the plushy couch, surrounded by pillows and comfy blankets as I tucked my sock feet underneath me.

"I'll come for a visit soon," I told her. "Promise. I'm just... I'm still settling into a routine here. And my weekends are pretty busy."

A sigh crackled down the line. "How's the new job going?"

"Good," I replied. Butterflies swirled in my stomach. "I temp on the weekends and then apprentice with Celadine during the week." I didn't dare tell my over-protective aunt that I usually met up with my boss in the dark hours of the night. But my first week of apprenticing went better than anything I could have dreamed of, and I wanted nothing to damper that joy. "It's just... everything is so new. I don't want to ask for time off just yet."

"You're entitled to time off, Avery," Tess said worriedly.

"Oh, I know. It's not like that," I assured my aunt. "Celadine's great. She's teaching me so much. And she works around my schedule with school and shifts at The Chocolate Kettle." Something warmed in my chest at the thought of working with her. Celadine was... extraordinary. For someone so young, she was wise beyond her years. She knew just about everything there was to know about the art business. I wanted to live up to her expectations. "Just let me prove my worth to her first, then I'll ask for time off and come home."

Julie stepped into my view and waggled a bottle of wine with an eager expression. I rolled my eyes but nodded with a grin.

"Uh, Tess," I said. "I have to go. I'll talk to you later, okay?"

"Okay," she replied. "Let me know when you can sneak away from your fabulous life and spend time with your dear ol' aunt."

I laughed. "I will. Promise."

I ended the call and tossed my phone on the coffee table as Julie took a seat and filled two wine glasses with her homemade brew. She handed one to me.

"Is this what we are now?" I kidded and swished the wine around in my cup. "Two winos living alone in the city."

Julie shrugged. "I wanna go out," she said over the rim of her glass. She chugged back a large gulp before adding, "There's a party on campus at my uni."

I chewed at my lip as I twisted the stem of my glass between my fingers. "I dunno, Jules."

"Oh, come on." She lifted her feet and snugged them beneath her on the couch. "It's one of the first nights your creepy boss hasn't monopolized you."

My eyes widened in mock disbelief. "You forced me to

take the job!"

"No," she said with a pointed tone. "I got you the *janitor* job, not the position under Celadine's wing. That was all you."

I grinned. "Yeah, I'm still not sure what it was I actually did to get that."

"She clearly saw how fabulous you are."

I gave her a look that said *yeah, right,* and sipped on my wine. I was getting used to the spicy aftertaste and the warm tingle it sparked all the way down my throat. "And she's not creepy. Not once you get to know her."

"I'm sure she is," Julie said in a brush-off way and pushed off the couch. She set her glass down. "Come on, we're going out." She held up a finger before I could pro-test. "Av', you moved to the city to shed that homebody life. You came here to start anew, to experience things, to become your own person—"

"Okay, okay!" I grumbled, but I couldn't help grinning. I stood up next to her. "Let's go."

The city at night was a sight to behold. Not something to fear. During the day, the downtown streets bustled with businessmen and city workers. The occasional tourist came to experience the historical place during the off-season.

But at night… it came alive with lights and music and people walking the concrete. Entire streets lined with pubs and dance clubs, people popping in and out of them as they carried laughter around in their groups. The air hung heavy with the scent of hot dogs and pizza, wafting from open pizza joints and wandering food carts.

Downtown Halifax was an experience, a destination, separate from the rest of the city. Buskers played fiddles down on the boardwalk that lined the harbor, and the sounds drifted up a few streets to where Julie and I walked to the frat party.

I could hear the party before I saw it. As we rounded the last corner, we emerged onto Inglis Street, where a row of campus housing sat near the massive university just a few yards away. It was an old brownstone. Garbage littered the front lawn, and things hung from a tree. The walkway crunched beneath my Blundstones–bits of food and broken glass–as we made our way to the wide-open front entrance. I'd never gone to high school parties, not like Julie did. Tess never allowed it. The noise from inside spilled out onto the crowded veranda and clamored against my ears, and I held my breath as we stepped inside.

"New meat!" some guy called out and raised his beer with one hand as he pointed at us with the other. He wobbled backward and lost his hat as his buddies caught him.

I looked at Julie, but she beamed. She loved being around people, around noise and dance and music. And I knew she really wanted us to fit in, to find our place here.

"Don't worry about those guys," she said to me and ushered me off to the kitchen.

Half-eaten pizza and open bottles of soda littered the countertops as people lounged about in small groups of chatter. She led me over to the dining room table, where people were playing poker. A couple people glanced up and looked at Julie with recognition.

"Julie!" one girl greeted. Half her head of black hair was shaved and combed to one side, and her blood-red lips were a stark contrast against her snow-white teeth. "You made it!"

Julie waved to them and then motioned to me. "This is Avery, guys." She looked at me with a smile as they all nodded as if they knew me. As if Julie had told them all about me. "And Av', these are… the guys. From my class." She began pointing at each of the six people that circled the table. Three guys and three girls. "Dom, Nathan, Chan, Margo, Shana, and Marty."

I lifted my hand and waved at them. "Hey, guys."

They erupted in overenthusiastic cheer and raised their drinks as they responded in unison. "*Hey, Avery!*"

I gave Julie a discreet look that said, *I know you set this up,* and took a seat offered to me. We spent hours playing round after round of poker. It didn't take long for me to settle in. Julie's friends from school were warm and welcoming and fun.

Drinks appeared in front of me, one after another until I couldn't sit still anymore and let Julie drag me to the living room, where everyone smashed around in a clumsy dance. I let loose, let go of the apprehension I constantly carried around. The hesitation I put forth before every decision. Tonight, I didn't want to be Avery the Sheltered Country Girl.

No, tonight, I was one of *them*. The kids who grew up around so many others their age. The ones who experienced the motions of public school and high school parties and dating. The trials of adolescence. People who weren't socially awkward or nervous about large groups of people or always chose the path of least resistance.

When one song ended, and I could practically hear the thumping of my heart in my chest, I realized just how much I'd had to drink. Too much. The room spun even though I stopped dancing and my stomach toiled. I needed air.

I tugged at Julie's sleeve as a new song pounded against the walls. "Popping out on the back deck for a minute," I roared in her ear.

She replied with a nod and waved at another person she knew from across the house. "I'll meet you out there in a sec!"

The music seemed to increase as I turned and made my way through the jam-packed rooms. As I reached the mudroom that held the patio exit, my phone vibrated against my thigh. I pulled it out to see the gallery number flashing across the screen. Why would Celadine be at the gallery at this hour? Or calling me, for that matter.

I swiped the button across the screen and put the phone tight to my ear to hear over the music. "Hello?"

Celadine's voice crackled through the line, but it was no use. The music was too loud. I opened the patio door and stepped out onto the crowded back deck where party-goers were barbequing.

"Celadine?" I said and pressed a finger to my other ear.

"Avery!" she said with impatience. But the surrounding noise was still too invasive. I could only hear every other word. "*Going… home… need… leave… telling… you…* "

"Sorry, Celadine. Celadine? I can't hear you. Can you text me?"

Before she could reply, someone slammed into me. A guy stumbling out through the patio doors with drinks held clumsily to his chest. Clearly too drunk for his own good. He continued to fumble on his feet, and I couldn't move out of the way quick enough as he pushed me to the edge, where a short set of stairs led down to the garden below.

I tried to push him out of the way. "Watch where you're going—"

We went over the stairs, but while I stayed on my feet, the guy rolled to the bottom, his drinks splattering and glass shattering. With a moan, he pushed himself to his feet and wavered in place as he eyed me.

"Hay," he said, his eyes barely able to focus on me. "I know you. New meat!" he erupted and threw his hands in the air. A few guys from the deck above, clearly his friends, repeated loudly, "*New meat!*"

"Uh, no," I said nervously. "Not *new meat*. I don't even go to your school."

I tried to skirt around him to head back to the house, but he stepped in my path. The guy was monstrous. Looming and thick in the shoulders. Definitely some kind of athlete. Probably football or hockey, by my guess. He reeked of beer and sweat, and his breath was moist as he clumsily leaned his face into mine.

"Where you goin'?" I shoved him away, but it was like trying to move a boulder. His hands gripped my sides, pulling me to him.

I wriggled in his grasp. "Let me go, you idiot!"

"Naw, it's a party," he said with a belch. His hand reached around to grab my ass as the other man-handled my wool sweater down to expose my bare shoulder. "You're supposed to have fun."

I reached into my bag and frantically rifled through the contents with one hand. Just as he leaned in to press his gross face to mine, I doused him with mace. An agonized scream deepened under his hands as he clasped them over his face.

"You *bitch*!" he spat and let out another long, tormented groan.

He wiped at his red, watery eyes–already swelling–and lunged for me. I stepped back too late, and his gorilla arm collided with the phone in my hand and sent it to the ground, where it smashed against a paving stone. I'd spent two months' earnings from my Etsy shop buying that phone outright.

"You asshole!" I yelled, but it only angered him more.

The guy fumbled for me, and I fell to the gravel path beneath me. He made a move to jump on top of me, but someone stepped between us. A tall figure, clad in black. The evening shadows seemed to absorb him but, when he turned to glance down at me from over his shoulder, I had to stifle the gasp that tightened in my throat. He was one of the hottest guys I'd ever seen in my life.

"You alright?" he asked quietly, his white teeth glistening in the bit of moonlight that filtered through the old maple trees. His sharp black eyebrow arched over painfully blue eyes. Eyes that cut through the shadows we stood in and locked on mine. I couldn't form a response, so I just nodded from the ground, mouth gaping. He turned back to the frat guy. "I suggest you leave."

"Leave? This is *my* house." He was so drunk he could hardly stand, and when his arm swung back, readying for a swing, my savior chuckled.

"You don't want to do that, boy."

"*Boy?*" the guy's swollen eyes failed to widen, and he rubbed them again. "Who the hell do you think you are?"

"You don't want to find out," he replied and casually smoothed the wrinkles from the sleeves of his fitted dark combat jacket.

The frat guy foolishly went to make another swing, but I hopped to my feet and doused him with more mace before a fight could break out. He screamed in agony, his fingertips pressing against his closed eyes as he blindly made his way back to the house. I could hear the faint mumblings of the word *bitch* and *whore,* but I didn't care. He was gone. And I could breathe.

Until my savior turned and faced me wholly.

I couldn't blink, couldn't move, or even speak. His striking looks held me prisoner, and I just stared at him like a fool. The silver moonlight reflected off his cerulean eyes, framed by the thickest, darkest lashes I'd ever seen on a guy. Or a girl, for that matter.

"Are you okay?" he asked me again. Concern wrought all over his face.

I blinked away the blur in my mind. "Uh, yeah. I'm fine." I nodded in the direction the guy ran off to. "Thanks for that."

He chuckled. A deep, raspy sound tickled my skin. "No

thanks necessary. Seems you handled it yourself."

I stood and watched as he bent with fluid ease and fetched something from the ground. He handed it to me. My phone.

I groaned. The screen was smashed. "Shit." I reached out and took it from his grasp, noting how blood trickled from my palm and soaked into the sleeve of my favorite sweater. I must have scraped it when I fell. "Ugh, could this night get any worse?" I bent to wipe the blood off on the grass just as I heard someone calling out to me from the deck above.

"Av'!" Julie spotted me and came flying down the steps. "What the *hell*? Did you *mace* someone?"

She helped me to my feet, and I glanced around for my savior, but he was gone.

"Yes," I said with spite. "He wouldn't get his hands off me! Even pushed me to the ground." I waggled my smashed device at her. "Broke my phone."

She clucked her tongue and glanced back at the house. "Asshole." I tucked the shattered phone in my pocket as she wrapped an arm around my shoulders. "Guess Tess was right about the mace, then."

I managed a smile as I discreetly searched around for the guy who'd tried to save me. "Yeah, don't tell *her* that, though."

✳✳✳

The next evening, I slowly made my way down the old iron steps that led from my apartment to The Chocolate Kettle below. I'd spent the entire day in bed, nursing a hangover from hell. I'd suffered greatly trying to get ready, but I wouldn't miss my time at the gallery for anything in the world.

Tomas smiled from behind the register as he wiped down the countertop.

"You look like…"

I grimaced. "Absolute garbage?"

He waggled his hand, and I managed a chuckle. "Can I get a large black, please? Oh, and add a shot of espresso?"

He turned and poured me a coffee and topped it with a lid before handing it over to me. I reached for my pocket, but Tomas shook his head.

"Employee perks," he said with a sweet grin. Tomas was the epitome of the boy next door. Always sweet and kind. Always makes you laugh. I'd only worked a couple of shifts with him, but he had me laughing the entire time.

I dropped the change into the tip jar before he could protest and took a quick sip of my coffee. I'd need it if I were going to stay awake for most of the evening.

"On your way to the gallery?" Tomas asked.

"Wouldn't get out of bed for anything less," I replied.

My empty stomach suddenly swirled, and I felt what little color I had from my face drain. Tomas fetched a chocolate bran muffin and handed it to me. "How did you know?"

He shrugged under his red Iron Man t-shirt and gestured dramatically to his face. "I'm Korean-Canadian. I was born with a trained eye to know when someone needs food."

I laughed and picked at the muffin. Letting my hindered taste buds get used to the sensation of food. I swallowed a pinch and waited to see how it'd fair in my stomach.

"Hey, so…." Tomas rubbed the back of his neck. "I was wondering what you were doing tomorrow." I must have looked alarmed because he quickly added, "You and Julie, I mean."

Sundays were one of the few days that Julie and I had no commitments, save for the couple of hours Celadine sometimes had me pop into the gallery. But she had mentioned nothing about this week. "Nothing that I know of. Why?" I noted the pink that flushed to his cheeks beneath his lovely brown eyes and batted my lashes jokingly as I leaned against the counter. "You know, you can just ask Julie to hang out. You don't need me as a buffer."

Tomas' cheeks reddened even more, but he grinned, owning his ploy. "I have no idea what you're talking about.

I played along. "Of course not."

He loosened a deep breath. "There's a Shakespeare in the Park thing tomorrow afternoon. Happens every year.

The drama students from Dalhousie perform it." Someone stepped up to the counter, and I moved to the side while Tomas served them. When they wandered off to a table, Tomas turned to me. "It's usually good fun." He added with raised brows. "There'll be food."

"Oh, well, in that case," I kidded and took a sip of my coffee. My stomach threatened to rise, but I stomped it down. Damn alcohol. "We'll be there." I didn't dare mention how Julie would be over the moon. I wanted to watch this love story play out naturally.

I said goodbye to Tomas and headed on my way. With some time to spare and a desperate need for a good dose of fresh air, I walked the few blocks to the gallery. The sun was just dipping below the jagged horizon, casting the bustling downtown district in deep orange and purple glow. By the time I reached the gallery parking lot–empty of all but one car–I'd finished my coffee and was buzzing with energy. But my heart sank when I spotted Helen exiting the front doors and locking up.

"Hey," I said and walked up to her. "Is Celadine not coming in tonight?"

"Didn't she tell you?" Helen's face twisted in confusion. "She had to leave town to deal with some urgent business matters."

My mind lagged as it rifled through the events of the weekend. Celadine *had* called me at the party, but I couldn't hear her over the noise before my phone was destroyed.

"She won't be home for a few days," Helen added as she began walking to her car. She called over her shoulder, "Enjoy your night off!"

As much as I loved my job, part of me was a bit relieved to have the night off. No amount of coffee was going to make me fit for work, and I was glad Celadine wouldn't have to see me like this. So, I headed back the way I came, but as I neared the streets that wound around my block, the remnants of espresso still coursed through my veins. I wasn't ready to go home yet. Music drifted up from the boardwalk a few streets down, the last of the local buskers before the chill of Fall crept in.

I grabbed a foot-long hotdog from a wandering cart and ate it in small, careful bites. Letting the grease soak up the mixture of old liquor and too much caffeine. I meandered about the boardwalk, enjoying the occasional fiddle player or acoustic guitar accompanied by a raw, crooning voice. I dropped what change I could find in my bag into their buckets and open guitar cases, then walked out to an empty pier to look over the harbor. The night sky echoed on the surface as lights of the city glistened in its reflection like colorful stars. I loved this city.

When the air chilled past the point of comfort, I zippered my leather jacket and made my way back toward the upper streets where I lived. As I rounded a corner near the end of the boardwalk, something rustled in the wild rose bush, and I stepped closer to see what it was. Probably a rabbit or a squirrel–a tiny blue light flickered deep within the leaves and thorns. A familiar blue hue, one I'd seen more times than I was comfortable with.

Slowly, I moved aside the outer brambles and narrowed my eyes to see in the darkness. The blue light flickered again and doused like a lantern going out. I kneeled to get a better look, poking my face in further.

Suddenly, something shot out of the bush, grazing my cheek, and fluttered around my head, tangling my hair. I shrieked and blindly swatted at the creature–bird, bat… whatever it was. Only when my hand collided with a tiny, solid object and I heard something smacking against the brick exterior of the building did I open my eyes. But it wasn't an animal I saw laying there in the mulch of the raised garden bed. I stared breathlessly at the tiny, crumpled body. The abnormally long and bony limbs, the iridescent wings…

It was… a fairy.

I don't know what possessed me to do it, but I took a few cautious steps closer. Unblinking, my chest heaving with tight breaths. I couldn't believe what I was staring at. It was no bigger than a small bird. Crumpled and twitching, unconscious. Voices and footsteps were nearing. I had mere seconds to decide.

My stomach rolled, and my head spun as it fought to process the reality of what was happening. But, when the shadows of the incomers stretched across the wooden planks to my left, I quickly scooped up the fairy and clutched it to my chest as I ran home.

Chapter Six

"Julie!" I called as I burst through the door to the apartment. But I was met with silence. "God damn it! Jules?" I checked her bedroom. Empty.

I wasn't sure why I wanted her to be home. Maybe to prove to myself that I wasn't crazy. That I truly held a fairy in my hands. I hadn't given it a second glance as I bolted home, but I could still feel its strange texture in my palms–the moth-like wings, the bony limbs, the leathery skin.

I closed myself in my bedroom and leaned against the wall to wait out the heaving of my breaths. I couldn't stop the tremble that jittered in my bones. I slowly peeled my shaky hands from my chest and glanced down at the creature in my hold.

The creature stirred, and I dropped it on my bed with a yelp. The tiny blue fairy opened its large black eyes, groggy and confused, and blinked up at me. For a moment, we just stared at one another in utter disbelief.

The fairy gave quick movements as it took in its surroundings, then hunched its shoulders with a hiss. "You captured me?" Any response I had dried up on my tongue. It tried to stretch its wings, but one was bent over, and it winced before hissing at me once more. "You *wounded* me?" It bared pointed teeth.

My back pressed firmly against the cool wall. "I didn't mean to." I managed a tight swallow. "You… you've been following me. Haven't you?" When the creature didn't respond and a tiny growl built in its chest, I grabbed an empty Amazon box. "Why have you been following me? Answer, or I'll put you in this box."

Another low hiss. "No mortal paper cage can contain me."

I paused as my eyes searched the room. Without a second thought, I grabbed a decorative birdcage I kept flowers in and dumped out the contents before tossing it over the fairy.

Its shriek was like a layered echo. "Iron!"

I dared a step closer. "Now, tell me why you've been

following me everywhere. I've seen your blue light before." I couldn't believe I was entertaining this delusion. The fairy fell silent but never blinked as it stared up at me from the cage on the bed. I fetched a stack of books from my nightstand and plopped them on top of the cage. "Fine. But you're not getting out until I get some answers."

I turned to leave, reaching for the doorknob when the fairy spoke. "I'm not following you."

I glanced over my shoulder. "Then why do you seem to be everywhere I am?"

"I'm... following the shadows."

My heart thumped hard in my chest as it raced. "W-what shadows?"

I knew exactly which ones.

"The ones that lurk all over the city in search of...." The creature seemed stunned as it struggled to find the end of its sentence.

I turned to fully face it. "In search of what?"

"I-I... don't know," it replied and placed a hand of long bony fingers over its forehead. "It hurts to remember."

I chewed at the inside of my lip. "You've hit your head."

The fairy gripped the bars of the cage, and a searing sound came from the contact. It fell back and nursed its hands before glaring at me with those black, almond-shaped eyes. "I want to leave."

"You shouldn't go anywhere with a head injury and

CANDACE OSMOND

a broken wing." I mulled over the situation in my mind. There was a fairy on my bed. *A fairy*. My mind struggled to process the information. Regardless, it was hurt, and it was my fault. "You won't last the night. You—" I loosened a deep sigh, "you should stay here until you're better."

Its eyes narrowed but widened as a thin, cloudy film flicked over them. "You invite me into your home?"

I nodded cautiously. "Will… I regret it?"

The fairy waited for a beat. No doubt contemplating how it would escape and pick out my eyeballs in my sleep. Surprisingly, it replied calmly, "No. I accept your offer."

"Just until you're feeling better and can fly out of here." My brows raised. "Okay?"

It nodded slowly, its unnaturally large and black eyes just staring at me. We both stood there in uncomfortable silence. Finally, I had to speak.

"So… what's your name?" I asked.

The scaly blue skin of its forehead crinkled. "I don't know." It let out a tiny, musical sigh and plopped down, defeated. "I can't remember."

Guilt fettered in my gut as I realized just how badly I must have hurt the creature. But I said nothing. I just grabbed my pillow and slid the case off. I poked it through the bars of the birdcage. "Here," I told it. "Get some sleep."

It accepted the cover without thanks, just watched me

leerily, and I decided to leave the creature be as I stalked out to the living room. There was no way I'd sleep in a room with that thing. Partially for what I feared it might do, and partly because I feared I was losing my damn mind. I closed the bedroom door behind me and headed for the couch, where I curled up in the fetal position and stared unblinking at the door.

✳✳✳

I was dreaming again. I knew because of how my feet seemed to float along the grass. I could feel the cool shadow of the trees and the dampness of night between my toes. Behind me, a party raged on. So loud, so bright. I didn't want to look at it. I wanted to stare at the shadows beyond the edges of the large backyard. Waiting.

Finally, he stepped out from the thick darkness. The unnamed man who'd saved me. Hair so black it seemed to gobble up the moonlight around him. Eyes so blue they put precious gems to shame. They peered at me from across the grass, and I let them suck me in.

His shape mesmerized me; tall with broad shoulders, the contours of his lean muscles evident under his perfectly tailored black combat jacket and dark jeans. He stood—old Converse sneakers on his feet—both his hands stuffed inside his pockets, and yet… he reached for me. His stare, it called to me, beckoned me to follow him. I took a few steps closer, my arm outstretched toward him.

Something grasped my shoulder, shaking me awake, and it sucked me from the dream in a blinding gasp. Immediately, I felt the sweat that covered my skin, how it clung to me under my clothes. The couch beneath me moaned as I pushed myself into a sitting position and found Julie standing over me.

"Too tired to make it to bed?" she asked.

I rubbed the back of my neck. "Yeah, something like that." My voice was hoarse. "Where have you been?"

Julie grinned. "Tomas asked me to go for coffee."

"And?" I smiled and fetched an old glass of water from the coffee table.

"And…" she shrugged," I like him."

"That's it? You *like* him?"

Julie rolled her eyes and headed for the kitchen. "I'm not looking for anything serious right now. I need to… finish growing into myself." She grabbed two fresh bottles of water from the fridge and tossed one at me as she came back and sat down in the chair across from the couch. "How was the gallery tonight?"

The gallery. God, that felt like eons ago. "Celadine's out of town for business, so I just went for a walk around the boardwalk before I came home."

She guffawed over a laugh as she cracked open her bottle

of water. "A walk? At night? By yourself?" I watched her take a swig and then clucked her tongue. "Don't let aunty Tess find out."

I laughed along with her but inside… I was wrought with nerves and rushing thoughts of worry. Of disbelief. Because, for once, Tess was right. Something lurked in the city. Shadows and voices, and angry little fairies. I drank some water to hide my expression.

I said goodnight to Julie and slowly headed for my bedroom. With trembling fingers, I turned the knob. The creaky hinges protested as I gently opened the door and stepped inside. I held my breath, my eyes immediately darting to the birdcage I'd left on my bed. But it was gone. No, not gone… on the dresser where I'd initially had it. Not a single flower out of place. The pillowcase returned to my pillow. It was as if nothing had happened.

Was I truly losing my mind?

If so—the blue light, the fairy, the shadows following me all over the city… was I subconsciously scaring myself out of living here? I let out the breath I'd been holding and tiredly changed into my pajamas before I slipped beneath the cool sheets.

Sleep weighed me down as my mind refused to let go of the thoughts of worry. I drifted off, exhaustion taking me. But as I plunged into the abyss of a dream, one thought carried with me, whispering a question in my ear.

Had my window always been open?

Chapter Seven

I awoke with a new sense of... *something*. Eagerness, determination. A stubborn will to never let my own mind scare me out of the life I wanted. I slept dreamlessly all night. Or... at least... I awoke refreshed, with no lingering tugs of a nightmare on my mind, no swirling thoughts or sweat coating my skin.

I yawned and stretched beneath the warm blankets as the early Saturday morning sun filled my bedroom. My window, still open, allowed a gentle breeze to coax across the room, and I inhaled the tinge of Fall approaching. This was heavenly. I could stay in bed all day and admire this lovely little place of mine. *Mine.* I rolled the word over in my mind. This bedroom, this apartment, school, it was all mine.

My phone beeped. Not a message, but a reminder I'd

set for myself days ago. I rolled over and swiped the screen to stop the annoying sound and groaned as I remembered what precisely the alert was set for.

I was meeting Maxine today.

One prof had assigned what he'd called a 'living assignment'. The city was full of artsy architecture, and we'd paired off to study it. Of course, he'd put me with Maxine. I rolled back and stared at the ceiling. I could do this. She was just a girl, like me. A person. Albeit the coldest person I'd ever met in my life, but a person nonetheless, and I would meet her in the coffee shop to discuss our project for class.

Julie and I bounded down the spiral staircase that led to The Chocolate Kettle below, and there she was. Maxine Carmichael, sitting ramrod straight in a chair near the back where a picture window cast her in a golden sunny glow. It covered her like a halo, outlining her dark shape and deepening the beautiful tone of her skin. No long black locks today or intricately braided strands. Maxine's hair was a massive rounded mohawk of tight black curls sprinkled with bits of gold that caught the sunlight like flecks of jewels. Her all-black sleeveless tube dress swallowed her right up to her chin, and she stared at me unblinkingly with those beauteous eyes.

Beside me, Julie halted with a shudder. "Jesus," she whispered to me. "Is that her?"

I nodded with a sigh. "Yep, that's Maxine."

She blew out a long breath. "Yikes. You weren't kidding when you said she was terrifying." I held up a finger to Maxine to indicate I'd be a minute and turned to the register with Julie to order our coffees. "Fucking gorgeous, though."

"Oh, she's like a gothic goddess," I agreed and set some change down on the counter for Penny, one of the day shift crew, and moved off to the side to let the line progress. "But, like, a goddess you *fear*."

Julie swallowed a chuckle as we turned and found Maxine's eyes on us. Waiting, brimming with impatience.

"I'll catch you later, k?" Julie said, and I gave her a nod as she skirted through the morning crowd for the door.

I took a deep breath, plastered on a smile, and walked over to the table where my guest waited.

"Maxine," I greeted curtly.

"You're late," she replied with a sneer and opened a large, thick notebook bound in black leather. "And it's Max."

The two statements clashed in my ears. "What?"

She set her pen down with an annoyed huff. "You're late. We were supposed to meet here fifteen minutes ago."

I slipped into the seat across from her. "No. I mean, yes, I know that. I'm sorry." I wrapped my fingers around the warm cup of coffee in my hands. "The other thing you said. Max?"

Her eyelids shimmered with black eyeshadow. "It's my name."

"Not Maxine?"

"Not if you wish to remain in one piece," she replied as coolly as a cat. Her perfectly manicured black fingernails casually turned the pages over. When I didn't answer, she set her pointed gaze on me. The whites of her eyes like pure moonlight around the pools of an abyss that anchored the centers. "Are we doing this or not?"

I shook away the scramble of thoughts in my mind. Maxine–*Max* always seemed to render me speechless, with little to no effort on her end. She was beautiful and intimidating as hell. The sliver of talent I'd seen just from peeking at her stuff online told me she was also far above my skill level. So why was Max doing a Foundation Year at art school? She didn't need it, clearly. She didn't seem to even want to be there. She rarely took part in class discussions, projects, or even hung around during break times. She constantly hid behind a wall of contrition. I wondered what was on the other side.

"Yes," I replied and fetched my own notes from my shoulder bag. "Let's figure out what we're doing for this project."

I could have sworn I caught the quickest tug at the corner of her mouth when she laid her eyes on my notebook.

I'd made it myself. Several of them, actually, and sold them in my Etsy store. But they were pink and purple with glitter and hand-drawn pixie wings and gold leaf marbling. Such a contrast against Max's leather-bound one; the soft black, an insignia of moon phases burned into the cover, its spine bound and tied with fraying straps of black leather. It was like pairing a Disney movie to a Horror film side by side.

"You make that?" Max asked with hardly a hint of actual interest as she took a sip from her steaming mug. She didn't strike me as the type to drink tea.

I ran my fingertips over the cover, remembering when I first came up with the idea and how excited Tess was. I smiled. "Yeah, I sell them in my shop."

Max just regarded me curiously, her eyes like a sharp rake as they scanned me over. An awkward silence held us in place, and I swallowed dryly.

"Did… you make that?" I tipped my chin toward her notebook.

"No."

I mulled my suddenly dry lips together. "I… saw your stuff." Max's face went blank. "Online. I checked out your work."

"And?" The reply carried the full intent of a warning. *Go ahead, mock me, I dare you.*

I attempted a casual shrug, but I'm sure it came off as uncomfortable. "It's… stunning."

Max's eyes narrowed. "Don't patronize me, Quinn."

"I-I'm not," I blurted. "I swear."

The back of her pen tapped anxiously against the paper in front of her, but she displayed no signs of being nervous. Max was like a wall of darkness, refusing to let anyone see anything behind it.

"Don't you mean it's *sickening*?" she said, clipped. "*Dark*? *Terrifying*? A *disgrace*?"

I gulped down a dry lump in my throat as her dark stare bore into me. But I refused to start this day cowering. I'd promised myself things would be different. I wouldn't live my life afraid. So, I went with compassion. I dared lean forward, reaching a hand for hers–for whatever possessed me to do so–but she flinched away.

"Is that what people really say about your art?"

Max said nothing as she stuffed her things inside her black suede shoulder bag.

"Just ignore people like that, Max," I tried to sound comforting. "They obviously just don't get it."

Something like regret flashed across her face. "Hard to ignore them when they're your family." She slung her bag over her arm as she stood up.

"Wait. Where are you going?" I asked. "We haven't even started."

She peered down at me as she stepped directly into the sun, casting her front in darkness as my eyes adjusted.

138

"I've already done all the research and planned everything out." She turned and headed for the door. "I'll email you the notes."

The sudden turn of events gave me whiplash, and I blinked through the confusion. "But you don't have my email!" I called after her, but she was already gone.

***

I turned the key over in my Vespa for the fifth time, but nothing happened. It was dead, and I could hear my aunt's voice in my ear, *don't forget to change that old battery*. I loved my bike, but it was nearing the end of its life, and I slunk down on the seat with a groan. I had to be at the gallery for my apprentice shift in ten minutes. Even though it was close by, I couldn't get there that fast on foot. I glanced at the pole that displayed the bus number just a few feet away from the entrance of The Chocolate Kettle and cringed at the thought of riding the bus. But it was my only option.

As the rain trickled from the skies, I tucked the bike key into my bag and stood under the sign as I waited for the bus. I could already see it coming from down the street. As it came to a stop and the accordion doors flung open, I took a deep breath and stepped inside. I dropped some change in the bin and took a spot near the back door. As the bus bounded off again, the force pushed me further into my seat, and my stomach rolled over.

I hated enclosed vehicles. Tess thought perhaps it was anxiety and a bit of claustrophobia when I was a kid. But it turned out to be good ol' fashioned motion sickness. I was prone to it, and it sucked beyond belief. Nothing curbed the inevitable wave that always rushed over me.

The bus made two stops along the way, but I paid no attention to the traffic of bus goers. I just had to hang on for a few more minutes. My fingers gripped the edge of the plastic seat beneath me as I put my focus on the gritty floor. I knew glancing out the window would cost me; it always made nausea worse. But I moved and leaned the side of my face against the cool glass. Beside me, someone filled the empty seat.

"You look like you're being held against your will," a familiar voice spoke.

No, no, no. Not now. Not while I was like... *this*. The deep husky tone was laced with amusement, and my stomach clenched at the sound. I turned my head slightly, enough to look at him. The hot guy from the party, the one who'd tried to help me, stared back with those unnervingly blue eyes.

"W-what?"

His soft pink lips widened into a smile that nearly took the breath from my lungs. "You look like you're dying. Are you alright?"

The bus took a sharp turn, and my stomach rolled. I stomped down the urge to vomit. "I'm fine."

Crisp leather replaced his casual combat jacket and crunched as he shifted in his seat. His jet-black hair slicked back neatly. "Sorry for leaving you the other night," he said. "Frat parties aren't really my scene."

I gulped down a belch that tasted like bile, and a sticky sweat coated my brow. With about as much grace as a seal, I wiped it with the back of my sleeve. "It's okay. I never got to thank you for... helping me."

Something flashed in those hypnotic eyes. Something like... anger. No, it couldn't be. The guy didn't even know me. But his gaze quickly softened as the corner of his mouth turned up in a grin. "You have absolutely zero color in your face. Are you sure you're—"

My stomach threatened to purge, and I clobbered over him to get out of the seat. I bolted for the side door near the back and pounded my palm against it. "Open the door!" I called to the driver. The sound of the bell dinging clamored in my ears, and the bus came to a screeching halt, nearly knocking me off my already unreliable feet. I attempted a glance back at the guy to give him an apologetic look, but the movement was my undoing. I shoved my body through the half-opened doors and barely made it to a bush, where I hurled my guts up. Behind me, the bus lingered, and I heard the call of the driver's voice.

"You okay, sweetheart?"

I remained bent over, letting the rest of the contents in my stomach spew from my mouth. But I waved a hand in his direction with a thumbs up. The doors closed, and I straightened in time to catch a glimpse of the hot guy staring widely at me from the window. Concern wrought across his striking features. But when he beheld the embarrassment on my face, I watched him erupt with a gutsy laugh as the bus pulled away.

I decided then and there that I hated him.

Rain thundered from the skies, drenching my skin through my clothes. Breath reeking like vomit, skin coated in sweat, rain soaking my hair and clothes, I covered my head with the hood from the sweater I wore beneath my jacket and walked the last few yards to the gallery.

My sneakers squeaked wetly as I trudged across the marble floors of the grand entrance, and near the back, Celadine twisted at the sound. She wore a deep crimson pantsuit, her many smaller braids tucked neatly into one large braid that bounced against her as she bound toward me. Her eyes alight with concern.

"Avery!" she said and gently touched my shoulder as she took in the sight of me. "What on earth happened to you?"

I thumbed toward the doors behind us. "My bike wouldn't start, so I took the bus, but that always makes me sick, so I had to walk, and it's raining…." I glanced down and beheld the state of myself. I wasn't fit to be in a place like this, a place so pristine and valuable. "Oh, god, Celadine. I'm sorry. I should have gone home to clean up–"

"No need," she replied with a quick shake of her head. She ushered me further into the gallery. "There's a bathroom and a change of clothes upstairs. Come."

She waved her hand, and I followed her to the upper level of the gallery. Where I'd never been before. I knew she hosted a rental space for artists to use. A sort of retreat. Most loaned the area for about three days. But it was almost always occupied. The talent that flowed through Gallery Danes daily was mesmerizing. Painters, writers, sculptures, artists of all sorts. Luckily, it was empty, I noted as Celadine fiddled with keys and let us inside the cozy apartment. She pointed down the hall.

"There's a bathroom on the right. And some clothes near the massage table."

My soaked clothes were now freezing. And I smiled with a quivered lip as I stalked past her and headed to the bathroom. I felt for a light switch with one shaky hand and flicked it on. Never-ending white marble surrounded me. Even the vanity was made of it. A bowl of Carrera on top.

I found a facecloth and snagged a fresh shirt from a small pile near what looked like a massage table. A pile of generic black t-shirts made of some glorious material that felt like a mix between silk and cotton. I painfully peeled my rain-drenched jeans and green plaid button-up before slipping a shirt over my head. A pile of loose, flared-bottom jogging pants sat next to the shirts. And I hauled on a pair of those, too.

I exited the bathroom with my wet clothes balled in my hands. "You wouldn't happen to have a bag, would you?"

Celadine grinned as she stepped forward, and her tattooed fingers took the clothes from me. "There's a dryer."

"Oh, I… don't want to be any trouble–"

She glanced over her shoulder with a disgruntled look. "Trouble?" She shrugged and opened one of the doors near the kitchen. "It's what it's for, isn't it?" A stacked washer and dryer and some empty baskets filled the tiny space. I stood and watched as my boss tossed my wet clothes inside the dryer and turned it on.

"Thanks," I said and admired the feel of the soft black fabric I wore.

"It's nice, right?" she said, her brows raised, waiting for my approval. I just nodded. "It took me forever to find just the right one for my guests."

"I like it," I replied and smoothed a hand down the sleeve.

"So," Celadine said, her tone changing the subject. "Tell me more about this bus ride."

Color rushed to my cheeks at the thought of seeing

that guy. Or rather… *him* seeing *me* like that. Throwing up in the bushes. It wasn't my finest moment. "What do you want to know?"

She studied me curiously. "Do you always get sick on the bus?"

I shrugged and watched her go to the small kitchenette and start rummaging through cupboards. "Buses, cars, trucks, you name it. If it's an enclosed vehicle, I'll get sick."

Celadine placed two China cups on the white marble top of a small island. "Enclosed?"

I approached and watched as she filled a kettle and ignited the gas stovetop. She looked so out of place in a simple kitchen with her striking looks. Yet, somehow, she seemed to fit. Like a work of art held against a bland background to showcase its beauty.

"Bikes are fine," I replied. "The fresh air seems to keep nausea at bay. That's why I drive a Vespa."

"And you've always been that way?" she asked and plucked a woven basket of various teas from a cabinet and slid it across the countertop as she motioned for me to take a seat.

I pulled out one of the round barstools and sat down. I fingered through the impressive tea selection and chose a vanilla-flavored one. Celadine put her elbows on the counter across from me and rested her chin atop her folded hands.

"Tell me more about your life," she said, her violet

eyes raking me over with a strange curiosity. "School, your friends, your family." As if realizing she might be prying a bit too much for someone meant to be my employer, she straightened and added, "You're my apprentice, I'm to teach you all I know, but I feel as if I hardly even know who you are." The kettle whistled, and she turned to fetch it from the stove. As she filled our cups, she said, "Are you enjoying life in the city?"

I thought of the shadows that seemed to follow me everywhere. The tiny blue fairy I'd had in my room... or thought I had in my room. I thought of Max and how I dreaded walking into class each morning for fear her death stare would one day actually kill me on sight. I thought of how Julie, my best friend and the driving force behind my decision to leave behind the country, and how she just seemed to fit in. How she'd already had friends from school, a guy she was interested in. It'd been weeks since our move to the city, and I still had yet to find my place in it all. Not entirely, anyway.

I wrapped my cold hands around the teacup and soaked up the warmth. "It's great. Everything's... great," I lied. But then I remembered... my promise to myself. To live without the thumb of fear pressing down on me. I'd told myself I would start embracing my new life. To stop scaring myself out of living here. Julie had her own classes, a temp job at the library, and Tomas... on some level. I had to find my thing. My place here. So, I smiled and asked, "What about your brother?" Celadine's already pale face lost what little color she held in her cheeks. "You mentioned having to deal with some business matters with him or something? Is everything okay?"

She put her teacup to her lips and nodded gently, avoiding eye contact, and waved a hand in the air. "Oh, it was nothing to be concerned over." She forced a sigh and smiled as she set down her cup. "The life of being an older sibling."

Tea warmed my inside as I swallowed another sip. "So, what's today's lesson in apprenticeship?"

Celadine's heavily ringed fingers fiddled with the rim of her cup. "For today, I'd love to discuss an upcoming showing I just booked."

"Oh?" I replied. "Anything good?"

She grinned. "It's a Mitchell showing."

A gasp turned over in my throat. Mitchell. That was the artist I mentioned in my interview. His stuff was unparalleled. "That's amazing! I'd love to help."

"More than help," she replied. "I'd like you to plan and organize everything. With my oversight, of course. I'll give you the gallery Visa with a breakdown of the budget and a list of things to be done. From there, it'll be up to you. So, are you ready?" She fetched a stack of papers from a boho-style shoulder bag I hadn't noticed she was carrying.

My nerves were racing. But I thrived on it. This was it. This was the beginning of my career, the path I'd been waiting for. With a deep breath, I nodded and took the papers from my mentor. My… friend.

"Yes, absolutely."

Chapter Eight

"I'm telling you," Tomas said as he took Julie's place at the pool table. He lined up his shot and looked at me from across the green. "Limited series is the way to go. From a filmmaker's perspective."

"But movies would be so much fun to make," I argued lightly as I leaned against my upright pool stick. I tipped my chin to Julie, who sat behind Tomas. She stuffed nachos to the side of her mouth as she met my gaze. "Julie. Movies or limited TV series. Which would you go with?"

Her eyes immediately went to Tomas's as if to say, *does it matter?* "I mean, there're pros and cons to both, I guess."

They switched places again, and Tomas came around

the table to argue his point like the film nerd he was. I loved it.

"With movies, you're forced to rush the storyline." His eyes were lit with passion. Passion for his art, for the thing he loved most in this world.

I stared back with nothing but admiration. This was what I needed. Busy, loud frat parties were definitely not my thing. But this... the three of us, all hailing from different corners of the art world–fine arts, media, and literature–gathered around a pool table under the dim golden hue of an old Irish pub, serenaded by the sounds of alt and Celtic rock.

This was the life I wanted. I knew it with such certainty. Especially after another dreadful week of facing Max's unwarranted anger each day, coffee spills and minor burns as I learned the ropes in the café, and the nightmares that fought for space in my mind as I stuffed it full of apprentice stuff.

Working with Celadine has been a dream, and my apprenticeship has only just begun. I wondered–hoped–it would be the starting point, the open door that would lead me to find my place here, in the city, in this new life.

Tomas continued, reeling me in from my own mind and anchoring me in the moment. "But with a limited TV series, you have the room to play." He took a deep, excited breath. "Room to fully develop the characters and storylines."

"But without the pressure to drag it out over several seasons," Julie piped up from the other side.

She'd grown tired of waiting for me to take my turn and retreated back to her giant plate of nachos. Tomas's cheeks flushed with red as he gave her that look. The one that said, *I think I'm in love.* I just gave a defeated eye roll and took my shot. I sank three balls, and Tomas let out a long whistle.

"You never said you were a sharpshooter." He casually flipped his short brown waves to the side and smiled.

I shrugged and rubbed the cube of blue chalk around the tip of my stick. "You should see me at bowling."

Tomas laughed as Julie just nodded over the plate of nachos. It was true. I killed at bowling. Around us, the gentle rock music that played in the tiny Irish pub suddenly stopped. The live band was getting ready to play, but they were still setting up.

"I'm getting a refill," I told them. "And maybe a hotdog. You guys want anything?"

Tomas shook his head, but Julie said, "Can you grab me a Coke?"

I left them leaning toward each other over the small bar table and made my way to the main bar across the pub. A semi-circle manned by just one bartender. I approached the worn oak edge and rested my elbows against it as I waited for his attention to fall on me as he made his way around to the three other people waiting.

When the bartender, a cheerful guy in a green plaid shirt, smiled at me, I placed my order and waited. But, as he turned away, I caught the deathly blue stare of someone across the bar, and my stomach clenched. Then threatened to heave as I watched him rise from his chair and saunter over to me.

"I see you made it," he said and leaned against the bar just inches from me. His black leather jacket, so perfectly fit his body, crunched as he shifted and leaned away. He stared at me with that grin. "The bus. You looked like you were about to pass out."

I realized then, my mouth... gaped open, and he must have mistaken my expression for confusion. I shook my head and reminded myself how to smile. "Oh, yeah. That. I... don't travel well."

He didn't reply, only lingered. Staring. Ogling was more like it. As if there were words written all over me, and he wanted to read every single one. I could feel my heart in my throat. "So... what are you, like, stalking me or something?"

His brows raised in delight. "Would you like me to?"

His wide pink lips turned up with a cheeky grin, and I ached to run my finger over the sharp lines of them. Knew exactly how I'd draw them. My heart rattled in its cage, and I swear… he almost seemed to hear it. Those dark blue eyes darted to that spot on my throat where I knew my pulse thrummed.

The bartender appeared with my drinks. "The hotdog will be another few minutes."

I just nodded, and he zipped off to serve someone else. I grabbed my beer as I pulled Julie's Coke close. "I'd rather not end up on a milk carton, thanks."

He straightened, and only then did I realize just how tall this guy was. With both of us upright together. He loomed over me, and I swallowed dryly.

His dark brows pinched together. "You think I'd hurt you?"

I took a sip to hide my nerves and shook my head. "I don't… I don't even know you."

He gave me a hesitant smile, a loveliness against the sharp contrast of his pale skin and dark looks, and held out a hand. I just stared at it.

"Cillian."

The name trickled off his lips like the word… *cookie*, and my eyes traced the sharp lines of them. Sketched them into my brain to no doubt resurface in my art later.

"What are you thinking about?" he asked, and I tore my gaze from his mouth.

Definitely not cookies.

I stared at his still-outstretched hand, gawked at the gesture, and then up at his awaiting face. Something in his eyes almost seemed to say—to beg, *don't take it*. Or was it just my measly sense of self-perseverance speaking to me? I took a deep breath, and, against all better judgment, I slowly placed my hand in his.

"Avery," I said and shook.

Cillian's long, cool fingers wrapped all the way around my hand. He eyed it, every finger, the paint caked under my nails. My cheeks warmed, and I slid my hand back.

"There," Cillian spoke. The sound was nothing but a deep rasp that caressed my spine. "Now you know me."

"And… *you* know *me*," I replied, my brows raised to convey the deeper meaning of my words. *Please don't stalk and kill me in the street.*

But I couldn't live my life afraid. Always missing out on… living. I refused to ever go back to the Avery I was mere weeks ago. The country girl who painted pictures of birds and fairies in her backyard. I'd moved to the city to have more. See more. Do more. Meet different people, friends, maybe even date. A concept I'd never really ever entertained until now. Not because Tess would have made it impossible, but because I had always been too preoccupied with my art. And home school isn't exactly the best method to meet guys. I'd been a nobody, a whisper of existence.

Until now.

So, I gave Cillian a smile and let out a laugh, playing off my tense behavior. But my cheeks still felt warm. I glanced over my shoulder at my friends, who suddenly found themselves fascinated with a spot on the wall. I rolled my eyes and turned back to Cillian.

"I'm with some–"

"Oh, of course." He waved a hand, signaling me to go on. "Don't let me keep you. I just wanted to say hello. You know, since you're not being harassed by some drunken idiot or losing your supper in the bushes."

Even though he poked fun at me, I could watch him speak all day. The way his too beautiful face moved. I fought not to stare at his mouth. So, I settled for those eyes. The ones I desperately wanted to paint. "Would you… like to join us?"

My hotdog appeared, and I cradled it to my chest with the two drinks. Cillian leaned into me, and I inhaled the cool, leathery scent of him. Frozen, captivated by his mere presence.

He said in a brush of air against the side of my face, "I don't think we're ready for that just yet. Besides, I was just leaving."

I watched as he backed away, grinning knowingly, his drink in hand. He tipped it up and took the last sip as he stared at me with delight over the rim. He placed the empty class on the bar and threw the bartender a wink as if he knew him–the returning wink confirmed–and then left me with the most devilish grin I'd ever seen outside of a cheesy teen drama as he slipped out the front door.

He was gone, but I couldn't shake the feeling that anchored me in place. Was it fear or lust? The fact that I couldn't tell the difference was enough to send a cold shiver down my spine, and I spun around as I headed back to my friends.

Cillian seemed to have some kind of interest in me. People just didn't have as many happenstances as we had. The party, the bus, and now here. But he felt… wrong. No, not *wrong*. I searched the bottom of my gut for the word.

Forbidden.

It was the only word that made sense to my rattling nerves. The strange tingling Cillian seemed to rouse under my skin. An itch I couldn't scratch. I took a long, deep breath and purged the encounter from my mind as I set Julie's Coke down in front of her.

"Who the hell was *that*?" she asked, her grassy eyes wide.

I shrugged coolly as I took a bite of my hotdog and stuffed it to the side of my mouth. "Just some guy I've seen around here and there."

Julie let out a long breath and chuckled. "I thought he was a figment of my imagination."

"He's pretentious," I said, suddenly annoyed in the aftermath of the encounter. "And he's painfully good-looking. That's not normal."

She nodded, and Tomas took his shot, sinking the white ball. His shoulders slumped as he walked over to where the ball popped out on the side of the table. "It's true. Definitely some kind of alien life form."

I nodded and sipped my drink, keeping with the bit. "Definitely. Clearly, he appears in the form I most desire because I'm the key to taking over the planet."

Julie howled with laughter, and I couldn't hold back, especially when Tomas joined in. He took another shot, and sank a ball then pointed his stick toward me. "Look, I'm not an expert on dating the male species, but I think it's safe to say that you'd be crazy to pass up that guy."

"Yeah?" I failed to stifle my laugh.

He held out an open palm. "Painfully handsome, hypnotic eyes, tall and lurky," he counted down on his fingers, "Movie star hair. How much more convincing do you need?"

I exchanged a look with Julie, and we both burst into laughter. "Not as little as you, apparently."

Tomas's cheeks reddened, but he squared his shoulders. "I'm confident enough in my manhood to know when to admit another man is, how do you say… " he waved a hand in the air with an exaggerated motion. "Hot as fuck?"

"I think I know bad news when I see it," I replied with an eye roll and took my shot, sinking two balls.

Julie hopped down from her bar stool and readied her pool stick. "I agree. A guy like that's either a serial killer or a heartbreaker."

"So, safe to say, I should just steer clear." I sucked in a long, deep breath.

We played a few more games of pool and shared more drinks before I had to fight off a yawn. I set my stick back in the holder on the wall and turned to my friends.

"I think I'm going to head home for the night," I told them. "I'm beat, and I've got a ton of stuff to do for the gallery tomorrow."

"You want us to walk you home?" Julie asked, and Tomas nodded from over her shoulder.

"Nah," I replied and shoved my arms into the sleeves of my army green jacket. "It's just a couple of streets over."

I left them chatting over a shared space in a corner where we'd played and headed out to the bustling street. One good thing about downtown Halifax, you're never really alone. The sidewalks were always littered with walkers–students and locals just going about their business.

I turned a corner, past a flourishing hedge of wild roses, but a loud rustling brought me to a halt, and I stared at the thick foliage as my pulse quickened. But nothing appeared. I walked faster, speeding for the coffee shop that I could already see up ahead. Shadows chased me across two crosswalks and floated up the old rickety staircase at the back of the Chocolate Kettle. I fumbled with my keys as the steps below darkened one by one. Each second passed like a needle to my throat. Finally, the key slid in, and I bolted inside the apartment before slamming the door shut.

Inside the dark porch, I pressed my back against the wall as I strained to calm my breathing. *It's nothing, it's nothing*, I told myself. I imagined it all. But, just as my heart began to settle, a loud *thunk* sound came from my bedroom. I plucked an umbrella from the hooks lining the porch wall and slowly crept toward my bedroom door. My knuckles were white as the handle moaned in my palms. I held my breath as I opened the door, and a gentle breeze blew in from the open window by my bed.

"Well, it's about time you came home," spoke a tiny, musical voice. My eyes darted to the mattress, and there it was. The blue fairy I'd captured before. So… it wasn't just in my mind. The fairy sat atop a small burlap sack as something wriggled inside.

"What do you want?" I asked. The umbrella draped across my front. I hovered near the door and reached out to close it. My eyes on the fairy.

It smiled up at me with a wide mouth of pointed teeth. Those all-black buggish eyes blinked. "You'll be pleased to know you didn't injure me beyond repair." She unfolded her boney legs and reached inside the bag. Those long, claw-like fingers pulled out a mouse by its neck, and I jumped back against the wall. "Oh, and I remember my name. It's Lattie."

The rodent squirmed and squealed in the fairy's grasp. I set the umbrella down and crossed my arms. "Yeah, and?"

Lattie's bottom jaw lowered, and she lobbed off the tiny mouse's head in a single bite. I fought the urge to vomit. I tried to look away, but she shoved bits to the side of her toothy mouth, blood now covered my white duvet, and said, "And yours is Avery Quinn."

***

Cheese, crackers.

"I think I'm falling for him," Julie said as she leaned against the old white fridge.

It took every ounce of willpower to look normal as Julie gossiped in my ear. I had to step away from my bedroom. I couldn't stand to watch the little beast eat a mouse on my bed. So, I mindlessly piled snacks onto a plate instead.

Grapes, a handful of cashews.

"I thought you weren't looking for anything serious?" I managed to say and added an awkward smile at the end. If she noticed I was behaving strangely, she said nothing.

"Who says it needs to be serious?" Julie plucked a grape off my plate and popped it in her mouth with a wink as she turned and headed to her room. "Night!"

"Night," I replied and gripped the plate of snacks before turning to my room.

I quickly shut the door behind me, balancing the plate with one hand as I stood just inside the quiet of my bedroom. Just to be sure, I used my lock for the first time. I couldn't risk Julie walking in on… I turned toward my bed as I gripped the plate with both hands and peered down at the blue fairy that sat waiting on my bed. No sign of the small animal it had consumed while I was gone.

I took a breath and sat down next to her. "Be quiet. My roommate's home now."

Lattie immediately picked over the array of foods I placed before her. "She doesn't like fairies?" She sniffed and poked and picked with a certain hesitancy.

I stared blankly at the wall. "Something like that." The sound of crackers crunching in her gnarly mouth ripped me from the haze, and I snatched a piece of cheese. She watched my every move with a calculated stare. "So, explain how this works."

Juices covered her hands and face as she gutted a grape and licked its flesh from her fingers. "You invited me into your home, trapped me in iron. So, now I'm bound to you."

"Bound to me?" I plucked a few grapes off the bushel. Lattie watched, her tiny nostrils flaring for a second. She was adorable and horrifying at the same time. Like something out of a Tim Burton film.

"Bound, together," she said slowly as if she thought me dumb. "Tied."

A manic guffaw escaped my chest, and I had to tell myself to blink. "So, I'm just *stuck* with a tiny vampire?"

Lattie stifled a shriek. "How could you say such a thing?"

"What?" I asked. "It was a joke…"

"Vampires are no laughing matter, Avery."

My breath hitched. "Are you saying that *vampires*… are real?" The fairy didn't reply, only stared wide and unblinking up at me. As if I were the ridiculous one. I chewed for a moment. "How do I… unbind us?"

"I'm not sure," Lattie replied after a breath too long, her black gaze gone wide and distant as she stared up at me. "I've never heard of it being reversed." Her pointy shoulders shrugged. "I supposed you could find a Fae Lord or a witch. Although those are extinct. Witches, that is. Fae Lords are few and far between, but there's a couple around."

I shook my head. Thoughts swirled in a dizzying pattern. "Wait. What are you saying?" I swallowed dryly. "What kind of Fae Lords are we talking about here? Fairies like… *you*?" Lattie just shook her head slowly. "And *witches*?"

If I were standing, my legs would surely have failed me. They felt like Jell-O as I pushed up against the white tufted headboard Julie made. It was one of her many DIY attempts that actually worked. Julie… I was stuck harboring this murderous little creature, and I couldn't tell Julie. Could I? I hugged my knees to my chest as if it could help keep the world from spinning around me.

Lattie fluttered her picaresque blue wings up to my knee and sat down, her long bony legs dangling as her heels bumped against my thigh. For a moment, we just stared at one another with equal fascination. From up close, I could see all the details of her. Her blue leathery skin seemed to breathe with every inhale and exhale. Some kind of shimmery dust coated every inch of skin from the top of her snowy hair to the tips of those long claw-like feet.

"How did you heal so fast?"

"Fae heal rapidly," Lattie replied. "As soon as I freed myself from your cage, it was only a matter of a few hours, and I was fine."

I just nodded, as if what she said made any sort of sense. Was I just amusing my delusion, or was there actually a tiny fairy in my room claiming the truth about magic and vampires and living shadows?

Slowly, I reached out, and she watched my finger as I stopped and silently asked for permission. When Lattie nodded, I brushed the edge of her wing with the tip of my finger, noting how delicate it felt, like a moth's wings. She shuddered at the touch.

"What," she breathed and hunched her back like a feral cat, "Are you doing?"

"I-I just had to… see if you were real."

"Real?" Lattie chortled. "I assure you I'm as real as you are. And so is the threat pushing across Ironworld." She pushed off my knee and flew over to the windowsill.

"Ironworld?"

She hunched, scanning the outside, but then peered over at me with an eye roll. "For someone with the Sight, you sure know nothing." Lattie's long and bony arm flew out and snatched a bird from the air with lightning speed.

I leaped across the bed and shooed her. "Don't! Let it go!" I tried to keep my voice below a strained whisper. The fairy dared look annoyed and released the bird back into the night. "And what do you mean… the Sight?" She fluttered over to my bed and patted the mattress next to her.

"Come, Avery Quinn. I've got a lot to tell you about your world." I had to tell myself to breathe as she spoke to me. "And the one beyond it."

Chapter Nine

poked the last stale cracker into my mouth and wiped the crumbs off on my black sweatpants as I balanced an open notebook on my upright knees. Lattie finally stopped buzzing around my bedroom like an ADHD-riddled busybody at some wee hour of the night and now relaxed, her wings spread out on my white duvet like silken drapes.

I had no idea what time it was. My blackout curtains blocked out every ounce of sunlight. But I didn't care. I had taken the red pill, I followed the white rabbit–or blue fairy– and there was no going back. I'd learned so much during the long hours of the night. Some big fight happened over five hundred years ago that tore the mythical lands apart. They've been divided and at odds ever since. A war-torn world.

She also told me that *If you feed a Fae, you'll never get rid of them. They're like stray cats.* I considered those words as I watched her pick over the remnants of the snacks on my plate.

"Okay, so you come from a place called Faerie where… fairies live?" I confirmed as the tip of my pencil hovered over my haphazard notes. I'd filled half the notebook during the night. Lattie sat upright and gave a nod as she sniffed for crumbs of the snacks we'd consumed. "But other creatures live there, too?"

She nodded again, tiredly. "Yes, all sorts. Battas, Ly Ergs, Trolls, Sirens." She waved a tiny blue hand as if the topic bored her. "But we're all Fae. Ruled by monarchs."

I flipped backward through my notes. "Yes, the monarchs. The… rulers?"

Another nod.

"Of different courts?" I wanted to get all the details right.

"No," she replied with a shake of her head. "There's only one. The High Seelie Court. The rest are Territories. Winter and Summer are the seasonal ones. Volatile but less… demanding. They balance one another."

"What about Autumn and Spring?" I asked. "Those are seasons."

"Those are merely a mix of the Fae that govern Summer and Winter. There are small domains that claim a place for

Autumn and Spring, but there's not enough Fae to rise to a Territory. It's mostly a motley mixture of the seasons. You want to avoid those places. They can be… unpredictable."

I stared at my notes, the pencil scratches that filled the papers before me. Page after page, I absorbed every word, story, and description Lattie told me in the night and spilled it all into my notebook.

Lattie found a broken piece of cookie in the folds of the blanket and shoved it in her toothy mouth. I flipped through the pages and noted a few question marks I'd left.

"But the other one, they don't have balance? The… Seelie and…"

Lattie let loose an annoyed sigh. "The High Seelie Court is the one that rules everything, with a scorned mad queen at the throne." She said nothing of her distaste at my constant questions. I wondered if it had something to do with the fact that I'd accidentally bound her to me. Did she *have* to answer all my questions? "Summer and Winter are the seasonal territories that help keep some semblance of balance in Faerie. Then… there are the other two territories. Dreams and Nightmares."

I flipped to a new page. "And Kings and Queens don't rule the territories. Only Lords, right?"

"Yes. Summer, Winter, and Nightmares each have a Lord at the helm. Holy people govern Dreams. Temples and libraries devoted to cataloging all our great knowledge dating back as far as our creation."

I filled the page as fast as I could with words and sketches. Lattie fluttered up to my knee and peered over the edge of the notebook. "No, no." She shook her little head and pointed at the middle of a drawing I made of the lands. "There's a lake here. Not land. The Seelie Court and four territories form a circle around it," she told me as her bony finger made a clockwise motion over the paper. "Seelie, Dreams, Nightmares, Winter, and Summer."

I tapped the eraser end against the page as I chewed the inside of my lip. "And... you mentioned there used to be a Seelie King that ruled *with* the Queen? What happened to him?"

Lattie shuddered at some dark memory. "At first, for as long as anyone can remember, there had only been a king. Orion, High King of the Seelie Court and ruler of all Faerie. Then a female named Mabry Solborn came along one day, out of the blue. She caught the king's eye and married him." Lattie's expression softened, and her massive black eyes flitted to the window. As if she could see past the drapes. "But he disappeared not long after their union, less than a year. Some say Mabry killed him. Others say the Dark Lord Oden did it. But it's all just rumors. No one truly knows what happened."

"He just disappeared without a trace?"

"The king, yes," Lattie replied and failed to fight off

a yawn, revealing dozens of those toothpick teeth. "But Mabry is now the High Seelie Queen. After her beloved king went missing, she went mad. Her grief consumes her still. She rules her court with a bloody fist and has pushed the rest of Faerie into ruin. So much so that it's a sliver of what it used to be. Fae have been fleeing to Ironworld for years in search of solace."

I shook my head as if it could whisk away the horrible images Lattie conjured in my mind. "But you said the metal in this world hurts you."

"Yes, it poisons our blood," she confirmed and stretched her too-long arms as her wings fluttered awake behind her. "But slow enough that we can withstand it for a mortal lifetime or two."

"That's… sad." Pity and grief filled my chest, but I was too tired to think of another word.

Lattie climbed back up my leg and stood on my knees, forcing me to set down my notebook. Her tiny hands tickled my cheeks as she pulled my face close. Her eyes were wide and stared right into mine. "Do not feel pity for us, Avery Quinn. It is far better to live a brief life of freedom than to live an eternity under the rule of a being such as Mabry."

I swallowed dryly. "Is she really that bad?"

Lattie released my face and sat atop my knee. "Yes, I'm afraid she is. But losing the love of your life and the heir to the throne all in one single swoop…."

"They had an heir?" I asked and readied my pencil. "A child?"

She nodded sadly. "Yes. A rumored son. But Lord Oden had killed the child the same night he killed Orion. Supposedly. But some whisper of the savior. The first and only born youngling of the two monarchs."

"What do they say?"

Lattie placed a hand on my notebook, trailing her fingertips over my notes and sketches, the drawings in the margins. "That the child lives. That the magic tasked with ending its life instead hid the child away. To only be found when they were of age. When they could return to Faerie and claim the Seelie throne." She blinked up at me. "To save us all."

I stared back at her, feeling the weight of the words she spoke, the longing she harbored for her long-lost home. The space in my bedroom seemed to close in, darkening around the edges of my vision. I could hear my heartbeat thrumming hot in my ears.

A loud knock at the door ripped me from the trance, and I stifled a yelp.

"Av', you up?" Julie bellowed from the other side of the door.

I scrambled to put away all my notes but remembered that I'd locked the door last night. "Uh, yeah, just woke up.

I'll be out in a minute."

"I'll put the coffee on!"

I sucked in a deep and cleansing breath as Lattie flew over to the windowsill and pulled back the curtain. Sunlight cut through the air, and I shielded my sensitive eyes from the blaring glow. Lattie and I talked all night and well into the morning, it seemed. Thank goodness it was Saturday. I would have been happy to curl up under the blankets and sleep the day away, but my phone buzzed with a reminder that I'd set for myself, and I cringed. I was meeting Max today to work on our project.

After I downed some coffee and breakfast with Julie—her too aware gaze raking me over with every bite—I said goodbye and headed down to the café to grab an espresso for the road and found Max standing outside, waiting. She stood as still as a statue, but the annoyed tap of her black gladiator sandal on concrete told me she'd been waiting a minute too long.

"You ready to walk the streets and admire some architecture?" I asked her with a heavy dose of morning pep.

Inside, I was a zombie. Desperate for the confines of my bed to drag me into a coma. But caffeine coursed through my veins, and part of me wondered what it would take to see a smile, even a hint of a grin, tug at Max's constant glower.

Her answering grimace told me all I needed to know. "Let's get this over with."

She shoved off the brick exterior of the coffee shop and smoothed out the blood-red silk tank top she wore over tight black pants that shimmered in the sunlight. Her lips, usually painted a matte black, matched the deep red of her top, and her hair hung in two immaculate braids that flanked her heart-shaped face. I could stare at her all day. Max was like a work of art.

But I cast aside that awe in favor of a retort, refusing to let her intimidate me any longer. "I'm surprised you haven't finished the whole thing yourself."

She narrowed her dark eyes on me. "What's that supposed to mean?"

We fell in stride together as we strolled down the sidewalk. "You did all the initial research and outlined the entire project without even talking to me, then emailed it to me like I'm nothing more than your lowly assistant or something. This is my project, too, you know."

Max shot me a sharp look. "This is our first extensive project from the course, and architects from all over the city are coming to watch us present. Excuse me if I do everything in my power to ensure I come out on top."

I sipped my coffee as we rounded a brick-clad corner.

"We ensure *we* come out on top."

She said nothing, but I saw how her fists clenched at her sides. It took every ounce of willpower not to ask Max why she was so angry all the time. I was sure the question would just lead to more pointed silence and death stares. She was beautiful, intelligent, stylish, and clearly well off on the surface. I wondered what must have happened to her to make her this way. To regard the world with such disdain.

But I held my tongue as we wandered downtown, making notes and taking pictures of all the historic architecture. The city was peppered with a mix of Victorian Gothic and Georgian designs, and it was hard not to stop and stare in awe of the splendor. The art, so well preserved and on display for all to see.

We only exchanged a few words the whole time, only about the project. I could see the restraint she struggled with, the desperation to take over and do everything her way. Max clearly wasn't used to working with others.

After about an hour, we had just about all we needed and walked side by side past a residential area tucked away on a street stuffed with massive trees. The greenery, already fading with the coming Fall, draped over the sidewalks and cast the houses in a cool shadow.

Max came to a halt outside an old but pristine Victorian Gothic revival mansion on a corner lot. The exterior was a deep purple with black trims and a wrap-around veranda on the main level. I saw a smaller semi-circle balcony of black wrought iron on the top third level when I glanced up. Thick iron gates protected the entrance, their pointed tops sharp enough to impale intruders.

"God, I'll never tire of the beauty in this city," I said and blew out a long breath.

Max chortled under her breath. "I'm surprised you've never seen this one." When she saw the confused look on my face, she rolled her eyes. "It is your boss's house, after all."

"Oh." I looked back at the house and saw it differently. Saw it as Celadine's and smiled to myself as I realized just how *her* it really was. Of course, this was where she lived. It was like the house version of Celadine. "No, I had no idea."

"How's the janitor's job going, by the way?" It was the first thing she'd spoken to me that wasn't related to the project.

"Good," I replied and felt my cheeks fill with heat. "I… I'm not just the temp anymore, though." Max's odious stare shot to me. "I'm apprenticing under Celadine during the evenings."

Her lips pursed as she took in the idea. "Well, isn't that nice for you, then?"

I swear, she couldn't make a compliment sound non-threatening if she tried. "It is," I replied. "Good, I mean. I'm learning a lot–"

She threw up a hand and looked away. "That wasn't an invitation to get chummy." I swallowed nervously as she stuffed her phone and notebook back in her bag. "Are we done here?"

My thoughts reeled. "I, uh, yeah, I guess so–"

And she was gone. Turned and strutted down the street before I even got the chance to register what was happening.

✳✳✳

The sun had just dipped below the horizon, leaving behind a violet-blue stain. I mentally checked that I had everything I needed as I locked the door behind me and cursed at my trembling fingers. I raced down the spiral staircase that led to the coffee shop below. The evening shift was just starting, and Tomas stood behind the counter as he tied his black apron. He flicked his head with a smile, tossing his floppy hair back from his eyes.

"Hey," he said. "Where you off to in such a hurry?"

My eyes burned as I looked at him and adjusted the strap of my leather bag. "I slept in." He gave me a dumbfounded look. "I took a nap this afternoon and slept too long. I had a bunch of stuff to do on a deadline for the gallery showing I'm planning." I checked my phone and grimaced. "Two of the places I need to get to close in less than an hour."

"Oh, that's a downer, for sure. Is there anything I can do?"

Tomas was too sweet. "Not unless you can be in four places at once."

He snapped his fingers with a mock frown. "Shucks. Don't think I can help you out there. Coffee?"

I exaggerated a sigh. "I guess it'll do."

He quickly poured me a to-go cup, and I waved as I turned to head out. Fishing for my keys with my free hand. But my new phone slipped from my pocket, too big to properly fit, and I groaned as it hit the floor. I bent and grabbed it in a quick swoop, so worried about screwing up my first solo show that I didn't see someone enter just as I sprung up. My cup lid flicked off, and hot coffee splattered on the floor.

My head shot to the person I'd bumped into, my mouth gaping with an apology, but I stopped short when I saw who stood before me. A stupid grin on his face.

I narrowed my eyes and stepped aside. "Cillian."

He tipped his head. "Always a pleasure, Avery."

I shook my head. "Why are you only around when I'm a mess?"

"You claim to be a mess, yet *I'm* the problem?" Those dark blue eyes glanced at the brown puddle on the floor between us.

Tomas appeared at my side, a fresh coffee in one hand, a mop in the other. "Don't you have somewhere to be?" he said and handed me the coffee.

Dear Lord, I could have kissed him. Tomas was just too good for this world. I laughed and accepted the cup. "I owe you one. Seriously," I told him as I hesitated and headed out the door. Failing to not look at Cillian as I did. Part of me hoped he'd follow me outside, where Tomas and the rest of the café didn't have to witness the way the guy made my face do embarrassing things.

But he never came.

The expanse of forest that stretched out before our street filled my vision with hues of orange and red under the near-black sky. Only a hint of navy touched the farthest point I could see. Fall was here already, early this year. I stood for a moment, breathing in the change in the air. The crispness crept in. I never enjoyed any of the seasons as much as I loved the actual changing of each one. New and familiar, all at the same time.

I swung a leg over the seat of my Vespa and turned the key over. And over. *This wasn't happening.* I tried again. And again. But nothing stirred within the old beast. I tossed my helmet in the basket at the back with a frustrated groan.

Cillian appeared at my side, and I rubbed a hand over my tired face. "Need a ride?" he asked. A coffee in hand.

He motioned to a matte black motorcycle just in front of me.

"No, I'm fine, thanks." I was in a sour mood and already hated myself for how I talked to him. But I hadn't been sleeping, and the all-nighter with Lattie left me with mere dregs of my patience. And now my bike was dead. Just when I needed it most. "You... don't even know me."

"Alright," he replied and sipped his coffee, his muscles shifting with a shrug beneath his black combat jacket. Beneath the...tight black shirt he wore. I tried not to ogle. Those cerulean eyes flashed with playfulness. "Take the bus. See how far you get on that rock-solid stomach of yours."

I resisted the urge to stick out my tongue at him and filled my mouth with warm coffee instead. Maybe he knew me a little. I checked my phone again. I was losing time.

With a deep breath, I said, "Fine." Cillian gave me a look that said, *And?* I pressed my lips together as I waited out the cesspool of butterflies in my stomach. "I would love a ride if it's not too much trouble."

He gave a mocking bow. "Never too much trouble for milady."

I rolled my eyes and turned to grab my helmet from the basket. Or maybe it was to hide the smile that spread across my face. I zipped up my emerald, green leather jacket to my chin. And only when I swung my legs over the seat of his bike, my breasts pressed hard up against his back, did I realize just how warm I was. It was like wrapping my arms around a chilly pillow.

"Where to?" he asked over his shoulder.

I had to think for a moment. "The Dartmouth Crossing. The two most important stops are next door to one another."

He gave the bike a rev. "Hang on."

We sped off through the city like a fucking nonstop bullet. I held a scream in my throat the entire time. My hands gripped his body, and I swear, I could feel the rumblings of laughter as we zipped in and out of cars. Somehow, Cillian missed every red light, and I was sure we were nothing but a blur across Halifax. What would have taken me at least half an hour on my Vespa took Cillian mere minutes on his bike, and we arrived at the Dartmouth Crossing Shopping Centre.

I climbed off the seat and let my legs balance for a moment, anger running rapidly through my limbs. "Are you *insane*?"

He removed his helmet and flicked back his jet-black hair that flopped atop his head. "What?"

My eyes bulged in their sockets. "You could have killed us!"

"Oh, please," he scoffed. "I've been driving like that for years. I know this city like the back of my hand. You were perfectly safe. I assure you." He gestured to the storefront behind me. "Plus, look! Time to spare."

I clutched the thick leather strap of my bag across my chest, mostly to hide my trembling hands, and walked as calmly as I could to the first store–a fabric shop–my body racing with adrenaline. And I wasn't sure if it was the lingering feeling of Cillian in my arms or the death ride he just took me on, but my heart refused to settle.

Even as I picked out fabrics for a custom order and set up delivery.

Or as I exited the store and saw him leaning against his bike, waiting. One long... muscular leg crossed over the other. I gave him a smile, but he only chuckled. As if he knew of the whirlwind of adrenaline that spun around inside of me.

Next door was the printer, and I had to get the order for posters and banners in today, or I wouldn't get them in time for the showing. I spent a good twenty minutes inside, poring over drawings, notes, and instructions with the printing clerk. I set the order and paid for delivery. When I left the shop, I let out a long breath and with it a heavy weight from my shoulders. My solo showing might not be a disaster after all.

Cillian called from the seat of his bike, "You ready for the next stop?"

I took a few steps toward him. "I'm good, actually."

Those nerves bubbled up again. But I stomped them down. *He was just a guy.* "Thanks so much for your help. I got the two most important things done. The rest can wait until tomorrow." I reached for my helmet. "I'll just take the bus back."

"Hungry?" Cillian asked. His face was just a few inches from mine.

This was the closest I'd seen his stunning eyes, and I scanned them, wanting desperately to figure out the hues, the tones, the pigments. How I might recreate it.

"What?" I said, blinking back to reality.

"Hungry? Food?" He made a mocking eating gesture with his hands, and I laughed. "Come on, consider it a thank you for saving your ass twice now."

I balked at the sudden audacity. "For *what*?"

Cillian shrugged. "Saving you from that man child who was pawing at you at that ridiculous frat party and giving you a ride to meet a deadline."

"I didn't ask for your help."

He raised a dark, challenging brow. "Would you rather I let Keg Stand Joe have his way with you?"

"I can handle myself," I replied and crossed my arms.

He sized me up dramatically. "Clearly."

I narrowed my eyes. It was growing daunting just keeping up with the guy. One minute he mocked me; the next, he played the hero, and after that, he seemed to despise me. It was torture.

"Look, I was just about to grab some sushi right over there," Cillian said, his voice soft and raspy again. He pointed across the parking lot. "You can join me if you like. Or you can brave the nauseating bus ride home and eat... what is it college kids eat these days? Ramen noodles? Mac and cheese?"

I loved sushi, and my stomach growled with betrayal. I wasn't in the mood to get motion sick tonight. And, while something about Cillian brushed my nerves, he seemed harmless. And the restaurant was an open public space. It wasn't like he was dragging me down a dark alley or anything.

I sighed. "Fine." I set my helmet back down, my shoulder grazing him. I swear I felt a shudder, but his face remained cool and collected. I looked him square in the face and grinned. "Only because I'm starving."

"Of course." He fell in stride next to me.

"And you're paying," I said and jabbed a finger in his arm.

He turned and looked at me, his dark hair falling to one side of his devastating face. "I'd never make a lady pay. Especially not one as regal as yourself."

I shoved at him. "And stop making fun of me!"

We entered the small sushi restaurant and took a private booth near the back that had a straight view to the front entrance, where a wall of picture windows faced the parking lot outside. I took off my jacket, then the thin red hoodie beneath, revealing my bare arms and a crimson tank top with gold chain straps. Without even looking, I knew Cillian's eyes were on me. Could feel them raking over me. The pale skin I bared, the chunky rings on each finger, the heaps of bangles and bracelets I wore.

I tossed my garments to the corner of my bench seat and slipped into it at the same time he mirrored the motion on his side of the narrow table. My gaze raised to meet his, and my breath fettered once again at the striking blue eyes staring back at me. A grin tugged at the corner of his mouth.

"What?" I asked, suddenly finding the menu in front of me super fascinating. I prayed the nerves I felt trembling my fingers didn't show as I gripped the laminated booklet tightly.

"Red looks lovely on you," he simply replied and picked up his menu. "It's your color."

My cheeks burned. "Yeah, I'm kind of limited when it comes to colors." I pinched a wave of my blood-red hair between my fingers. "Red, green, navy," I shrugged, "Sometimes gold."

"Black goes with everything," Cillian replied.

I set my menu down with a cheeky grin. "I assumed that color was only reserved for you."

He didn't get the chance to give an equally sarcastic retort as our server appeared next to the table. "Welcome to the Jade Garden. What can I get you?"

Cillian motioned for me to go first. *A gentleman*, I noted to myself. "I'll have a green dragon roll, one yam roll, and a side of veggie spring rolls, please." She scribbled on her notepad and nodded before tucking my menu under her arm. She turned to Cillian.

"I'll have two salmon maki and an order of the House Nigiri," he told her politely and folded his menu before handing it to her.

When she was gone, Cillian shifted in his seat and fixed his stare back on me, his fingers steepled in front of him as he assessed.

"What?" I asked, suddenly conscious of every part of me.

"You don't like real sushi?"

"I didn't realize I'd ordered off the pretend menu."

A ghost of a smirk. "You don't eat the raw stuff?"

I shuddered and shook my head. "Not a fan. I prefer my food cooked."

"I suppose you like your steaks well done, too."

I wrangled my hair up off the back of my neck and twisted it into a hair tie in preparation to eat. "Wow. A daredevil on the motorcycle *and* a psychic? Quite the date I've landed."

Cillian's thick dark brows raised. "This is a date?"

My lips pressed together as I stomped down a whimper of embarrassment. "That's not–I didn't mean–"

He chuckled as he leaned back, and my mortification rose from my gut. Under the table, my fingernails dug into my palms. *What was wrong with me?*

"So, tell me something, *date*," he said.

I gave him a look that said, *oh, shut up*, but I couldn't help myself. I hid my smile with a sip of water from one of the glasses the server had quietly slid onto the table. I wiped the moisture from my lips with the back of my hand. "What… do you want to know?"

"Anything," he replied and slipped out of his leather jacket. I had to focus on keeping my breathing calm as my eyes combed over the corded muscles of his arms beneath a thin black t-shirt. "All I know is that you keep your circle of friends small, you're an artist, you look good in my favorite color." He witnessed how that same color suddenly filled my pale face, and something danced in his eyes. "And you've got the stomach of a sickly child."

"Hey!" I shrieked, but we chuckled together. "Wait. How did you know I'm an artist? I never told you that."

His blue eyes darted to my fingers. The smudges of charcoal on the underside of my right hand, the old bits of paint under my nail-polish-chipped nails. I slipped them beneath the table.

"Don't hide them," he told me. "To create such beauty with your hands is a talent befallen on very few."

"How do you know I create beautiful things?" I challenged and took another sip of water. "Maybe my work is atrocious."

"Maybe," Cillian replied and leaned back with a wink. "But I doubt it."

Our food arrived, and I wasted no time digging in. I was starved and hadn't had sushi in ages. I shoved some to the side of my mouth and said, "I was raised in the country." Cillian gave me a questioning look as he ate. "A thing about me. The city is… all new to me." *Among other things.* He nodded slowly, considering. "Your turn"

Cillian swallowed and held both hands out. "What would you like to know?"

I shrugged. "What do you do? For work."

He dipped a piece of sushi in soya sauce and said, "I'm curious. What is it you *think* I do?" before stuffing it in his mouth.

I picked up a small, serrated knife to cut through one of my spring rolls. "Male model?" Amusement flickered in his eyes. "A plant hired to follow me around and annoy me endlessly?"

Something outside caught my attention through the front window, and I froze. Cillian responded, but his words breezed in my ears as the thunderous beating of my heart clamored wildly. I stared unblinking at a strange, gray, bony creature crouched on the edge of a garden planter just out front of the restaurant. Its dark and leathery arms whipped out and plucked a passing bird from the air, crushing the life of the poor animal.

But that's not what had my heart in my throat.

It was the way the creature seemed to… *see* me. Its black eyes narrowed with promise as they cut through the restaurant and bore into me. I felt all the color drain from my face, and the only thing that ripped me from the trance was the sudden searing pain in my finger. I glanced down at my hand. The knife, I'd gripped the blade, and drops of crimson dripped onto my napkin.

"Oh, shit!" I said, and the knife clattered to the table as I hastily wrapped my finger with a fresh napkin.

Cillian's eyes widened, and his hands gripped the edge of the table in front of him. He must have thought I was absolutely insane.

"Sorry," I told him and inched out of the seat. "Excuse me, I'll be right back." I ran off to the bathroom to clean my wound and wrap it better. The cut was actually small, just deep, and the bleeding stopped after a few minutes of pressure. But when I returned to the table… he was gone. A wad of twenties left in his place.

Disappointment flooded me. I scanned around to see if he was still there. At the front, near the buffet, a glance out the front window. But I noticed his jacket was also gone and I knew... he must have decided that the strange girl from the country was not a great idea after all.

With a sigh, I fetched my jacket and hoodie, swiped the money Cillian had left, and paid the bill on my way out. Part of me hoped he was just outside, out of sight, waiting. But a new level of disappointment washed over me when I found the strip of concrete outside to be empty. No sign of that terrifying creature, either. *What the hell was that?*

I began to second guess my own sanity again. I wondered then how I must have looked. To Cillian. My gaze went distant, wide-eyed, as I'd gripped the sharp blade of a knife... I should have known better, should have listened when I'd told myself he was way out of my league. I mean... I didn't even *have* a league. I was a loner, a quiet country mouse in a city too big and loud for me. I was a freak. No wonder he left.

I would have, too.

Chapter Ten

I sat up in bed, settled against the headboard behind me, sketchbook in hand, as a low hum of some alt-rock station played in my bedroom. After I'd braved the bus ride home and waited out the dose of nausea that nearly took me down, I'd mumbled some non-verbal response to Julie's question about my day and swiped a banana from the basket on the table as I made a beeline for my bedroom. Now I sat in near silence, aside from the whisper of music, the lights reduced to the lamp beside my bed, and mindlessly poured my thoughts and worries onto paper.

Try as I might, I just couldn't get Cillian out of my head.

I hated how any form of speech became a daunting task around him. How my heart fluttered wildly with every look he offered. I didn't even know him. But… is this what it felt like for *everybody*? To like someone. Was I crazy for letting myself fall for a total stranger when he could so easily disappear from my life? Today was the perfect evidence of his ability to leave on a whim.

I let out a groan, and the back of my head bonked off the headboard. I should just forget him altogether. Purge him from my mind. Save me the heartbreak. I glanced down at the paper on my lap. Only to find that I'd sketched a pair of eyes, over and over, all across the spread. I didn't need the aid of color to know whose eyes they were.

I slammed the book shut.

I needed a distraction, but from someone who wouldn't ask questions like Julie would. A gentle October breeze floated in through the open window, and I realized it'd been a while since Lattie had come… I wanted to say *home*, but this wasn't her home. I'd blindly trapped her in this magical attachment to me. But I felt a sense of… *responsibility* for the creature. As murderous and terrifying as she was.

To avoid the inevitable questions from Julie, I threw on a hoodie and crawled down the fire escape outside my window. When my boots hit the concrete below, I headed off in search of Lattie. I had no idea where she went when she wasn't at home with me. The only leads I had were the spots I'd seen her before we met. In the park's tree line– which I wasn't venturing into at this hour of the night. I made a quick and fruitless sweep of the boardwalk down at the waterfront. And the alleyway between the clubs on Argyle Street.

As I trekked back up a few streets from the waterfront, I turned down Argyle and headed toward the nightclub. When I reached the mouth of the alley, I glanced around to make sure no one was watching as I gripped the worn stone corner and peered inside. It was pitch black, with heaps of black garbage bags catching the moonlight from above. No movement. No sound. But… I *felt* it. A pulsing from inside the building. Not the mundane nightclub to my right, but from the brick encasing the alley. Deep and thrumming, a bass that burrowed and echoed inside my chest. Luring me in.

Slowly, I stepped inside the alley, trailing my hand over the rough stone, looking for… I wasn't sure. A sign, a door, something that connected to Lattie. That night with Julie, I swore I saw something. A flicker, a glimmer, a… crack of light in the dark wall near the back. At the time, I was drunk and had chalked it up to just that. But now, I realized, with this Sight Lattie claimed I had, I must have seen something otherworldly. I just wished I knew how to tap into it again.

My finger dragged along all the cracks and crevices until the cool stone seemed to warm, and when I reached a hot spot, I pushed it like a button of sorts. I stood back and waited, hoping, holding in a breath as I stared into the darkness. After a moment, a distinct click sound clanged in the air, like a heavy deadbolt sliding open, and I released a sigh of relief. A rush of panic immediately followed it as the outline of a door formed in the brick, and it pushed open.

A shadowed figure stood in the purple-blue light that filled the space around him. I squinted and strained my eyes to adjust. He was a man in every sense of the word. Except for the pointed shape of his ears on either side of his bald head. I bit down on the gasp that tightened in my chest.

"Who are you?" he asked.

My mind raced for a response. "I'm... here to meet a friend."

He stepped into the moonlight, and I could see his features a bit more clearly. A slender, pointed nose, broad shoulders covered in a long leather trench. His bald head glistened above thick, dark eyebrows, and he grimaced as he seemed to... sniff the air around me.

He gave a slight groan and picked something from his belt. A vial of purple liquid that glowed like a lava lamp. He shoved it toward me. "Drink."

My face pinched in disgust. "You can't be serious–" He grunted with suspicion and took a step closer. I panicked and swiped the vial from his hand. If he realized I wasn't Fae–if he discovered I was trespassing and snooping… I wondered then what kind of fairy he was. One of the terrifying kinds that Lattie told me about? Did he come from the same place that the bony creature outside the restaurant came from? I didn't want to find out. I just wanted to find Lattie.

I downed the contents of the vial. The taste of black cherries, laced with a metallic tinge, coated my throat, and I failed to stifle the ugly cough that gurgled from me. The fairy said nothing, only watched me expectantly, almost as if he were waiting for something to happen. But, aside from the burning in my gut, nothing happened. And I gave the guy a look that said, *there, happy*? He wordlessly stepped aside to let me pass.

I didn't know what to expect from drinking a strange vial of fruity liquid and entering a hidden room behind a brick wall, but it wasn't *this*. It wasn't the great expanse of a dark nightclub packed with people swaying and gyrating against one another. But here I was, standing in the porch area as others filed in behind me, seemingly appearing out of nowhere.

But they weren't people at all. Pointed ears, abnormally long limbs, gargantuan heights mixed with other very non-human dwarfish shapes. Cat-like creatures crawled along the massive system of rounded ventilation, snaking the looming ceiling above. Smoke misted across the floor, absorbing and reflecting the neon lighting in fractals on different surfaces. A fairy nightclub. While searching for Lattie, I'd stumbled into a creepy fairy nightclub, and I suddenly realized just how human I was. It'd only be a matter of time before someone else noticed.

The deep bass of the eerie music thundered in my chest like a drum. Carefully, I avoided contact with anyone and circled the perimeter, my eyes squinting and scanning the space around the many bodies. Looking for anything that resembled Lattie. But there were no familiar shapes in the crowd.

Suddenly, a part formed as the dancing Fae moved to either side of the club, and down the center of the divide, a pair of black eyes burrowed in a pale, dirty face stared back at me. Oily black hair framed her features, melting into the leathery wings she kept tucked tight, and inky shadows crawled over her whole body as her black, clawed hands flexed at her sides. I had no idea who or what she was, but her hypnotic stare told me one thing: she knew me. Wanted me. Her very presence lured me in with a dark promise. And that promise was death.

I forced a breath to fill my too-tight lungs and shook my head, scattering the strange hold she seemed to cast over me like a loose net. A quick glance to my left and right told me I had two options. Stand and face whatever this creature was or run for the back exit. I'd never make it back to the door I entered without crossing her path. So… I took off.

I reached the back door marked EXIT and slipped through. Only when the heavy metal door closed with a secure click did I finally take a breath and shuddered away the remnants of the eerie sensation that clung to my skin. I turned and stopped in my tracks. This wasn't an exit at all. I stood in a long, narrow hallway. The walls were dreary gray, black doors lined each side. Unmarked.

Shit.

The sound of several footsteps from behind the door at my back gave me no choice but to bolt down the hallway. I didn't dare a look as I heard the door creak open. I blindly chose one of the random doors, thanked the heavens it wasn't locked, and slipped inside another room. But only another horror faced me.

Cages, so many cages, lined the walls and stacked on top of one another. Inside… fairies. Tiny ones, just like Lattie. I walked along the front of them, peering inside, searching for my friend. They were quivering in corners, hunched in fetal positions. Some even looked near death as they lay on the floor of their cages. My heart broke as I beheld them. Too small and sickly to even muster a sound at the sight of me. I could see their once lush colors now drained and dulled to a lifeless gray.

Near the end of the line, they hooked the caged Fae up to various needles and tubes, all draining the blood from their tiny defenseless bodies. One of them shakily lifted their head and gawked at me with pleading eyes. Eyes like Lattie's. I couldn't imagine her here, like this, like a lab rat. My heart clenched in my chest.

I had to do something.

A loop of chunky iron keys hung on the wall, and I wasted no time swiping it, but there had to be a dozen keys on it. Frantically, I rifled through them, trying to eye the one that looked small enough to fit the locks.

"It's the brassy one," a meek voice whispered. A small and red-colored fairy, like Lattie, but with longer, heartier limbs. Only, instead of leathery wings, this creature had panels of skin folded between its limbs. It crawled to the iron bars and gripped them with a pained expression as it peered up at me. I held up the brassy key. "Yes, that one."

I wasted no time unlocking as many cages as I could. I knew time was precious, knew someone would be along any minute to check on these creatures, to… collect the blood being taken. The quiet of the narrow warehouse area slowly filled with whispers of awe, words of gratitude and disbelief, and the gentle clanking of locks falling to the floor and iron cages creaking open.

When all the Fae were freed, they swarmed at my feet in an enormous group, looking up at me with those other-worldly eyes. Some headed for the wide loading door, while a small few remained in their cages, too sickly to move. I slipped out of my hoodie and tied the drawstring closed at the neck to form a bag of sorts and gently placed them inside.

"Who are you?" asked the crimson fairy as its long, clawed fingers wrapped around my leg. "Why are you helping us?"

"My name's Avery," I replied and gave it a smile. "A… friend."

Wetness filmed its large black eyes. "This is a kindness we won't forget."

"Who did this to you?" I asked and began walking toward the loading door. I bent and gripped the handle. "Why are they taking your blood?"

"Bad people," it told me gravely and shook its head. "Bad, bad people."

I hauled open the loading door, but I discovered we weren't alone as it moved up and slipped into the brackets above. A truck backed up to the loading dock, and a man hopped out of the passenger side. No, not just any man… the guy I'd bumped into in the alleyway that night.

"What are you doing!" His eyes widened at the sight of me, and a gasp froze in my chest.

The dozens of Fae crowded at my feet, the bundle of sickly ones I cradled in my hoodie… I was stuck with nowhere to run. I searched around in panic, my heart kicking wildly for me to just drop everything and run. But I couldn't just abandon them. I had no choice but to head back into the nightclub.

But the guy hopped up onto the landing before I could make a run for it, his intimidating stance forcing me back further into the warehouse of the club. He grabbed my one free arm, the one not holding a hoodie full of tiny Fae. Realization struck his expression. "Hey, wait, don't I know you?"

"Let me go!"

I tried to wiggle free, but his grip was firm, and my shoulder socket protested with every tug I gave to free myself. Panic festered in my chest. Vomit threatened to rise. I wriggled again and stomped the heel of my boot down on his foot as hard as I could, nearly dropping my hoodie and the poor creatures inside it. His grip loosened, and I darted for the club door just as the driver of the truck appeared to check out the commotion.

But I wasn't fast enough.

The guy was clearly Fae as he sprung toward me with an otherworldly speed. So fast, it was nothing but a blur to my mundane eyes. His large hand gripped my arm again, tugging me back. But this time… it burned. A blinding white light burst from the touch, and a scream erupted from me as I was forced to look away. Then, suddenly…

It was over. The light disappeared, leaving us all in thick darkness as my eyes adjusted. Two figures were on the floor. Unconscious, I realized as I blinked away the burn on my retinas. Thankfully, the Fae I'd rescued were fine, all staring up at me in bewilderment. Waiting.

I didn't have time to process what had just happened. *Did he just knock himself out?*

"Come on," I whispered to them all and ushered the group to follow as I headed for the loading door. "Let's get out of here."

One by one, I helped them down from the short leap to the ground. Some jumped, some climbed down, just a few actually needed my help. The smaller, wingless, and seriously injured ones. Under the intrusive light of the city, I could see how they were all a range of colors, damped and dulled from however long they'd been caged up. Their magic was probably non-existent. Some of the festering wounds and fresh scabs told me as much. I knew very little about fairies, but Lattie told me they're supposed to heal fast. Caged in iron for however long… who knew how much time these precious creatures might have had left.

I somehow managed to sneak the group of fairies to the safety of another alleyway a few buildings down. The late hour was on my side. We didn't pass another living soul. When we all dipped into the shadows, I pressed my back to the wall and slid to the concrete. My limbs shook with adrenaline and the aftershock.

A tiny, clawed hand wrapped my wrist, and I glanced to my right to find the red fairy, its color already beginning to seep back into its leathery scales. In the streetlight filtering in from the sidewalk out front, I could see the feminine feline appearance rounding out. As if the distance put between her and the nightclub was all she needed.

"Thank you," she said with tears in her eyes.

The fairy gently pried the bundled neck of my hoodie from my death grip and set it down, peeling away the fabric to show the few tiny Fae inside. They moved around in a squishy pile, like a litter of puppies. So sickly, so small, so defenseless. My heart squeezed, and I carefully stroked one of their soft bellies.

"Will they be alright?' I asked.

The creature nodded and looked at the little ones with a motherly glean. "Yes, thanks to you. The younglings will live."

"Younglings?" I balked, and my throat tightened. "These are... *children?*"

She nodded. "Yes, bred in captivity. I feared that's all their immortal lives would amount to. Caged and beaten and broken. Used for their most precious resource." When I just stared unblinkingly, it continued, "Blood." The fairy cooed at one of the stirring younglings. "The very magic that makes them."

"Is that what those people were doing?" I felt sick. "They were… taking your blood?" The fairy nodded again. I swallowed nervously. *Bred in captivity*? "How… long were you all caged?"

"Months," she replied. "From what I managed to keep count of. There were days that just… they're a blackened spot in my memory. But it's been at least eight months since they captured me, and some of my kin were already there when I first arrived." I must have looked confused because the fairy clarified with a smile–how it could even manage a smile was beyond me–and placed a hand on my arm. "A Fae gestation period is much shorter than that of a mortal. We produce younglings several times a year. High Fae… two or three times, if they're able."

"Able?"

"High Fae are known to have difficulty reproducing. Which attributes to their scarcity."

"Oh," I replied as if I understood any of what the creature was even saying. My fingers still trembled, and I stuffed them tightly between my knees. "So… what now? Can I help you get somewhere?" I didn't dare entertain the idea of bringing them home with me. Hiding Lattie was a task in itself. There had to be more than two dozen here of all shapes, colors, and sizes. Some as small as a kitten, others as large as a spider monkey. Like the red one.

"We're all water Fae," the creature said. "I just need to get us to water, and we'll be fine from there."

The harbor front was just two streets down. Hiding one fairy was fine, but an entire entourage? Most of them sick and injured, unable to walk. I glanced around the alleyway we hid in, noted the heaps of boxes and garbage bags. An old, rusted cart sat outside one of the back doors. I began rifling through the junk and emptied a couple of damp cardboard boxes, one for each tier of the trolly.

"Here," I said. "It's not glamourous, but I can get you all to the water without being seen."

I began helping some of them into the boxes, but the fairy hopped up on edge to peer more closely at my face. "Why are you doing this? Why are you... helping?"

I shrugged with a shoulder. "I couldn't just leave you all caged up like that. It's sickening what those men were doing."

"They're not men," the fairy said, and a sigh fettered from its chest. "Humans can't possibly be so cruel."

I thought of my parents. How they were gunned down during an evening stroll in the park, with a baby in their arms. *If it weren't for my aunt...* I shook my head as the fairy leaped down to the ground. "Humans can be savage and heartless, too. Trust me." They nodded thoughtfully and began softly unwrapping the folds of my hoodie to scoop out the younglings. "Don't." I kneeled and put a gentle hand on its leathery back. The fairy looked up at me expectantly. "Keep it. Make sure they're warm and secure until you find a safer place to hide."

Her eyes gleamed over. "What is your name?"

"Avery Quinn," I told her. I wondered what Lattie would think of all this. "A... friend."

"Well, Avery Quinn, friend." She bowed her head. "I am Vassia. And this kindness will not be forgotten. Every Fae across the waters will know, and this debt will be repaid."

My heart squeezed at the thought of these defenseless creatures worrying over repaying me. "Vassia, there is no debt. I swear. I'm just trying to help. I have—I know one of you. A fairy named Lattie." Something like recognition flashed in her eyes, and she leaned back, almost as if she were sizing me up in a new light. "She's my... friend. Of sorts. Do you know her?"

"Yes," Vassia replied hesitantly. "I know Lattie. A lot of us do. I... had no idea she'd been sent to Ironworld."

"She wasn't sent," I said. But then realized I wasn't entirely sure where Lattie came from and how she got here. She'd once mentioned something about following the shadows, but I'd never truly asked beyond that. "I found her. Or... she found me. I'm not really sure." I let out a nervous laugh, my mind suddenly whirring with how little I knew of the creature I was stuck with. I sighed. "I have a sort of responsibility to her."

Vassia didn't reply. We had the last of Fae placed inside the boxes, and she followed as I pushed the trolly to the alley's mouth. I took a quick glance to my left and right, ensuring no onlookers were coming down the sidewalk. The coast was clear, so I pushed off and made my way to the waterfront as quickly as possible.

Once we reached the edge of the water, I helped Vassia move all the Fae from the boxes. I stood and watched as they all flourished at the first touch of water, their strength returning, their colors bleeding vibrantly back into their skin. Vassia was the last to go, the younglings clutched to her chest, and she turned to me before she dove into the water, a strange look of yearning on her face. Before I could manage a goodbye, she was gone.

***

After snoozing my alarm several times, I slogged out of bed. All-nighters and nightmare-filled sleep were wearing on me. I took a quick glance in the mirror above my dresser and immediately averted my eyes at the sight of the bruises forming beneath them. I ran a brush through my ratty red hair until it resembled something that would pass as non-feral and covered myself in my red bathrobe before heading out to the apartment, where the smell of coffee lured me.

But it wasn't Julie who stood in the kitchen. It wasn't even… a human. A cold gasp solidified in my throat as I stood just outside my bedroom door and stared at the be-ing rummaging around in my kitchen. Feminine and pure white from head to toe. Skin like a Roman statue, stark snow-white hair cascaded down her back like threads of silk.

I swallowed nervously, unable to blink. She had no idea I was standing there, and I watched in disbelief. I noted a pair of delicate white wings tucked neatly at her back as she moved about. She finally spun around, a frying pan in hand, and saw me. I backed up a step as she smiled so lovely, her crystal white eyes blinking widely between two delicately pointed ears.

"Morning!" she greeted with a musical voice layered with something familiar.

Panic coursed through me. "What… who are you? How did you get in my house?"

The fairy's beautiful face pinched in confusion. "Av', what are you talking ab–" The slight bit of rose in her dainty cheeks washed away, and her white eyes bulged from their sockets. She set the frying pan down cautiously, never taking her eyes off me. "Avery." She took a step clos-er, and I retreated. She held up both empty palms. "Av', it's me. It's Julie."

I shook my head. Words evaded me. This was just another dream, another nightmare.

"Can you see me?" she asked. I only managed a shaky nod. "Like... *see* me?" I nodded again but then assessed my ways out. Julie blocked the only exit. "Let me explain—"

I bolted back inside my bedroom and locked the door behind me before shoving the dresser up against it. My chest heaved and burned with frantic breaths. What was happening to me? Why were there fairies *everywhere*? I had to get away. My head swirled, refusing to settle. I slid open my window without another thought and crawled down the fire escape.

I ran in my sock feet through the city, up and down the beautiful historic streets of downtown Halifax. My heart burned in my chest. I had no idea where I was going. I just had to... go. Get away from it all. Some part of me, however small, still wondered if Lattie was a figment of my imagination. That the Fae I rescued last night was just part of some twisted nightmare.

Until now. Until I beheld my best friend standing in our kitchen. But she wasn't my best friend at all. Julie was... Fae. Some sort of ethereal, snow-white being. So different from any fairy I'd ever seen. I wondered, as my feet paddled down the sidewalk of a quiet street, just how many other Fae there really were.

Then my thoughts wandered as I blindly walked. Julie lied to me. For years. Did she seek me out when we were kids? If so, why? What purpose did she have to insert herself in my life? She always said that she spent her childhood as an orphan, bouncing from family to family until the Ryans stuck. But it was also the same time she'd met me.

My mind tightened and swirled, throbbing at my lobes. I had no clue what was happening to my life. Fairies seemed to pop up everywhere. Some good, some… not so good. But, as much as I entertained the idea that Julie might have ill intent, I couldn't bring myself to believe it.

A canopy of orange, red, and yellow filtered the street. Some of the oldest houses in Halifax were on this street. I stopped in front of that Gothic Victorian corner lot. Celadine's. I stared up at the intricate black trim work, the deep violet wood siding. A rounded turret made up the front left corner, adorned in several round windows, like giant portholes.

I don't know what brought me here. My mind still fought to catch up with the rest of my body. But here I was, outside my boss's door, at the crack of dawn. *In my bathrobe*, I noted as I glanced down with a disgruntled sigh. The iron gate moaned as I pushed it open and stepped inside the quiet property of Celadine's home.

A crow gently cawed from the top of a maple tree, the sound trickling down through the black-purple leaves.

I walked toward the spacious front porch; long garden planters built of stone on either side of the short staircase. Black flowers and succulents of all sorts of varieties spilled out of them. A gothic garden. I smiled. How fitting for Celadine. She was like a gothic goddess, so striking, so beautiful with her never-ending tattoos over pale skin, her violet cat eyes, the heap and tangle of braids and twists and beads that she kept swirled atop her head.

I pinched the old brass door knocker between my fingers and gave a few taps on the door. I suddenly regretted coming here. I felt like a fool. What would I say? How would I explain the state of my appearance? What could have possibly driven me to walk here in my sock feet and bathrobe that wouldn't make Celadine think I was insane?

The deep plum-colored door swung open, and Celadine stood just inside the shadow of the covered porch. Words dried up in my throat. She looked… tired. I'd never seen so much as a wrinkle in her clothing before, let alone *tired*. Her violet stare behind her cat-eye glasses was puffy with remnants of broken sleep. Her skin seemed even paler than usual.

"Avery," she croaked sleepily and curiously scanned the space behind me. "Is everything alright?"

I hugged myself tightly. "Yes. I mean, no. Not really. I just… I'm sorry for showing up at your home like this. I just… need someone to talk to."

Without hesitation, she flung the door wide open—her navy silken kimono flowing in the breeze—and ushered me inside. "Of course. No need to apologize." I stepped inside, and she closed the heavy door behind me. She glanced at my sock feet and lifted her trailing gaze to the red robe I wore, but she said nothing of it. "Come, sit down."

Celadine led me further into her home with a gentle hand at my back. The front porch opened to a massive sitting room filled with Victorian furniture and gothic décor. A white tufted sofa sat mirrored to two black wingback chairs; a brass coffee table topped with white marble anchored the space. The deep charcoal walls were intricately designed with golden wainscotting on the lower half and peppered with antique sconces between abstract paintings. Celadine's own art, no doubt. Everything sat in the dim lighting of several lamps and sconces. The thick black curtains were all drawn closed.

"Here," she said, motioning to a chair. "Sit. I'll make some tea."

I folded my jittery hands in my lap, suddenly very aware of just how out of place I was here in my boss's home fit for royalty. I waited while Celadine prepared tea in what I assumed was the kitchen just off of the large sitting room I was in. The sounds of clanking and water pouring echoed off the walls. It was only a few minutes, but it was enough for my mind and body to catch up with the adrenaline that'd brought me here. I melted into the black velvet chair, brushed my clammy hands over the stiff arms, and thought about Julie.

She lied to me. Everything else aside—the fact that she wasn't human, that she might not even be my friend—the lie hurt. That she either deemed me unworthy of knowing her secret or didn't think she could trust me with it. That hurt.

Celadine appeared with a brass tray balancing two delicate black China cups rimmed in gold. Steam billowed up from each. She set down the tray and took a seat in the second wingback chair, angling her body toward me and leaning forward to add sugar and milk to her tea.

"How do you take yours?" she asked me.

I blinked through the fog in my brain. "Uh, just milk, please."

I watched as she added a healthy pour of milk to mine and accepted the warm cup and saucer when she handed it to me. Celadine then leaned back in her chair.

"Now, tell me," she said. "What troubles you so much that you ran here without shoes or clothes?"

My cheeks heated. "I feel like an idiot now," I admitted. "I just… freaked. And I didn't know where to go."

"What happened?"

I sucked in a deep breath through my nose. "Have… have you ever had someone in your life suddenly turn out to be… not what you thought they were?" I cleared my throat. "I mean, not *who* you thought they were?"

She studied my face. "As a matter of fact, yes. I have."

I sipped the tea and rifled through my thoughts. "What did you do? How did you deal with it? How did… you forgive them?"

Her tattooed hand closed into a fist, and she dipped it to her side below the arm of the chair. "I think that entirely depends on circumstance. Some things… some *changes,* are unforgivable. I would judge the matter based on the person's actions." I let her words roll around in my mind. "This person you speak of… a friend?"

I just nodded.

"And this friend is suddenly not who you thought they were?"

Another nod before I sipped my tea again.

"Was it a change beyond their control?"

I thought for a moment. Julie was… Fae. But she must have been born that way. Certainly not her fault. But my train of thoughts circled back around to the same conclusion. I didn't care that she was a fairy. I care that she lied.

I sucked in a deep breath. "She was… born like it. It's the lie, the hiding of it that threw me for a loop."

"Well," Celadine replied and leaned back as she held her cup and saucer close to her chest. "It seems that communication is needed. Go talk to your friend. Give her a chance to explain before you write her off completely."

A rush of guilt struck me. "Oh, I would never–" And there it was. The answer that had always been there. I would never cast Julie aside because I knew she'd never do to me. And yet... I ran away at the sight of her. The *real* her. I set my cup down. "I should go."

A clanking sound came from the kitchen, like something falling to the floor. Celadine's eyes went wide and shot to me.

"Is someone else here?" I asked and stood from my chair. "I'm sorry, Celadine. I just barged over here with no notice. I had no idea."

"No, it's fine. It's–" She stood and placed a gentle hand at my back, ushering me toward the door while casting worried glances over her shoulder. "My... cat."

"You have a cat?" I asked as we reached the front door.

Celadine swung it open, and her shoulders hunched at the sound of more noise coming from the kitchen. "Yes. The bane of my existence, really," she replied through gritted teeth. But she flashed me a smile. "Are you okay to head home?" Her violet eyes raked over my attire.

I glanced down at my sweatpants and tank top under the red bathrobe. "I'll be fine. The good thing about a college city is that there's always someone running around in their pajamas." I returned her smile, oddly at ease with myself. My nerves finally settled. "I'll blend right in." I stepped over the threshold onto the beautiful, covered porch and turned back to my boss. My friend. "Thanks, Celadine."

She nervously glanced over her shoulder toward the interior of the house but whipped me a tentative smile. "Yes, of course." More noise sounded from that kitchen area, and she narrowed the door opening. She raised her brows and said, "I'll see you Monday evening?"

I nodded. "Yes, definitely. We can go over what I've done for the Mitchell showing so far."

She closed the door further. Only a sliver of space allowed half of her panicked expression to show. "Excellent. Yes, see you then."

Before I could reply, she closed the heavy wooden door.

After a few deep breaths, I turned and began the long walk back to the apartment. I needed it. The walk, the movement in my limbs, the time to wrap my head around all my settled thoughts. Julie was Fae, and she hid it from me for years. This much I knew. The rest–the how, the why, the… what it all meant… I had so many questions. I halted on the sidewalk, just a block from the apartment, as I realized one awful thing. I didn't even give Julie the chance to explain. I didn't ask a single question.

I just ran.

My heart squeezed in my chest as I looked ahead, down the busy street toward The Chocolate Kettle where we lived above. Julie was there, inside, probably beside herself.

Probably crushed at the way I behaved, how I seemed to have rejected the actual sight of her. But I didn't. I ran from the betrayal, not from who or what she was. I didn't even care about that. But how could I prove that to her?

Suddenly, it dawned on me. I ran for the old brick building and climbed back up the fire escape, where I fumbled over the window ledge and fell to my bedroom floor. I rummaged through the stack of sketchbooks and papers next to the bed and grabbed one book in particular before I reached for the doorknob. I allowed myself one long breath in and out before turning the knob and opening the door.

Julie was there sitting in the oversized chair that seemed to swallow her up in her human form. Her crystal blue stare cut across the space and found mine. It glistened with everything I expected to find there–questions, worry, guilt. She said nothing as I slowly made my way over to the plushy sofa across from her and set the book down on the coffee table between us. She didn't take her eyes off me. She didn't even blink.

I cracked open the half-filled scrapbook, revealing notes and drawings of the Fae world. Every detail Lattie had told me. "For the record, I didn't run because of… what you are." Julie averted her gaze and fixed it on the book, her eyes widening as she realized what filled its pages. "I ran because it blindsided me. It hurt me. And…" I loosed a sigh and leaned back on the sofa. "And after the night I had—"

"What is this?" Julie said, stricken with awe as she leaned forward, her fingers slowly reaching for the book.

I pressed my lips together until she looked at me. "I think my questions come first." I motioned to my scrapbook. "Then I'll answer yours."

She squared her shoulders and sat back in the chair. "Fair enough."

"For starters, what are you?"

Her face remained still. "Fae."

"I know that," I replied. "But… what *kind* of Fae?"

"A Changeling." The words were curt, but I caught the slightest hint of a tremble in her bottom lip.

"What's a Changeling?"

Julie braided her fingers together in her lap. "It's hard to explain—"

"Try me."

Panic flashed across her lovely features, and she stilled herself with a deep breath. "When some Fae younglings are born, they're sickly. And rather than nursing them to a healthy state, the parents often switch them for human babies."

I focused on every breath that passed through my body. "But how do human parents not notice?"

"The Fae babies are given a glamor," Julie replied. "A

powerful one. To make them appear human. They often die of unknown causes before the glamor wears away."

"But you didn't."

Julie's eyes locked on mine as she nodded. "I have no idea where I was first abandoned. I don't know who my actual parents are. All I know is that I lived. I survived whatever sickness I was born with."

My mind struggled to piece the thread of events together. "Who were the parents they left you with? What did they do when the glamor wore off?"

But, as I spoke the words and witnessed the painful memory surface on Julie's face, I regretted asking.

"I don't know. I have no memory of being with a family. All I know is that the glamor never wore off," she said just barely above a whisper. "Not at first, not for years. I was... found in a dumpster when I was barely a year old and given to a Catholic orphanage where I stayed until I was seven. I'd already learned that I was different by then. I could run faster, climb higher, was stronger than any of the other kids my age." She chortled to herself. "Heck, more so than any adults, even." I stared quietly, letting my best friend comb through her most personal memories, realizing with every word she uttered just how painful it must have been for her. "I, uh, I was nine when I accidentally dropped the glamor. I was laying in the grass looking for four-leafed clovers when I heard one nun scream."

She shuddered.

"It took me a moment to realize she was screaming at the sight of me. Pure white skin. Eyes too white, too large for my face. And… wings." Julie wrapped her arms around herself and lifted her distant gaze from the floor between us. "I ran. I ran for days and days until my legs couldn't move. But dropping the glamor gave me the Sight, and I saw creatures all around me in every crook and corner of the city. I watched them tear apart animals and eat their insides. I saw Fae touching humans everywhere, without them even knowing, pulling at their hair, cutting them, kissing their lips. The city was full of rampant creatures, and mortals just went about their days like everything was normal. Totally unaware. I was constantly running from them. I hid away in the back of an old pickup truck one night, under the safety of a tarp. I hadn't slept for days and must have completely crashed because the next thing I knew, the truck was moving. It came to a stop at a quaint little house in the country. I heard footsteps coming around the truck and panicked. All I remember was closing my eyes so tightly and praying that the glamor would appear again." Julie paused to smile at the memory. "And it did. Somehow, I made it work. Because when the tarp lifted and I stared up at the faces of Tom and Evelyn, they didn't scream and run."

Run. Like I had done at the sight of her.

Guilt coiled in my gut. "So, what happened then?"

Julie tilted her head. "Well, I think you know the rest. Tom and Evelyn took me in. They'd combed through every missing kid's report they could find, called all the necessary sources and authorities. But no nine-year-old girl was reported missing with my description. And, since they never could have children of their own," Julie shrugged happily, "they kept me. Raised me. Showed me what it was like to be loved."

"So, they have no clue?" I asked.

She shook her head.

I chewed at the inside of my cheek. "When we were growing up, you'd come in here every chance you got. Why? If the creatures you saw here were so terrifying…." I thought of the nightclub I'd broken into last night. It felt like years ago. "Why come back here?"

"I was searching for others like me."

It hadn't dawned on me that there'd be others. Ones like Julie. "And… did you find them?"

A sense of pride animated her face. "I did. And more."

I leaned back and crossed my arms, contemplating what to ask next.

"Look," Julie said and shifted to the edge of the chair. "I know you're freaked–"

"Shouldn't I be?" I snapped stonily. "Has our whole friendship been a lie?"

"No, I swear, Av'," she quickly assured me. "I'm still me. I'm still Julie. Every moment of our friendship has been true and real. The only difference was that... I was never the human girl you thought I was."

"Why didn't you just tell me?" The words came out with a squeak.

"I wanted to," she said. "So bad. You have no idea. But... it was decided that it'd be a bad idea."

I raised an eyebrow. "Decided by whom?"

The corner of Julie's mouth turned up with a knowing grin. "One thing at a time."

I grimaced and narrowed my eyes at her, but she just laughed.

"Av', it took you months to get over the fact that they changed the actor who played that guy on Game of Thrones."

I threw my arm up in protest. "Why would they change him? They didn't even try to find someone who even looked similar!" Julie just stared at me with a look that said, *see my point*? I let my hands fall to the arms of the chair in defeat. "Fine. Fair enough."

"Look, the point is that now you finally know," she said and relaxed with a long, pointed exhale. As if she'd been holding in that breath her whole life. "I swear, I'm still me," she added and placed her hand over her heart. "So, the ball's in your court now."

A long pause hung silently in the air. I could hear only the sounds of the bustling downtown seeping through the windows. Julie rose from her seat and headed to the kitchen, where she began making tea, leaving me to sit by myself and sort through my thoughts in peace.

Julie wasn't human.

I still had so many questions, but only one for myself. *Did it change anything?* As I watched her carefully come back to the living room with a tray of cups and a teapot balanced on top, the answer blared across the forefront of my mind. No, it changed nothing. Not about our friendship, anyway.

Julie resumed her spot across from me and sat with her hands between her bouncing knees. Although she wore a human glamor, I could see it now. The…otherworldliness holding still beneath her skin. If I strained, I could see through it. Could see her Fae appearance. With time to process, to hear her story, I could finally sit and admire what she truly was. Beautiful. Ethereal. Like a living snowflake.

I cleared my throat. "So…" Her head snapped up at the sound of my voice. As if she'd been afraid that I wouldn't speak to her ever again. "Do you have, like, magic powers or anything?"

She visibly relaxed for a moment, then her ocean eyes lit up with a grin. She flicked her wrist, and the teapot hovered over the two mugs. I watched with awe as Julie filled both perfectly. Then did the same with the honey. Two little spoons stirred the tea and set themselves on the table. All without a single touch from Julie. I looked at her. Her face was expectant, her chest slightly heaving.

I just smiled and said, "Cool."

Julie shrunk with a sigh. "Okay. My turn." She sat upright and leaned forward to look at the scrapbook I'd laid out. "Where did you get this?"

I swallowed dryly. "I made it. I'm… in the process of making it."

She shook her head, her face blank. "How?"

"I… I've been harboring a tiny blue fairy in my bedroom. Her name is Lattie." I couldn't stop spewing words. "I accidentally bound her to me, and I can't break it. I was terrified of her at first, but–" I shrugged. "She's kind of cool, I guess. In a non-threatening but murderous way."

Julie mulled it over. "Sounds like a Pixie. Annoying things."

My heartbeat quickened. "But it's not just her. I've been… seeing things."

Her eyes widened. "I knew it!"

"Knew what?"

"You have The Sight," Julie explained. "I always had a hunch you did. From the moment we met as kids, I knew there was something about you. I could sense it. And then your art." She shrugged. "All whimsical and magical. It was too similar to my actual world to be a coincidence." Julie took a moment and shook her head. "I tried so hard for years to get you to see through my glamor. But you never could. And I never dared drop it in front of you, in case I was wrong."

My cheeks flushed hot. "I'm sorry. For running."

She waved it off. "It's all good. We've both been keeping secrets, it seems."

I glanced at my scrapbook and closed it.

"I wonder what the trigger was," Julie mused.

"What?"

"Something must have triggered your Sight to see through my glamor," she replied. "It's a pretty strong one."

I thought of last night. The weird drink I had to consume before being allowed in the nightclub. All those fairies I helped escape. I stared blankly at the space behind her. "The drink."

"The wine?" Julie quipped. "I'd been practicing brewing it for months. I finally got it right, and I'd hoped it would reveal your Sight. Did you drink some more?"

"No." I shook my head. "It wasn't your wine. And it… it's not just you who I saw."

"What other kind of stuff have you been seeing?"

I struggled to think. "Shadows, flashes of light." A

shudder ran down my spine. "And last night…"

She tilted her head. "You mentioned that before. About last night. What happened?"

I rubbed my hands over the fuzzy fleece of my red pajama pants. "Well, Lattie hadn't come back for a while, and I was restless, so I went looking for her." I sucked in a deep breath. "I remembered that night you and I went out when I was standing outside that alley…." I blinked through the images that flashed through my mind. The guy I'd bumped into was the same one–the same *Fae* that blinded me in the nightclub with that light. Knocked himself out, as well as the goon who was with him. I shuddered. "I, uh, saw a sliver of weird light, so I went back to it, hoping to maybe find a clue to where Lattie was. But I found this… nightclub. Only it was full of these horrible creatures, and the bouncer made me drink this weird purple vial. Afterward, I began to see things. Inside the club." The creepy woman, surrounded by darkness, how the crowd parted for her like the sea, giving her a direct line to me. I fought back the wave of nausea that swarmed over me.

"Do you think you could find it again?" Julie asked. Her focus seemed to have shifted to something else as her face lit up with anticipation.

"What? No. Haven't you been listening? That's a party I *never* want to go back to."

Julie grinned. "That wasn't a party. I'll take you to a real Fae party."

"Oh, I don't know—"

"Just trust me," she said and rose from the chair to stand next to me. She peered down at me; her hand extended in silent invitation. "Don't you want to see more of my world?"

Chapter Eleven

A full moon shone down over the never-ending flora of the Public Gardens, a gorgeous, gated park downtown. So beautiful, they often used it for wedding photos, first dates, and an escape for those looking for a peaceful stroll through flowers and ferns. But we apparently searched for something else entirely. Through the violet shadows of the quiet park, we searched for a place. A fairy party.

Julie led the way as I nervously looked for park patrol. The Public Gardens were only open during certain hours of the day and always closed at night. But as she'd scaled the black iron gate, I'd found myself following her. Desperate to see. Julie had sworn that the creepy nightclub I stumbled upon wasn't what all fairies were like. They were most definitely from the Territory of Nightmares. The gathering she now led me toward promised to be the total opposite, and I blindly followed her in hopes she was right.

We snuck through the twisted trees and gardens, lined with quaint benches and ornate lamplights. A man-made pond sat still as glass near the back, and we headed for it. When we approached the water's edge, Julie gave me one last look before she bent to swish her fingers through the water. At her very touch, the water turned... shiny. I had no other word for it.

Silvery dust seemed to spill from her fingertips, and I watched in unblinking awe as the substance spread like liquid glitter. Rippling outward until it seemed to reach an invisible wall and then moved up and around us, peeling away the thin veil of glamor that covered us like a massive dome. My eyes burned at the sight. The beauty that revealed itself.

Slowly, the veil crumbled away, falling to the grass like a gentle, star-dusted snow. The dull, grayed landscape of Ironworld melted away, and in its place... colors like I'd never seen before. And yet... familiar. Golds flecked with sunlight, green that shimmered to purple. An image flicked across the forefront of my mind.

The paints Julie had given me for my birthday.

I looked at her as the last of the veil fell, to say... something. Anything. But as my mouth gaped with empty words, the glamor around her also dissipated, and she stood before me as she did earlier that day. White as the driven snow, every single inch of her. And here, amongst the magic of her kind, she glistened like crushed diamonds in the moonlight. Her crystal blue eyes were the only reprieve from her starkness.

The last of the veil touched the ground just as a set of ethereal wings stretched out behind her. And a snap of sound clamored in my ears, like suddenly blasting the volume on the TV. Fiddles and flutes and harps played festive music as Fae of all sorts danced about the water's edge. Some perched on rocks and stumps and little handmade stools as they sipped from miss-matched mugs.

They hardly seemed to notice as Julie and I appeared out of nowhere. A few quick, uninterested glances slipped our way, but they just nodded happily at the obviously familiar sight of Julie and went back to enjoying the party.

Everything was brighter here. The grass was greener, the air sweeter, the moon and stars like a canopy of twinkle lights. Julie just stood patiently, watching me with admiration and pride in her blue eyes.

I glanced around, taking in all the unfamiliar faces, unique shapes, and colors of creatures. A group of young, humanoid Fae waved to us from a picnic table and recognized them. Not in this form, but small things like their eyes, their smiles. They were Julie's friends from her class.

Dom, Nathan, Chan, Margo, Shana, and Marty.

When I finally spoke, the words came out like a dry whisper. "What is this place?"

Julie motioned around with a hand. "This is The Sanctuary." She took a slow, deep breath. "This… is what I found when I came looking."

"And they're all Solitary, like you?"

She nodded and glanced around. "Changelings that have never even seen the glory of our homeland. Displaced Fae that have been driven from their homes and forced into Ironworld. We all gather here in the Sanctuary's safety whenever we can. To let our exhausting glamors drop, to revel in the moonlight." She shrugged with one shoulder. "And in the sunlight sometimes. But daytime's trickier, with the Gardens open to the mundane world."

She began circling the party, and I followed. "So, how do you all stay hidden?" I asked. "I mean, here *and* in Ironworld? Just the glamors?"

Julie plucked two glasses from a long buffet table and poured wine from a pitcher. "Glamors, wards, other bits and pieces of magic," she replied and handed me a glass. "Some never leave the sanctuary."

I followed her line of sight to the rim of shadows around the gathering, the places where the light did not reach. A cluster of canvas tents sat huddled together, propped up with sticks, logs, and rope. Above them, in the swaying treetops, tiny houses made up a strange little village.

I shook my head in awe and slowly turned around as I beheld the array of fairies before me. "How…" I stared into Julie's eyes. She knew what I meant. "*How*?"

"The Sanctuary sits in a pocket of reality," someone replied. Someone, not Julie.

We both turned to find a woman—a fairy—standing there. At first glance, she appeared human, but it only took a split second to see she was otherworldly. Delicate, pointed ears peeked out from the mass of cotton candy pink waves that flowed to her waist. Creamy skin that shimmered ever so slightly from a pearly green to gold to a lovely red. As if a dusting of powdered gasoline covered her. But it was her deep-sea blue eyes that truly captivated me. Large and deep in their shadowed sockets, they gleamed with age behind the beauty. Wisdom. She was ancient.

Julie motioned to the fairy. "Av', this is Moya. And Moya…"

The pink-haired fairy goddess smiled and sized me up and down as if she could smell the naivete on me. "This must be Avery, then." She pinched the side of her olive-green slip dress and wiggled it back and forth. Half a dozen gold bangles clanged against her long, bare arms. She extended a hand to me. "Julie's told me all about you."

Julie sucked in a breath. "I've been close friends with Moya for over two years now. We… help find displaced

Fae first coming to Ironworld. To help them adjust, settle, find homes."

My eyes widened. "*That's* what you've really been doing in the city?"

She nodded with a tentative smile. "Yeah."

I thought for a moment, and the only question that seemed to form properly in my scattered mind was, "So, if you never came to Ironworld, what part of Faerie would you have been from?"

Julie tipped her head back as I watched her remember, and we both gave a single nod. My scrapbook. My fairy grimoire. I knew more than Julie thought I did. But she suddenly sighed in relief. As if just realizing she didn't have to hide anything from me anymore. I couldn't imagine the weight of that secret. All those years.

"I'm not sure," she replied in a breath and switched glances with Moya as the maiden sipped from a flute of wine. Julie turned back to me. "I've never been to Faerie. That I recall, anyway. I was taken when I was a baby and left in the streets of Ironworld. But…" She slapped her pale white arms at her sides and tipped her head. "I'm told I'm a shoo-in for a Winter Fae."

I turned to Moya. "And you're…"

Her head tilted as she flashed those unearthly eyes at me and swooshed her glass delicately in front of herself. "Summer Fae." She held up her hand and shrugged. "But also, not. It's… a complicated story."

"Moya wasn't born on land," Julie attempted to explain, glancing at Moya to get a nod of approval to explain her story for me. "She's from the sea."

My jaw fell open. "Wait. Do you mean…like…a mermaid?"

Moya smiled and sipped more wine. Her gold bangles jangled together with every move. "Yes. I was birthed under the sea." She sucked back the dregs of her glass and set it down on a table. "A very long time ago. But I grew… bored. Too many years, knowing there was a growing world up here." She cast her glance to the sky and closed her eyes as she inhaled deeply with a sigh of admiration for the magical blanket of night above us. "So, I left and came on land. I found the Summer Territory first. Spent years there. I fell in love, even." Moya looked me square in the eyes. "That's why I pledged myself to the Summer Lord and declared myself Summer Fae. Denouncing my ties to the sea."

"Denouncing?" I asked, my throat dry. I glanced into the glass that Julie had handed me and sipped. It was so different from Julie's homemade wine. It still burned like liquid sunshine, but with more hints of pear and apple.

Moya leaned in. "My father is the king of the sea. Or part of it, anyway. Has been for–" She waggled her hand in the air. "A few thousand years."

I lowered my gaze and focused on the pebbles in the grass as I waited for everything to settle on me. But it only took a moment to consider. Lattie, Julie, Moya, this place... magic—I loved it. My heart burned in my chest.

This was the best day of my life.

I let out the most prolonged breath as if casting away the remnants of my hesitancy. A swarm of colorful pixie-looking fairies buzzed around in a cluster, moving from person to person. "What are those?"

Julie and Moya both scowled with annoyance. Moya's glass was suddenly—magically—full again. "Nixies," she said and took a long sip. "Busybodies. They know just about everything going on in both Faerie and Ironworld because they're always about. Like mosquitoes. Just say nothing around them you wouldn't want others to know."

I recognized the shapes and features of some of them. "I've seen them before. And other small fairies. In the nightclub. They were being held in cages."

"You never mentioned that," Julie said and blinked widely at me.

I rolled my eyes. "Forgive me if this is all a little overwhelming. I'm processing things as fast as I can." Julie shoved at my arm with a half grin that I returned. I looked at Moya. "I let them all out. Led them to the safety of the harbor because this red colored one named Vassia said they were all water fairies."

Moya laughed. "The sneaky devil. She wasn't wrong. All of Faerie can be reached through the waters that connect our worlds. You see, Faerie is almost as vast as Earth. A replicate, of sorts, a mirrored existence on the other side of the water. Oceans, lakes, ponds."

I downed what was in my glass.

Her forehead pinched in thought. "Those Fae won't forget what you did."

I wasn't sure if that was good or bad. I stuffed my hands in the pockets of my navy hoodie. "So… who caged those fairies? What were they doing?"

"We're not sure," Moya replied. "But more and more Solitary Fae are going missing each day. We've been dealing with it for months now. This nightclub you mentioned. What else can you tell us about it?"

I rifled back through my recent memories. "I remember everything being dark. The lights were blue and purple. Dark smoke covered the floor. Eerie music with a deep bass vibrated everywhere. Like some kind of creepy rave." I shuddered.

"Can you remember anything else?" Julie asked. "Details. Images. Names. Conversations. Did Vassia tell you anything?"

I shook my head. "It happened so fast. This bouncer guy made me drink this purple liquor shot before I went in–"

"You drank the purple liquid?" Moya asked, suddenly sizing me up curiously. "And you remembered everything the next morning?"

I nodded as my thoughts came to a halt. "Yeah, and I even saw through Julie's glamor. Why? Is that bad?"

"I would think quite the opposite," Moya replied and drank her wine. "But I suppose it depends on how you look at it. The club is called Umbra, and the purple liquid is bewitched. Harmless," she added at my raised brows. "But if a human ever does somehow come by the club, the purple drink makes them forget all that had happened in the Club of Nightmares. But…" The sea maiden cocked her head to the side as she looked me up and down. "It appears to have no effect on you."

A layer of self-consciousness burned beneath my skin, and one look from Julie told me she knew how I felt. When I didn't reply, Julie said, "What else can you tell us about the club? What did you see?"

My throat tightened. "There were these guys."

My best friend's body straightened and tensed. "Guys?"

I nodded and sipped from my wine. "Yeah. Two of them. They… they were Fae, I think. They tried to blind me with this light–" My mind seared as I recalled the events that already felt like eons ago. I shook my head. "I don't know. It was all so–" I gasped, my eyes wide. "There was a truck!"

"A truck?" Moya asked and inched forward.

"Yes." I pressed my lips together. "A white truck, like a delivery kind. And there was a symbol on the side."

"What did it look like?" Moya tensed and crossed her arms as she held a breath.

"I didn't get a good look," I said. "We were running, and I was trying to round up all the fairies… but it was some kind of animal." I picked up a stick and drew it in the dirt. A canine head. "A dog or something."

They exchanged a glance, and Moya nodded. Julie rolled her eyes with a hefty sigh. "No, not a dog. It's a wolf."

"A wolf?"

She nodded. Her hands on her hips. "Therians. They basically rule the city. Heck, the country, even." When she saw the confusion on my face, she added. "Werewolves." I felt my expression pale, and Julie laughed. "Not like you think. They're people, but also shapeshifters. You wouldn't know a Therian from the next person in Ironworld."

"That doesn't make me feel any better."

Moya smiled. "The myth is that they used to be able to change into anything they wanted. But, somewhere along the way, they enforced a Lycan form and now…." She shrugged the arm not holding a drink. "That's just what they are."

"Also, some of the richest and most powerful beings in Ironworld," Julie said with a hint of annoyance. I wondered just how much they dealt with Therians. She leaned back against the edge of a picnic table. "We've suspected them of kidnapping Solitary Fae for some time now. See, Faerie is the birthplace of mythical creatures, but Ironworld has its own beasts. Therian shapeshifters, for one. Although, they originally came from Faerie, hundreds of years ago."

I swallowed dryly. "And… vampires?"

They both gave me a similar look. One that said, *what?*

"How do you know about vampires?" Julie asked me.

"Lattie mentioned it," I replied and chewed at the corner of my lip.

Neither of them spoke, leaving me in a comfortable silence as I processed my way through it all. My entire world was transforming at lightning speed, and I could barely keep up. But I wanted to. Deep down, part of me screamed to be heard. *This is what you've always wanted!*

Finally, Julie had enough of the silence. She huffed a sigh, but when I glanced up at her, she smiled. "The world is not what you thought it was, Avery."

"I'm beginning to realize that." And the very thought brought a grin to my face.

Moya's many bangles chimed in the air. "Can you show us where you entered the club?" she asked.

"Go *back*?" My insides twirled.

"You'd be perfectly safe, I assure you," she replied with a lazy smile. "I just need to see the entrance." Those ancient eyes flashed at me. "You'd be doing a good thing, Avery. If you're correct, you could help save a lot more lives."

It felt good to help save those fairies from the night-club. And the rush of it lasted for hours afterward. I'd gone home to bed, where I laid wide awake for hours, vi-brating with the aftershock of what happened. I wanted to feel that rush again. I wanted to have a purpose, to help in a way that was bigger than myself.

My chest rose with a deep breath. "Let's go."

I followed Julie and Moya away from the lovely sounds and smells of The Sanctuary. We stood at the edge of the glamor that protected it, and I watched in continual awe as they stepped over the threshold. We emerged on the other side—the Ironworld side—and the sharp, blaring noises of the city clawed at my ears.

The late-night hour cast a dense, dark blanket over the jagged lines of historic rooftops and business centers. The black pavement beneath my feet gleamed wetly, reflecting the white moonlight that filtered down through the clouds. The city was like a dark jewel, but it was nothing compared to the magnificence of my fairy companions.

I turned around as Julie and Moya's human glamors fell into place. Julie's snow-white features melted away, replaced by the familiar appearance of my best friend. Moya still wore her olive-green dress and golden accessories, and she still looked like... her, mostly. Striking and otherworldly. But gone were the pointed ears, those deep-sea eyes dulled to a lovely gray, and her cotton candy hair no longer fell to her waist. The pink had dimmed to a mundane strawberry blonde. And was now cropped short at a sharp angle that sliced along her jawline.

She caught me ogling, and I said, "How... if I have The Sight, why can't I see through your glamors now?"

Moya lifted her bare arm and turned it in the moonlight. "You can. You just don't know how to remove it. Your eyes are lazy, and your mind doesn't know how to use The Sight yet." She stepped into a sliver of lamplight. "Focus on me. Open your mind. Train your eye."

"Which one?" I asked, confused.

Moya chuckled. "Your mind's eye. Try to open it. Search with your mind and find the block, the closed window."

I glanced at Julie, and she gave me an encouraging look. I inhaled slowly and closed my eyes as my thoughts wandered. I walked around the great expanse of my mind, searching for some sort of window or door. But there was nothing. It was like wading through mud. But there, beneath the walls and layers that blocked me from my own mind... I sensed something. A pulsing.

I let out the breath I'd been holding in and opened my

eyes. "I can't." Julie tipped her head with concern. "It's there. I can feel it. But it's too hard to grasp."

Moya smiled knowingly. "In time then." She turned and looked on toward the bustling city before us. "For now, just lead me to this nightclub."

We walked the streets, up and down sidewalks, until the three of us scaled along the giant brick exterior of the building that contained the multilevel mundane nightclub Julie and I had gone to weeks ago. I brought them to the alleyway between it and the next building, and we slunk into the shadows as we headed right to the back, where a pile of soggy boxes and a heap of overfilled black garbage bags sat.

"This is it," I told them and pointed at the bare back wall. "I saw this… sliver of blue light right there and touched it. The doorway opened, and the bouncer appeared."

Moya pressed her palms against it and ran her hands along the brick, her ear tipped toward it. I stepped back and stood next to Julie. She gave me a cautious look, and I realized then just how quiet she'd been this whole time. Was she nervous? Did she want me so immersed in her secret world? Or was she just observing me, watching how I reacted to everything?

"I can't find it," Moya finally said and stepped away from the wall, carefully avoiding the piles of garbage. "It's gone."

I shook my head in disbelief. "How can they just move an entire club like that?"

"The door is gone, but the club is still here," she explained. "I can feel it thrumming with magic. Some things, such as this nightclub and The Sanctuary, exist in a shadow realm. Not Ironworld, but also not Faerie. But some kind of in-between. Like a closet. A pocket of... nothingness." We all walked to the mouth of the alley. "See, portals and doors can be ripped in the fabric, but they can also be moved. The dark energy of Umbra, I can tell it's there, just heavily guarded now."

I grimaced. "Because of me."

Julie finally spoke. "I'm sure they would have moved the door eventually, Av'. If they're smart, they'd re-ward the entrances regularly."

We stood on the empty sidewalk, and I leaned against the cold stone exterior of the building. Being out so late at night, I could see only a few people walking the quiet streets.

"So, what do we do now?" I asked.

"Nothing," Moya replied. "We do nothing but wait for the next lead. Something's taking the Solitary Fae from Ironworld, and now we know for sure that the Therians clearly have a hand in it. I'll start there." She smiled at us. "For now, go home and rest. I'll be in touch when I know more."

And just like that, she was gone. A light dusting of iridescence glittered to the ground in her wake. My eyes bulged at the empty space left behind.

"What... where did she go?"

Julie laughed. "It's called wisping. She can travel the fabric of the world."

I considered it for a moment. "That's... convenient."

Julie just chuckled. "Can you do that?"

She shook her head. "No, I'm afraid my magic is limited to animating beverages and covering blemishes." She smiled nervously but masked it with an exaggerated sigh as she slung an arm over my shoulders. "So, have you decided if you forgive me for lying to you yet?"

The day had been a rollercoaster of events. But I wouldn't change it. Not for the world. I spent most of my simple life in the country, dreaming of something more. A life, adventure, exploring what it meant to live. And... the universe delivered. How could I turn my back on it now? I smiled at Julie and tugged her arm tighter over my shoulder. "Come on, let's go home."

Chapter Twelve

I never begged for death before. But I'd almost welcome it as I fought off another yawn from my desk. My stomach rolled, protesting at the lack of food in it. But I couldn't even think of eating after my alarm went off, and I'd only managed a couple hours of sleep. In one weekend, my entire world turned upside down. Fairies, werewolves, vampires, hidden sanctuaries, and missing Fae. It all felt like a twisted dream, but I knew it was real. All of it.

After the weekend I'd had, walking into class this morning felt odd. Plain. Mundane. Almost… almost as if this were the world that wasn't real. Everyone just went about their business. The prof spewed off today's lesson from the front while I fought off the coma that threatened to crash down on me. I was thankful I sat near the back.

But it came with its annoyances.

To my right, I could feel Max glaring at me as I failed to stifle a massive yawn. I gave her a quick glance through watery eyes.

"What?"

Class ended, and she rolled her heavily shadowed eyes as she slapped her books and papers in a pile. "It's a wonder you've even noticed me sitting here," she replied and guffawed with distaste. "Why would you even bother coming to class if you're just going to sleep the whole time?" She slid her stuff into her bag and stood up as she glared down at me. "It's making me look bad. Sitting next to someone like that."

Maybe it was the sleep deprivation. Or perhaps I'd just had enough of Max's high and mighty attitude. I clumsily grabbed my stuff and stood to face her, matching the look she was still drilling into me. "It's not all rainbows and sunshine sitting next to someone like you, either, y'know."

Max leaned back; her expression twisted with revulsion. "*Someone like me?*"

I groaned and headed for the door with everyone else.

"What's that supposed to mean?" she called after me. I just kept walking. "Quinn!"

***

My energy was to the dregs by the time I walked into Celadine's office that evening. But we had so much to go over for the big showcase. I didn't have the heart to postpone in favor of sleep. I rubbed my eyes, but the surrounding skin was tight and dry. Celadine cocked her head to the side as she examined me, and I took a seat in the leather chair across from her desk and gave a tired smile.

"Long night?" she asked with a grin, her tattooed fingers tipped with deep purple—almost the same as her eyes—splayed out on her desk.

"Something like that," I replied and tried to ignore the croak in my voice.

Celadine frowned. "Are these late nights not working for you?"

I sat at the edge of my chair, my hand out toward her as I shook my head. "No, no. I swear. I'm... totally fine with the hours." I sighed and relaxed back in the chair, gripping my accordion folder in my other hand. "I just had a crazy weekend."

She eyed me for a moment and then stood from her black wingback chair. I watched as she walked to the quaint butler's bar nestled in the wall. An electric kettle blew steam into the air, and Celadine grabbed it and poured us two cups of hot water.

"Thanks," I said to her back. She glanced over her shoulder in question. "For talking to me about my friend this weekend. And for not thinking I was insane for barging in on your home like that."

She spun around and leaned against the counter. "Nonsense. You're welcome any time."

I just nodded in thanks.

Celadine adjusted her cat-eye glasses, fetched two tea bags from a tin, and plopped them into the cups. "So, you've had no trouble securing everything you need for the showcase?" she asked and stirred around the tea bags with a spoon.

"No, not at all." I mindlessly picked at the chipping maroon nail polish I wore and admired my boss.

She neatly arranged her heap and tangle of hair in a giant beehive of braids. My boss was someone unlike anyone I'd ever known or even seen before. The silken one-pieces, the never-ending swath of braids and dreads, sprinkled with chunky beads of silver and wood. The intricate tattoos seemed to cover every inch of her, save for her face and parts of her neck. I could stare at her for days. She was a visual wonder. An eclectic, gothic beauty. And I knew…

I had to paint her someday. If I could ever drum up the nerve to capture it on canvas.

Celadine grabbed a jar of honey from the floating shelf

above the little countertop as I opened my folder of paper-work and receipts. The first one I saw was for the printer, and I groaned inwardly.

"Actually, I nearly missed the cut-off time for the custom printer order," I admitted. "But I found a ride at the last minute."

Her dark brows rose as she came toward me with two steaming mugs. "A friend?"

I quickly grabbed two wooden coasters from a stack she kept on her desk and set them out. "No. I mean, yes. Kind of. I don't really know him. But I've… seen him around."

She took her seat. "Be careful out there. The city is a beauty, but she can also be a beast."

I laughed to myself. "Don't worry. He totally ditched me. I went to the bathroom, and when I came back, he was gone."

She almost looked relieved. "His loss."

I stared down into my tea and inhaled the scented steam. French vanilla. I'd mentioned it a few weeks ago, how it was my favorite. In fact–Celadine had been bringing snacks and beverages and books to share with me almost every time we'd met. As if she'd been making a note each time I mentioned something I liked. I smiled at her from the rim of my cup. She was quickly becoming more than just my boss or my mentor even. Celadine was… most definitely my friend. Someone outside of the crazy mythical world I'd recently uncovered.

I set my cup down on its coaster and began organizing my paperwork on the desk between us. Ready to go over all the details. But Julie's reminder before I'd left the apartment sprang into my mind.

"Oh, before we start," I said, and Celadine raised her brows in wait. "Tomorrow night. I was wondering if you wouldn't mind rescheduling our apprenticeship lesson."

"Oh?" she replied and shoved her tea aside to drag my paperwork toward her. "Everything alright?"

"Yeah, there's just this concert—"

"Say no more," Celadine cut in and shuffled all the papers together in a neat pile.

"Are you sure?"

"Yes, of course," she assured me. "I sometimes forget you're still so young. A college student." I didn't dare say how she was clearly only a few years older than me. "You shouldn't miss out on these moments. Besides," she held out her hand for the rest of my folder, and I placed it in her grip. "Gives me time to go over everything."

My stomach wrung with guilt. "You don't want to discuss it all now? While I'm here?"

A coy grin tugged at her mouth, and she adjusted one of the many chunky rings she wore. "No, I'm sure it's all fine. You've been following the instructions I gave you?" I nodded dutifully. "Excellent. Then I'll review everything and just let you know if I have questions." Those violet eyes flashed with amusement. "Now, go home and get some sleep before you pass out in my office."

My cheeks warmed. "It's that noticeable?"

"I've seen dead bodies look more alive."

Even though I knew she was kidding, a shudder ran through me. I shook it off and stood from my chair. The only thing animating my legs was the sheer will to make it to my bed and the sudden promise that it would be soon. I smiled and said goodbye to Celadine as I made my way back through the gallery and out the front door.

I barely remembered the winding drive home, but when I pulled up in the modest parking area across from The Chocolate Kettle, I thanked the heavens I made it in one piece. With my helmet tucked under my arm, I entered the café, intent on saying hi to Tomas before I made a beeline for my bed. But someone else had his attention. A swath of black leather and broad shoulders leaned over the counter–and my heart sprang to life as a pair of cerulean eyes sparkled at me.

Cillian's wide smile taunted me as I ignored him, and I looked at Tomas behind the counter they'd been chatting over.

"Hey," I greeted with a sleepy smile. "How was it tonight?"

Tomas wiped at the butcher block. "Good. Had a

couple of rushes, but it's been quiet overall. Coffee?"

"No, I'm good. I'm actually headed to–" I was hyper-aware of Cillian's presence, how he casually leaned against the edge of the wooden top, watching, waiting for me to notice him like a sly cat. I wouldn't dare give him the satisfaction. He'd ditched me during our… whatever it was. I felt like an idiot around him. "I'm calling it a night. Are we still on for the concert tomorrow?"

Tomas brightened his already cheery expression. God, he was like a breath of fresh air. Always. There wasn't a nasty bone in his body. "Definitely. I'm pumped. It's the last outdoor concert of the year, and I heard Dallas Green's in town and might make a surprise appearance between sets." His big, brown almond-shaped eyes shifted to Cillian, who was still watching us with a smirk as he sipped a coffee. "I, uh, I hope you don't mind, but I invited Cillian."

My stomach clenched, and I dared cast him a side glance. "Oh? You… know him?" I asked Tomas.

Tomas and Cillian's chuckles echoed between them. "Not really," my friend admitted. "But Cillian's become a regular. And we've been chatting for weeks. When I learned he's a huge Sons of Galloway fan, I had to invite him."

I finally set my full attention on Cillian, and he straightened, his height towering over me like a looming shadow. "You're a Sons of Galloway fan, are you?"

Cheekily, he grinned down at me, flashing a perfect

set of teeth, and I was grateful he couldn't hear my heart thrumming nervously in my chest. "Yes, massive fan, actually."

"What's your favorite song?" I tested.

He hesitated, igniting a smirk from me, but he replied, "Well, I loved *Ether* until their 2018 album came out, and now, I think my favorite song might be *Crescent Sun*."

His deep blue eyes locked on mine, almost daring me to keep challenging him. But I wouldn't give him the satisfaction of biting. I oafishly clapped his arm, knocking that stupid smirk off his face for a split second. "Great! I hope you enjoy the concert, then."

I gripped the leather strap of my shoulder bag and nodded goodbye to Tomas as I turned and headed for the winding metal staircase that led to my apartment.

"Oh, I'm sure I will," Cillian called after me.

I stopped on the first stair and gripped the railing; Tomas's innocent expression was wrought with confusion as I fixed my gaze on Cillian's dark stare from across the cafe. "Let's see if you can stick around to see the end."

Perhaps it was the exhaustion brimming around my mind, or maybe I was just fed up with being the meek and shy Avery Quinn I'd always been, but I didn't give him the chance to retort. But as I scaled the stairs, his answering chuckle tickled my spine, and I hastily closed the door behind me.

***

The sun was a stain of deep orange beneath the blanket of twilight that fell on us as we made our way toward the harbor front the following evening, lured by the lights and sounds of the outdoor concert. Scents of steaming hot-dogs, spilled beer, and crispy beaver tails—deep-fried dough covered in copious amounts of sugared toppings—filled the air, and my stomach danced with glee. I loved this city. It had so much to offer. Good food, music, theater, art. A culture I belonged to.

Not to mention the secret mythical world hidden behind a veil of magical glamor.

They blocked off the vast parking lot between a brewery and a row of restaurants, and they set a large stage on one end. The place was already filled with people, jiving to the pre-show of budding local musicians. Some kind of all-girl rock group that played catchy melodies mixed with heavy metal. There was no shortage of talent in this city.

Julie and Tomas walked beside me, cautiously flirting, and I immediately went for the refreshment truck that sat parked near the edge of the concert, next to a few food trucks that billowed steam and sounds of fat spackling in deep fryer vats.

The early autumn air was already chilling with the

lowering of the sun, and I was grateful I'd worn a thick, red plaid button-up over my torn jeans. My long red hair cascaded over my shoulders, draping down across my back and hugging the chilled skin of my cheeks.

Julie appeared at the edge of the lineup and handed me a ten. "Grab me two beers?"

When I'd finally made my way up the line, the next opening band began to play as I made my order at the counter. I balanced two large plastic cups of beer, and I cradled them to my chest with one arm as I drank from a third with the other. Julie relieved me of the two she bought and handed one to Tomas, who was peering around at the faces in the crowd.

"Looking for someone?" I asked while I happily swayed to the gentle tune of some Irish shanty.

"Yeah, Cillian said he'd meet us here," he replied and sipped from his beer.

The orange smudge on the horizon at the end of the harbor was nearly gone, and early evening was entirely upon us. The loose strings of patio lanterns cast an umbrella made of golden balls of light, reflecting on the faces of the concert-goers, glistening in the tiny wet spots on the pavement beneath my red Doc Martens–leftover from the day's sprinkle of rain.

I ignored Julie's questioning look as I let out a guffaw and spoke over the rim of my plastic cup. "I wouldn't get your hopes up. The guy's about as reliable as a wet paper bag. He probably ditched you. He has a tendency to do that."

"Do I, now?" a deep, raspy voice spoke up from behind me. Its sound tickled all the way down my spine, and a slight yelp escaped my lips as I spun around. Cillian's coy smile gleamed in the lantern light.

I tried to hide the way my throat bobbed with a nervous swallow and tipped my chin upward. "Well, you don't have the best track record."

"How long am I going to be paying for that one incident?" he said teasingly. A swath of silky black hair fell across his forehead, and I had to crush my hand into a fist to stop myself from reaching out to move it aside.

"*One* incident?" I balked with exaggeration as I comfortably slipped into the witty banter we always seemed to fall into. "The frat party, the pub, the bus—"

"The frat party I'll give you," he cut in, his thick dark brows raised. Julie and Tomas had conveniently moved closer to the stage. "But the bus was all you and the pub… I'd said goodbye, didn't I?"

My reply was a grumble and a shrug as I sipped my beer. Over Cillian's shoulder, I could see Julie stealing a glance back toward us, and I rolled my eyes as I failed to hide the grin that tugged at my mouth.

"Regardless," he continued and leaned closer. The scent of leather and crisp night air nearly took my breath away, and I closed the bit of distance left between us. His cool breath tickled my suddenly warm cheeks. "I apologize for leaving at the restaurant. I got an urgent call from work."

It pained me not to watch the way his mouth moved with every word, and his knowing grin told me he knew it. He knew the effect he had on me, on probably every woman he crossed paths with.

"Yeah, I saw the bills you left," I replied.

Cillian held both arms out. "Then I fail to see the issue."

It was utterly impossible to be mad at him in person.

I just laughed and shoved at his chest as I slipped by him. "Come on, let's get a good spot before the show starts."

Cillian followed close behind me as I wove through the growing crowd and sidled up to Tomas and Julie. She gave me a quick look that asked, *everything cool?* And I nodded happily. The four of us quickly melded into a never-ending circle of conversation. Turns out we all had a lot in common. Especially Tomas and Cillian as they dove into a deep discussion about some tabletop game Tomas loved. Apparently, Cillian had always wanted to try it, and Tomas wasted no time inviting him to the next game night he held with his buddies.

We danced and jumped around to each song as we filled our bellies with tap beer and street food. I tried not to stare, tried not to look at Cillian every other second… but I was weak. Everything about him lured me in, called to me like a dark melody only I could hear. But I didn't dare let myself feel embarrassed with each flitting look because, every time, every glance… his eyes were already on me.

As if they never left.

Julie and I had wandered away at some point, between bathroom breaks and drink refills. Sons of Galloway filled the stage after the opening acts, and we danced around to the tunes we loved so much. In the breath of silence that cut the air between songs, Julie put her mouth to my ear.

"I think that Cillian guy likes you," she said.

My stomach twirled with butterflies. "Isn't he too old for me?"

Julie shrugged out of her white knitted sweater and tied it around her waist, revealing flawless bare arms beneath a white tank top. I wondered then how much of it was glamor. I strained my eyes, but I couldn't see through it. "He's not that much older, Av'. Besides, we're not children. You can date older guys if you want to." Her nose scrunched up teasingly. "Unless you're just looking for excuses."

I gave her a look that said, shut up, and I turned to face the stage with the rest of the crowd. But something heavy sank to the bottom of my stomach. Was I making an excuse to keep Cillian at bay?

I considered it as I mulled my lips together and searched the crowd for our male companions. They stood a few feet away, conversing with another group of concert-goers. Even though he was only a few years older than us, he made sweet Tomas look like a child as they stood together. The way he towered inches over everyone, the way he carried his strong, broad shoulders on top of a lean, muscled frame, and the usual black attire he wore so perfectly fitted to that body.

As if he sensed me staring, Cillian's deep blue gaze found mine through the moving crowd and flashed with something that tickled the pits of my stomach. A look of hope, of... desire. Laced with hesitancy. Something warmed under my skin, and I shuddered. Maybe I *was* making an excuse not to let him too close, simply for fear of how hard I knew I'd fall.

I turned and faced the stage with Julie as a new song struck up, one of my favorites, and we both danced despite the way my tired legs protested. I lifted my arms above my head, my eyes closed as I let every note fall on me.

Tap beer filled my veins, and I suddenly felt light on my feet as I danced. I needed this. The normalcy of it all. I could almost forget that the city was hardly more than a mask for the dark, mythical world hidden beneath. Almost.

"You look beautiful when surrounded by things you love," Cillian's bottomless voice rang in my ear as his lips brushed the skin of it.

I spun around to face him, careless and taken by the music. I gave him a smile, one that invited him to come closer. And he did. His wide hands carefully took me by the waist as we danced together. When the song slowed during a bridge, I slung my arms around his neck, surprised by my sudden boldness. But, if being in his presence sent my heart fluttering wildly, touching him ignited something beneath my skin. A thirst for... *more*. To be closer. To feel every part of his tall, sturdy body. Like an iron statue in my hands.

I tipped my head back, revealing the length of my neck, and my mess of crimson waves hung behind me. I felt his arms tense at my curved back, and he pulled me close, swinging me upward to meet his chest. My head swarmed lazily with beer, and I smiled stupidity up at his dark, curious expression.

"How did you know this was my favorite song?" I spoke above the music, careful to not touch my lips to his ear for fear I might not have the strength to hold myself back from taking the perfect lobe in my mouth.

Cillian's whole body shivered with a chuckle. "I didn't," he said. "It's actually mine."

I swayed back and forth in his arms. "See, why don't I

believe you?"

"You don't have to." The words carried a challenge of some kind. To pry further. He *wanted* me to get closer.

I searched his eyes for any sign of deceit, for a hint that he was playing me. "Are you making friends with Tomas to get closer to me? Because he's my *actual* friend, and if you hurt him–"

Cillian's hand gripped my waist tightly, and I stifled a pleasant yelp as he grinned and tucked his face to my ear. "Would it be so terrible if I were?"

God, he could say anything, anything, and that voice would undo me. But I stilled, cutting through all our light-hearted repartee. "Yes. Yes, it would."

But Cillian continued to converse with that carefree demeanor he so loved. "And what do you mean, *actual friend*?" He put a hand to his chest and leaned back with a feigned offense. "Am I not your friend?"

I stepped back and took a deep breath as I batted my lashes. "That remains to be determined."

Cillian's laugh was loud and infectious as it carried past the song's end and filled the air around me. I nodded my head toward the edge of the concert where the refreshment trucks were.

"I need some water," I told him and raised my brows in a silent invitation.

He offered his elbow, and I slipped my arm around it

as we wove our way through the crowd. When we merged at the edge of it all and stepped into the spacious area beyond the concert-goers, Cillian tightened his arm, holding my hand closer to him.

"I've loved Sons of Galloway since they were playing on street corners," he said. "My job keeps me... very busy and away from the city," he continued, and I listened intently, eager to gobble up any minor detail he was willing to offer. Cillian let loose a sigh. "It's hard to find time to make friends. Tomas is someone I see almost every day, and we just got to talking. We have a lot in common."

I looked up at him through my lashes. Comparing Cillian and Tomas was like setting night and day side by side. I couldn't imagine what they truly had in common. But who was I to judge?

"So, what *do* you do for work?" I asked. "We never got around to that part of our... " I didn't want to imply the word date again. "Uh, at the restaurant."

Cillian's body vibrated with the chuckle he stifled as we stood in line for drinks. "I work in sales."

"Figures," I chortled.

"What's that supposed to mean?"

"You've got all the charm of a salesman," I replied.

He grinned and arched a perfect eyebrow. "You think I'm charming?"

"That's not what I meant—" Julie appeared and tugged

at my free arm. I turned to find her and Tomas covered in neon paint splatters, heaving for breath as she handed me a bottle of water. "Bless you!" I said and put the bottle to my parched lips. But I choked down a burning cough. "This is vodka!"

"I come prepared!" Julie laughed and pranced in circles around a lovestruck Tomas. Her long platinum hair danced behind her, catching his face and spinning him in awe.

My best friend was enigmatic and bursting with carefree joy. She always made the most of everything, always found a way to squeeze the most fun out of something. It was that childlike wonder that she always seemed to behold the world with that captivated me so many years ago. Being around Julie was… addicting. But part of me wondered how much of that influence she was aware of. If any of it stemmed from her Fae existence.

"Actually, I think I've had enough for tonight," I said and handed the bottle back to her, but she was barely aware I was even there. Tomas gave me an apologetic look and took the bottle from me. Cillian's hand gripped my waist, hugging my side closer to him. My breath hitched, but I caught Julie's eye and said, "I, uh, I think I'm going to head home."

She came to a halt and gave me a frown. "Aw, really? But the night's still young!"

Every fiber of my being wanted to stay, dance, and

revel in the music. But I was getting closer to Cillian…. and he wasn't running. "I have class tomorrow," I told her, raising my voice as the next song struck up. "And so do you!" I reminded her with a laugh.

Tomas leaned in and spoke to the side of my face so I could hear. "You guys head back. I'll make sure she gets home after a few more songs." Julie flung her arms around his neck and draped off of him as she danced.

I smiled in thanks and waved them off as I turned to leave, Cillian close to my side. I hadn't invited him, but I wanted to. I wanted to bring him back to my apartment, to be alone with him. I wanted to get closer, to have his arms around me, his hands on my skin. His lips on mine. But how did I tell him that? Was it implied? Did he want me to invite him to my home?

By the time we walked up the few streets and reached the apartment, I still hadn't figured it out. But he was still there, walking with me. He stopped at the base of the steps in the back alley, and I turned and looked down on him from halfway up.

"Did… did you want to come in?" I asked, cursing my warming cheeks.

In the darkness of the alley, he nearly disappeared, save for his pale face that caught the moonlight. He flashed a smile and gripped the railing. "I'd love that, very much."

Cillian waited patiently as I drunkenly fumbled with my

keys and let us into the quiet apartment. I prayed Lattie wasn't there but kept a distance from my bedroom door just in case. Or perhaps part of me was too nervous of what might happen if I led this man—this perfect, gorgeous, beautiful man—into my bedroom.

As my head spun under the heavy blanket of booze that ran through my body, I was relieved to be away from the noise of the concert. I may have had more than I could handle. I went to the kitchen for water while Cillian cautiously circled my modest home, looking at books on the shelves, the art—my art—on the walls.

"Do you want anything?" I asked. I had to press my lips tightly to stifle the sound that turned over in my throat at his answering look. A dark stare cut across the room with delight. I held up my glass. "Water?"

Cillian shook his head gently. "No, I'm good. Thanks."

He wasn't closing the distance. Wasn't making a move. Was he being a gentleman or waiting for me to be the first? My head spun again, and I focused on breathing in and out, deep breaths. In and out.

My gaze flitted to the balcony door. "I think I need some air. Join me?"

Cillian nodded in response and quietly followed me onto our tiny balcony overlooking the enormous park across the street. Winding with walking trails, stuffed with flowers readying for the Fall, and sprinkled with lamplight.

I stood and gripped the metal railing as I sucked in a long, cooling breath and Cillian sidled up next to me. Our arms brushing. His broad hand wrapped around the wrought iron ledge with mine, and I didn't give myself the chance to back out.

I slowly shifted my hand over his and turned to face him. Cillian peered down at me from beneath a curtain of silky black hair that fell across part of his face. Those cerulean eyes locked on mine, and my body stilled as my lips parted. My gaze dropped to his waiting mouth, and I leaned in ever so slowly.

This was it.

But all my hopes and wants hurtled to a stop the instant his hands swiftly gripped my upper arms and held me in place, preventing me from closing that gap and placing my mouth on his. My heart screeched to a halt as embarrassment crashed down around me. I didn't know what to say, and... neither did Cillian as his mouth gaped wordlessly. His expression was wrought with sympathy.

I didn't want his pity.

The front door burst open and in stumbled a giggling Julie, herded by an apologetic Tomas who found my panicked face from across the apartment and out the patio door. He thought he was interrupting, but, really, he was saving me from my moment of mortification.

I didn't give Cillian so much as a second glance before

I swiftly stepped across the threshold and disappeared behind my bedroom door, where I passed out on my bed in a whirlwind of regret. But not before I heard the distinct sound of retreating footsteps and the front door closing.

I was a fool.

Chapter Thirteen

I barely slept. The beer coaxed slumber I fell into only lasted a few hours before I stirred, my stomach growling, my mouth parched. Compared to Julie's homemade wine, a few beers were nothing. But I'd fallen asleep in my clothes, even my shoes, so I shed everything in favor of an old, oversized t-shirt and scavenged some leftover Chinese food from the fridge before scurrying back to my room where I now sat. My back up against the headboard. My sketchpad in my lap.

I mindlessly scrawled the pencil tip over the paper, my thoughts wandering to... so many things. Like Lattie. I hadn't seen her in days, and I worried that maybe the people she was running from caught up to her. Or had that dark nightclub–what was it Moya called it... Umbra?

—capture her? I wondered if Moya could help me find where Lattie was.

Then there was last night. I'd replayed the balcony scenario over and over in my head, trying to see where I went wrong. Why he…rejected me. I was no expert—it was hard to date in our tiny town, Tess's tight leash aside—but I could have sworn he was into me. Perhaps he was just a shameful flirt. Maybe I was better off.

But he was friends with Tomas, which meant… I'd cross paths with the blue-eyed devil again. A groan rolled over from within me, cut short by a gasp as the sounds of clanking pots came from the kitchen. I crawled across my bed and peeled back the corner of the curtain. Sunlight poured in. I must have been awake for hours.

I headed out to the apartment to find Julie in her white flannel pajamas, filling the coffeepot as scrambled eggs cooked on the stove. Beneath her clothes and mundane appearance, her true form glimmered. As if her glamor were weak. I realized I still had my sketchpad tucked under my arm, so I set it on the table as I sat down.

"Morning," I said. "Hungover?"

Julie smiled tiredly, and the toaster popped. "Morning." I laughed at the agony in her tone and watched as she plucked two pieces of toast onto a plate and then replaced them with two fresh slices of bread. "Hangover's an understatement. I can barely hold my glamor."

"Can I ask you a question?"

She half-turned to look at me as she worked. "Sure," she replied hesitantly.

"You almost always wear white." Julie looked relieved that my question was merely about her attire. "Why is that? Is it… do you prefer it because it's so similar to how you truly look?"

Julie was quiet as she piled eggs onto the plate. Ever since I discovered her secret, she'd been careful not to talk about it too much—about any of it, even the world she came from. I didn't know if she was scared, nervous, or was just being cautious about feeding me information at my pace. She walked over and set it in front of me, her glamor like static around her outstretched hand. I gave her a look of thanks.

"It's… just easier," she finally said, her long blonde ponytail falling over her shoulder as she leaned against the back of a chair. "Yeah, I wear mundane clothes. But I can create a whole new glamor from nothing, but it's hard and takes so much energy. Especially if I want to keep it up every day. But I can also create a glamor from something that already exists."

I just nodded, awestruck. My best friend… a fairy. A stunning picture of ethereal perfection. How lucky was I to touch her world? To have this peek inside.

"I… could change it up, though," she added. "If the

white's too drab," she drawled mockingly and tipped her head back as her white pajamas morphed and turned to a sheer robe lined with fur around the bottom and the over-sized sleeves. With a snap of her fingers, a crystal blue bled into it. With a grin, she snapped her fingers again, and the entire thing changed into a pair of jeans and a blue blouse. She twirled and did a curtsy.

I laughed and picked at my toast just as hers popped in the toaster. "Jules, the white is totally fine."

She shrugged and grabbed the coffeepot and set it on the table. "Better than my Fae form, I suppose."

Her joking demeanor tucked away, and she averted her gaze. I realized then… how Julie never really could be her true self in her life. Not at home, at school. Not even with me. Until now.

"You know," I croaked and shoved a bite of eggs to the side of my mouth. "If it takes so much energy, you don't have to wear the glamor around me."

Her sky-blue eyes darted to me. "It… doesn't freak you out?"

I leaned forward and gave her the most profound look of love as I placed my hand over my heart. "The opposite. Jules, you're *the* most beautiful thing I've ever seen in my life."

Tears rimmed her eyes, but I broke the emotional tension before we both erupted into tears. "So, uh, when did

Tomas go home?"

She quickly passed a finger under each eye and cleared her throat. "Late. A few hours after we got back." She poured herself a cup of coffee and grinned at me from over the rim. "And Cillian left shortly after you stormed off to bed." I grimaced at my plate. "He… didn't make a move last night?"

My cheeks burst with heat. "No, I did. But he shot me down. Guess I must have read all the signals wrong."

Julie plopped some eggs on a plate with her toast and sat down across from me. "Well, he's a damn fool for turning you down. Maybe he's gay," she added with a chuckle. "It would explain his painfully good looks."

A moan turned over in my throat. "He's not *that* good-looking."

She laughed at my sketchbook, and I gawked at the images I'd mindlessly drawn. Those dark eyes, the silken hair, the wide, sharp jaw. It was Cillian. All over the page, right down to the finest detail.

I rolled my eyes and stood up in a huff as I tucked it back under my arm. "I've got to get ready for class."

***

The rest of the week went by in a blur. Mainly because the gallery showcase on one of my favorite artists was at the end. I stared in the mirror as I applied my makeup for the event. My stomach brimming with butterflies.

Not to mention... Lattie had yet to return. I worried for her, and it grew with each passing day. Every night, I left the window open, hoping she'd come home. But she never appeared. Did those shadows catch up with her? I hadn't seen them myself. Not for days. A fact I was eternally grateful for. Classes were going great, smooth—Max barely even looked at me. We now worked on the project separately. Aside from a few quick exchanges of yes or no answers in class. Which was fine by me.

But I almost craved the distraction this week. For something... anything to take my mind off the fact that tonight was my first big showing. An event completely put together by me. Yes, Celadine helped and guided, but in the end...this show was mine. This was my first test. The thought both unnerved and elated me.

I set down the bronze-pink lipstick and stepped back as I beheld my reflection. I'd taken inspiration from Moya and wore a long, silky slip dress of emerald-green. Much darker than her olive-colored one, but with my stark red hair—which I left cascading down over me—to contrast and a slew of chunky gold accessories, I felt like a goddess. I took a deep, calming breath and let that affirmation wash over me.

No, I felt like a... *woman*.

A person with purpose and talent—a talent that's on display for everyone to see tonight. Yes, the artist's work will be the focus, but beneath it all... me. My vision. My choices in fabrics and décor and food and music. I'd been setting a stage for weeks, and tonight the show would start.

I walked out to the apartment where Julie and Tomas waited. Whatever conversation they'd been having immediately stopped as two pairs of wide eyes gawked at me. Julie wore a skin-tight, long-sleeved white dress that hugged every inch of her from chin to floor. A thigh-high slit up the side revealed similar gold gladiator sandals to the ones I wore. Tomas kept it simple in a gray pair of slacks and matching shirt he left unbuttoned at the top, the collar comfortably laying open around his neck. His usual straight, floppy dark hair was combed and slicked back.

"You guys look amazing," I said, suddenly feeling like a fraud. I never dressed up. Grungy nineties fashion mixed with a just-rolled-out-of-bed look was my go-to. Compared to Julie, who looked like she was born in her outfit—perhaps she was, maybe it was a glamor—I felt like a kid dressed up in her mother's clothes. I wrung out my fingers at my sides and held a smile as I sighed nervously. I couldn't let my nerves get the best of me. Not tonight.

"You're not too shabby yourself," Tomas replied with his usual light-hearted tone. I could have been dressed like royalty, and he would still throw glances at Julie as if she were the moon. He only had eyes for her.

"Av'," Julie took a step toward me and took my hands, lifting them above my head with a gesture to do a spin. "You look like a goddess. Green is definitely your color." I spun, and she released me.

"I don't think many goddesses are gingers," I said and pawed at the ends of my hair.

Julie rolled her eyes and fetched a small white clutch from the table. "Yeah, only Athena." I grabbed a golden fur scarf from the back of a chair and wrapped my neck tightly. "Aphrodite. Freyja—"

"Okay, okay." A laugh turned over in my throat, shared by Tomas, and I took my place beside them as we turned and headed for the door. "I get it."

Julie slung an arm around my shoulder with a grin. "Tonight is going to be amazing. I promise."

"Plus," Tomas added, "You've got us. If it's a disaster, we'll burn the whole thing down, and no one will ever know."

"Glad I can count on you guys to commit a felony for me."

"What are friends for?" he replied, and we left the apartment in a cloud of laughter.

We arrived during the soft opening before the actual show began. Guests filed in neatly, their expressions and sounds of awe resounding off the sets already. I stood at the edge of the vast front lawn with Julie and Tomas on each arm and stared at my work unfolded.

Flanking the pristine paved walkway was the divided lawn I'd filled with local musicians from the universities. Harpists, violinists, and pianists serenaded the guests as they walked the grand path set for them.

Thousands of twinkle lights cast a blanket of stars in swoops that seemed to never end as they bound and looped around the entire property. Weaving in and out of doors and windows, off balconies from above. I'd set up some of the artist's older pieces, some abstract sculptures, to offset the musicians and remind the guests what was in store for them. The gallery itself was a work of art. It made it easy to dress up, especially with the creations from one of the most talented artists in the Maritimes at my disposal.

"Av'," Julie almost whispered, her jaw hanging low as she beheld everything with wide eyes. "I feel like I'm in a dream. This is absolutely stunning."

"Just wait until you see inside," I replied, brimming with pride. All my nerves had settled when we arrived, and I was suddenly eager to share my work with the world. I just… had to see it for myself.

We reached the grand front doors that were propped open. Helen stood with a leather clipboard and checked each guest's name as they entered. She just nodded to me, and we stepped aside in the foyer just inside the doors.

"I'm going to check on the set-up and make sure it's all good for later," Tomas said.

"Yes, of course," I replied and motioned toward the area where all the cords and electrical were kept hidden with tape and carpets and a temporary wall. "And, hey?" He halted and raised his brows. "Thanks. For… helping."

"Are you kidding?" he asked. A slight squeak in his voice. "*You're* helping *me*. I'm surprised my prof didn't steal this project away from me. This event is going to look good on my resume."

Julie and I laughed. "Well, thank you, nonetheless. To-night wouldn't be half as amazing without the audio-visual setup you created. And it definitely wouldn't have been in the budget if I had to hire a studio."

Julie nudged me with her shoulder. "We just love to make you look good."

Tomas bounded off toward his elaborate mess of equipment borrowed from school, and I took Julie fur-ther into the gallery. Heaps of black silk draped from the vaulted ceilings, creating endless backdrops for some of the key pieces–stunning abstract sculptures gleaming with gold. Or… what looked like gold. The artist was now working with clay infused with gold pigment. The result was something that looked like it belonged in the palace of the gods, which happened to be the theme for the night.

Guests in evening wear muddled about, admiring the work and chatting quietly amongst their groups as they sipped from champagne flutes and nibbled on the refreshments. Julie and I stood at the edge of the main room, outsiders taking it all in. I could feel her eyes on me, and when I turned, her expression burst with pride.

Then something caught my eye a few feet away. No, not something… someone. A certain caustic woman who nearly disappeared against the dark backdrops that filled the room. Max. She picked at the table of fresh fruit with an upturned nose.

"Excuse me," I said to Julie and calmly walked over to Max. But Julie followed close behind. Silent and supportive. "Max, what are you doing here?"

Her answering glare was enough to make me want to wither away. "Matt Mitchell is one of my favorite artists."

I shook my head. "No, I mean, *how* are you here? This is a private event with a guest list I curated myself. I don't remember seeing your name anywhere on it."

She raised her chin with a bored expression. "There are no doors closed to me in this city," she said as if that were answer enough. I just stared unblinking at her until she rolled her eyes and deflated with a sigh. "You might remember seeing my mother's name on the list. She gets invited to everything where money's involved."

"So, why isn't she here then?" Julie asked from over my shoulder.

Max gave her a look that said, *how dare you speak to me, peasant*, and didn't even bother replying to her as she set her looks-to-kill on me. "My mother has no appreciation for art."

Even though her daughter was an artist? An amazingly talented one at that?

Max plucked a grape from her near-empty plate and popped it in her mouth. She gestured stiffly to the room. "Nice show. Your boss has outdone herself."

As if summoned, Celadine appeared from the shadows Max stood in, like a spill of ink. "I had very little to do with this at all." She released her hair from its usual tangle atop her head and covered her bare arms, the only skin showing–save for her face–against the dense black one-piece she wore. Its flowy legs billowed around her feet. She placed a cool, delicate hand on my shoulder as she turned and faced Max. "This was all Avery. Every bit of it. From the lighting to the very grapes you hold in your hand."

Max almost looked pained as she forced a smile that didn't quite suit her. But she set the plate of fruit down with distaste. "Well," she wiped her hands together as her stare drilled into me. Her dark lipstick set on frozen lips. She couldn't even muster up a compliment for me. Not even in front of the woman she admired, the woman she wanted to be. Any remaining fear I had of Max dissipated, and I only felt pity for her now. For having to harbor such angst and jealousy. It must have been exhausting.

She turned on her heel and stormed off. No part of me was even surprised.

"Well then," Celadine said and blew out a huff of air. "I'm glad I didn't hire her after all."

"You were considering it?" Julie balked.

Celadine eyed my friend with delight, that purple gaze raking over every inch of her. "Only for a moment, and only because her mother is one of our largest benefactors. But after meeting with Avery," she gave me a wink, "I knew what the right choice was. I mean, just look." Celadine waved her palm around at the gallery. "It was a genius idea to use the local talent hiding in the schools. I never would have thought of it. This might just be one of the best showcases the gallery has ever hosted, and at a fraction of the usual cost."

My cheeks flushed at my boss's kind words.

"Av's the best," Julie piped in as if it were a matter of fact.

"Oh, Celadine," I said, motioning to my best friend. "This is Julie, my friend I told you about." *When I showed up unannounced at your house.*

A look of realization washed over her, and she offered a hand. Julie shook it happily. "So nice to finally meet you.

Avery's told me so much about you."

"Same," Julie replied. "Avery talks about you all the time. I'm going to see if Tomas needs help," she said to me and waved to both of us as she left.

I nodded. "Let me know if you guys need anything."

Celadine observed Julie as she wove through the crowd in search of Tomas. Someone called out to my boss before I got the chance to thank her for the kind words.

"Ah, another one of our wonderful benefactors," Celadine whispered to me with a hint of sarcasm. "I'll find you later. Go, mingle." She handed me a flute of champagne. "Have fun. Enjoy the showing. This is your night just as much as it is the artist's, Avery. Don't be afraid to tell them who you are."

"Thanks, Celadine." I smiled and tipped the glass to my lips as she disappeared.

I took a moment alone to fill my lungs and will my heart to settle. Not from nerves but from excitement. Everything was running without a hitch, my vision laid out smoothly. Sounds of awe and praise floated around the room. Falling on my ears as I swayed in and out and around the guests.

I spent some time meeting and greeting, explaining details about specific pieces, ushering guests to washrooms, refreshments, handing out drinks. I was everywhere all at once, and the non-stop rush elated me. I practically floated across the floors of the gallery. I couldn't wait to tell Tess about tonight. She'd be here if it weren't for trade show season. But she was off showing the province all about her stellar gardening and landscape skills.

Suddenly, the lights went out with a clang that resounded through the building, casting the entire gallery in complete darkness. Gasps and loud whispers of confusion filled the air, but only for a moment as new lights–spotlights set on the sculptures, bringing them to life–popped into place.

Rope lighting dimly lit the traffic flow on the floor so guests wouldn't trample over one another and offered a guide around the show. The musicians changed the tempo of their delicate melodies to deep notes of epic music fit for the gods as the layer of sound effects Tomas created thundered. Lightning, wind, the clash of titans and beasts. It wasn't just a show. It was an experience. I kept to the outskirts of it all, rounding each space and room, watching my work come to life in a whole new way.

It filled me to the brim with joy, but something tugged at a tiny part of my mind. Darkness more profound than the shadows I stood in. A sinister feeling that beckoned me to turn and search for it. I strained my eyes as I failed to see in the room's darkness, but I felt the tug, and I followed it. Past the tables heaped with fruit bowls, in and out of the preoccupied guests. With every step I took, the tug grew deeper, harder, practically dragging me along.

Then, just as quickly as it appeared, the tug was gone. I stopped and spun around, searching for its source. The lights seemed to change, altering, lighting a path right across the gallery as the crowd even seemed to mindlessly part, leading me right to the back exit… where a figure stood. Shrouded in the darkness that seemed to emanate *from* her, two sinister eyes stared at me. Beckoning, calling, luring me to come closer. And I knew… I stared into the face of evil.

The woman—*creature*—from Umbra.

My feet were not my own as they carried me toward the eerie woman, her features sharpening with every step. Wide eyes that seemed to bleed blackness, matted oily hair that hung in knots and heaps around her shoulders. Shoulders that shrugged with the weight of wings—a pair of leathery, bat-like wings—their tips pooling on the floor around her.

While humanoid in form, her body was out of proportion to be anything from my world. Ironworld. Limbs just slightly too long, fingers with an extra joint… one of them now curling over and over as she drew me closer.

Just as I came within a few feet of the creature, she spun around and slipped out the back door. I followed. My mind was trapped behind mental bars, unable to control my legs. My chest was tight with fear. Sweat tickled the surface of my skin. But I disappeared through the same door like a damn fool.

I was halfway down the back lawn of the gallery, gobbling up every cool, fresh breath of air I could, hoping it would clear my mind from the trance the woman had me held in. But it was a firm grip around my arm that finally stopped me. The fog cleared as my mind snapped into place, and my chest suddenly heaved with anxious breaths.

"Avery," Cillian said, concerned. "What are you doing out here? Where are you going?"

My trembling mouth gaped open as I fought to find the words to describe what had happened to me. But I couldn't. I felt cold, empty… unfinished. A shiver chattered over me, and I hugged my bare arms tight to my body.

Cillian slipped out of his black blazer and slung it over me. "You're freezing out here."

As the last of the fog melted away, I blinked and stared up at his beautiful face, those almost navy eyes glistening down at me. Then I remembered the guttering feeling of rejection. I slinked out of his embrace. One sleeve of his jacket slouched to my elbow.

"What do you care, anyway?"

At his sides, I saw his hands clench and wring out. "I care a great deal more than you know."

I guffawed and stole a quick glance toward the gallery before letting my gaze fall to the dark grass beneath us.

"Then why didn't you kiss me the other night?"

His stare bore into me, pleading. "I'm many things, Avery, but someone who takes advantage of a drunk woman is certainly not one of them."

Something in my belly warmed at the way he said *woman,* and I swear, he almost seemed to sense it.

Cillian stepped closer, his cool breath trickling down across my face. With a sly grin, his fingertip whisked the exposed skin of my arm. He leaned in, pushing my hair aside with his face as his mouth almost touched my ear.

"Because, when I *do* kiss you," he whispered deeply, igniting a flame up my spine, "And, believe me, I *will* kiss you. I want you to remember every second of it." He pulled away, only enough to face me, and the look of desire in his eyes nearly took my breath away. His dark brows waggled. "I know I will."

I didn't have the sense to hold in the slight laugh that came from somewhere inside me, and I playfully shoved at him. Cillian smiled and adjusted the sleeve that slouched down over my arm.

"So, I'm forgiven?" he asked.

I feigned a troubled sigh and tipped my head back to look at him as he leaned closer. "I suppose."

"You look like a vision tonight," Cillian's deep, raspy tone practically purred. "I couldn't keep my eyes off you."

His hypnotizing mouth was dangerously close to mine,

and a hot gasp filled my throat as I parted my lips. But then a thought blazed across my mind, and I put a hand on his chest as I shook my head.

"Wait, how did you get in?" I asked. Cillian immediately stepped back, his expression seemingly laced with regret. Like he'd been caught in a lie. "It was invite-only. You have to be on the guest list. A list I curated myself and checked a thousand times this week." He wouldn't look at me. "You were not on it."

Cillian opened his mouth, ready to explain, but a panicked voice rang across the lawn, stealing his attention. I spun around, following his line of sight, and Celadine stormed across the grass, her black silk dress billowing behind her.

"Cillian! What are you doing?" she yelled.

He immediately tensed and stalked toward her, leaving me frozen in place. Why was she so angry?

"Cellie, don't start–"

"No!" she said and shoved at his chest as they came together. Her violet eyes were wide with anger. "I told you not to do this to me. I begged you, Cillian. Not after everything…" Celadine's eyes found mine, and she took a deep breath. "I told you to stay away from *her*."

I gasped as she pointed at me, and a different kind of fog filled my mind as I dipped into a new panic. Was

Cillian Celadine's boyfriend? I swallowed nervously. *Husband*? Mortified, I slowly backed away. I couldn't go back to the gallery; I'd have to pass right between them. My only option was the dense thicket of trees that filled the space between the gallery and the next street over. Home, I'd go home where I could die of embarrassment in solitude.

I slunk away into the darkness and let the thick cover of the trees take me. But that was a mistake. I wasn't alone in here; I could *feel* a presence. An eerie voice cooed in the air, trickling into my ear, muddling all other sounds. A slight stench of rot filled my nostrils.

And she was there. One moment… nothing. The next, I was mere inches from the terrifying woman that had tried to lure me from the gallery. A lump formed in my throat. *And in the nightclub.*

"Finally," her voice, like claws on my mind, seeped into the air. "You're a difficult one to obtain."

She seemed to be everywhere, all at the same time, and I spun in place to try and catch a solid glimpse of her.

"*Obtain* me?" I replied shakily. "Why? Who are you? Why have you been following me?" And, as I spoke the words, I knew… this creature *was* the shadows I'd been seeing everywhere.

A sneer caressed my skin as she continued to circle slowly. "He'll be so pleased I've found you."

"Who?" I choked. "What are you talking about?"

She appeared in front of me and shoved her face to mine. Inhaling the air around me like some kind of animal. This close, I nearly gagged on the stench of charred flesh and decay. The stench of… death. Her clawed fingers tipped black–as if she had driven them into thick ash–twirled a curl of my hair as she dragged it across her long, pointed nose.

A low groan purred in her throat. "Perhaps I'm mistaken." She gripped my arm and shoved the sleeve of Cillian's jacket up to expose my wrist. I froze in place, unable to take in a full breath. The tip of a claw traced a line across my flesh, and she cackled madly. "Of course, I could just bleed you and make sure." She mumbled to herself in thought. "But he would be displeased at that."

"Avery!" Cillian's voice speared through the trees like a siren's rescue, and my heart thumped to life, begging me to go to him.

Move, you idiot!

The clawed hand in the dark abruptly released me, and the creature was gone, leaving me in the stark, cold darkness of the trees. The slight note of a deep cackle slowly disappeared with her. I couldn't wait around for her to come back. I had to go. My feet clumsily led me out of the trees and back toward the gallery, where Cillian came running across the lawn, Celadine close behind.

He skittered to a stop, grasping my arms, scanning me over with a frantic examination. "Christ! What were you doing in the woods?" he asked, his steady hands holding my face. My jaw trembled as I stared blankly. I saw him look over my shoulder at the edge of my vision. Into the trees... as if he knew something had been in there with me. His hands firmly gripped my upper arms, yanking me from the trance, and I looked up at his worried face.

"Avery," he said calmly now, brows raised. "Are you alright?"

Before I could answer, Celadine stepped up to his side, slightly less angry than she'd been mere moments ago but still upset, nonetheless. Calm, but her jaw tight. "Cillian, we're not done here."

Those blue eyes closed tightly as he gritted his teeth. "Oh, I think we're quite done."

Tears brimmed, and I shook my head as I stepped out of Cillian's embrace, and I looked at my boss–my mentor. My *friend*. "Celadine." I shook my head, trying to find words. "I'm so sorry. I'd no idea... nothing happened... we're not...." I could only manage a deep look of pleading as I gripped myself. I was coming apart at the seams. I couldn't deal with whatever *this* was, plus the fear still inhabited my body. Residual from the grave encounter I'd just had in the thick of the woods. All I could do was tell myself to breathe. "Please don't fire me."

Celadine blinked, all traces of anger now gone. "Fire you? Why on Earth would I fire you?"

I shrugged tensely, looking between the two of them. "I'm not with him. I mean, I'm not... we're not... if you guys are together–"

Celadine let out a laugh of surprise that pierced my ears, a single noise that hung with disgust, and her violet eyes blinked at Cillian. I dared a look at him. I wanted to shrivel with mortification. He stifled a laugh.

I could feel my face blanking.

Celadine tipped her head to the side and leaned toward me. "Avery, Cillian is my twin brother."

"Brother?" I said, my throat dry.

I glanced back and forth between them, looking for similarities. And, suddenly, it slipped into place. The dark hair, while Celadine styled hers much differently, it was there. The inky tone. And then the sharp jaws, soft and pale pink lips that melted away into high cheekbones. Wide cat-like eyes framed with dark lashes and perfectly thick brows. From what I could tell, most of Celadine's pale skin was covered in tattoos of all kinds. But Cillian's skin was flawless by the little I'd seen. Pale and creamy and gleamed in the moonlight.

I shook my head. "Then why are you so upset?"

Cillian cleared his throat. "Cellie likes to think she's the boss of me and...." He exchanged a look with his sister. "And she didn't want me fraternizing with her beloved apprentice."

She seemed to sigh in relief. "I didn't want him scaring you off, is more like it," she said to me but narrowed her eyes at him.

"But Avery is an adult and can decide for herself," he countered, arms crossed casually. "As can I." When Celadine refused to reply, Cillian grinned in delight. "Now, if you'll excuse us, I think Avery would like to go home."

I straightened, my stomach rolling. "Yes, but the showing–"

"Was a hit." Celadine touched my arm. "There's nothing else for you to do. I can take care of the gallery tonight. You go home and get cleaned up, rest. You deserve it." Her brows pinched in the middle. "Avery, you're white as a ghost. Are you okay?"

I most certainly was *not* okay.

But I managed a nod. My arms inside Cillian's jacket were nearly frozen in the late-night air. "I'm fine. I just... I think I need some sleep."

He buttoned up the coat right to my neck, and I found him smiling down at me as I tipped my chin up. "Come on, I'll get you home."

I clung to the back of him as he drove us to my apartment, just a few quick minutes from the gallery. But he was careful, took his time. Didn't weave in and out of traffic. By the time we got to my place, I had found myself wishing for his crazy driving just to take my mind off of what had happened earlier, even for a moment.

I swung myself off the bike after we stopped and looked at him with a ghost of a smile. "No parlor tricks tonight?"

He smirked and balanced himself on the bike, one leg on each side. "I thought you didn't like my maniac driving?"

I shrugged and walked up the first couple of steps. "Do you want to come up for a bit?"

For a second, there was hesitation in his dark blue eyes. But he nodded slowly and moved off the bike. His leather jacket hanging open. "Do you want me to?"

The image of those creepy black eyes flashed across my mind. Followed by the stench of death. A shiver rushed over me. "I don't want to be alone."

For a moment, it seemed like he wanted to ask me more, but he just followed me up the stairs and into my dark apartment. I flicked on the kitchen light and a floor lamp in the living room. The bottom of my dress was heavier now as it dragged across the tile floor, and I realized the bottom hem was soaked in mud from the woods. I groaned.

"I'm just going to change," I said over my shoulder and motioned to the living room. "Make yourself comfortable.

I'll just be a minute."

I shed the dress and the sandals. Tossed all the chunky gold jewelry on the dresser and slipped into my favorite pair of jeans. My options for shirts were between three half-clean band t-shirts and a plain black tank top. I cursed my lack of clean laundry, as well as my juvenile taste in clothing, and threw on the tank top before heading out to the apartment.

Cillian waited on the couch. Stretched out like a cat with an ankle across one knee and both arms over the back of the cushions. He immediately sat forward and cupped his hands over his knees. The corner of his mouth tugged upward. "I never really got the chance to finish telling you how absolutely stunning you looked tonight. Like a fistful of gems. I couldn't take my eyes off you."

Something stirred in my gut at the thought of Cillian watching me at the gallery.

"Geez." The sofa sank with my added weight as I tucked my hair behind my ears and sat beside him. "Maybe I should have stayed in the dress."

He grinned wickedly. "You look just as tempting now." He failed to not look me up and down and guffawed to himself. "Trust me," he added in almost a whisper.

This close, face to face, all I could do was stare into those hypnotizing blue eyes. So deep, like the depths of the sea on a sunny day. But here, in the dimly lit living room we sat in, they almost looked black. It was so eerily quiet in the apartment, and I suddenly wished I'd turned on some music or something, anything to take away from the rampant sound of my beating heart flailing around in my chest.

We were alone.

I was *alone* with Cillian in my apartment.

And he was looking at me like I was... *desirable*.

My breath hitched. "Do you want some tea?" I immediately regretted the words. Why was I such a spaz?

Cillian's mouth–his warm, inviting mouth–curved upward. "Do *you* want tea?"

"No." I shook my head and pressed my lips together, a movement he watched very closely as he slowly leaned closer. My heart sped up even more. "I definitely don't want tea."

"Me neither," he said through a coy smile. His fingers carefully took mine, moving sensually to trace lazy lines on the back of my hand.

Only a few inches separated us, and I gobbled up the nearness of him. The feel of his skin on my hand–my arm. His leg pressed up against mine on the couch. Those eyes stared at me with a look that said so much. And I hoped the answer reflected in mine. Cillian's cool breath brushed over my face.

But I couldn't stop my mouth from spewing more

words. "Did you mean what you said? Back at the gallery, about kissing me?"

"Yes, every word."

My hand moved over his knee, and I gripped his hard thigh. Cillian cupped my face in one hand, his thumb brushing the skin of my too-warm cheek. His touch was cool, soothing, and I turned my face in his palm, pressing my mouth to it.

The sensual moan that turned over in his chest vibrated in the bit of space between us. Space that lessened even more as he moved closer, that wide mouth just a hair from mine. My lips parted, and I sucked in a sharp breath of air–cool air that spilled over his bottom lip.

The door barged open, and I yelped. Cillian immediately tensed and shuffled to the end of the sofa.

"Oh my god!" Julie said as she sped across the apartment, eyes alight with panic. "I was worried sick! I couldn't find you anywhere! Are you okay?" She plunked down on the couch to my other side. "Why did you leave?"

"Shit." I cringed. "I'm such an idiot. I should have asked Celadine to tell you."

The cushions shifted as Cillian stood up and cleared his throat. "I'm, uh, I'm just going to head back and see if Cellie needs any help at the gallery."

"Are you sure?" I practically floated across the floor as I walked him to the door. He stopped in the open frame and leaned against it. I lowered my voice. "You can stay, you know."

His cerulean eyes flickered to something over my shoulder, and they glistened with a bit of amusement before falling on me again. His expression wrought with a deep look of longing, one that made my breath still in my chest.

"Until next time," he whispered and placed a gentle kiss on my cheek.

And then he was gone. I shut and locked the door but then stood there staring at it. Julie appeared at my side, and I turned to look at her. She raised her pale brows, confusion all over her face.

"Cellie?"

Chapter Fourteen

Julie blew out a long, exasperated breath as I finished explaining everything to her. How the guy I was falling for was also the brother of my boss and mentor. I told her about each time I'd crossed paths with him and the events that had led to tonight.

She hugged a pillow to her chest as she rocked back on the sofa. "So, Celadine's not mad, then?"

I shook my head. "Not that I can tell. I mean, yeah, she was a bit peeved at her brother for not listening, for not staying away from me." I rubbed my hand over my lips in thought. "I'm still not entirely sure what's going on between them. I mean, why would she get so upset about the possibility of him dating her apprentice?"

Julie shrugged. "Maybe something happened in the

past? Maybe he'd dated a previous apprentice of hers, and it didn't work out?"

I considered it. I suppose that would explain Celadine's apprehension. To put all that work and effort into molding someone, only for them to leave due to a broken heart. I swallowed dryly.

That could be me one day.

A commotion came from behind the closed door of my bedroom. Like something falling to the floor, and both Julie and I whipped our heads in the direction of the noise. Another series of banging and clanking echoed inside my bedroom, so I leaped to my feet and swung the door open to find Lattie on the floor, wrestling with a fabric bag she fought to keep closed in her tiny hands.

She hissed up at me, and I gave her a scolding look. "Where the hell have you been?"

"I was hunting," she replied and lost her grip on the bag. A kitten scurried out.

Wide-eyed, I caught it in my hands and cradled the shivering thing to my chest. "Lattie! You can't eat people's pets!" The cat meowed in my arms. "Birds and mice, fine. But no cats!"

I didn't need to turn around to know Julie stood right behind me, quietly observing everything. Lattie's big black, almond-shaped eyes fixed on her over my shoulder. But she said nothing of my friend's presence.

I walked over to the window and carefully set down the cat on its four legs and waited for it to crawl down the fire escape before I spun back around to the murderous little creature now sitting on the edge of my dresser. Her long, blue legs dangling.

"You've been gone for *days*," I said to her. "I nearly got myself killed trying to find you."

"Like I said," she replied through pointed, gritted teeth, "I was hunting. It's what my kind does. And *you* just lost my supper."

"Lattie, I will not let you drag back the neighborhood cats to eat in my house," I scolded. "If you're going to be doing that, then keep it away from here."

"Fine." She crossed her too-long arms in a huff and then cocked her head to a wide-eyed Julie standing in the open doorway. "Care to explain?"

I heaved a deep sigh and rubbed my hands over my exhausted face. So many moving parts to my life, and I felt like I had no control over any of them. "This is Julie," I said and then laughed tiredly. The cat was out of the bag– both literally and figuratively. "My roommate I told you about. She's like you. She's Fae."

Lattie blinked at me and then at Julie. "Is that so?"

Julie nodded once. "Yeah, Solitary. Raised in Ironworld." She tipped her head, examining my tiny blue friend. "Strange, I've never seen you around."

Those little blue wings puffed out as Lattie hovered in the air between us. "I'm not Solitary. I came from Faerie shortly before I met Avery."

"Well, it's nice to finally meet you," Julie said with all honesty.

Lattie fluttered over to her, swirling around her head, touching her hair, and sniffing her skin. She then looked at me, her face pinching. "What did you mean before, when you said you nearly got yourself killed looking for me? Killed how?"

I explained to Lattie all about my run-in at the night-club Umbra. Her withering expression told me she knew exactly what club I was talking about. Julie just listened intently, knowing what had already happened. But then I realized… I hadn't told her everything about that night.

I sighed and plopped down on the edge of my bed. "And there was this woman. A creature, or… something. I don't know what she is or who she is. All I know is that she's been following me pretty much everywhere."

"Wait, *what?*" Julie tensed.

"I forgot to mention it before. I think I was in shock." I chortled. "Still am. But she was at that nightclub, stalking me. And again, tonight, at the gallery. She keeps trying to lure me away with her."

"What did she look like?" Julie asked sternly.

Bringing the image of her to the forefront of my mind

made me cringe. "Black, everywhere. Dripping with it. A witch's cackle. Eyes so dark they almost seem pit-less." I pressed my lips together. "And wings like a bat's. Leathery, big, all torn up. They drag on the ground when she walks."

Julie and Lattie both gasped in unison.

"I take it you've heard of her?" I asked.

"Av'," Julie's voice was an icy whisper. "Why didn't you tell me?"

I pointed to my head, brows raised. "Shock, remember? My little human brain can barely keep up with any of this. And to be honest, I thought… maybe I was losing my mind." Lattie's expression fell sadly. "Why? Who is she?"

They exchanged a look, and Lattie hovered in the air next to my face. "Evaine. The creature you describe is undoubtedly Evaine. She's one of Faerie's most lethal assassins for hire."

I froze, my limbs tense with fear. "Jules?"

My best friend nodded solemnly.

"Could your presence at Umbra have maybe attracted the wrong attention?" Lattie questioned.

I thought for a moment. "No. She's been following me long before that."

Julie began pacing. "When did you first start noticing her?"

"In Tess's garden one evening, just before we came to the city. I was painting…"

"What was the painting of?" Julie drilled.

"Just the usual whimsical stuff," I replied as I struggled to pull up the memory "Some sort of castle, far in the distance, over strange treetops."

"Where is the painting now?"

"Still at Tess's." She brimmed with anxiousness, making me nervous about whatever was calculating in her brain. "Why? Jules, what's going on?"

She glanced at Lattie, and the little blue creature nodded dutifully. "I think we need to see it."

***

The sun was barely up when we drove to Tess's cottage the following day. Julie squeezed onto the seat behind me as I drove the short highway on my Vespa. Lattie said she'd meet us there. How she knew where to go, how to find Tess's house, was beyond me.

The gravel crunched beneath the hot tires as I turned down the long, narrow driveway that led right up to the quaint country cottage, tucked neatly away in a thicket of trees and shrubs. Scents of exotic flowers and unpicked apples, along with some kind of baked goods, wafted by my nose before I even had my helmet off. Home. It smelled of home. Julie stopped and took a deep breath as she stared at the front porch.

"You ready for this?" she asked me quietly.

I took a steadying breath. "Yeah, I am. I just want answers." Her sky-blue eyes glistened as I stared into them. I gave her a reassuring smile. "I'm not afraid anymore."

"Girls!" Tess called from the front door, now swung open. She clenched her pink wool sweater at her chin. She barely contained her blonde hair in a messy braid that hung down over her shoulder. "What are you doing here?" She immediately fell into a bit as she twisted her face into a withering frown and hunched her back. She shuffled stiffly toward the railing and adjusted invisible glasses. "It's been forty years. I hardly recognize you. Have you come to see your dear ol' aunt?"

We erupted into laughter. A good, hefty laugh that stirred the stress in my gut, so it wasn't just some big lump. It was good to be home.

"Just had some time and figured we visit for the day," I told her and bounded up the stairs with Julie close behind. "Feel like some company?" I wrapped my aunt in a tight embrace.

"What's that?" she replied, still in her crone's voice, and cupped her hand to her ear as she pulled away from me and hauled Julie in for a clumsy hug. "You'll have to speak up, dearies. The years have not been good to my failing ears."

Julie and I exchanged an amused look, and I rolled my

eyes as we filed inside. "Yeah, yeah. I get it." I squeezed Tess's hand. "I'll visit more. I promise."

Her face gleamed with a smile, and she said in her normal voice, "I'll make some tea."

While Tess noisily brewed a pot of tea and prepared snacks in the kitchen, Julie and I hunched over my back pile of unfinished paintings in my bedroom. The door shut and locked behind us. A gentle tap on the window reminded me who else came with us, and I hauled it open to let Lattie in. She buzzed around my room, taking in the new surroundings, and then hovered in front of us over the stack of canvases.

"It should be here in this collection," I said quietly and began rifling through them. And then a second time. "No, it can't be." I spun and dug through the bottom of my closet. But it was empty. I turned to Julie and Lattie. "It's not here."

"What do you mean?" Julie asked.

My shoulders tensed. "It's gone. The painting that Evaine saw me working on in the garden that night. It's not here."

Julie chewed at the inside of her cheek. "Maybe Tess moved it?"

"Lattie, stay here, okay?" I pleaded. "And try not to make any noise."

She nodded and set herself on my handmade quilt as

she poked around at the collection of paintings. I secured the door behind us and headed back out to the house. Tess was just moving a tray to the dining room table stacked with a steaming teapot and cups and spoons.

"Hey Tess, did you move any of my paintings?"

She straightened and gave us a curious look. "No. Not that I can recall. Why?"

I played it off like it was no big deal and sat down with as much of a carefree expression as I could manage. "Oh, it's just… I never finished it, and I was hoping to take it back to the city with me."

She squeezed a heap of honey into her mug. "Which one? Maybe I moved it while I was cleaning."

Julie shot me a look of warning that said, *watch what you say*.

I averted my gaze from my aunt's inquisitive stare and slowly prepared my tea. "It's, uh, just some dark treetops with a whimsical castle in the background."

Her face paled as she thought, her expression gone blank. "No. I can't say I've seen it."

"Are you sure?" Julie pressed.

Tess glanced between us, and I could see all light-heartedness was gone. She was my overprotective aunt once again. "Is something wrong?" she asked tersely. "Did something happen? Are you being safe?"

"What?" I let out a nervous laugh and leaned back in

my chair stiffly. Nothing got by her. "No, everything's fine, Tess. Chill."

Then a thought occurred to me. I had some sort of evil fairy assassin after me. If my knowledge of crime fiction was any bit helpful, I knew what that meant. It would only be a matter of time before Evaine began to hurt the people I loved just to get to me. I couldn't let Tess know I was in any danger whatsoever. She'd insist I move home immediately. And, while I'd love nothing more than to slither back to the safety of her nest, I couldn't lead Evaine to my aunt.

I took a deep, steadying breath. "I just… Celadine had mentioned wanting one of my pieces. I thought she'd like that one if I finished it."

She considered it for a moment. "Well, at least stay for supper. I'm hitting the road again soon with the Home and Garden Show and won't see you for weeks."

Something inside me sighed in relief at that. Tess would be gone. Far from here. Safe.

Julie cleared her throat. "We should actually head back." She gave Tess an apologetic look. "We've got classes in the morning."

"Oh, *please*." My aunt's face turned down with the most exaggerated frown. "This is the first time you girls have come home to visit since moving to the city."

I threw Julie a side glance, and she nodded. "Okay, we'll stay," I gave in and smiled.

Julie leaned forward in her chair. "But only if you make your tarragon rice!"

Tess chuckled and stood up, overlapping the flaps of her sweater across her body. "How could I deny that? I just have to run to the store." She drained her tea to the dregs. "I'll be right back."

She was barely halfway down the driveway when Lattie poked her head out from my bedroom door. "Is she gone?"

"Yeah," Julie replied and shoved off her chair. "But we're staying a while. You should head back to the city."

Her massive black eyes blinked up at us, laced with concern. She set them on me. "When were you in Faerie?"

"What are you talking about?" My face twisted with confusion. "I-I've never been to Faerie."

The tiny blue creature cocked her head toward my bedroom, motioning us to follow. When Julie and I stood just inside the room, Lattie pointed at my paintings that she'd laid out on display across my bed.

"Ly Erg, Batta," she said and pointed to each one. "This is the Matton Forest. This one here is a beach in the Summer Kingdom where mermaids often come to visit."

My eyes were dry as I blinked, and my throat protested with a dry swallow. "Wait… are you saying these are actually things from Faerie?"

Julie said nothing as she slowly approached the bed and

examined the paintings–paintings she'd seen a hundred times–now taking them in with a whole new light. Her home. A home she doesn't remember, had never returned to. Her fingers reached but never touched as she slowly circled the bed.

"Lattie," I said. "How could I possibly paint images of a world I'd never seen before?"

"I do not know." She shook her little head. "But I'm certain. These are but mere glimpses, but I'd recognize the imagery anywhere."

"It can't be," I said, mostly to myself. Because the truth was blaring in my face. "My work always comes from dreams or… just my imagination."

We stood in the stark silence of my childhood bedroom, and the weight of the discovery began to sink in for all three of us. My chest heaved with a burning, anxious breath.

"There's only one solution I see here," Lattie cut the silence. "You're some kind of Oracle."

"Oracle?"

Julie's head whipped to me, her face alight with understanding. "A mortal Seer." The words spilled over her lips in a whisper.

Lattie's wings carried her around the room, and she then hovered in the space before me. Her depthless eyes examined every inch of me. "We've not seen one in a few centuries. The last mortal Seer predicted the war between Fae and Therians. He saved the king's life."

"Av', that might explain why Evaine wants you," Julie piped up. "Maybe she's been hired by someone, this apparent person, to track down a Seer. It would explain *so* much. In fact… it would explain everything. How you can see these things and how you have the Sight, the ability to see through glamors."

The impossibility of the notion clashed with my rational mind. The words she spoke… felt true. As if she were peeling away layers of secrets with every syllable. My eyes rimmed with wetness. "But what would someone want with me? I don't even know how to wield it. The… *Sight*. And everything I've ever *seen* it's from the past. I can't predict the future."

Julie began to pace. "Maybe you just don't know how. Maybe whoever hired Evaine knows how to use you—"

"*Use* me?"

My best friend's face became stricken with regret. "Oh, Av', I didn't mean…."

"Yeah, you did," I said, lowering my gaze to the floor as I let it sink in. "You meant it because it's true. Which means…"

Lattie placed a delicate, long-fingered hand on my shoulder as she looked at me with pity. "There's a powerful Fae after you," she finished.

"When we first met, you said you weren't following me. You were following the shadows. You were following Evaine." Desperation flowed in my veins, and I begged the universe for a different reason. That this was all some sort of coincidence.

She suddenly seemed nervous. "Yes, I was hunting one night and saw Evaine speaking to someone in the shadows near the edge of the Matton Forest. The other person was heavily cloaked, and I couldn't see them. But they were discussing the Therians and Ironworld. I'd never been, and the Therians had existed long before my time. I'd never seen one before. I was curious, so… I followed her."

"And what was she doing?" I pressed. "What did you find?"

Lattie's bug-like eyes darted back and forth between us, and her slender throat bobbed with a nervous swallow. "You. I found you."

Chapter Fifteen

"No, no!" Lattie squeaked in her terrifying but musical voice as she sat on Julie's shoulder and read the book in her lap. She threw a pointed finger at the page. "That's all wrong."

Julie slammed the book shut and slapped it on top of a teetering pile we'd already read through the last few days. "That's what you've said about all of them!"

Lattie fluttered in the air and hovered over the coffee table that sat between us. "It's all just mortal myth and speculation. Have you no actual libraries?"

"Not like in Faerie," Julie replied and plucked another from the pile of unread texts on the floor. She'd pulled everything she could find about Oracles from the public library and used bookstores and hauled it all home for us to study.

I gnawed at my thumbnail; the dark green polish long chipped away. "Do you think Moya could help us?"

"Moya?" Lattie perked up. "The sea witch?"

Julie shot her a look. "She's not like that anymore, and you know it."

"What am I missing here?" I asked.

Julie sighed and adjusted herself into an upright position. "Moya's... old."

"Ancient," Lattie added with a guffaw.

Julie narrowed her eyes at the creature. "No one actually knows how old she really is. She existed in a time that predates—" She shrugged. "All of us. Some say she's as old as the sea itself."

"So, she's not really Fae?"

"Oh, she is," Julie said with certainty. "The story is that she crawled out of the ocean centuries ago, running from her father the King of the Seas, from all the horrible things he made her do and became part of the Summer Territory after pledging herself to the Summer Lord."

"Pledging? So, they're *together*?"

"No, no," Lattie chimed in. "It's not like that. The Summer Lord loves only one. The Lady of Summer. But..." Her black eyes flitted to Julie. The fact that they both knew these details told me it was a tale widely known amongst their kind.

Julie leaned forward with a sigh; her hands wrung together on her lap. "The Lady of Summer disappeared the night of their union. The Lord has been searching for her ever since to make his territory whole. But it's been years, and no one's seen so much as a trace of her."

A chill crawled over my skin. What a wicked, cruel world they all came from. But it wasn't much different from my mortal one. There's always pain and loss. But this particular loss, the Lady of summer's disappearance, seemed to bring about a tangible sadness.

"I knew," I said, veering away from the topic. "Some part of me could tell that Moya was ancient. I could see it in her eyes."

Julie brightened. "I bet she could help, too. Better than the fairy tales we're wasting our time with here." She scowled at the piles of old texts strewn about. "I'll call her." She snapped her fingers, and a puff of black smoke drifted upward. She noted my slack-jawed stare. "It's a spell, of sorts. A call out. If Moya's on the Ironworld side of the realm, then she'll hear it and know to come."

"Only on this side?" I chewed at my nearly non-existent thumbnail. It looked so jarring against my otherwise normal nails. But gnawing at it had become a new habit of late. A coping mechanism while I processed the lightning-speed of events that changed my life before my eyes.

"Yeah, pretty much," she replied sadly. "My magic

doesn't reach all the way to Faerie."

Something like remorse hung in her tone, and my heart ached for my best friend. For her loss. She was born into a world that rejected her before she even got a chance to live. I couldn't imagine feeling like that. Like... knowing where you come from but having no place there.

Before I could say anything, a long, slender leg stepped into the room... out of thin air. Moya. Her entire body, clad in a lovely midnight teal dress—the same color as her eyes—slicked to her body like liquid silk. Black mesh covered her arms beneath the coppery pink waves that cascaded down over them.

My jaw hung open. "Okay, *how* do you do that?"

"I open the fabric of space and time and walk through it," she replied matter-of-factly.

"Of course." I nodded, my hand over my mouth, trying my best to pretend what she said didn't blow my freaky mortal mind.

She turned to Julie, and her forehead crinkled. "You called? Everything okay? Did you hear anything about Umbra?"

"It's Evaine," Julie told her. "It appears she's been hired to capture Avery."

"What would someone of that caliber want with a small mortal girl?"

I cringed at the description. Was that how they saw me?

I supposed I might have seemed fragile, useless… *new*. Compared to their powerful, immortal selves. I didn't like it. I didn't want to be small.

Lattie hovered in the middle of our little circle. "Avery is an Oracle."

Moya pinched her brows at the tiny fairy. I piped up. "Oh, this is Lattie."

The sea maiden didn't even comment on Lattie's presence and gawked at me. "A mortal Seer? Are you certain?"

"No, not at all," I said with a jitter. "We have no proof."

"Av'," Julie tipped her head. "Come on… "

"Well, we don't." I crossed my arms.

Moya took a seat at our modest kitchen table and draped one long leg over the other, revealing a small slit in her dress. "I know little about Oracles or Seers." Her polished gold nails clicked on the table. "But I know someone who can help."

"Oliver?" Julie quipped and paced between us.

"He's been alive since before the Great War."

"Great War?" I asked. The new information swirled in my head.

"Yes, long before I left the sea, Faerie was nearly destroyed by a massive, internal war. Creatures of all kinds wanted to have an equal stake in the lands, but the High Fae wouldn't have it. They killed anyone that they didn't drive away. I've only heard stories of the ancient time, but

Oliver was there. If anyone had information about an Oracle, it would be him."

I exchanged an equally confused glance with Lattie and asked them, "Who's Oliver?"

Julie folded her arms with a smile. "Are you ready to see more of my secret world?"

***

More of her secret world translated to a rickety old cottage deep in the woods. But not my woods, not a forest from Ironworld. I'd watched as Moya pinched the invisible fabric of time and opened a seam of sorts for us to step through. Immediately, the air was different. Lighter. Filled with the static of magic. The moon shone above, but its light reached father, deeper.

"What is this place?" I asked. My neck craned so I could see as much as I could while we headed for the cottage.

"Another one of those pockets I told you about," Moya replied. "Oliver's home exists here as a safe haven for displaced Fae in Ironworld to seek help."

"Help?"

At my other side, Julie added, "Oliver's a Healer. Treats both Fae and mortals alike."

The cottage itself was clumsily made of mismatched stones, stacked and held together with mud and other strange things. An overly patched roof made of sticks and sheets of thick bark hung down over the corners. Covering one of the glassless windows on one side. A fire raged inside; I could see its burning glow through the few cut-outs in the walls.

We stepped up onto the lopsided front porch, and it moaned under our weight. Strings and spits of various things dried all around. Herbs and flowers and strips of what looked like some sort of meat.

Moya didn't even knock, and we stepped inside the warmth of Oliver's cottage. Scents of freshly baked bread, brewing concoctions, and what smelled like stew immediately hit my nose. The items drying and curing outside were nothing compared to what I found inside the home. More of it hung from the thick wooden beams in the ceiling, over handrails, along the hearth that sat snuggled in a wall above a firepit. Over the flames, a giant black cauldron steamed and bubbled with something. Probably that stew I smelled.

A figure emerged from the next room, and I tried my best not to gasp as I gawked at them. At their pure otherworldliness.

"Nice of you to knock," he grumped in a deep bellow. A tall man–no… a troll–stomped over to the cauldron and dumped something inside. I didn't know how he avoided everything that hung from the ceiling, but he did. His gargantuan height weaved in and out of obstacles without even paying attention. As if he knew exactly where every single herb or piece of jerky hung. He dusted off his thick hands and grumbled under his breath as he peered at Moya and Julie, then noted my presence. "Who's this?"

"A friend of ours from Ironworld," Moya replied. "She needs your help."

"Does she have payment?" he grumped and pulled out a sizable handmade chair from the table. It scraped across the floor, and I swear the whole cottage moaned as he set his weight on it.

"Oliver," Julie scolded mockingly and circled the table. With both palms placed on it, she leaned forward and eyed him with a smirk. "She's my best friend." The corner of her mouth turned up even more. "And an Oracle."

"An Oracle?" a voice–no… two voices, layered on top of one another like an echo–cooed in my ear. My head whipped around, but no one was there. I felt the delicate touch of a hand caress my shoulder. "A mortal Seer? We've not seen one for a long time."

I stepped toward Julie, my breath frozen in my chest. I searched in the cottage's dimness for the sources of the voices. But only swift shadows moved along the edge of the candlelight that filled the room.

Julie laughed. "It's okay, Av'. Aya, Brie?"

Two figures stepped out of the darkness along the wall.

Similar to Moya in shape and features, but their appearance was starkly different. Hair of navy ink pinned back neatly in thick braids, skin of a blue-gray pallor. I mean, what skin I could see next to the tight strips of multi-colored leather that covered their lithe bodies. Weapons of all sorts—arrows and hooks and tiny daggers—were discreetly strapped to their torsos, arms, thighs. But those eyes, two pairs of wide, curious eyes, gawked at me, and I shuddered under their milky stare. Like the eyes of the dead.

Julie pressed up against my side. "This is Aya and Brie, Moya's sisters."

"The Shades," Lattie whispered in awe.

"Shades?" The word rasped from me.

"We're untethered to this world." The identical sisters smiled widely as each one flanked me, sizing me up and down, sniffing my hair, noting everything from my clothes to the old Converses on my feet to the chunky jewelry I wore. As if they'd never seen a human before.

"Uh, hello," I said to them and recoiled as one got a little too close to my face. I realized they had no scent, no breath that I could feel. They produced no sound as their leather boots walked over loose floorboards. "I'm Avery Quinn."

"I apologize for my sisters' strange behavior," Moya said and tugged at their sleeves, motioning for them to back off. "They're new to this world. To *your* world," she added.

"We've never had the pleasure of meeting a mortal face to face," one sister spoke, and I wondered how anyone could tell which was which. "Only from afar."

"And never able to ask them questions," the other said.

"Like what is a toaster?"

"What is the purpose of a balloon?"

"Enough," Oliver grumbled from over the vat of stew he now stirred. His massive size turned and stood before me. Two beady eyes tucked away in folds of his peachy-gray skin peered at me from over a stubby, thick nose. "So, you're an Oracle?"

"Apparent Oracle," I corrected and ignored Julie's eye roll. "I'm hoping you can tell me more about it."

Everyone took seats around the room. Oliver by the fire on a rickety wooden stool that disappeared beneath his vast body. "That depends," he replied. "What type of Oracle are you?"

I stuffed my hands in my pockets. "There are different types?"

Oliver chuckled quietly. "What are the signs?"

"Just… flashes." I shook my head at the thought. "Weird dreams. Most are blurry, and I fill in the blanks with my imagination."

"But what sort of things do you see, specifically?"

"A flash of a wing–a leathery bat wing. Blue grass.

Pink sandy beaches. The sharp tips of a castle over trees. Strange tiny creatures." I looked to Lattie for help.

Lattie sighed indifferently, "Ly Ergs, Batta's." She waved her hand and fluttered around a flank of meat curing over a fire. "Yet she's never actually seen any of it with her own eyes."

"But everything I *see*," my throat was dry, "It's all so murky. Like I'm only getting the bits that manage to seep through."

"Interesting." He rubbed his chin thoughtfully between his finger and thumb. "There may be a mental block. Most likely because you're mortal. I have a way you can open your eye, though."

He stood and fetched a small wooden box from a high-up ledge and opened it on the table to reveal a collection of glass tubes and leather satchels filled with various things.

"Actually… " I stole a glance at Moya and Julie. "Is there a way to do the opposite? To close the *eye*?" They all stared blankly at me. "I don't want to be used as a tool. Or worse, a weapon."

The Shades gasped in unison from the corner. "It doesn't work that way. It's a gift you were born with."

I guffawed. "A *gift*?"

Julie stood and came to my side as she addressed her friends. "How can we learn more about it? Like, how can we help Avery? Right now, she has no clue how to manage her ability."

Oliver considered for a moment. "The only mortal Seer I've ever known lived hundreds of years ago. And the Seelie king kept him tucked tightly under his wing the whole time. But we all knew he saw things no one else could, so much so that...."

He almost seemed to regret his words.

"What?" I asked anxiously. "What happened to him?"

The troll mulled it over with a grumble under his breath. "It drove him mad. The visions." At my wide-eyed expression, he added, "But the king pushed the Seer. Too much, too far. Mortal minds are delicate things, and you can't force magic through them like that. Your ability seems to come naturally, when it wants, and when you allow it. If you nourish your gift, it will nourish you."

I folded my arms tightly to mask the quick rise and fall of my chest. "So, I have no choice but to embrace it?"

"Is there a way we can find out who might be seeking Avery and why?" Julie pried.

He picked at the flank of juicy meat hanging by the fire and shooed Lattie away from it. "If it's Evaine who's been hired to fetch her, then only a higher Fae would be behind it, could afford the price to hire her. So, it's a Lord or the mad queen."

An icy feeling touched the bottom of my gut. "You guys said the last Oracle predicted the war, right?" A resounding nod. "And they also saved the Seelie king?"

"Yes," Moya replied softly, already catching on to where I was going. Her deep-sea stare fixed on me. "Among other things."

"Then it's possible… the mad queen…." I could barely say the words.

An audible gasp bounced around the room. But, as shocked as they may have sounded, only looks of pity stared back at me. The poor, naïve, mortal girl with an evil fairy queen after her. They felt the truth I edged at.

A moment of silence filled the room. But then Moya stood from where she sat.

"Lattie, you spy around the Summer lands and listen for any whispers of a war brewing. Oliver, get in touch with your contact that surrounds the Winter borders and see if they know anything." She turned to her sisters. "Aya, Brie. You both know what to do." I shuddered at the thought of what exactly it was they did. "I'll head to the Seelie Court now to see what I can find."

Then she turned to Julie and me with an overly en-thusiastic smile that failed to comfort me the way I knew she thought it would. "And Avery. I suggest you stay put in Ironworld. Don't make any sudden changes to your routine. If Queen Mabry is after you and Evaine spies for her, then we don't want to tip her off that you're privy to her plans. Stay home as much as you can. I'll prepare some wards to place around your apartment." She gripped my upper arms and peered into my eyes to urge her words. "Don't go anywhere alone. Stay away from the shadows. Understand?"

I just nodded. All I could think of was how my life was defined by this. By the need to protect me from the possibility of danger. I'd grown up a sheltered and inexperienced girl because of it. Only this time, there really was something to worry about. There indeed was something sinister lurking on the dark streets, waiting for the perfect opportunity to kidnap me, kill me… I still wasn't entirely sure. But one thing was certain, I'd stumbled into a whole world of trouble.

***

The prof droned on about our upcoming projects. I'd only been half-listening, for my mind was elsewhere. A far-off world where everything you could imagine stalked about. Vampires, werewolves, fairies… everything you could ever expect from the myths. But they weren't myths.

And neither was an Oracle.

A thick black binder crashed on top of my desk, and I nearly fell off my seat.

"What the hell?" I gasped.

Max glowered down at me. Her tight, oversized bun only made the expression starker. "It's my notes and works for my half the project." She wore a deep crimson pair of pants, held together with a seam of crisscrossed straps of leather that ran up the outside of her legs. She crossed her bare arms as a black sleeveless turtleneck gobbled up her long neck. "You remembered, right?"

Oh, that's right. I was supposed to stay behind with her today to put together our two project halves and finish it up. I quickly stifled the look of awe. "How could I forget?"

"So, are we doing this or not?"

We moved next door to a room with long tables fit for laying out a large project. They mostly used it for group work, but it was far better than our small desks in class. My binder was nowhere near as profound as Max's. In fact, it wasn't even a binder; I'd assembled it all in a duo-tang and slipped everything into individual plastic sleeves, all organized with color-coded dividers. I actually put a lot of work into my portion, my half, and still… it was nothing compared to what Max had done. She was a perfectionist and then some. A fact I was surprised to discover I admired.

I let her lay everything out and fuss over the final, assembled version, only speaking a few words now and then. But it didn't matter. I was barely listening. Half my mind still drifted to thoughts and worries of the dark fairy that currently hunted me down. For reasons I had no idea.

The project with Max seemed like such a useless concept in the grand scheme of my now tragic life.

"Quinn!" Max spat and snapped her perfectly manicured nails in front of my face. "What's the matter with you?"

I blinked away the fog from my mind and adjusted on my stool. "You wouldn't understand."

She sort of snorted as she gripped her hips. "You assume I'd actually care. I'm just concerned about your ability to finish this project with me. I'm not afraid to admit that I'm a sadistic perfectionist, Quinn. This needs to be exceptional."

"Look, Max, I get it," I said evenly. "I want this to be good, too. And it will." I swept my hand over the table, palm up. "It *is.*"

I swear I saw her visibly relax. It was so minor, most probably wouldn't notice. But her usually tense shoulders slumped slightly, and she let her hands fall to her sides. I decided to set aside my stress over mythical beings for a moment and give Max my full attention. It was only fair.

We dove into the work. The object was to study the historic architecture around the city and the modern and then create our own plan for a new, artistically driven building that combined both. Hence, the project partners. Two people coming together just like the two styles. A couple of hours into it, we took a break and snuck into the small canteen area that served coffee and snacks during the day and made a small pot of coffee.

And I thought I might have caught the slightest glimpse of a smile, a real genuine smile, on Max's face as she eyed the basket of individually wrapped brownies. For a moment, I thought she'd take one. But her face twisted with hesitation, and she relaxed her fingers before wrapping them around the Styrofoam coffee cup I handed her.

I grabbed two brownies and shoved them in my hoodie pockets. Max didn't say anything, but I heard her laugh under her breath as she followed me back to our table. I tossed her a brownie when we sat down. But she waited until I'd had mine half eaten before opening hers and cautiously taking that first bite.

Max's eyes fluttered behind closed lids, and she moaned. "I know these are absolute garbage, but they're so fucking good."

"Maybe I should have left some money," I said between chewing.

She scrunched her nose and stared out the window as she took another bite. "My mother has donated enough money to this school. I think I can take a few cookies."

I remembered Celadine saying that Max's mother was one of the gallery's most prominent benefactors. "So… you're like rich or something?"

Those eyes turned dark, and she tossed me a glare. "No, my *mother's* rich."

I cowered inside. "Touchy subject?"

She didn't even bother to answer.

"Sorry," I offered and busied myself with my cup of coffee.

After a moment, she sighed and said, half interested, "Tell me something about you."

"Me?"

"Sure, why not." It didn't sound like a question.

I sucked in a long breath. "I was raised in the country by my aunt. There's not much to tell, really. I lived a pretty boring life." I shrugged. "Until now, I guess."

"Lucky." Her perfect brows rose and plummeted.

"There's nothing lucky about losing your parents to a random street murder before you even knew them."

I was just as shocked as she looked at my words. I rarely, if ever, spoke of my parents. And never felt the need to defend their death. But something lit inside me at her tone. I was certainly not lucky. Yes, my childhood was lovely under Tess's roof. But my parents *had* been murdered for no good reason, and now evil fairies hunted me down.

"I didn't know." Max's face was stone. "I'm... sorry."

I dragged my teeth over my bottom lip. "It's fine."

Silence hung between us as we averted our gazes and sipped on our hot coffees. Outside, the sounds and lights of busy streets came to life with the falling of early night.

"Do you miss them?" she asked quietly. Still not

looking at me.

No one had ever asked me that. "I know I should. I know… I should have this time in my life where I mourned their death. But how can you miss people you never really knew? I was an infant when they were murdered."

"Did they find the shooter?"

I shook my head solemnly. "No. It was labeled a cold case. My aunt was with them, but she'd run with me in her arms before she could get a good look at the guy. The only details she had to give the police were that he had a young voice, a masked face, and took their money."

"That's really shitty." She finally met my gaze, and I swear I found the slightest hint of sympathy in her big brown eyes. And, for some reason, I couldn't help but laugh. I wasn't sure if it was a hopeless reaction to the doom and gloom that filled my life or because Max's attempt at connecting with another human being was even sadder. Her brows rose in surprise, but she soon threw in a laugh with mine. "I'm bad at this."

I waved it off. "We all are." I swept a glance at our project. "I think that about does it, though. I'm happy with the way it turned out."

She examined it all with a satisfied sigh. "Me, too." She cocked her head and narrowed her eyes at me. "How are your presentation skills?"

I gave an eye roll over the rim of my coffee cup. "I

think I'll manage."

We gathered up our things and headed down to the main level entrance, the only one left unlocked and monitored by the after-hours security guard. We stepped outside, and I inhaled the fresh night air. But then it hit me. Nighttime. Darkness. Shadows.

Evaine.

I froze in place and peered up and down the sidewalk. Max halted a few feet away and threw me a look over her shoulder. "Quinn?"

"The, uh, nighttime just makes me nervous." I backed up against the door. "And I forgot my bike today."

Max clenched her jaw as she seemed to consider something, mindlessly dangling her keys with one hand. Then she cocked her head toward the only vehicle on the street—a black Jeep—with a sigh. "Come on, I'll give you a ride."

I was immensely grateful because Max still drove around with the canvas top removed, even though we were well into Fall. I happily let the chilly breeze wash over me, keeping my car sickness at bay, but it only took a minute to shiver against its touch. Max didn't seem to be bothered by it, though. Her naked arms still bared, not a goosebump to be seen.

In minutes, she pulled up to the café, and I pointed to the alley behind the building. She veered into it and came to a halt. I reached for the door handle, but she grasped my sleeve, her eyes fixated on something outside.

"Wait."

"What's the matter?" I asked and followed her line of sight to find a tall, dark figure leaning against a parked motorcycle. My heart thrummed, but my stomach relaxed.

She tipped her chin tersely. "You know that guy?"

"Yeah, he's… a friend." She gawked at me in disbelief but said nothing as she released my sleeve. "Do *you* know him?"

Her shadowed face twisted with contrition. "No, he just gives bad vibes."

I laughed. "So do you, and yet here I am. Letting you give me a ride home."

She flashed me a poisonous look. "You're *welcome.*"

The laugh filled my throat as I stepped out of the Jeep. I shut the door and turned to say *thank you,* but Max sped off, kicking up bits of gravel in her wake. I sighed and shook my head as I turned to face Cillian.

"Friend of yours?" he asked cheekily and shoved off his bike where he leaned.

"Something like that." I couldn't help the way my eyes scanned every inch of him. Damn, he looked so good all the freaking time. It was almost unfair to the rest of us. "What are you doing here?"

He grinned devilishly and loomed over me, letting his lovely scent of cool night air and leather envelop me. "I thought, perhaps, we could grab a coffee. Or something to eat?"

"Is that so?" I gave him a playful smile and tipped my face upward. "Are you planning to ditch me after the first bite this time?"

Something about what I said made him grimace. "How long will I be paying for that one?"

"Planning to stick around, are you?"

"For as long as you'll have me."

I knew we were just exchanging witty banter, but something about the change in his tone, the casting aside of humor as he stepped closer, our chests nearly touching, made my stomach tighten with anticipation. We were finally alone, with no one to interrupt us. His wintery breath cooled my heated cheeks, his thumb brushing along one of them as he cupped the side of my face.

I was long lost in those pools of deep blue when he whispered, "I'd very much like to kiss you now."

My answer was removing another inch between us, my hand eagerly slipping under his open leather jacket as I splayed my fingers over the dip of his hip. His breath hitched at my touch, and I watched as his lips parted ever so slightly, making their way for mine.

My eyes fluttered closed just as Cillian's mouth met mine, and I melted in his arms. One hand combed into the hair at the side of my head. The other firmly planted at the small of my back. All I wanted was to disappear into his embrace as his mouth devoured mine, and he pulled me closer. Slow and sensual at first, but I felt that hunger building. Mirrored by my own. I wanted him. More than I'd ever wanted anything in my life.

I pulled back with a sharp exhale and, when I opened my eyes, Cillian was already staring down at me. He trailed his thumb over my tender lips with an admiration that tickled something at the bottom of my gut. And suddenly… the reality of my life came crashing down over me.

I stepped out of his cool embrace, my skin searing in all the places that his touch had met. "I'd love to grab a coffee or some food with you, Cillian." I stilled my breath. "But I've had an incredibly long day and an even longer weekend. I'm… I should stay in tonight."

He examined me with a scrutiny that made me flush, and I wondered if he could see the signs under the cast of night. The dark circles beneath my eyes, the new pallor of my skin. I had barely slept more than an hour since Oliver's cottage.

His brows pinched together. "Is everything alright?"

I nodded, but even that simple gesture was a lie. "I just… " Just *what*? What could I possibly say to him? In fact, with Evaine after me, it wasn't safe for *anyone* to be around me. Not until we figured out what the creature wanted. I took another step back. Cillian noted it with distaste. "It's, uh, it's actually best if we don't see each other for a while."

He seemed thrown, and I didn't blame him. He'd just given me the best kiss of my life, and I followed it up with a rejection. "We're seeing each other?" His attempt at humor didn't hit the mark.

I rolled my eyes and tipped my head to the side. "You know what I mean."

"If you're not interested, Avery, then just say the word. I'll leave you be. I don't want to make you feel uncomfortable."

I abruptly shook my head. "No, you don't, I swear. I just…" My dry eyes suddenly burned with the wetness that rimmed them. I stole a glance around, the shadows of night unnerving me. I was involved in a world he'd never understand. A world that could get him killed. A chill ran through me, and I shivered it off.

Cillian came closer, tense with concern. "Avery," he almost whispered. "Are you alright? Is someone trying to hurt you? Is there something I can do?"

He looked at me with such longing, such care, that it nearly broke my heart. I gently shook my head and faked a yawn. "I appreciate the concern, but I'm honestly just tired, and I've got some school stuff coming up that's going to occupy a lot of my time. It's just not fair to you or anyone for me to…." I gestured at him with exaggeration.

"Start something right now."

Those blue eyes raked over me, examining. *Searching.* "Are you sure?"

My chin bobbed up and down a little too anxiously. I hoped he didn't pick up on it. Cillian's expression softened with a coy smile as he sauntered closer and leaned into me, his lips brushing across my cheek as his mouth found my ear. "Then, when you're ready to start, you come to find me." He placed a kiss on my cheek, and I felt it burn all the way down the center of my body, where the sensation pooled between my legs. He stepped back, leaving me breathless, and I watched as he walked to his bike and swung one long, muscled leg over the seat. The metal beast sank with his weight, and he glanced up at me. The perfect sight of him made my breath still in my chest. "I'll be waiting.

Chapter Sixteen

Days went by. I felt so alone and scared. Lattie and Moya were somewhere deep in the lands of Faerie to spy anything they could find about any mention of Oracles and who might have hired Evaine to kidnap her. I mourned the loss of my future. Well, the one I had planned, anyway. How I'd been a fool to hope for such things. School, an art career, my foot in the door at the gallery, the possibility of dating for the first time in my life.

Every ounce of me wanted Cillian. He was the first guy I'd ever had an interest in. The first one that had ever looked my way. But how could I have a relationship with someone when half my life was now rooted in this mythical world of danger?

A pile of old texts that Moya had hastily borrowed

from the Territory of Dreams laid on the coffee table. I spent every waking hour pouring over them, and all I found on Oracles were a few meager facts. I couldn't find the exact age of the last one, but it said he was officially the King's Oracle for nearly three hundred years. A *mortal man...* lived well over three hundred years. I wasn't sure what that meant for my own mortality.

One normal and reliable thing I had in my life was my few weekly shifts at the coffee shop with Tomas. He was just wholesome. Nothing ever got him down, and his personality was infectious. We made work a game. Seeing who could sell the most coffees. Betting which chocolaty dessert sold out first. Scavenger hunts to count how many times we noticed something—old men in sweater vests, soccer moms, hipsters. Tonight was people with beautiful smiles. We'd counted twenty-seven by the time the last customer left.

I was about to lock the door when Julie barged in. Her cheeks were frosty pink from the Fall evening air. Although she put on a cheery demeanor for Tomas's sake, I could sense Julie was eager to tell me something. She practically bounced on her feet.

"Hey, guys!" she said and rubbed her icy hands together. "Any coffee left?"

"Yeah, we haven't dumped the pots yet," I replied, eying her curiously.

But she averted her gaze. She knew I could tell there was news to be shared, but not in front of Tomas. He disappeared behind the counter for a moment and came back with a steaming cup for her.

"Thanks." She flashed him the widest smile, one she only wore for him.

Tomas looked at her like she was some sort of precious thing. "Twenty-eight."

"What?" Her brows pinched innocently.

"It's nothing," I said with a laugh and tugged at her sleeve. "Come on, let's go upstairs. You cool to close up, Tomas?"

He nodded, slowly tearing his gaze from Julie. "Yeah, it's cool. I'll see you guys later."

I followed Julie up the spiral staircase and called down to Tomas, "I owe you one!"

Once we were safely in the privacy of our apartment, I could see why Julie had been brimming with eagerness when she first came into the café. Moya and her sisters waited in our living room. Well, Moya was in our living room with Lattie perched on the arm of the sofa. The Shades wandered about the place, eyeing things with the utmost curiosity. Still strapped to the nines with leather and weapons, but their already corpse-like complexions were now see-through.

Julie must have noticed me staring at them. "When in

Ironworld, the Shades are invisible, even without a glamor. To the untrained eye, they aren't even there." She hung her heavy coat on the hooks by the door, and our three guests turned their heads toward us. "But the fact that you can see them means your Sight is getting stronger."

"I'm still not sure if that's good or bad," I mumbled as I made my way to the couch and plopped down.

Moya shifted in her seat, folding one long olive-green pant leg over the other. She wore a tight golden corset over the silky slacks, baring her arms, and I admired the way her otherworldly skin tone caught the lamplight. "It's good, darling. Don't worry."

"I bet the person hunting me down thinks so, too," I guffawed.

"There's no talk in the Seelie kingdom about an Oracle or anyone seeking one," was her answer. "And I tracked Mabry's movements for days. Nothing is happening there. She's just a madwoman on a throne, terrorizing her kingdom. She has no interest beyond that."

One of the Shades stood behind the couch. "Oliver reported nothing from the Winter border. They're silent."

"Why just the border?" I asked while also wondering how to tell which one was Aya and which was Brie. I had to come up with some tell. "Why didn't he enter the Territory?"

Julie sat down in the poofy chair across from us. "The

Winter Lord is an old, paranoid crank who goes to great lengths to protect his Territory from Mabry's reach. It's heavily guarded and warded, and no one even knows how to actually enter."

The other twin sidled up to her sister. "You must be invited and then guided to the palace through secret passageways."

"So, we have nothing?" I asked, my heart sinking.

"I might have stumbled upon something," Lattie spoke up, and we all turned our attention on her. "It's not much, but it's something. A few Summer Fae said they heard whispers of Evaine spending an awful lot of time in the Territory of Nightmares."

Everyone, except for me, exchanged a knowing glance. My shoulders touched my ears. "What does that mean?"

Julie looked at me with such deep pity that I wondered just how bad this dark Territory was. "It can only mean one thing, Av'. That the one who's hired Evaine to hunt you down isn't Mabry. It's the Dark Lord of Nightmares. The question now is *why*."

A memory tickled the front of my mind, and I leaned forward. "When Evaine cornered me outside the gallery that night, she said something…." I struggled to remember the exact words. "Something like *he'll be so glad I've found you*."

Moya only had to look at her sisters, and they gave her a

dutiful nod. "We'll do some spying in the Dark Territory."

And then they were gone. As if they'd never been there to begin with.

"Okay, question," I said. "How do I tell them apart?"

Julie and Moya laughed, but it was Julie that answered, "I had a hard time at first, too. Aya is slightly taller, not by much. Like maybe an inch. And Brie has a scar above her right eyebrow."

Moya stood from the couch and adjusted her stylish corset. "I think what we need to focus on is learning more about your abilities, Avery."

"How do we do that?" I spoke. "*I* don't even know anything about them."

She exchanged a look with Julie, and my best friend gave a nod of approval. Moya smiled at me. "I think it's time we pay a visit to The Blood Reader."

***

Apparently, the Blood Reader was an ancient being that could tell your past, present, and future just from a drop of your blood. And, as it turned out, we could find him in The Black Market, an eclectic storefront downtown that sold things like hemp sweaters and fake shrunken heads and every type of incense you could imagine. But, as I stood quietly while Moya spoke with the shopkeeper, I realized it was all just a front to hide the real Black Market.

We headed for the back through a thick beaded curtain, and Moya led me to an old wooden door hinged with thick iron. She yanked it open, and immediately I was met with sights and sounds and smells, unlike anything I'd ever experienced.

Tables and booths stretched on as far as the eye could see, all lined and huddled in a farmer's market fashion. It must have been another strange pocket in reality. Because, according to the exterior of the mundane building, we should have been standing in a storage room.

Creatures of all kinds mozied about, shopping and bartering with merchants. Humanoid Fae, trolls, dwarves of some sort, and tiny pixies busied the market carrying bags and crates of goods. As we walked, I noted the various goods from each merchant.

Delicious soups and stews, dangling chains beaded with glowing jewels, skinned and headless animals curing over vats of things steaming. The air smelled of a mix between sweet and sour and… something else. Something I'd come to know. The static tinge of magic.

"What is this place?" I said, awestruck.

"It's The Black Market of Ironworld. Solitaries and other creatures mingle here to trade and buy goods. Things they need but could only get in Faerie. Most merchants grow or make their goods, but other stuff, hard to get stuff, is smuggled in daily."

Moya led me to a private booth near the quieter back end of the market. She moved aside a thick black curtain to find a sightless being–its eyes long gouged from its head, grayed leathery skin covered all that I could see. It was sitting diligently at a table. Alone. As if it were waiting for us. A devilish sneer upturned its red-stained mouth as its long, boney fingers splayed across the table. I noted how they were stained. As if dipped in blood and had been left to dry for a century or two.

"Moya Seaborn."

"Hello, Reader," she greeted sternly. I kept tucked to her side.

"It's been a while since we last spoke. How have you been, dear? Still wandering the Summer lands, or have you returned to the water?"

Moya held a terse expression. "I made my choice many years ago, you know that."

I wondered then about her past. I knew she'd fled the sea centuries ago. But why?

"Have you come to ask me a way home?" the Reader pried.

She pressed her lips together. "I have no need to return to the depths of my birthplace, Reader. Now stop taunting. I'm here to elicit your services."

The creature leaned back in its chair, sniffing the air as it did so. "You request a reading?"

"Yes," Moya replied and motioned to me. "For my friend here."

"I require payment."

Moya flicked a strange-looking coin onto the table.

The Blood Reader shot from its chair, and I saw how it only wore a tattered pair of pants. Its bare feet paddled over, and it inhaled the air around me. A long, grotesque breath. It took my hand and mulled it in its own in a flash with long, scratchy fingers. Dragging those bloodied nails over my tender flesh.

"Come sit."

I obeyed and took the seat across from it at the table while Moya hung around the flap of the curtain door. The Reader took my hand again and moved with lightning speed as its arms swept over the surface of the round, wooden table. With one of its sharp nails, it sliced a gash across my palm. I gasped in pain, but one look at Moya's staid expression told me this was to be expected.

The Blood Reader squeezed the edges of my hand until crimson oozed to the surface, and it took a long, generous swipe with a finger before bringing the taste to its mouth. I tried to hide my cringe of disgust and remained quiet as the creature worked. Those pitless eyes stared into the abyss of nothingness as it leaned back, its face slack.

After a moment, its blank expression became animated once more, and it faced me.

"I cannot Read you."

Moya put both hands on the table. "Why not?"

The creature sized me up with an unnerving hunger. "The girl's blood is… new."

"New?" I croaked. My throat was parched. "You mean young? I'm only eighteen."

The Reader shook its obscure, bald head. "No, no, dear girl. You are… new. But old." It cocked its chin to the side. "Your blood is not human nor Fae. It's something else entirely."

Then it was true. The weight of it pressed down on me. I really was this apparent Oracle. A human with a magical ability. I swallowed nervously and glanced up at Moya. She motioned to the door. It was time to go.

She opened the flap of the tent for me and turned to flick another coin toward the Reader. "For your discretion."

We exited the tent and emerged back into one of the busy alleyways of the Black Market. I fixed my distant gaze on a nearby booth where a Fae woman with skin of darkened bark spun glittering lengths of glowing wool into spools. I focused on it, letting the image of it anchor me in place because every inch of me wanted to drift away. I wrapped my arms tightly around myself.

Moya placed a gentle hand on my shoulder. "At least

now we know for sure."

"Know what?" I balked, my gaze still distant. "What we already knew?"

"What we suspected," she corrected me, and something about her tone actually stilled my nerves. "Now that we know for certain, we can move forward. I think a trip to the Territory of Dreams is in order. Spend some time combing the archives. See what we can find…"

As the sound of Moya's voice trailed off, making way for the sudden pounding pulse that filled my ears, I fixed my crazed stare at a booth near the end of the alleyway. Away from most patrons, those close enough hissed and cowered away from the man standing there, exchanging money with a merchant. A man with hair as black as night, a shape and stance I'd never mistaken. Not in a million years because I knew it. I knew him.

I watched with clenched fists as Cillian paid the human-looking merchant a wad of cash and was handed a small crate of something. My heart skipped a beat when I realized what was inside it. When Cillian lifted a blood bag to his lips. At the same time, I felt fresh blood dripping down my wrist, oozing from the wound the Reader had inflicted.

Cillian halted and sniffed at the blood bag curiously, then sniffed at the air around him until his eyes found mine across the market and widened in horror. He dropped the basket and sped over to where I stood with Moya, who was still droning on about a trip to the Territory of Dreams.

I tensed and slowly shook my head. Unable to tear my unblinking stare from Cillian as he approached. Heaving breaths burned in my chest.

"Avery, what's the matter?" Moya noted and then hissed at Cillian as he came to a halt mere inches from us. With a protective hand, she shielded me. "You've no business here, vampire."

I cringed inwardly at the word.

He glared daggers at her. "My business is where I put it." His tone was clipped, but it softened as he looked at me pleadingly. "Avery, what the hell are you doing there?"

Moya, confused, glanced between us. "You know this man?"

Words were like ghosts on my tongue as my eyes locked on those deep pools of blue, a blue I'd come to love so, so much. They felt like betrayals to me now, shiny bait used to lure me in. I shook my head. "No, I–I…don't know him at all."

Pain flashed across his beautiful face.

I managed to back away, tugging at Moya's arm. "Come on, let's go."

She asked no questions, only turned and fled the market with me. I didn't look back, didn't see if he stood and watched me go. But part of me knew…he did. I could practically feel his pained stare clawing at my back with every step I put between us. But he never followed.

We made it all the way home, and if Moya had spoken a word the whole way back, I wouldn't be able to note a single one of them. For my mind was elsewhere. Gone. She left me at the door, and I entered the apartment, brushing past Julie with a murmured excuse of being tired and that I'd explain in the morning. I bolted for my bedroom, where I clasped on my bed in a fit of silent tears.

Not only had I learned that I truly was some sort of mortal Seer with a dangerous Fae after me, but I also discovered that the first guy I'd ever liked was actually a–I could hardly bring myself to even think of the word.

A… *vampire.*

Chapter Seventeen

I don't think I'd closed my eyes the entire night. I feared Cillian would appear at my windowsill. Even as the sun cleaved the sky, I still lay there, restless. Too shell-shocked to allow myself to sleep. I lay in the sun for hours as my mind spun with thoughts. Pouring over every single encounter I'd had with Cillian and revisiting them all in a new light. How he seemed to just appear out of nowhere and always seemed to know where I was or when to show up. How he'd bolted the second I'd cut my finger at the sushi place. And then… how I'd only ever seen him at night. Another thought occurred to me.

Celadine.

They were siblings, which meant… was she a vampire, too? My beloved mentor. My friend. How could she be a viscous, soulless creature of the night? As much as I didn't want to admit it, the truth had been there the whole time.

Celadine only worked nights. Was painfully beautiful, just like her brother. Pale skin that always felt like a cold doctor's touch. So, it was true. Celadine and Cillian Danes were vampires. And I'd been a fool enough to put myself right in their path. Was this how they lured their prey? With smiles and friendship. With seductive whispers and loving touches?

The thought made me want to vomit.

I heard the apartment's front door open, and I stole a glance at the clock by my bed. Julie was home from school already? I peeled the blankets off with great effort and headed out to the apartment.

"You stayed home today?" She swept the thick strap of her bag over her head and set it down on the floor.

I nodded tiredly and made a beeline for the kitchen. "Yeah."

Julie watched me with a careful look. "Av', is this about what the Blood Reader said? Do you want to talk–"

The front door blew open, and Max barged in, so fast and furious that I hardly had time to process the anger wrought on her face. "You better be fucking dying!"

"Woah!" Julie leaped between us, and Max shot her a venomous look.

"What the hell, Max?" I squeaked. "You can't just burst

into someone's home like that—"

She looked me up and down. "Two arms, two legs, I assume a *god damn heartbeat*!" She shoved at my chest. "Where have you been all day? I called you a million times!"

I turned my phone off last night. And then it hit me. A deep, regrettable sigh washed over me. "Shit… the project."

Max's crazed eyes widened, bulging with the whites of them. "Yeah, *shit the project*! We were supposed to present today. *Together*."

"Max, I'm so sorry," I said with all honesty. I felt like the lowest low.

"Don't bother," she said and flung up a hand. "This is why I don't do group projects. This is why I never put my shit in someone else's hands." She shook her head with a disgusted chortle. "People just always fucking let you down."

She spun on her heel and slammed the door on her way out, knocking one of the pictures clean off the wall where it smashed to the floor. Julie immediately fetched the garbage can, and I walked over to help, my limbs stiff with the aftershock of hurricane Max.

We picked up the bits of glass and metal in silence, but after a few painfully quiet beats, Julie said quietly, "You wanna tell me what that was all about?"

"Max and I were supposed to present our modern art

and architecture project to the class today," I replied. "The prof had some of the top designers in the industry come to sit in, too. I think... I think Max was actually looking forward to it."

"So, why didn't you go?" Julie asked. "Doesn't seem like something you'd forget."

Frustration burned in my gut as I stood up. "I'm just... it's a lot, Jules." I couldn't fend off the tears that swelled in my eyes.

Without a second thought, my best friend swept me into a tight embrace, and I melted in her arms. "I know, and I'm sorry."

"For what?" I leaned back and swept a finger under each eye.

"For waiting so long to tell you what I suspected," she replied and let go of me to discard the refuge from the broken picture. "I'd had a hunch for years, but I was so worried to say anything. First, I thought, well, what if I was wrong? Then I thought, what if I'm right and you get so scared that you never want to be my friend again." She rubbed the back of her neck. "I spent so long worrying over whether I should tell you that it just got to the point where it was too late. We'd been friends for years, and I didn't want to do anything to risk that. So," she shrugged, "I waited. To see if you'd figure it out on your own."

I managed a lazy smile. "The wine helped."

"Yeah, I may have nudged you from time to time." She took a shaky breath.

"Listen, Jules. No matter what's happening or what we might discover about this ability I have, just know that nothing will ever change our friendship. I promise." Her whole body seemed to relax, and my heart squeezed at the thought of my friend harboring any worry over the friendship we had. It was staid. A constant. "Please never doubt that. I think I just need some time alone. Preferably in bed." I rustled up a chuckle to lighten the mood. "My puny mortal brain just takes a while to process it all."

Julie laughed. "Well, don't take too long. There's so much I want to show you."

I nodded and grabbed a throw blanket from the back of the couch to wrap around myself as I headed for my bedroom. "And I can't wait to learn more about your world. In time."

I reached my door as Julie said, "It's your world, too, you know." I glanced back at her. "You belong to it just as much as I do."

With a tired sigh over a thankful grin, I turned the knob and disappeared into my room. Because I couldn't let her know that my sour mood had nothing to do with her world or my newfound abilities and had everything to do with the fact that the guy I'd been seeing turned out to be a predator. I needed time to reel.

Lattie landed on my windowsill and knocked on the glass with a curious expression. I hauled up the old slide window and let her in.

"Why was it closed?" she asked and plopped down on my bed.

I slammed it shut again and eyed up and down the street below. "Just a precaution." I tightened the blanket around me and laid down next to her as she stretched out her long limbs. "Lattie, what do you know about vampires?"

She let out a tiny sound and flipped over to look at me. "Vampires?"

I loosed a deep sigh. "Yeah. Tell me everything you know about them."

She blinked a few times before settling back down at my side. We both stared tiredly at the ceiling. "Well, they're ruthless and soulless, for one."

"Is it possible for them to be good?"

"They're beautiful for a reason. They're predators, luring their prey with dazzling smiles and ill promises of immortality. But they're most definitely not your friend, Avery. They're not your lovers." She yawned. "They rarely even Make their prey. A vampire in Ironworld only has one thing on its mind. Where their next meal is coming from."

I considered all that she said with a stony gaze at the ceiling. I thought back over all the events that led me to this moment, this crossroads with Cillian and Celadine.

The job posting. I'd wondered how I got the job over so many other more qualified candidates. How Celadine swiftly lured me closer with the offer of an apprenticeship.

And then Cillian. He'd followed me all over the place before even approaching me for the first time. His smell, his touch. Even the sound of his voice. It all affected me. Swayed my will until all my thoughts were consumed by him.

I wondered when they'd planned to do it. Kill me. Eat me. Drink me. Whatever it was they did with their prey. Would they have locked me up and toyed with me for a while, or would it have been a swift death? I'll never know because it ended here. All of it. I wouldn't give them the chance to lure me any closer.

I sat up and bounced on the bed as I fetched my laptop from the little bedside table and fired it up. Before I talked myself out of it, I typed up my resignation and emailed it to Celadine. Satisfied with my decision, I closed it and swung off the bed, tossing the blanket.

I needed some normalcy.

***

I drove the hour-long trip to Tess's house in the country. Home. I went home. It was the only place I could think of that was free from all the chaos that currently consumed my life. Every minute I drew closer, I could feel my nerves melting away.

But Tess wasn't home when I arrived and, when I called her cell, I got an automated message reminding me she was out of town for the Home & Garden show. She wouldn't be back for weeks, but I stayed, anyway.

I needed the quiet.

I took a long bubble bath. Only stepping out when the water turned too cold to tolerate. Then I prepared some snacks and grabbed a beer as I headed out to the garden patio. My sketchbook tucked under my arm. The sounds of JJ Wilde boomed from my phone as the sun set, and I smiled happily as Tess's garden automatically came to life with millions of solar-powered twinkle lights and patio lanterns. I rocked back in the lounge chair and kept doodling mindlessly in my book. I hadn't been this content in weeks. Not since…

And just like that, my thoughts became consumed once again. I fought to swat away the images that burned into my mind. Demanding to be seen. Celadine pouring over years of notes to teach me all that she knew. Cillian's blazing white smile that always took my breath away. How every fiber of my being had screamed that they were dangerous when I'd first met them.

But I'd ignored it. Chalked it up to me just being nervous and inexperienced. Their goodwill behavior and seemingly normal lives had convinced me. And Cillian… I just assumed his presence always set my nerves on fire, not because he was a predator but because I was so irrevocably attracted to him.

I huffed out a sigh and slammed down my pencil.

Who was I kidding? I wanted them probably as bad as they wanted me. But for different reasons. While they most likely viewed me as a meal, I looked at them as two people I so desperately wanted to get closer to. Even if it was all a seductive lure. A predator move.

Celadine was everything I'd ever hoped for in a mentor. She was my friend; she would have opened doors for me I may not have ever reached in my lifetime. She taught me so much about the art world, giving me the best leg up to start my career. It killed me inside to even consider that it might have all been a show. That she'd go to such great lengths just to drink my blood.

And then Cillian…

I glanced down at my sketchbook and groaned. I'd done it again. Black hair, the way it fell like a silky curtain across his forehead. The shape of his cunning eyes. The line of his jaw. I filled the pages with glimpses of him. I tossed my head and closed my eyes with a loud grumble but inhaled deeply. And I swear I could smell his inviting scent of leather and night air in the breeze.

"You forgot that I have a little freckle above my left

eyebrow," spoke a voice that sent my eyes flying open and my chair rocking back on two legs. He grinned sadly and pointed at the drawings. "Right here."

I slammed the book shut and flew to my feet. I backed up to the patio door, putting as much distance between us as I could.

"How did you find me?"

"Oh, I don't think you're ready for that answer."

"No?" I challenged brazenly, clutching my scrapbook to my chest. "And when would I be ready, Cillian? Right around the time you planned to tell me you're a *vampire*?"

His expression hardened. "I was going to tell you."

"When." The word was more of a demand than a question.

But he didn't seem to have an answer either way. He just stared at me. He looked so beautiful in the twinkle lights. It almost hurt to look at him. And I hated myself for even thinking it.

"You quit?"

"What?" I said, my tongue gone completely dry.

"The email you sent to Cellie," he reminded. "You gave her your resignation?"

"What did you expect?"

Cillian's shoulders slumped as he leaned forward in the chair, bracing his forearms on his knees. "Everything and nothing."

"What the hell is that supposed to mean?" He refused to reply, and something burned in my gut. Rage. I was pissed. "Please leave."

He stood from the lounge chair, palms out in surrender. "Avery, if you'd just let me explain–"

"I said leave." I inched further down the exterior wall of Tess's house, a movement he noted. "Leave here, leave me alone. Don't come to the coffee shop, don't pester my friends, and don't make me feel bad about leaving my dream job. Trust me, I already hate myself for it."

"Then don't leave," he replied with a hint of desperation. "Don't quit. Cellie needs you."

"Does she?" I retorted. "Need me for what? Does she plan to get close to me, make me fall in love with the job, with her, with *you*… and then eat me for dinner? Is this some kind of game to you guys?"

He rolled those blue eyes. "That's not what we–"

"I've already given my answer. Now leave."

But he didn't. He just stood in place like a freaking statue, like a dark spill of ink against my aunt's beautiful garden. The sight of him almost broke me. I sucked my lip inside my mouth to stifle the sob that threatened to erupt.

"Avery, please," he gently begged. "If you won't talk to me, that's fine. I get it. I'll deal. But don't do this to my sister. She doesn't deserve to lose you. It'd crush her."

My eyes brimmed with tears. "Put yourself in my shoes. What would you have me do, Cillian?"

"Just talk to her. Even a phone call."

I chewed at my lip. "Give me one good reason why I should. A *real* reason," I added when I saw he was about to dive into more pleading.

"We're not like the others of our kind," he offered sincerely. And part of me believed it.

"So, you guys don't prey on humans or drink blood?"

"Well… it's more complicated than that."

"But it's really not," I said and released my death grip on my book and set it down on the table. "You either drink human blood, or you don't." He just stood unmoving. Staring at me. "Is this something that can be explained in less than sixty seconds?"

He slowly shook his head, and that bit of hair fell across his forehead. "No, I'm afraid it's not."

He shoved his hands in his pockets. I ached to touch him and chastised myself for feeling that way. He just looked far too inviting. *It's just his predatory lure.*

I sucked in a deep, cleansing breath. But it did no good. "Then I'm not ready to hear it." I folded my arms. "I want you too badly to let you linger while I process everything."

His sharp inhale had my eyes darting to his parted lips. "You… want me?"

I looked up at the night sky. "I don't think that's really a secret at this point." I tipped my chin back down. "But… you're a *vampire*, Cillian." A crazed laugh escaped. "I don't even know what to do with that information. I'm still processing *fairies*."

His stunning face twisted curiously, then he nodded back once as if to say, *ahh*. "Julie. And the little blue creature that crawls in and out of your window."

I nodded absently, trying to hide the lightning speed of which my brain processed the fact that Cillian knew about my mythical friends while also considering that he knew which window was my bedroom.

"How did you know?" I asked him. "About my friends?"

He looked unsure. "I could… smell them."

My eyebrows raised. "Oh? And how do my friends differ in smell from me?"

He braved a step closer, and I let him. A fact that made him visibly relax. I could probably touch him if I reached far enough. I stuck both hands under my arms and made the mistake of meeting his gaze. Those deep pools of navy blue stilled my breath in my chest.

"Well, for starters," he said in a deep, raspy purr. "Julie smells like sunshine wrapped in the static of magic." Cillian leaned ever so slightly. His face dangerously close to mine. Only a few inches separated us. "Whereas you, my dear Avery," he made a show of inhaling the air around me, "Your glorious scent makes my skin crawl and my

CANDACE OSMOND

head spin. You make me want to devour the world around you just by being in your presence."

Dead air hitched in my throat as he came even closer, his own luring scent enveloping me. And like a mouse caught in a trap, I froze as his lips brushed the searing skin of my cheek with a feather touch, and he whispered in my ear, "but I can wait."

I don't know what came over me. My hands were not my own, nor my feet as he leaned away, and I stepped toward him. My fingers clawed around the back of Cillian's neck, and he stilled as I planted my lips to his in a crushing hold. But I fumbled in my haste, and my tooth broke the skin on the inside of my lip. I could taste blood.

And I was kissing a vampire.

Cillian's entire body tensed, and his iron grip closed around me like a vice, hauling my body to his in a crushing embrace. I couldn't escape, even if I wanted to. His hands raked through my hair, as mine did to his. And I slipped my tongue inside his panting mouth. A mouth that seemed to devour mine in a never-ending hunger as he sucked the blood from the wound. It charged me. I felt on fire with a searing current that blazed throughout my body.

I backed up until we pressed against the patio door. The cool glass sent another sensation shooting down through me. I gasped into his mouth and whimpered as Cillian thrust his hips ever so slightly. I could feel him hard against me, and I moaned, a purr that vibrated both our lips.

He bit down harder, drawing more blood, and I froze. Immediately ripped from the sensual daze. I pushed at his iron chest to no avail. It took a second push to break the bloody kiss, and I wavered in place with a heavy inhale. Rewarding my lungs with air. Cool wetness dripped down over my chin, and I wicked it away with the back of my hand.

And then I looked at him.

Gone were those night-blue eyes I loved so much. Only pits of black stared back at me. And there he was, the monster. A minor change, but enough to remind me why I left the city.

"We can't do this," I said, my hands clenched into fists.

Cillian blinked a handful of times, and I watched the blue seep back into his eyes and the whites restore. So they weren't contacts after all. He looked at me with remorse. "Avery, I'm so sorry—"

My hand shot up. "I need time, Cillian."

"Of course," he quickly replied and wrung a hand through his hair, slicking it back into place.

He was just too much to look at, and I closed my eyes tightly, tipping my head back against the glass. A light brush of air kissed my face, and I opened my eyes. He was gone.

I took a seat, my hands shaking in my lap. Matched to

the buzzing that hummed over my skin. I could still feel his lips on mine. *I'd kissed a vampire.* It was intense. And brutal. And dangerous. And… I reached up and touched my trembling fingertips to my swollen lip…

…I absolutely craved more.

Chapter Eighteen

I stayed at Tess's house all weekend. Just me and my thoughts. I actually got sleep. Cooked myself a couple proper meals. I nourished myself, something I'd neglected to do since moving to the city and taking on so much. School, two jobs, the apprenticeship, then juggling it all with the discovery of a mythical world operating right under our noses.

I needed to recharge. So, that's what I did. And I returned to the city anew.

I beamed as I headed to class. Two coffees and two muffins in my arms. Tomas opened the doors for me.

"Doubling down this morning?" he kidded.

"I'd certainly need it for how much sleep I've been getting," I replied. "Although, I caught up on some this

367

weekend."

It was so refreshing having a friend who was just human. Nothing more, nothing less. A pure and uncomplicated human friend. Tomas was a breath of fresh air.

"How was your visit with your aunt?"

Some time alone was exactly what I needed to put the whole fairy thing in perspective. I smiled. "She wasn't home, so I just vegged all weekend in silence." I knew what I was. A mortal Seer. An Oracle. Julie was a Changeling. Lattie was… whatever she was. Some terrifying yet adorable, carnivorous pixie. Moya, once a mermaid, was now a member of the Summer Lands. Her sisters were some sort of otherworldly Shades. Oliver, a troll and a magical healer.

They were good people. I knew it, felt it. And I wanted to learn more about this world I've found myself inexplicably linked to.

"Well, you missed out on an epic weekend," Tomas said with a laugh. The sarcasm was light.

"Yeah?" I quipped, and we turned one of the last corners before we would have to split to our classes.

"Oh, yeah. A Tolkien marathon. I think I might have bored Julie to near death, though. Could have really used you there."

"Did you tell her Viggo actually broke his foot in that scene where he kicked the helmet?"

"Yeah, she didn't even care!"

I laughed as we came to a stop where the hallway split in two. I was right. He was left. "Some people just can't appreciate art when they see it, Tomas."

I listened to his chuckle as we parted and bounded for class. I was a few minutes early, but I planned it that way. For today, anyway. Because I knew stickler Max would be there. She pretended not to notice me as I came right up to her and set one of the coffee and muffin combos on her desk.

"What's this?" she balked. Her hair was long black curls that hung to her elbows today.

"Peace offering," I told her. "Amends for standing you up with the project."

She pressed her lips into a thin line and narrowed her black-rimmed eyes at me. "It's going to take a lot more than baked goods and some crappy coffee, Quinn."

"Fine." I reached for the coffee and muffin, but she snatched them away.

"But it's a start."

I failed to hide the grin that plastered across my face and took my seat next to Max.

Small victories.

Days crawled by. Without my job at the gallery and the nighttime apprenticeship, I had so much free time on my hands. So, I picked up a few extra shifts at the coffee shop. But it still wasn't enough to fill the void packed with worry. By Friday, I'd had enough. And when Julie suggested we go to the Sanctuary in the park for drinks, I happily approved. It was warded, and I felt safe there.

We found it just like before, and a party exploded around us. I let the lively music take me away as Julie swiped two flutes of wine from a table and handed me one. We leaned against a large tree. I was beginning to love this place. Before long, we were four drinks in and dancing about. I twirled with trolls and skipped around with higher Fae. Those busy-body sprites spun around me like a whirlwind, tousling my hair and tickling my skin.

I let loose, let myself fall into place there. In a world I'd now come to accept as part of my own. I belonged to it, as Julie had said. And she was right. I could feel it in my blood, in my bones.

The wine swirled in my head. I nearly floated along the grass as I moved off to the side to break from dancing. I plopped down on a worn stump and watched Julie get taken by the music and Fae around her. Fiddles played a jaunty tune, and she danced with her hands in the air, dragging colors through it like watercolor paint. She'd completely let down her glamor and paraded around like some sort of ethereal angel, and all I could do was stare in awe. She was a sight to behold.

A voice called from the trees that sat in the dark that rimmed the party. My heart sprang to life because it sounded like Lattie. I searched the crowd for my tiny blue friend, but she was nowhere to be found. I stood up and followed the call of the voice, a twinkle in the air, a cry for… me.

Averrrryyy…

I burst through the trees in a frantic search. My feet stumbled as I hit the damp sand of a small crescent that curved the dark side of the small lake. But there was nothing, no one. Just as I turned to go back, there was a movement on the water. A slight ripple on its surface. I stopped and squinted in the dark. A pair of black eyes poked up from the water and blinked wetly at me.

"Hello?" I asked.

The eyes became a head as a strange horse-like creature emerged to its neck. I froze. I knew what creature this was. I pulled quick glimpses from the pile of texts Moya had borrowed from the Territory of Dreams. I'd skimmed a section on various Fae creatures. This was a kelpie.

"Avery."

"Yes?" I replied hesitantly.

I knew the creature thrived in the waters. Often swamps and small lakes where people frequented. People… because it loved to torture its prey. With the upper body of a horse and the lower body of a sea serpent, kelpies were known for luring their prey into the water, where they then drowned the person and sucked the marrow from its bones.

"Why don't you come into the water where I can see you better?" Its voice was like eerie music I'd never heard before. Seeping into my ears like warm oil.

"No, thanks," I replied, shaking the mesmerizing hold it had on me. "You won't be drowning me today, kelpie."

Wet steam huffed from his snout, and the creature emerged even further, revealing black scales that looked like they were dripping with black tar. "Not even to save your friend?"

"My friend?"

"Avery!" Lattie's panicked voice echoed in the wind.

My heart raced. "Let her go!"

"Come into the water and trade for her."

"I told you," I breathed heavily, "That won't be happening."

"Are you sure about that?" Its gaze averted downward.

I was up to my knees in water. But I didn't recall moving from the safety of the beach, I hadn't taken a single step. Terror struck me, and I turned to bolt but found the kelpie's power held me in place. I was in its domain now. The creature floated closer. I struggled to tear my feet from the mud they were stuck in, but it was no use. I may as well have been cemented in.

"Don't come any closer!" I demanded. But the kelpie

only chuckled darkly. Its tail rose from the water and gently touched my hair with its tip, trailing down my arm.

"Such a pretty thing," it cooed. "Shame for it to go."

"H-how did you get here?" I asked. "This is a sanctuary for Solitary Fae."

"Am I not Solitary?" it preened. "I answer to no Lord, no ruler of courts. I govern myself, as I have since the beginning of our time."

I narrowed my eyes, refusing to let my fear fill my scent. A detail I'd read about the kelpie. "What's it going to take to let me go?"

"Offer another in your place."

"No," I replied, and remembered how most Fae loved to make deals and trades. "But I'm willing to make some sort of trade."

"What do you offer, Avery Quinn?"

I cringed at the sound of my full name on its lips. "What do you want?"

"Marrow."

"What *else* do you want?"

"Blood."

I rolled my eyes as impatience toiled in my gut. "What else do you want that doesn't require the loss of life?"

The creature dipped below the water, and panic seared my veins as I searched for it. Silence fell, and all that could be heard were my labored breaths, and a fog spilled from my mouth. The kelpie then popped up right next to me, its fish stench bombarding my nostrils.

"That bracelet of yours is quite lovely," it cooed again. "I do love trinkets." It ended the word with a snake's hiss.

I glanced down at the bracelet Tess made for me. "The next best thing to marrow and blood is… a piece of jewelry?"

"It's not the object itself but what it represents," the kelpie said. "It means something to you, yes?"

I swallowed wetly. "Yes, it was a gift. But how did–"

"Then I want it."

I turned it over my wrist, contemplating. "And you'll let me go?"

That massive horse's head nodded and huffed more wet steam. "Yes, for your bracelet, I'll free you from my bind."

Without another thought, I slipped it off my wrist and held it out for the beast.

It slanted its head, showing me its oily mane woven with various things. Bones, jewels, children's toys. I shuddered at the thought. "Would you mind weaving it into my hair?" Its tail swished in the distance.

With trembling hands, I reached out to tie the bracelet to its slick, wiry mane. The strands were so sharp they sliced my fingertips. A few drops of blood hit the water when I pulled away, and the creature immediately flew into a frenzy. Moving with lightning speed as it gripped me with its tail. I fought and struggled against the crushing hold and let out one mighty scream before it yanked me beneath the water.

I could tell I was drowning almost immediately. I'd expelled every ounce of air from my lungs with that last cry for help, and now my lungs burned for breath, filling with the murky lake water. But I didn't give up. I'd fight until the last drop of life seeped from me. I kicked and pulled and pushed at the thick tail, but the kelpie dove deeper, dragging me to the bottom of the lake. The water was cooler down there, but it still burned in my lungs all the same.

With the last of my life, I gripped the thick, scaly tail in my hands, and a strange but familiar light formed under my palms, spreading outward, burning in its wake. It was as if the kelpie's scales possessed a magic of their own, glowing and searing and blinding with an otherworldly light.

There she is!

She's come back!

It's not her. She's a human.

Look closer. She doesn't know.

She doesn't know...

The whispers surrounded me, coming from all directions. Like that night I fell in Tess' fountain. What were they talking about? Who were they?

He knows. He'll come for her yet.

But the death grip around my body loosened as if the light... bothered the beast, and I frantically kicked for the surface. I broke through and gasped for air, filling my waterlogged lungs, desperate to live. I managed to take a few deep breaths before the kelpie claimed me again and yanked me back down to the depths, where two eyes peered at me through the murkiness, a darkness so thick it had to be supernatural. The sinister stare cleaved the water, heading straight for me.

Evaine.

I panicked and gripped my scaly prison once again, and that blazing light formed beneath my palms, but this time... I was in control of it. It grew brighter and brighter until even I couldn't see anymore. I let it pour from my hands with no kind of damper. A force building. I closed my eyes as the pressure grew too much. And it blasted me out of the water like a shot out of a gun. My body slammed onto the beach. Harsh rocks and bits of sharp sand dug into my skin, and lake water purged from my lungs as the sound of the world slowly came back to me.

"Avery!" Julie's voice reached my ears, and I flinched. But it was her, really her. Not some illusion of sound from the kelpie. Julie ran to me and dropped to her knees at my side. "What were you thinking?" she balked, and Lattie fluttered up from behind her. "Never go into the water with a kelpie!"

I couldn't answer her. I still coughed, gurgled bits of water, and I deflated on the beach as I rolled over. Moya was there now, too. Appearing next to Julie. Lattie had the good sense to actually look concerned as she cast her gaze out over the now quiet waters.

"I heard your voice," I croaked with strain. The tinge of blood stained my raw throat. Lattie whipped her head to me, eyes wide. "The kelpie told me it had you."

"You… you braved a kelpie to save me?"

"It was a trick," Moya said. "That's what it does." She peered down at me. "Are you alright?"

I nodded and pushed myself into a sitting position. "Evaine." The memory nearly knocked me back down. "Evaine was in the water."

The three of them whipped their heads toward the lake in search.

"I see nothing," Moya said, unsure. "But I wager it's best we leave."

"Av'," Julie said quietly as she helped me to my feet. "What was that blast of light?"

I stared at my trembling hands, no evidence of burned flesh to be found. But I could still remember what it felt like on my skin to wield the light in my hands. My throat tightened as all the possibilities crashed down over my tired mind. I looked up at them. *Me*, I thought, but couldn't say.

My jaw was heavy. *It was me.*

Chapter Nineteen

I sat on our couch after I'd changed into dry black leggings and a navy wool sweater. My chin rested on my knees as I attempted to rub some warmth back into my feet. But it was no use. My fingers were just as cold. The moisture from my hair soaked into my dry clothes. I could still smell it. The lake water. Cold and dirty and musty.

Julie sat just as silent as me on the other end of the couch. The only sound to be heard was the ticking of the clock that hung in the kitchen. Moya stepped inside from the patio, and my eyes shot to her.

She sauntered over to where we sat. A golden fur cowl around her neck. Her eerie pink hair was half pulled back and held in place with kelp green combs lined with pearls.

"I'm all done," Moya said. "I couldn't do the coffee shop, but I warded both entrances to your apartment, as well as every window and the patio door."

I loved the way her hair gleamed with magic right to the tips. The way it caught the light, unnatural and beautiful. A sight I desperately wanted to paint. The layers of iridescence. And, in that moment, I loved my ability. The Sight. To see these otherworldly things as they truly were.

Minus the kelpie.

I swallowed tightly. "Thank you so much."

"And might I suggest a trip to the Territory of Dreams. *Soon?*"

Yes. I needed to know more about my newfound magic. "Definitely."

"Excellent," Moya replied and plucked some nuts from a bowl on the table. "Just give me a few days to secure some time in the temple."

I couldn't wait a few days. But I didn't want to push. I just nodded in thanks and made a mental note to pay a visit to the Blood Reader myself.

"What should we do for now?" Julie asked eagerly.

Moya shoved a handful of nuts to the side of her mouth. "Just go about your regular lives. Stay away from shadows or roaming alone at night. The apartment is an iron cage. The wards you already had in place were good. I just built off of them."

I exchanged a look with Julie, and she shook her head. "We didn't have any wards in place."

The sea maiden tipped her head in a very non-human way. "Well, then you either have an unknown ally, or someone wants you kept their little secret. A mortal Oracle? I'd say word's spread by now."

I couldn't imagine who might be our ally. No one else knew. Which only left the idea that someone was homing in on me. On my ability. To use me for themselves. To… keep me a secret. I cleared my throat. "Do… do vampires have the ability to place wards?"

All three heads whipped in my direction. While I could see Julie's confused expression from the corner of my eye, Moya tipped her chin up in realization. "The man in the market."

I just nodded.

"What are you talking about?" Julie shifted where she sat and unfolded her legs from beneath her.

I took a stilling breath and flexed my fingers in my lap. "Cillian and Celadine are vampires." I struggled to get the word out.

Julie's eye slowly bulged in the sockets, and her hand came up to cover her mouth. "What?" She shook her head. "No, that's not possible."

Moya then grabbed an apple from a small basket on the countertop and bit into it as she watched Julie piece things together.

"It was a shock for me, too," I said with a tickle in my throat.

"No, I mean, it's not possible," Julie urged and dragged herself across the sofa to face me. "I would have known."

Moya pointed a finger with the hand that held the apple, brows raised. "Yes, that's true. I didn't feel it in the market. I'd only known because I smelled fresh blood on his breath. Plus, his general appearance." She rolled her eyes, and I knew exactly what she meant. Too perfect. Too beautiful. A predator in every sense of the word. "Although, his eyes were not black."

"Black eyes?" I questioned and pulled the ivory knitted blanket from the back of the couch, bundling it to me as I recalled the kiss. The one that left Cillian's eyes black.

Moya tossed a grape on the floor, and Lattie chased it like a cat.

"Vampires are known in our world for their black eyes. And, because Fae are natural prey to vampires, we have an extra sense to protect ourselves."

I rubbed at my face. "An extra sense?"

Julie fidgeted with the sleeves of her white hoodie. "Yeah, sort of like a spidey sense. It's almost like a little *ping* of nausea when we're close to them." I blinked at her. "I never got that around either of them."

"At all?" I wondered why I still questioned it because

part of me knew there was truth there. Cillian and Celadine must be different.

"Are you sure they're vampires?"

I mindlessly reached for my swollen lip, and Julie let out the tiniest sharp inhale, and our eyes met. An understanding passed between us, and my eyes glossed over. Julie stood up and put on a smile for Moya.

"Thanks so much for helping us out."

"Of course," Moya replied and wiped her hands together as she chewed the last of her snacks.

Something Lattie once told me, a small passing detail, poked the back of my mind. *If you feed a Fae, you'll never get rid of them. They're like stray cats.* Moya said her goodbyes and was gone in a poof.

Julie immediately spun to me, her smile fading. "Tell me everything."

I collapsed back on the sofa with a huff. "I don't... I don't even know where to begin."

"Start with the facts," she said and sat next to me, her expression moving with concern. "How did you get that fat lip? Did he hurt you?"

"No," I replied with a cringe. "Not... exactly. I found out what he was, and I freaked."

She nodded in understanding. "That's why you went home."

"Yeah, I just needed to get away from it all, y'know? To

clear my head." I pressed my lips tightly in thought. "But then he found me. He *knew* how to find me. He showed up in Tess's backyard, wanting to talk. To convince me not to quit my job–"

"You quit?" Julie balked, and I just gave her a tipped look. "Oh, right, yes. Vampires. Continue."

I shook my head, assembling my thoughts. "One thing led to another, and I kissed him."

"*You* kissed *him*, or he kissed you?"

"I kissed him," I said begrudgingly. "And turns out, I'm not that great at it." I'd kissed guys before back home in our one-horse town. But they'd been innocent pecks of teenage curiosity, nothing like the hot, passionate show Cillian and I put on. "I clumsily smashed my mouth to his, and my lip cut on my tooth. And... the blood..." I could hardly finish the sentence. The vivid flashes of his cool mouth on mine, his teeth biting ever so slightly, his tongue sucking the blood from my wound. All the while... he still kissed me. The most mind-blowing kiss. "Anyway, I told him to leave. And he did."

A long period of silence hung in the air. Even Lattie, perched on the arm of the sofa, was quiet. Julie gnawed at her thumbnail, her gaze distant.

"So, your boss and boyfriend are vampires," Julie seemed to say to herself as if she just couldn't grasp the fact. But she lived in this world, this crazy mythical world.

Why was it so hard to believe?

"He's not my boyfriend." The words cut like a knife, and my heart squeezed.

She took a deep breath and exchanged a quick glance with Lattie. "Well, what do you *want* him to be?"

"Does it matter what I want?" I said hopelessly. "He's a vampire. I'm nothing more than a meal to him. This whole time… he's been setting the trap."

"But it makes no sense. I've been around vampires before. I got nothing when I was around the two of them. I didn't even suspect they were otherworldly at all."

I hugged my knees to my chest and stared at my best friend with glossy eyes. "What do I do, Jules? Cillian and Celadine had inexplicably woven themselves into my life. I can quit my job, I can tell Cillian to leave me alone, but will that really stop them?"

"I think the real question is if it's even necessary. I mean, it feels a little over the top, the way they've sought you out. The time they've both invested into gaining your trust."

"I've never known a vampire to drag out a kill so long," Lattie finally chimed in. I cringed at the word kill. As if I were nothing more than a cornered deer. "They're known to be civilized when they want to be. When they need to be. But good?" Her head shook sadly. "I'm not sure."

"How can I get the answers I need?"

Julie stood and paced with a pondering look. "We do a little recon."

"What?"

She grinned. "You know where they live. Let's go. Sneak around, listen in. Peer in windows. See how they behave when you're not around."

"Jules, it's the middle of the god damn night."

She shrugged cheekily and fetched her coat from the back of a chair. "Perfect time to spy on vampires, then. Don't you think?"

***

Even though I'd nearly lost my life to a kelpie or the fact that the sun would be up in a few hours, Julie and I trekked across the quiet downtown with Lattie in tow. My mind was spinning. Questions, so many impossible, unanswered questions. It didn't feel real. That I had... magic. Power of my own. This blinding, burning light that lay dormant under my skin. I wondered how I'd made it my whole life without knowing, without it surfacing in some way. One fact pounded in my chest; there was no way I could wait for Moya to get me into the Temple of Dreams. I needed answers now.

"Jules?"

"Yeah?" she replied absently as she scanned the empty streets.

"Would you go to the Blood Reader with me?"

She skidded to a halt. "What, right now?"

"No, no," I replied. "Tomorrow?"

Understanding filled her expression. "Yeah, of course. I have a shift in the cafe, but right after?"

She had to work tomorrow, and here she was, traipsing through the city in the middle of the night with me to spy on vampires. I didn't deserve her. "Thanks." I checked the street sign just a few feet away, barely visible under the dimming streetlamp. "It's just the next street over."

We crept up to the dense, perfectly trimmed hedges that surrounded the outer iron gates of Celadine's Victorian mansion and ducked below the cover they provided, only peeking over the surface to look for any sign of movement.

Most of the windows were dark, but a few on the main level glowed with a soft yellow light that spilled out into the gothic garden boxes under the windows. I adored this house, so dark and lovely with its pristine historic features. The wrap-around veranda was painted black to match the ornate trim work that crawled over the deep purple exterior. I glanced at the curved glass sunroom and guffawed at myself at the idea of a vampire needing such a thing.

"What if they spot us?" I whispered to Julie and Lattie.

"Do vampires have, like, special abilities or anything?"

"Some do," Julie replied, her eyes narrowing in the dark as she peered at the house. "Some don't. And they're all different. I've heard of vamps with the ability to fly, others with super speed, cloaking, hypnotic powers—"

"Mind reading," Lattie added.

"*Mind reading?*" I swallowed nervously, suddenly second-guessing what we were about to do. I wondered then if Cillian had those abilities. It would explain how he always seemed to know where I was or what I was doing. Or my favorite band, favorite food. I felt the color drain from my face. "Let's do this before I change my mind."

We snuck around to a bald spot in the hedge, and Julie touched the black metal fence. "There're no wards." Before I could form a reply, she gripped a picket in each hand and curled her fingers around them until they… disappeared.

"How did you do that?"

She wasted no time stepping through the opening she had just created. "Just another parlor trick," she said. "Come on."

I followed her, and Lattie fluttered close behind as we snuck through the darkened yard. We crept over to one window with light inside. The kitchen. It appeared to be empty, so we moved to the next one.

A beautifully decorated living room, similar to the front room I'd sat in. Dark wainscotting lined the walls, and gothic golden-brass fixtures hung from them. Stark white tufted furniture was arranged neatly, and Celadine draped across the long Victorian style sofa, dressed in a black silk kimono as she sipped on a glass of red wine with boredom.

Was it blood?

Cillian stood leaning against the wall, his body tense, his arms folded tightly to reveal parts of his muscled forearms. My breath caught in my throat as I stared at him. And another figure occupied the room with them. A man. Older, but all the key features of a vampire. I noted the absence of black eyes, though. Just unnatural baby blues in shallow pits, a stark contrast against the all-black suit he wore. He looked like the devil incarnate, come to Earth to make a bargain.

"I urge you to consider my offer," the man spoke to Celadine, who remained on the couch like a lazy cat.

She seemed so unbothered by him. "I've already given you my answer, Botwood. Several times. I have no desire to become a token member of your little council."

The man, Botwood, clenched his fists at his sides. "To-ken–*little* council…" He stopped and took a deep breath. "Vampires are flocking to the city in droves, from all around the world. You've no idea what we're trying to establish here, Miss Danes."

Cillian pushed off the wall. "And we don't care to

learn." He stood a solid foot taller than Botwood and glared down at him. "We want no part. We never have." I drank him in, every inch of him. "It's been made very clear what you all think of my sister and me. For years now. And we're perfectly content remaining on the outside where you've pushed us." He took a few intimidating steps closer to Botwood, the black long sleeve shirt stretching over his tightening muscles as he pushed the sleeve up to his elbows. "But now that we're useful to you and your cause, you think we'll take whatever scraps you give us?" He laughed darkly. "It's not happening. Get out."

Botwood straightened his back as he stared challengingly up at the vampire that loomed over him. "Mr. Danes–"

"Oh, don't pull that Mr. Danes bullshit with me, Botwood. I said, get out. I'd advise you to listen before my hospitality expires."

The man opened his mouth to argue more, but Cillian's hand moved in a flash and gripped him by the throat, lifting him off the floor. The sound of his neck cracking was impossible to ignore. I stifled a gasp in my mouth, but it was enough to make the two vampires inside whip their heads right to where I crouched outside the window with my friends.

"*Shit, shit, shit*," Julie hissed and began ushering me out of the way. "We need to leave. *Now!*"

We clumsily backtracked the way we came and took off

running the moment our feet touched the sidewalk. Lattie soared high above us. My heart beat wildly as my chest burned with heaving breaths. But I didn't stop. Wouldn't stop until we were safe behind the wards Moya placed around our home. While the recon trip confirmed what we already knew–that Cillian and Celadine were vampires–I still had so many questions. About them, about me.

Like why, although I knew he was a bloodthirsty creature of the night who could lift a full-grown man by the neck with one arm... I still wanted him. More than I'd ever wanted anything in my life.

Chapter Twenty

I slept all the next day. Well, it was more like a deep, induced coma brought on from over exhaustion and mental trauma. Either way, I was grateful for it. Not just because I'd desperately needed sleep, but I knew I never would have sanely waited for Julie to finish her shift in the coffee shop so we could see the Blood Reader together. Even now, as I paced my bedroom floor in wait, there were still twenty minutes before she would be home.

So much had happened in such a small amount of time, and I obsessively pored over everything in my mind as I paced. Aside from the fact that an evil hell fairy was hunting me down, just in the last forty-eight hours… the kelpie attack, learning more about Cillian's secret. Vivid flashes of a black leathery wing, tar dripping eyes, those thick and oily scales as the kelpie's tail constricted my body, and my lungs filled with water. And then… the light. *My* light.

Or was it?

I stared down at my empty, shaky palms. How did I do it? How did I summon that light, and how had it never presented itself before? Not once in my life until I became exposed to this mythical world.

A cool breeze blew across my bedroom, and I looked up to find Cillian sitting casually on my windowsill. My blood stilled in my veins as I stared in disbelief at how soundlessly he'd appeared. Like a ghost.

Or a vampire.

"How… you can't come in here," I managed and blindly reached for the knife I'd begun keeping under my pillow.

He arched a curious, brazen brow and swung his legs over the edge, placing one leather boot on the floor. "Can't I?"

The wooden knife handle groaned in my hand as I gripped it tightly at my side. I shook my head and backed away, putting as much space between us as I could in my modest bedroom. "No, I mean, we have wards–"

He guffawed and set his other foot down. "Not very good ones, then."

No, they were solid. Moya had made them herself. *Anyone with ill intent will not be able to enter.* The sea maiden's words rang in my mind. But Cillian had entered without a hitch. Which could only mean… he truly meant no harm.

Then why were my senses suddenly on high alert?

He remained near the window, seemingly unsure whether to come any further. "Spying on me now, are you?"

My throat tightened. "How did you know?"

He tapped his nose with a sad grin.

"Let me guess? You could smell us?" I replied with a bit too much sarcasm.

"You," Cillian said pointedly, and those killer blues shot to my face. "I could smell you. I could be in a room full of Fae, Avery, but if you're there… " He took a deep, exaggerated inhale and shook his head. "And now that I've… tasted you–"

I cast my palm up to stop him. I looked away, biting down on my lip to keep from screaming at the memory. The one of Cillian's mouth on mine, his teeth gripping my bottom lip as he laid the most passionate kiss on me. Such a bittersweet mix of emotions stirred in my chest.

"That man," I said quietly, fixing my stare on the carpet. "Did you… kill him?"

"I try not to be a monster, Avery." The pain in his tone made me look at him, and he tipped his head, giving me a pleading look. "And Botwood's no more a man than you are. He's a vampire. Older than even I am."

I let his words settle on me. "And, how old are you, exactly?"

Cillian lowered his brow and looked at me through those thick dark lashes. "You sure you're ready to know that?"

I raised my chin slightly, my face stern. "Yes." A lie. I wasn't sure I was ready for any of it.

His beautiful face hardened. "Maybe I'm not ready then."

Impatience suddenly flooded through me. Enough of the word games and secrets. I was done with it.

"So, what *are* you ready to tell me then?" I angled the tip of the blade in his direction, and he eyed it with a lazy smirk. I wondered then if a stake would have been a better choice of weapon.

His shoulders slumped beneath his leather jacket. "I wanted to tell you I'm sorry," he said. "I want to crawl on the floor and beg for your forgiveness."

"For what?"

His chin pointed at my still-fat lip, and I self-consciously brought my hand up to cover it, embarrassed at the memory of how I'd behaved that night. A literal predator had his mouth on mine, and all I could do was demand more.

"That was my fault," I said, barely above a whisper. "I'm sorry."

He dared take a step closer but halted as I stiffened against the door at my back. "You have absolutely nothing to apologize for, Avery. *Nothing.*" My eyes locked with his as they widened at me. "You hear me. Nothing. You should never have to apologize for what I am."

I let the affirmation sink in. "Would you have stopped?" I wasn't sure I even wanted to know the answer. "If I hadn't pushed you away at my aunt's house, would you have stopped?" *Before you killed me*, I wanted to add. But didn't.

Cillian's wide mouth parted slightly as he sighed warily. Seemingly weighing his answer carefully. "Yes."

"You swear?"

"Yes," his voice deepened, and my stomach clenched. "If you understand just one thing, let it be that I'd never hurt you. Never. I… couldn't. Not since the first moment I saw you."

"At that frat party?" God, I have had so many cringeworthy moments since moving to the city.

"No," he replied and stared off thoughtfully. "In Cellie's mind."

A toady wince choked in my throat. Was Cillian one of those mind-reading vampires Lattie mentioned? God, my thoughts weren't even safe around him, then.

"I can't see inside your mind if that's what you're wondering."

I arched a brow in question as my thumb rubbed against the hard, leathery hilt of my knife. "Can't you?"

"No, just my sister's."

I said nothing to that. I just waited for him to explain. Cillian's chest rose and fell.

"Cellie and I are linked. Mentally. And sometimes… emotionally. We can sense one another's pain, our happiness. Everything. When I learned she'd found a human to—" he cleared his throat, "get attached to, I was furious. Because it's not fair to me for her to take risks like that. If something ever happened to you, she'd be crushed, and I'd be forced to endure that pain. So, I began picking images of you from her mind to learn what I could about you so I might scare you away." He let that settle over me for a moment. "But I couldn't. Not when I saw what lurked in the shadows, watching you. Not when I saw that you so blindly surrounded yourself with immortal creatures. I watched you on the grass at that party, and I knew… I *knew*… I had to protect you at all costs." That navy stare set on me with such yearning that I wanted to weep. Cillian relaxed against my dresser, ankles crossed. "So, ask me whatever you want, Avery. Whatever questions plague your thoughts. Let me wash away those worries. I'll never lie to you."

I couldn't bring myself to answer him or say anything at all. The solemn declaration wrapped me in a whirl of thoughts and emotions, and I struggled my way to the surface, where I could think clearly. Cillian was so tempting, so beautiful, so alluring. Every word he spoke was like a call to something deep inside of me. Deeper than my own soul.

I could hardly stand being in the same room with him. This midnight predator, this immortal creature disguised as a man who just poured his heart out to me. If it weren't for the slight tremble in my legs, I might have forgotten where I was, standing in my bedroom.

All I could think about was how much I wanted his hands on me, touching my skin. A blaze of warmth trickled down my torso and pooled between my legs, and I clenched my thighs tightly. I wondered if he could tell the effect he had on me. The desire I harbored for him.

His fiery stare was answer enough. His fists clenched at his sides. Not in anger, but almost as if he struggled to reign in that same desire that mirrored in him. His muscled chest heaved ever so slightly, and I ached to run my hand over the defined lines of it.

I couldn't bring myself to face the big questions, so I settled with, "Is Sons of Galloway really your favorite band?"

Cillian reeled back with a silent chuckle and gave me a look that said *of all the questions*. His soft pink lips widened with a grin. "Yes." I didn't bother to hide my look of surprise. "One of them. Top five at least."

"Are you going to bite me?" The words rushed out as if with a mind of their own. "I mean, do you have a need to?"

Cillian's Adam's apple bobbed with a dry swallow. "Among other things, yes." Those predator eyes darted to my neck, and a tiny gasp caught at the back of my throat. He quickly added, "But I would never–I mean… I can control myself if that's what you're worried about. I'm not some blood-sucking monster."

Everything Cillian said felt right. Felt *true*. If only his expression didn't reflect the word he'd so carefully avoided.

But. I'm not a blood-sucking monster *but*.

"I actually have a question," he said.

I shot him an incredulous look and swept my hand through the air between us. "Oh, please, by all means." I could only imagine where this was going.

"What were you doing at my house in the middle of the night?"

"Looking for answers," I replied honestly.

"And? Did you find what you were looking for?"

"No." I chewed the inside of my cheek. "I only left with more questions." I stole a glance at my sketchbook on the bed, thankful it was closed, knowing it was full of images of him. Questions, questions, questions. Manifested in a notepad nearly filled with them. Cillian utterly consumed me.

"Well, when you're ready for answers, you know where to find me," he replied, and a cool breeze caressed my face as I looked up to where he was standing, mouth open and ready to really talk. To tell him I was ready.

But he was gone.

The front door to the apartment opened and closed as Julie's voice called out my name. I grabbed my green leather jacket from the back of the door and headed out to meet her with a sigh. I couldn't afford to fall prey to the distraction of Cillian. Not now, not when I had my own questions to be answered.

It was time to pay a visit to the Blood Reader.

✳✳✳

"Okay, don't tell him what you're after," Julie said in a low tone as we wove through the people at The Black Market. Steam shot up and out from a cauldron of soup at one merchant tent, and Julie expertly avoided it without a second glance. Her attention focused on me. "The Reader is still Fae. They're…tricky. Don't give him anything to work with, or he might find a way to lie to you."

"So, what do I say?" I could see the familiar black tent up ahead.

"Just ask for a reading and tell him to look closer, see what he can find."

I squared my shoulders as we reached the tent, and Julie pulled open the flap as I stepped inside. She followed close behind, and, just as before, The Blood Reader sat at a small round table. As if waiting for us. Aside from some sort of Fae light that lit the space, nothing else occupied the tent, a fact I'd been too shell-shocked to notice before.

The bald, sightless male inhaled deeply in our presence. "I require a mighty payment for the answers you seek, my child."

Julie said nothing as she tossed three of the same coins Moya had on the table. I made a mental note to ask about those later.

The Reader's long, pale, bony hand swept the coins across the table toward him. His blood-stained fingertips curled over them. He grinned and waved at a chair that suddenly appeared. "Your hand."

This time, I sat and placed my hand in his upturned palm with more confidence.

"I've read you before," he said. "Recently."

I leaned forward. "I wish for another. A… deeper one. I'd like you to see what you can find."

The Reader yanked my arm, bringing my wrist to his grotesque nose—nothing more than a slight bump on his face with two uncomfortably long vertical slits that opened and closed with every breath. He cocked his head as if listening to something we couldn't hear, and that grin turned wild.

Without releasing my arm, he fetched a small wooden

box from the floor at his feet and flipped it open on the table. A tiny golden dagger in a dark wood hilt lay nestled in a pool of small vials. Vials of just about everything. I had no idea what any of it was, but colors across the rainbow stared back at me. I desperately wanted to capture them on canvas.

In a flash, the tip of the dagger flicked across my palm. Blood oozed to the surface as I stifled a wince, but those bony fingers curled over my entire hand as he squeezed at the sides. His free hand grabbed a vial, one filled with white dust, and popped the cork with his sharp teeth.

"What is that?" Julie tensed at my side.

"Sands from the land of Summer, blessed in the Temple of Dreams," The Reader replied. "Very hard to obtain. But I just need a single grain," he added and tapped the vial gently over my wound.

A single grain of glittering sand fell into the blood that covered my palm, and immediately a blinding light filled the tent, pulsing from my hand in a blanket of gold. I shielded my eyes, as did Julie, but The Reader stared unblinking in wonder.

And with a vicious lick of his tongue–too quick for me to even cringe–darkness fell on us again. No, not darkness. The regular dim of the tent from before. So stark in the wake of the light that had just burned our eyes.

"What was that?" I asked. My voice didn't sound like

my own.

"Sunlight," the Reader replied.

"What?" Julie breathed, relaxing her arms.

"Summer sunlight, to be exact," he added with half a sneer. "You've got Summer blood. So slight, I couldn't pick it up before. But I see it now. The crumb." He slicked his lips. "It's stronger."

I swallowed nervously. "Would *using* magic make it stronger?"

The muscles around his pit-less eyes moved as if he could actually see me. "That would do it."

"So, are you saying that the more I use it, the stronger it will get?" I asked.

He sat stiffly as I glanced up at Julie, who wore a look of concern.

"It's very likely." His tone had a playful hint. "Aren't you going to ask me what else I saw?"

I whipped my head in his direction. "What do you mean?"

"Sometimes other images come to me during readings. Things I never sought." A devilish sneer.

Julie moved so close she brushed my arm. "Get to the point, Reader. What did you see?"

Those dark holes widened in delight, and he cast his arms out dramatically as if putting on a show. "Darkness."

"Darkness?" My stomach clenched, and I leaned closer.

"What's that supposed to mean? Like… death?"

"No, not death." His expression turned distant. "Something else entirely. The darkness, it's a living thing. And it calls to you." He snapped out of the trance that seemed to take him away and faced me directly, the corners of his blood-stained mouth reaching his eyes. "Avery Quinn."

"How did you–" The word died on my lips as I exchanged a panicked look with Julie. I'd never told The Reader my name. But I supposed he could see just about everything. I clenched my jaw. "Tell me more about the darkness. Is it Evaine? Is it the mad queen? The Dark Lord?" I slammed my fist on the table. "Something *else*?"

"Av', let's just go," Julie said uneasily.

The Blood Reader knew my name. It was only a matter of time before word got back to Faerie, and I'd have more than just Evaine to contend with.

"No," I said firmly and twisted in my seat. "I came here for answers. I'm tired of spinning with questions about my own damn life." I narrowed my eyes at him. "Tell. Me."

The Reader, unfazed by my determination, leaned back in his chair that moved with a life of its own as the spires grew and curled behind him until it became a small throne of sorts. He flipped my coins over the backs of his fingers. "Your time is up."

"I've got more money," I said desperately and shot a hopeful look at Julie, who gave a quick nod.

"Oh, I don't think you possess the fortune I require for those answers," he taunted with an eerie coo.

Shadows moved outside and shifted across the floor where the tent's fabric didn't touch the floor. "Come on, Av'," Julie said nervously, eyeing the shadows. "Let's get out of here."

I stood and slammed both hands on the table. "No! I came here for answers, and you didn't give me a single one!"

The Reader's bloodied lips pulled back over its teeth. Challenging. I'd pushed too far. "Don't be throwing demands around my home, girl. Did I not tell you what's in your blood? The power you possess?"

"This power. Will it help me? Can I use it against the darkness?"

"Yes and no."

"What kind of answer is that?" My eyes bulged. "Tell me something useful!"

Julie tugged at my arm, hauling me closer to the exit. "Av', come on—"

"You'll find your answers in the Temple of Dreams."

Everything came to a halt, and I exchanged a quick glance with Julie before eyeing The Reader. "In Faerie?"

"Your time has expired."

And he was gone. Table and all. We stood in an empty, dark tent, and I followed Julie out into the bustling crowd of The Black Market. But it was all a muffled noise in my ears, competing with the hot thumping of my pulse. I hugged myself tightly, brimming with emotions.

"Are you okay?" Julie asked calmly. My eyes stung as they glossed over. "Oh, Av', it's okay, don't cry—"

"I'm not crying," I said curtly. "I'm pissed. I'm overwhelmed. The more I seek answers, the more questions pile up." My gaze wandered to the dark booth at the end of the aisle where I'd once seen Cillian buying blood. "And the less I know about myself." The angry tears spilled over and ran down my cheeks. "How did you do it?"

"Do what?"

"When you realized you weren't normal," I replied. "How did you cope? How did you… go about figuring out who you were?"

She gave me a comforting smile and tilted her head to the side as she stepped closer, lowering her voice. "I've always been the same… me. I'm Julie. Yeah, finding out I wasn't human was a bit of a surprise, but deep down, I kinda always felt it. That I was different. I think it's why I jumped from foster home to foster home so much and always ended up back at the orphanage. People were naturally uneased around me. Until I met the Ryans. And I'm still discovering who I am, *what* I am. What I can do. It's not something you figure out all at once." She rubbed my upper arm with care. "But one thing I can promise you is that you won't go through it alone. Not like I did."

I cupped my hand over hers on my arm and returned her smile, immediately feeling better. "Thanks." Then I remembered Moya's suggestion to go to the Territory of Dreams. "Have you ever been to Faerie?"

"No," she replied and shook her head. "I'm Solitary. I belong to no Court or Territory. I have no place there." She waited a beat before continuing. "Plus, I'm willing to bet you can't get a decent cup of coffee there."

I laughed as I wiped at the wetness on my face with the back of my sleeve and blew out a cleansing breath.

"So, what next?" Julie asked.

"I have no idea," I said. "Wait for Moya to arrange that trip to the Temple of Dreams for me?"

"Well, until then," she grinned, "Shall we go shopping?"

"Shopping?"

She held up a small, light brown leather pouch and jingled it. The sounds of coins came from within. "Where do you think I got those paints I gave you?"

"I meant to ask about those coins, actually."

"They're made from precious metals mined in the mountains of Faerie," Julie began. "The raw material is pressed into coins in the Territory of Dreams and then circulated throughout the lands. The ones found here in Ironworld are worth a lot more than they are in Faerie, though. As you can imagine, they're hard to smuggle over."

I peered around at the market in a whole new light. The endless booths and merchant tents, packed together in haphazard lines, all boasting a range of goods. An old, withered Fae female, her hunched back covered in a knitted shawl, hovered over another smaller Fae as she mended her shredded wings with a glowing thread. The booth next to her displayed shelves of trinkets I didn't recognize. Strange things that looked like otherworldly versions of candles and kitchenware.

"So, how did you get them?" I asked.

She shrugged as we began walking past tables. "Odd jobs, various magical services."

"I thought your magic was limited to twirling coffee and an awesome glamor?"

She threw me a sidelong smirk. "I may have a few other tricks up my sleeve."

Indeed. I took in the booths with greater detail as we walked. Fae poured magic into bottles and passed it over the counter in exchange for those same coins. Food merchants with black cauldrons boiling with skinned legs of weird creatures sticking out. Animals unlike any I'd ever seen before hung from hooks and ropes, drying and curing. A healer of some sort mended an arm bent at an unnatural angle. I cringed at the sound of bones crunching back in place. But the person didn't flinch. Magic. It was everywhere here.

I considered then how I wasn't that different from them. These wondrous creatures. I had untapped magic and an ability to see the past, present, and future. I just had to learn how to wield it. Now that I knew what lay dormant inside me, I wanted nothing more than to nourish it. Wield it. Use it. I wouldn't be so vulnerable, so weak with control over my power. I could have a fighting chance against Evaine, against whatever darkness the Reader saw in my future.

Cillian's beautiful face flashed across my mind's vision. I wanted him. That was undeniable at this point, but he was powerful. He was a vampire. A creature of the night. *And I possessed the power of the sun*, I reminded myself. *I could kill him.*

I had to figure out how to use and control my power. I just hoped the trip to Dreams gave me the answers I sought.

"Hey, isn't that the Botwood guy?" Julie said and came to a stop.

I followed where she was staring. A familiar man stood at the same booth near the edge of the market that Cillian had once stood at. I squinted through the dim lighting and steam of the area and recognized the guy from Celadine's house.

"Yeah, it is."

She hushed me and pulled me off to the side as she eyed him warily. "And he's at a Therian merchant's booth."

"How do you know that? Do you have some sort of extra sense for them, too?"

She shook her head. Those sky-blue eyes locked on Botwood. "No, I can't tell a Therian from the next person, but the symbol on the crates by his feet." She pointed. "Look."

I narrowed my eyes at the stack of three small crates at his feet. A black wolf's head stamped on their sides. "That's the same symbol I saw on the truck at Club Umbra."

We crept closer, using tent flaps and stacks of goods as cover. The merchant opened one crate he set on the counter, and Botwood peered inside. He reached in and pulled out a bag, inspected it with a pompous sort of curiosity before placing it back inside with a single nod.

"And how many are ready to distribute?"

The merchant said, "Twelve hundred crates, sir."

Julie and I listened intently, just one booth away.

Botwood handed the merchant a wad of cash. "Be sure this gets delivered to the council on thirty-fifth."

"He must be talking about the vampire council," Avery whispered. "The one he was trying to get Cillian and Celadine to join."

"And I bet my life those crates aren't filled with human blood," Julie replied in a hiss.

I considered it for a moment. "You think it's Fae?"

"Connect the dots, Av'. You saw a Therian truck at a

Fae nightclub. A club where you also found all sorts of Fae in cages. And now we see a vampire ordering a shipment of blood from a Therian merchant?"

"But why would the Fae willingly treat their kind that way?" I asked. "Don't they hate vampires and Therians?"

"They do," she said and gnawed at her lip. "Come on, follow me." Botwood was gone, and she tugged at my arm as she sneakily led us around the booth. We crept as close as we could, and Julie crouched down as she rolled her hands together, forming a white ball of static in her palms. It turned to glitter, and she blew on it with a gentle breath, causing the particles to float toward one of the unattended crates, where it melted away into the wood.

"What was that?" I asked.

"A tracking spell," Julie said and turned away from the booth. I hastily followed her. "Wherever that crate's going, I'll know.

"And what then? You plan to barge into a vampire council and demand answers?"

She looked at me with more confidence and determination than I'd ever seen her display. "Not alone."

***

We barely had time to contact Moya before Julie's tracking spell was triggered. We brought her up to speed—

on the vampires and my trip to the Reader–as the three of us followed whatever magical tracking signal Julie felt or heard. Right to the vampire council.

An old stone structure with spires and arched windows of stained glass. We snuck around and peered in the windows. Nearly every room was vacant of vampires but full of wooden crates with a wolf's head stamped on the side.

I've never liked what I found peering through windows.

We found a vantage point in the thicket of trees that surrounded the back of the building, where a loading dock hung open, lights blaring out as three guys loaded crates onto a truck. The same truck I'd seen at Umbra. Moya narrowed her eyes at two men who stood near the front of the truck, and a third man hopped out of the driver's side.

"Sullivan," she spit.

"Who?" I squinted over the hedge and immediately shot back down. "Fuck. That's the guy from the nightclub," I whispered.

Julie paled. "It's also the brother of the Dark Lord."

My heart hammered in my chest, and I clenched my clammy palms. "Wait. So, the brother of The Lord of Nightmares is driving around with a Therian shapeshifter, delivering Fae blood to the vampire council?"

The three of us exchanged a wide-eyed glance and then shared a long exhale.

"It would appear so," Moya said, shock lacing her tone.

It was a lot to digest. The convolution of it all. So many mythical races, all despising one another, create this circle of hate and volatility. "Again, don't they all hate one another?"

"Aw, can't we all learn to get along?" a deep, raspy male voice spoke.

We spun around to find Sullivan standing there. Deep brown eyes that melted away in his brown hair and thick eyebrows. I noted his worn leather jacket had a splatter of blood dried to it. He grinned cheekily and eyed me. "Hey, don't I know you?"

My body froze. I'd run into this guy—Sullivan—three times now. None of them good.

Moya tossed him a vulgar gesture. "You're a disgrace to your kind. How do you sleep at night?"

Sullivan stuffed his hands in his pockets and tipped his head with a knowing smirk. "Upside down in a cave. How about you, sea witch?"

Before she could form an answer, two other vampires came out of nowhere and knocked Moya in the back of the head with a club.

"What the hell?" Julie balked and glared daggers at Sullivan.

He wiggled his fingers with a grin. "Now, now. The sea witch is perfectly fine. Just can't have her bippity boppiting you three out of here, now. Can we?" A knife appeared in his hand, and he twirled it around. "I mean, not before I ask a few questions, anyway."

"We don't know anything about anything." Julie spat and sidestepped toward me.

He stalked around us, turning us around in place. I wasn't about to take my eyes off him. "See, why don't I believe you?" He motioned to the truck in the distance. "Regardless, you've seen too much."

"You hunt and harvest your own kind for profit?" I said, surprised at my own voice. "You're a disgrace to Fae."

He let out a bark of a laugh. "Oh, you're spitey." He pointed at me. "I like you."

He continued to pace around us. More vampires appeared, closing us in, eying us like a meal, and panic fettered in my chest. Moya was out cold. She couldn't wisp us out of here. Julie claimed her powers weren't much better than parlor tricks. How were we going to get out of this?

Then I remembered... I had magic. *Sunlight.* And we were surrounded by vampires. But how did I summon it? It had been a fluke before, driven by emotions. I searched within myself for something different, something that shouted *this way! This is how you do it!*

But I was empty. As if there were nothing but a cavity in place of where I searched for it. Our only hope was to stall until Moya came to.

"Does… does your, uh, brother know what you're doing there in Ironworld?" I dared to ask, my lip trembling slightly.

He examined me with a full up and down sweep. "What do you know of my brother?"

"I know who he is. I doubt he'd approve of you selling the blood of his people to vampires."

Dark chuckles moved through the crowd of vampires. "You clearly don't know my brother, then." He motioned tersely to someone. "Take them."

Julie and I fought the entire way to the large open space of the front half of the building. And I realized it was clearly once a church. How ironic. It took a vampire at both our heads and feet to get us inside. A bloat of air chuffed from my lungs as they tossed the three of us on the cold stone floor before an altar where five vampires sat in a row of chairs. Each sitting stiffly with black robes pooling at their feet.

Blood seeped from the back of Moya's head, and we immediately scrambled to her unconscious body as we stared back at the creatures glaring down at us. Glaring as if we were nothing more than vermin, with eyes as black as night.

"Who are you?" demanded a female vampire with a tight blonde bun atop her head, held in place with an intricate bramble of black iron.

"People in the wrong place at the wrong time," Julie

assured her. "We'll just leave, and you can pretend we were never here."

Sullivan stepped forward, hands in his worn black jeans. "They were lurking around the bushes, watching us."

The female narrowed her all-black eyes. "Why were you spying?" When we didn't reply, she continued, "Why is Moya the Maiden with you?"

A male shifted in his gaudy seat. "Did the Lord of Summer send her?"

Julie was like a steel box, refusing to give them anything. My mouth gaped open as words blindly spilled out. "We… know nothing. I swear. We don't have the answers you're asking for. And we didn't see—"

"Well, if you have no answers, no information, then you're of no use to us," the male said as his fellow vampires sat by idly. He regarded them before nodding a chin to someone at the back of the spacious room, and a swarm of vampires closed in on us. Trapping us in a circle of blood-thirsty predators. The male on the platform grinned wickedly. "Except for one thing."

My heart pounding, I looked to Julie with a hopeless expression and reached for her. She grasped my hand, and the female vampire snapped her fingers once, signaling the swarm to close in more. A mix of black eyes and ones with varying colors of contacts widened with delight, and white teeth flashed. They were going to eat us.

Julie and I huddled closer over Moya's body, and she whispered, "I'm sorry," before ducking her head down in defeat. What could we do against a circle of a dozen vampires?

But I wasn't ready to give up. I gripped both her hands tightly and closed my eyes, searching for that speck of sunlight that roamed around in my body. That drop of power I possessed. *Please*, I begged it. *Help me.*

Something warm blossomed in the gallows of my gut, so slight I nearly missed it, but I dove for it, for its warmth and protection, and I clutched it. The ball of light grew and grew, flooding my body and pulsing at the seams that held me together. Almost as if asking for permission. I gave a mental nod, allowing that power to explode from my pores like a sun flare. The pressure and force were almost too much to handle. And my back arched as a scream erupted from somewhere deep inside me. A scream matched in sequence from voices in the room.

Then, like an elastic band pulled too tight, my power snapped back to me, and I collapsed on top of Moya's body. I felt her stir under my weight. Slowly, I peeled my eyelids open and looked at a stunned Julie; her face gone utterly white as she gawked at me in disbelief. Both our chests heaving.

Ash rained down on us and, as I tore my panicked stare from my best friend and we both took in the scene around us, I noticed we sat in the center of a perfect circle of ash. The vampires were gone. All except the ones sitting in chairs on an elevated platform.

Sullivan appeared from behind a closet door, his expression like Julie's. Only he smiled and pointed at me. "You!"

Moya groggily came to, and I saw the rushing impact of the scene snap her to full attention. She tensed and looked at us. Then to Sullivan with a glare. "Traitor."

"You're one to talk, sea witch," he replied. "Looks like you've been holding out on us." Those brazen eyes glided to me.

Julie grabbed me and touched Moya's back. "Go!"

In an instant, we were gone. The last image I saw was Sullivan running toward us. We plopped right in the middle of our apartment, where Moya immediately collapsed on the couch. The rush of magic, so much magic… left me humming.

"Are you okay?" Julie asked Moya, whose skin had lost that coppery shimmer. Dark circles formed beneath her eyes.

Lattie appeared, and we brought her up to speed. Moya already looked better, the magic replenishing and seeping back into her skin.

Julie turned to me with a thoughtful expression. "Is that what you did with the kelpie? The light thing?"

I shook my head. "No, what happened with the kelpie

was absolutely nothing compared to what I just did."

Moya sat up, all signs of wear gone. She was radiant. "That was you? The vampires, the… ashes." Her deep-sea green eyes widened at me. "Did *you* do that?"

I nodded. "I went to see The Blood Reader again. He told me–showed me–that I have Summer blood in my veins." I stretched out my fingers in front of me. "I can summon sunlight."

Moya stared off as she took it all in. A smile tugged at the corner of her mouth.

Julie paced. "I should have done something. I should have been able to…."

"To what?" I shrugged. "Jules, we're fine. We got away."

Her eyes glossed over. Her cheeks flush. "No, I should have done… *something*. You shouldn't have had to kill all those vampires. I totally freaked. If you hadn't–" She turned to Moya. "Can you teach me to wisp?"

"Yes, I can. But it'll take some time."

"Whatever it takes." Julie squared her shoulder. "Things are changing. Stakes are higher. My magic can only do so much to protect myself and Avery. I need to be able to get us out of a bind at any moment."

"Then I'd suggest learning from the best. Aya and Brie taught me. I'm sure they could teach you much faster than I could."

Julie nodded dutifully. "Sounds good."

I cleared my throat. "Moya, can you take me to the Temple of Dreams soon? The Reader had said I'd find answers there. About what I am, what I can do."

Moya smiled. "Of course. I'd just confirmed everything with a priestess today. We can go now, or do you wish to wait?"

It didn't take a second thought. "No. I want to go as soon as possible." It was the middle of the night, but there was no way I could sleep. "I'm done not knowing who or what I am." I remembered then, Julie, how she'd never visited her homeland. "Will you... come with me?"

"To Faerie?"

"Please?"

She beamed. "I'd be honored."

I gave Moya a single nod, and she gripped both our hands.

And then we were gone.

Chapter Twenty-One

We stepped out of the milky fabric of space and time right into the hollowed hallway of a castle. No, not a castle. I glanced around, shielding my eyes from the blaring sun that forced in through the stained-glass windows, arched with pointed shapes and trimmed with stone carvings. Not a castle, but a temple. The walls reverberated with the hum of deep chanting, a calm hum that caressed my nerves.

"Come," Moya said. "This was the only route I could secure on such short notice. We can't waste any time."

We fell into step on each side of her, and Julie asked, "How did you wisp directly into the temple? I thought there were wards up the wazoo?"

"There are," she replied with a knowing smirk. "But I

have a friend here."

I remained silent as we sped down hallways and around several corners. My mind and body still thrummed with the aftermath of using my unknown power. We passed several tall figures draped with golden cloaks that dragged on the floor behind them. They didn't raise their hidden faces at us as if we weren't even there, and I wondered if Moya had some sort of glamor over us.

We seemed to be slowly spiraling down through the belly of the temple. Past holy people, altars of candles and Faerie symbols, statues, and elegant carvings set in the stone-built walls. Open arches replaced the stained-glass windows, letting in a warm, sweet breeze laced with floral hints and something familiar. Something I couldn't quite place but tickled some dormant part of my memories.

A smattering of rooftops wound around luscious fauna outside and far below the temple. A village, an entire town, skirted the temple, but I couldn't make out the smaller details. We must have been hundreds of feet up. The Temple of Dreams was a tower.

"If the Territory of Dreams has no Lord or ruler, how do they govern themselves?" I asked. "How—why do the other Territories stay away?"

"It's protected," Moya replied as we descended to lower levels. I could feel the cold of the earth creeping in. "The Seelie King, long ago, before he disappeared, set the most powerful wards around Dreams to protect what's most valuable to us. Our knowledge, our histories. So, no one with ill intent may enter."

"And the people govern themselves. Living peacefully with one another. Mostly farmers and holy people." Julie studied everything with the same wondrous awe that I did, reminding me she'd never been here. She'd studied her homeland, knew almost all there was to know about it but never stepped foot here. I wondered what she was feeling.

Moya led us down a few more levels until the stone beneath my feet felt sturdier, solid. A ground level. A cloaked figure waited for us by a large wooden door held in place with thick, golden hinges. Moya walked right up to them and bowed her head.

"Solenna," she greeted.

The priestess gripped her hood and pulled it back, revealing her face. Beautiful and ethereal but regarded us with ancient wisdom. Skin and hair the color of clouds melted together behind eyes rimmed in gold. She smiled at her friend.

"Moya Seaborn," she said. "You'd said the matter was urgent, but I had not realized just how soon you'd be coming."

"Is it ready?" Moya asked hopefully.

Solenna nodded with a calmness I admired. "It is." She

swept a hand toward the wooden door. "I haven't done a Revealing in a few decades. What a treat." She glanced between Julie and me. "Which of your companions will I be working with?"

Moya took one step toward me. "This is Avery. We believe her to be a mortal Seer. But she also possesses a dormant power. We'd like to find what's blocking her connection to it as well as its limits and how she might wield it."

I bowed my head. "Thank you for helping."

Solenna smiled. "Of course. It's my pleasure. Shall we?"

She gripped the large lever of the door and hauled it open. We followed her into a spacious candlelit room empty of furniture or windows. A golden circle was painted on the stone floor. She guided me with a gentle hand into its center as Moya and Julie remained by the wall.

Solenna took both my hands in hers as she turned, and we faced one another. "I'm going to do a Revealing on you. It's a simple process that won't cause you any harm. I'm simply going to connect with your magic and follow it to reveal more. Alright?"

I just nodded, surprised at how safe and calm I felt in her presence. Her fingers curled around my hands, and the same humming I'd heard when we first arrived pulsed from her chest as she closed her eyes. Something like static crackled where our skin touched, and I focused on my breathing, keeping it steady and calm while Solenna channeled magic through me. I could feel it, her power, like a hunting dog sniffing curiously inside me. Stirring my belly and creeping around my mind.

She dropped my hands, and our eyes opened in unison. But her face was wrought with concern.

"What is it?" I asked. "What's wrong?"

"There's a block, indeed," she replied, sizing me up. "Something keeping your magic contained. But it's…" I tossed a quick glance at Julie and Moya, who waited patiently. "There's a Made bind. Someone wove it into your being. To hide not just your power, but to hide… you."

"Who would do such a thing?" Moya asked. "To a mortal girl." She arched an eyebrow at me. "Your aunt?"

Julie and I let out a chortle, mine a little more nervous than hers. "Tess? God no, she doesn't even believe in ghosts, let alone magic." I mulled it over for a moment. Why had my parents been murdered in the night? The killer was never found, and no motive could be reasoned. "Could maybe my parents have known? Maybe they did it to protect me? To keep me away from the magical world. If they'd known I would be some sort of Oracle…."

"It's possible," the priestess said. "The only way to know for sure is to find the one who performed the bind."

"But that's impossible." I shook my head.

Julie uncrossed her arms and stepped closer. "What

sort of being could perform such a thing? A Lord?"

"Yes," Solenna replied. "Also, a Healer."

Moya paced around the painted circle we stood in. "All magic leaves a mark. An essence. A... map. If a Healer was the one who contained your magic, then another Healer could map it out more easily than anyone else." She urged me with her eyes. "We could possibly find the origin, the mark left behind by the creator. With it, we could release your full power."

I chewed at my lip as I stared off in thought. Then it hit me. "Oliver."

She smiled. "Yes. I'm betting Oliver could help you learn more. That is... if you want to."

It only took half a second to consider. "I do. I need answers."

Solenna rolled back the sleeves of her cloak. "I can aid in your search. While I can't remove the bind, I can create a way around it to your magic. If you're ready."

I took a deep breath. "Yes. Whatever it takes. I'm ready."

Once again, the priestess held her hands out, palms up, and I placed mine on top of them. She wrapped her fingers around my hands and closed her eyes, but the painted circle on the floor lit up with a golden hue this time. The light grew and rose around us like a wall, and when it met at the apex of a dome that formed above my head, Solenna disappeared, along with the rest of the room, leaving me in darkness.

"Hello?" my voice rang out in the blackness and echoed back to me. I crept around, my footsteps loud and clamoring. There were walls, somewhere in the darkness, for sound to reverb off of. As if I wandered about in a pitch-black warehouse, empty of everything.

Almost everything.

Far in the distance, a speck of golden light formed on the floor, and I followed it. Beckoned by its silent call. It grew the closer I got, taking shape and form. A rose. A single golden rose, glowing with the light of the Summer sun.

The image flickered, and I blinked to focus. As the flower grew, its shape morphed into something else entirely.

Tiny sobs trickled outward, and I realized, as I finally reached the light, that it was a figure… a person, huddled in the fetal position on the floor. Not covered in the glow, but *made* of it. But the person was… me.

I kneeled down. "Hey, it's okay," I cooed gently and placed a hand on its back. *My back.* The figure responded to my touch and turned over to reveal my own face, stained with golden tears, staring up at me. I smiled and tipped my head in wonder. "You don't have to be alone anymore. I've found you." I offered my hand, and she just stared at it, like a scared stray, unsure of what to do. I inched closer, and she flinched. "Don't be scared, it's… it's me," I told her and placed my palm to my heart. "You've been waiting for me, haven't you?"

After a moment, she nodded. Her gold-rimmed eyes glowing with wetness.

I smiled. "I'm here now. I'm sorry it took so long for me to find you."

I offered my hand once more.

My light form reached out with trembling fingers, and the moment the tips touched my own skin, she exploded into a plume of golden rays. Each one shaped into a curled finger that dove for me, forcing itself into my body through every single orifice. Filling every crack of my existence. It was warm, too warm, but I relished in it. Like a missing piece of me had finally been put in place. I was... whole.

I stood in the darkness, me and the light-form now one, flexing my hands and arms in front of me. Strength and power hummed over my skin and under its surface.

"Avery!" someone called in an echo. Moya.

I searched around me, but there was only darkness. Thick and murky, slowing my every movement.

"Avery!" someone called again. Julie.

The sound of my name rang off the confines of the mindscape like a bell. Clamoring back to my ears. I walked and ran and searched, reaching blindly for the exit. Panic fettered in my chest.

"*Avery!*"

And just like the release of a drain, it sucked me back to reality. Only it wasn't the same as I'd left it. The window-less stone room we were standing in was now shrouded in impending darkness, a dense shadow crawling across the floor with clawed tips.

Solenne kept it at bay with a shield of crystal white magic as she swung her arms in the air while Moya and Julie toed the circle I stood in, panicked and wide-eyed, desperate to get to me. But I realized… they couldn't enter the ring.

Without another thought, I lunged for Moya's urgent hand just as Evaine smashed through the priestess's cover of magic. The ear-gouging sound boomed off the four walls as bits of rock crumbled to the floor. Julie gripped my arm and shoved me behind her as she and Moya stood with Solenne and formed a new shield of magic.

Evaine's solid form manifested from the inky shadow, rising from the floor as if absorbing the darkness. Only… she wasn't as I remembered from Ironworld. No, this was a beast unlike anything I'd ever seen in my life. The skin of a corpse. Matted black hair that almost looked like it was made of black smoke, with two twisted horns of raw bone curling upward through the mess. Wings of war-tattered leather dragged on the stone as her soot-covered feet padded across the floor, her wild eyes fixed on me, and she crooked a clawed finger with a devilish sneer, revealing rotten teeth.

Death incarnate.

"You've no business here, hell fairy!" Solenne bellowed and blasted a shot of white light at Evaine, forcing her back. But not enough. "You know the laws of this Territory."

Evaine cocked her head unnervingly. "Just hand over the girl, and I'll gladly be on my way." Her lips curled back in a frightening attempt at a smile.

"I'm not going anywhere with you," I spat, surprised at my own audacity. She could crush me in the blink of an eye, no doubt. But I would not back down. I would not show fear again.

"You have some nerve coming here, Evaine," Moya spoke as if they were old friends… or old rivals, and Evaine rolled her eyes. "I suggest you leave—"

Four inky whips shot out from Evaine's body, whipping through the air and wrapped around each of us like elastic bands. The black tendril choked the life from me as I gasped for a breath that wouldn't come. Evaine dragged me across the floor in the blink of an eye, my arms tight at my sides while my friends yelled for the hell fairy to stop. I kicked off the floor as I reached her and drove both feet into her gut, but it was no use. She was as solid and unmoving as a boulder. Pain shot up through my legs, buckling my knees. But something stirred inside of me. Something warm and assuring.

I felt my newfound power thrumming under my skin, and I took a deep breath. *Do it*, I whispered to it in my head, as if my magic had a mind of its own, and in an instant, my skin burned. The stench of seared and rotten flesh filled my nose, and Evaine let out a piercing scream as the thick ribbon around me loosened.

She reclaimed the other restraints, and my friends rushed to my side, ready to fight. But Evaine's sinister cackle stopped us all in our tracks. She backed away slowly, eyeing each of us, but giving me a look laced with a promise. And as quickly as I could blink, she was gone. Her unnerving laughter was nothing but a whisper in the air.

I turned to everyone. "So, that was Evaine?" The creature I'd encountered in Ironworld was hardly a Halloween costume compared to what I just witnessed.

Moya straightened, her face tight with anger. "In all her glory."

"I thought she couldn't get past the wards here," Julie said.

Solenne ushered us out of the room. "She must have tracked your magic, Avery." She closed and locked the door behind us. "And bypassed the wards somehow."

"That would suggest she knew I had magic at all," I replied.

"Evaine's shadows are always listening," Moya said. "That's why she's the best assassin and spy in all of Faerie." Her brows moved in consideration. "Perhaps the entire world."

I could hear my nervous swallow in the tense silence that followed.

Solenne turned to me, her lips pressed tightly. "Tell me it worked. The circle. Did you find the answers you were looking for?"

In response, my magic stirred inside. "I… did. I found a way to my power, but it's like… it's like it's not mine. I don't control it. It almost has a mind of its own."

Julie exchanged a look with Moya and then to me. "I think it's time to pay a visit to Oliver."

***

"Mapping a bind?" Oliver said as he blew out a long breath, his eyes distant in thought. "That takes some work." The troll's large leather boots clunked on the floor as he walked to the hearth, removed a boiling pot from the spit, and set it on a stone base next to it.

"Can you do it, though?" I asked. "Is it possible?"

Aya leaned against the door frame in the cottage as Brie sliced an apple for them to share. "Oliver can do it. He can do anything."

He guffawed. "Your faith in me will be my undoing." Aya chuckled and popped a piece of apple into her mouth. Oliver set his wrinkled gaze on me. "Creating a bind would be easier, but even then... I haven't done one in a couple of decades. I'll need time to gather some supplies and some time to unfold the map."

"How much time?" Julie asked from the table where she sat next to Moya.

He grumbled under his breath. "A couple weeks, perhaps."

"What do you need from me?" I asked.

"Aside from a few drops of your blood," Oliver replied. "Nothing. I'll let you know if it works."

I didn't hesitate to agree. I stood patiently as Oliver pricked my finger and drew blood into a vial.

"So, what do I do in the meantime?" I said as Julie rose from her chair and came to my side, ready to go home.

Oliver glanced at Moya before giving me a grave look and a shrug. "Stay alive."

***

Things like classes and shifts at the coffee shop seemed trivial compared to my new chaotic life filled with magic and danger. Almost as if it weren't even real. I felt like I was walking onto the set of a boring movie as I entered class on Monday.

Max grimaced as she took in the sight of me, and I knew why. I'd seen it for myself in the mirror that morning. Dark circles under my eyes, skin pale and tight from sleep deprivation.

"Jesus, you look like shit," she said as I took my seat and let my bag plop on the floor.

"Good morning, Max," I replied tiredly.

Her dark brown eyes immediately went to my lip, still red and swollen from the encounter with Cillian in my aunt's backyard. It felt like it happened in another time. So much has happened in the days since.

"Are you dating that guy?"

My brows touched as I pushed myself off my desk and sat up straight. "What?"

"The guy from the alley." Max gestured to my overall appearance with distaste. "Did he hurt you?"

I'd been to school several times since the incident with Cillian, and my lip and Max had said nothing. I must have looked worse than I thought.

"No," I replied flatly and let my hair fall around my face to hide what I could. "I'm not dating him."

"Good," Max said and turned in her seat to face forward as the prof entered the room. "He seems like a dick."

"You didn't even speak to him."

CHAPTER TWENTY-ONE

"I don't need to. I know a jerk when I see one."

I shook my head and laughed under my breath. "I assumed that's what you thought of everyone you meet."

Unmoving, her gaze set at the front of the class, she replied, "Not everyone."

I hadn't really considered how Max never seemed to talk to anyone. Not in class, not out in public. Not unless she absolutely had to. I'd never seen her with friends. But she talked to me. Quite a bit. In her own morose way.

Was Max my friend?

I swallowed dryly and fetched some supplies from my bag as I considered it. I couldn't afford to bring anyone else into my crazy world. It was too risky, too dangerous for everyone involved.

Screw that!

I came to the city to have a life, and I'd be damned if I'd shy away from it now for fear of… myself. I wanted to make friends, have a job, and go to parties. And… I wanted Cillian. A sense of absolute filled me, and I took a deep breath. I knew what I had to do. I had to learn to master my power, to control it. Not just for Cillian or Max or anyone else, but for myself.

Chapter Twenty-Two

The sky had turned a navy blue when I climbed the old wooden staircase behind the coffee shop. The sounds of cars cruising by the mouth of the alley filled the air as I fished around in my bag for my keys.

And suddenly, he was there.

Just like that. Cillian stood halfway up the stairs, gripping one side of the rickety railing. I didn't gasp this time. I didn't even care that I wore sweatpants. "Are you going to talk to Cellie?" he asked, his eyes glistening as they blended with the night.

My fingers gripped my keys inside my bag, and I held my breath. But the sight of him, below me, staring up with that promising glare... undid me. I let the keys fall to the bottom of the bag and gave him a smile. His shoulders relaxed at the sight.

"Not yet." I folded my hands in front of me. "I don't know what to say to her."

He dared a step closer. I didn't move. But my breaths came easy, and I waited for him to take another.

"You can trust her, you know," he said and placed a hand over his heart. "Trust... *us.*"

I glanced to the side, to where a small garden had begun growing. Flowers of every color, all along the edge of the old brick building. "I know."

The railing moaned under Cillian's weight as he leaned into my line of sight. The corner of his mouth turned up ever so slightly. "Have you figured out what you want?"

His words carried a weight I never realized would be there. What did I want? Cillian was a vampire. *And sunshine literally crawls beneath my skin.* Since moving to the city, I discovered so much about myself. That I wasn't as alone in this world as I'd always thought. That I had powers and magic, all the things I'd painted my whole life were real and before me. In all the chaos, one thing was for sure.

I wanted him. I wanted to be with Cillian, despite the odds against us.

I wasn't afraid of him anymore. But now... I feared my untamed power and what it could do. To him. To Cellie. I could kill them both if I wasn't careful. But I wasn't alone. I had help. Friends. Moya would help me hone my magic if I asked her. I was sure of it. And Julie, she'd help me in a heartbeat.

I brightened, and he took the last few steps, carrying with him the scent of leather kissed by night. He loomed over me, and I devoured his presence.

"I know what I want."

Cillian looked hopeful but hesitant. He leaned in, examining me closely, and slowly placed both arms on either side of my head as he reached for the door behind me. My heart beat wildly. It was all I could hear. And I was betting he could hear it, too.

Cillian closed his eyes, listening. A deep hum rasped from his throat, and he put his lips to my collarbone.

"The sound of your heart beating is so lovely."

I swallowed dryly. "Let's keep it that way."

Cillian pulled back and stared me straight in the face. God, his beauty made me want to freaking weep. "Does that mean…."

I looked up at him through my cold lashes, unable to hide my thoughts in my expression. *I want you, Cillian.* My breath caught in my throat as he leaned in and placed a kiss on my mouth. My mind struggled to keep up with my body, and I wrapped my hands around the back of his neck, pulling him closer. It was like taking that first breath on a cool winter's night. Yet, his mouth was warm. As if his very breath was chilled.

I bit his lower lip, and a mix of a laugh and moan rumbled through his body as he leaned his whole body against me. We slipped to the side, in shadow. But my heart nearly stopped, and Moya's words rang in my mind. *Evaine's shadows were always listening.*

In a gasp we both shared, I tore myself from Cillian and stepped back into the light.

"What's wrong?" he asked.

I hugged myself as I paced the tiny, rickety landing. "Actually, now that I think—"

"Don't you dare finish that sentence." Cillian's face twisted with a flicker of pain. And I knew... he'd walk away if I changed my mind. No matter how much he didn't want to. He sighed. "Give me one good reason why not."

I looked at him for a moment, weighing my options. I held out my cupped hands and begged the light to come. The tiniest ball of sunlight formed in my palms, and Cillian hissed as he backed away.

"That's why," I said, and the light disappeared. He gawked at me with the deepest look of awe mixed with a hint of—was it betrayal? "I'm sorry. I'm not... you're not the only one of us who's dangerous."

"What are you?" he asked, bewildered.

I shrugged. "Human, for all I know. I've got someone looking into it for me." Words I never thought I'd hear myself say. "But there's Fae blood in me somewhere, from far back. Some ancestor had sex with a fairy. Who knew?"

Cillian relaxed and smiled. "Indeed."

"I'm not saying no to this," I told him. "I just wanted you to know. First, before things progressed."

He shook his head, and a chunk of hair fell across his forehead as he leaned in closer, reclaiming that space between us. "I can't stay away. I've tried." His fingers gently combed my cheek. "I can't stop thinking about you. I can't settle with just *knowing* you. I have to be in your life, now even more than ever." He cupped my face in his hand. "You're worth the risk."

"The risk of death?"

"If I knew for a single second that you truly wanted to be with me, despite it all, I wouldn't care what reasons you had not to. I'd never leave your side."

My eyes brimmed with tears. "You think I don't want to be with you? God, it *kills* me not to be with you, Cillian. I can feel it, scratching under my skin every time I think about you, which—" I flapped my hands at my sides. "Is every damn minute—" He grabbed my face in both hands and slammed his mouth over mine in a crushing embrace.

My fingers wandered as I gave in to the kiss, to the power of it. Wiping away all that I was. It was just Cillian and me. Nothing else mattered. The very air around us seemed to still.

I found the hem of his black shirt and crawled my

hands beneath it. He tensed at my touch, but it only intensified the kiss. Cillian pressed me up against the door, and one hand dropped to below my jaw, holding my face as his tongue swept over my parted lips. A slight moan twirled up through my chest, and he smiled against my mouth.

I wanted to tell him the rest. The part where some evil hell fairy is hunting me down. It was dangerous to be with me for so many reasons. But I couldn't say anything, couldn't bring myself to conjure up a single word as Cillian enveloped me in a cloud of inky darkness. I stole the breath from his mouth as his right knee wedged between my legs, prying them apart while his hand slid into my pants.

Thank God I wore sweatpants today.

The tips of his fingers swept back forth over my hot skin, just inside the waistband. As if asking for permission. I rolled my hips ever so slightly in response, and Cillian dipped his open mouth to my neck as his fingers skimmed over my nerves. I tipped my head back and stifled a cry.

"Don't," he whispered heavily in my ear. His body moved and swayed against my body with every pass those fingers made over me. "No one can hear you. Or see you."

The words both unnerved and elated me. I let out a small cry of pleasure when his fingers finally plunged inside. Cillian leaned back, just enough to meet my face, and I stared into those endless pools of cerulean. A color that was quickly becoming one of my favorites.

We watched one another with matching breaths, and his thumb rubbed circles around my most sensitive spot. He pressed himself against me with a deep groan—I could feel the size of him rub against my inner thigh, and it was all I could do to stomp down the urge to gasp too loudly. A new delicious fear filled me.

"Oh, God, *Cillian*...." I rasped into the skin of his neck while his lips dragged over mine.

Those fingers knew exactly what they were doing. A rush of warmth flooded me, but not quite reaching the edges, and I rode the high, the motion of which Cillian moved us. Pressed up against the cold door, a wave of motion moving as one.

I buckled beneath the pressure of my building orgasm and fought back a moan. Cillian's mouth was slack as he leaned back and watched me, something seeming to build within him, too. Even though my hands splayed on the door behind me, bracing for what was to come.

I filled his hand in warmth, and we both exhaled long and hard as our eyes locked. And, right there, just humming beneath the surface of my skin, I felt it. My power. The static of magic and sunshine. Almost like a satiated cat. And for a moment, I felt... in control of it. The feeling elated me. Joining the high I was already on.

The culprit backed away, eyes dark and wild and fixed

on me. A grin tugged at one side of his mouth as he tipped his chin up and slipped one finger in his mouth... then slowly dragged it out. I held my breath as Cillian took one step closer and leaned into my ear, brushing the side of my face with his as he did. My eyes fluttered closed.

"I'm not going anywhere," he whispered.

A cool kiss touched my cheek, clashing with the hot goosebumps that scoured over my body as I opened my eyes.

And he was gone.

***

"I think I can control it," I said to everyone that filled Oliver's cottage. I shifted in my seat at his round table and stared right up at Moya, who hovered on her feet. "If I had some help. Just to get me started."

"Well, I'm happy to help you," she replied and waved an arm before crossing both over her chest. She gestured with a tip of her head toward her sisters, who lay sprawled over a wooden window bench together as they shared some kind of fruit I'd never seen before. Like watermelon crossed with pomegranate. "Aya and Brie would have a thing or two to teach you, as well."

Aya snickered and shoved a mouthful of fruit to the side of her cheek. "Absolutely. When we're not busy teaching this one to wisp."

I looked to Julie across the table, and she rolled her eyes. "You mean *failing* to teach me."

Brie swung both legs down to the floor and stared at Julie. "You'll get it. It takes time."

Julie just nodded solemnly.

"I didn't know you were having issues," I breathed. "Everything okay?"

She nodded. "It's fine."

Aya sighed, and I thought she would join in reassuring Julie, but she looked right at me. "Julie wants to be an expert immediately. She lacks the patience it requires to learn how to literally grasp the fabric of space and time." Aya's dark eyes flashed to Julie then. As if to say, *duh*. Even though she was a solid form in Oliver's cottage, I couldn't help but envision that ethereal, smoky skin I saw at my apartment. The sisters were dark and cunning beauties. I wanted to draw them.

Oliver's oafish feet clonked back and forth across the rickety floorboards as he worked. Still trying to map my bind. Julie told me he'd been at it non-stop.

I reached out and touched his arm as he passed me, two vials of some strange herbs in his hands.

"Thank you," I told him, and he nodded down at me.

"Thank me when I can figure this out," he replied.

"No luck yet?" I asked.

He grumbled gently and fussed with a mess of things on his desk beneath a window. "I've yet to start the mapping. I'm still gathering and preparing a few things I need." Oliver tried to smile as if he'd forgotten how to. But it never reached his eyes. Those two deep-set troll eyes. "But once I do, it shouldn't take long."

I returned his smile and the slightest twinkle danced in his one eye. "Well, thanks either way. For trying. For helping me."

Aya and Brie stood on one side of me, finishing a semi-circle with Moya and Julie, with Oliver in the back. Brie sheathed a dagger she'd been polishing. "You're one of us now."

"Yeah," Aya added. "One of the team."

Moya and Julie exchanged a look that almost seemed to say, *finally*, and Julie shrugged with a laugh as she looked at me. "We take care of each other." Her throat bobbed with a suddenly nervous swallow, and she raised those perfect dirty blonde eyebrows. "So… you in?"

I'd never had a group of friends. Never had a large family. It had always just been Julie, Tess, and me all my life. I'd never had a need or even a second thought for anything more. But as I regarded the group of misfit Fae in front of me, I knew. There was no question in my mind.

"I'm in."

***

I cupped my warm mug of tea to my chest as I stepped out into the crisp night air of the balcony. Cillian waited in one of the wooden lawn chairs, and I twirled inside at the sight of him. But I was determined to play it cool. I closed the patio door, muffling the sounds of the TV Julie and Tomas watched.

"Fancy meeting you here," I said and inhaled the steam that wafted up from my tea. My red wool sweater scratched the nylon of my black leggings, but I was grateful for its warmth against the Fall evening.

Cillian leaned back in his chair and tucked his hands behind his head. "I figured you'd venture out here at some point."

"You know, we have this thing called a front door." I didn't bother to hide the cheeky grin as I sauntered closer, my knee rubbing against his. "And I also have a phone."

His hands immediately went to my leg, wrapping around the upper part. His fingertips caressed my inner thigh as he stared up at me.

"Forgive me," he said with a coy, raspy whisper and tugged me closer. "I'm old-fashioned."

An old-fashioned… *vampire*? Because I didn't know of any men who just showed up on a second-story balcony.

"You're forgiven."

I stood between his legs until he pulled me down onto his lap–gently, mindful of my tea. I didn't feel his body even move beneath my weight. It was like sitting on a rock that bent and molded to me.

His thumb caressed my ear as the rest of his fingers wrapped around the back of my head. "I've missed you." The words brushed over my lips before his mouth found mine in a kiss.

"It's only been a day," I replied through a grin.

Our foreheads touched. "Long enough."

Something silvery moved in the corner of my eye, and I shifted on Cillian's lap to look up at the sky just as another one blazed by. A shooting star.

"Make a wish," I said with a content sigh and rested my head on his chest, still looking up at the sky.

He said nothing, only held me tight.

After a moment, he finally spoke. "You know, they meant something to my people. Shooting stars." I loved how the vibration of every word hummed against me. "They were a symbol of hope and new beginnings."

I sat up and turned to him. "Tell me more. About your... people. Tell me where you came from. Your past."

Cillian flashed that white smile at me. But something like sadness glistened in his eyes. He moved part of my escaped ponytail behind my ear. "That would require telling you my age."

CHAPTER TWENTY-TWO

I set my mug down on the table next to us. "I want to know. I'm ready."

His hand found the hem of my sweater and slipped up my back. He traced a lazy circle over my skin. Then he took a long breath.

"My sister and I were born in a village somewhere in Scandinavia before it was the region you know it to be today."

I picked through my brain for a map of the world. And I rifled through my thoughts for bits and pieces of what I knew. "So... Vikings?"

Cillian seemed hesitant.

"Older than Vikings?"

"Not much older," he replied, his face just inches from mine.

I stared into those hypnotizing blue voids, and I saw it. The depths of his life. A pair of eyes that carried wisdom and experience and such a sizable chunk of time.

I couldn't look away. "How much older?"

His whole body rose and fell beneath me with a heavy sigh. "Cellie and I will turn... four thousand years old next summer."

Those fingers stilled at my back. He waited, holding a breath, surely expecting me to run away screaming. But I just shifted closer and wrapped my arms around his neck, bringing my lips right up to his.

"Are you scared?" he asked softly. "I'd understand if that's too much. The age, the time–"

"Tell me more," I whispered against his mouth and placed a kiss there.

He waited for my kiss to end. But his embrace tightened. As if he were afraid that I'd change my mind and go.

"We grew up in a small village," Cillian began. "We weren't the nomadic Vikings you know of. We didn't roam the seas, pillaging and conquering. We were a peaceful lot, for the most part. There were warriors, mostly for protection against other tribes. But there were also healers, mothers, fathers, teachers, cooks. And… witches."

"Witches?" My brows raised.

"Our mother was the high witch," he continued. "With my sister under her wing. Until… a vampire rolled into our town." I tensed, but Cillian held me close. "He killed so many in the dead of night. Cellie and I woke up to the sound of our mother's scream and rushed over to her cabin, only to find his teeth clamped down on her neck. Cellie and I tried to fight him off. It worked, he let her go, and she scrambled away. But we weren't so lucky. The vampire snapped our necks on the spot."

I pushed away from him. "*What?*" I wasn't expecting that. I'd assumed… a vampire turned him and his sister. "So…." I blinked through the confusion. "How?"

Cillian gave me a grave smile. "The village warriors

managed to take down the vampire in the end. And our mother used its blood to perform some sort of spell–a ritual–to bring us back to life. Only…."

"You came back as vampires."

He nodded, and I kissed the side of his mouth to assure him everything was fine. "But we're slightly different from your average, heartless killer."

"Oh, God, please don't tell me you drink animal blood and sparkle in the sun," I gasped sarcastically.

Cillian tipped his head back and let out a howl of laughter. All dread gone from the moment. He squeezed me in a crushing embrace and planted his mouth down on mine. A kiss that devoured.

He pulled away, taking my breath with him. "No, I can spare you that." He cleared his throat. "We don't prey on people. I buy my blood from the Black Market."

"What about Celadine?"

Nothing but love filled his gaze. Love for his sister, his twin, the one that'd been with him since day one. "Cellie's special. Before she turned, she learned so much from our mother and quickly became a powerful witch. When she turned… she didn't feel the desire for blood. I mean, she could drink it if she wanted to, and it would satiate her. But it's energy she wants most. Creative energy is the best."

Realization swept over me. "The gallery."

"Yes, the gallery. The trove of talent that she curates

there. She was even once in love with an artist."

"Really?" I asked, and Cillian nodded. "A human?"

He nodded again. "His name was Derek, he was a tribal tattoo artist she'd met a few hundred years ago, and she loved him more than anything in the world." He flashed a grin. "I mean, aside from yours truly." I slapped at his chest. "But, when he died… his death consumed her, and, with the mental bond between us, I just couldn't stand to be around her for decades. I'd only just come back a few weeks ago when I could feel her pain lessening. When I realized *why* it had been lessening, that she'd found something… someone to fill that void in her heart."

I gasped. "Wait, what? *Me*?"

Cillian gripped my chin between his thumb and finger. "Yes, you. She adores you like a sister. She wants to teach you everything she knows. About art, about everything."

I thought then how one of my worries was that Cillian was immortal. He'd live forever, essentially, and I would just age and die. But now, I wasn't so sure of my actual lifespan. If the Fae blood and abilities granted me a longer life or not. The last mortal Oracle lived hundreds of years. I stared at Cillian with a hopeful look. I wanted to live a longer life, to spend it with him. As crazy as that sounded.

But he deserved to know how dangerous it was to be with me.

"Cillian." The dread in my tone made him stiffen. "I–if

we're going to be together, it's only fair for you to know everything about me first."

He visibly relaxed. Did he actually believe I'd scare that easily? His backstory was practically a bedtime lullaby compared to what now circled me. His large hands cupped my body in his arms and squeezed me tight.

"A bit of sunshine and magic isn't exactly alarming, Avery." His fingertips dug into my behind. "It only makes you even more tempting."

Warmth pooled between my legs, and I squeezed them together as I traced his bottom lip with my thumb. "No." I planted a kiss there. "Not that. I mean, it has to do with that, but the real danger is this hell fairy named Evaine. She's an assassin that someone in Faerie hired to hunt me down."

Anger flared in his eyes, and a subtle growl rolled over somewhere deep inside of him as realization swept over his beautiful face. "The creature in the woods outside the gallery that night."

"How did you—"

Cillian tapped his nose.

My smile didn't reach my eyes. "That's why I wanted to keep my distance from you. To keep *her* away from you and Celadine. We don't know who hired her or why, exactly. Just that she's determined to lure me away to Faerie." I shrugged inside my oversized sweater. "Now we're thinking it's something to do with the fact that I'm also some kind of mortal Seer."

Cillian's face lit up with wonder. "An Oracle?"

"You've heard of it?"

His gaze turned distant for a moment. "Yeah, a long time ago. A mortal Oracle had escaped Faerie after the Great War, slipped away under the protection of the Therians, apparently."

"What happened to him?"

"No one knows," he replied. "My guess is he eventually died. Being mortal, I doubt his life was long."

I shook my head. "But it was. He'd lived for centuries before the war. In the Seelie King's grasp."

"Oh, well, I'd say the Oracle probably died an unfortunate death then," Cillian said gravely. "Ironworld is full of diabolical creatures. Something as rare as a Seer... I can just imagine what his blood went for on the Black Market alone."

I shivered, and Cillian shifted in the chair, suddenly realizing the weight of his words. His mouth gaped apologetically. "Avery, I didn't mean—"

"Yes, you did," I told him. "And you're right. Which is all the more reason to really consider whether it's worth the risk of being with me."

Cillian's hand wrapped around my back as the other slowly slid between my thighs. "Avery, it's going to take a lot more than that to scare me off."

"You mean…" I hesitated a moment, carefully weighing my words. "Impending doom aside, don't you prefer me to be…*human*? I mean, I am. Human–"

His dark laughter rocked through me, and I melted in his arms as Cillian buried his face in my neck. "I'd take you in any form. But knowing you have Fae in your blood explains why my own sings around you."

"Yeah?" The word came out in a crackle.

His skin brushed against my face as he slowly brought his lips to hover over mine. "Your very existence drives me mad. I don't know whether I want to eat you or be inside you."

His words were like a dark promise that reached the farthest corner of every one of my nerves. A gasp froze in my mouth as his came down over mine and devoured. Slow, sensual, and claiming. His hand slid higher up my thigh but waited for silent permission. My choice. It's always been my choice with Cillian.

I slipped my hand over his and guided it closer. He was growing beneath me already, his impressive size pushing against my bottom. I gently moved over it, teasing, and Cillian let loose a deep growl that seemed to envelop me with desire.

Noise from inside the apartment reminded me of where we were, and I glanced over my shoulder.

"Do you want to go?" he rasped in my ear.

A hot tremble rocked through me as his fingertips touched the apex of my thighs, taunting my opening through my leggings. I nodded.

In a flash, Cillian was on his feet with me tucked tightly in his arms.

"What are you–"

We took off into the sky like a bolt and moved through the sky so fast I couldn't even open my eyes. In a single breath, we landed on the rooftop terrace of Celadine's Victorian mansion a few blocks away. Through a wall of glass patio doors, I could see a small apartment adorned in dark wood, stone, and leather textures. A bachelor pad. This must have been where he lived.

He set me down but braced the space behind me with an outstretched arm. My head spun, but I focused on breathing.

"That's how you appeared in my aunt's garden that night and then disappeared without a trace." I stared up at him. Not a hair out of place. "You can fly?"

"I can." A chill crept over me as the cool night breeze tickled my skin. "So, what'll it be?"

He let silence hold the space between us as I digested the new fact and the question that meant so much more than a question. Cillian would never push me to accept him, would walk away if I met my limit of supernatural surprises. But as I let myself get lost in those pools of navy blue, I knew there was nothing he could do or say to turn me away. I only wanted more.

"I figure my life is destined to implode at some point. Whether that's good or bad, I don't know." A sigh jittered in my throat. "So, I may as well live my days as happily as I can." I leaned into him and kissed his chin. "I'm yours, Cillian."

His whole body relaxed with a sigh and drew me in with both arms, crushing me to his iron chest. He tipped my face upward with a finger under my jaw. "And I've been irrevocably yours since the first moment I saw you."

My hands slipped beneath his shirt and grazed the soft, toned muscles of his back. "Then prove it."

With a coy smile and a hungry look in his eyes, Cillian lifted me up, and I wrapped my legs around his waist. He carried me with ease toward the door, and the apartment moved in a blur at the edges of my vision before I felt the soft cradle of a bed beneath me. Black silk sheets surrounded us. The scent of leather and fresh soap filled my nose, mixed with the cool scent that always seemed to waft from Cillian's skin.

He stood at the foot of the bed where my legs dangled, and our gazes locked as he slowly removed my leggings and wool socks. I sat up and slipped off my sweater to reveal the olive-green lace bra I wore. My eyes dipped to where the crotch of his black jeans bulged, and I sucked in a quick breath as Cillian undressed in front of me.

If I thought he was beautiful before, it was nothing compared to the god that now stood before me. Cillian was a sight to behold. A looming expanse of moon-kissed skin over lithely moving muscles. I tried not to look but failed, and my throat went dry at the size of him.

"*Holy shit.*" I wasn't sure if it was thought or whisper, but his crooked smile told me the answer.

My bent knees trembled as he lowered himself onto the bed and removed my underwear in one swift movement. His nose touched my thigh and ran the length of it with an inhale that sent goosebumps racing over me. I tipped my head back the second his cool breath touched my most sensitive spot—arched my hips as his warm tongue slowly caressed it.

"*Cillian….*" I dug my fingers deep into his black hair. Pulled at its roots.

But he continued, and a guttural moan escaped as a shutter raked through me. Finally, he raised his head, his expression wild as he dipped his mouth to my breasts and tore down the straps to free them. I cried out again when his hand moved between my legs and picked up where his mouth had left off.

"I'd never let anything happen to you," he said in a breath against my sternum, making my nipples harden. I tipped my chin down, and he stared up at me while my body moved ever so slightly with his hand. "You don't have to be afraid of Evaine. She won't get past me."

An unexpected dose of brazenness flooded me, and I tightened my legs around him as I flipped us over. A ball of sunshine formed in my palm, but Cillian didn't flinch. *Trust.* That was trust that he showed… that I felt.

"I'm not afraid of her," I said. Surprised at my own declaration. But it was true.

I formed the light into a blade, reigning in the outer glow until it was a solid ember, and held it as close to his neck as I could. Cillian didn't blink as he stared into my eyes.

He leaned forward just a hair. "Then I'll fight by your side." A grin tugged at his parted mouth. "You, gorgeous, spiteful, delicious creature."

I kept the blade at his neck as I lifted myself onto the tip of him. He sucked in a sharp inhale. My back arched as Cillian's hand cupped both my breasts and slowly rolled my nipples between his fingertips. Waiting for me to proceed. Going at my pace. It made me want to drive the length of him into me, but I knew I'd regret it. This was going to take a moment.

Slowly, inch by inch, I lowered myself down over him. Down, down, until he filled me, and I braced my hands on his hard chest. My fingertips dug into his flesh as I rolled my hips and a curse seethed through his teeth.

"*Fuck*, Avery." He gripped my sides.

Wetness dripped down over him, allowing me to quicken the pace, to take it when his body began to move with mine. Driving himself further into me. Unintelligible sounds erupted from me in a stream of moans. Every inch of my body burned with the building of my climax, and I felt its twin rushing through Cillian as his whole body tensed and his hands tightened on my upper thighs to the point where I knew there'd be bruises there tomorrow.

I soaked up the energy and released it. And, as we rode that seemingly never-ending high together, I could only think of one thing. Whatever was waiting for me, whatever sinister creatures lurked in the shadows, I could face it all. Tomorrow.

With Cillian by my side.

Epilogue

The tendrils of a dream held me in place as I stared down at a room in a dimly lit castle. Walls of stone and floors of rustic boards. A man sat in a throne-like black wingback chair, draped to one side of it in boredom. Snow white hair fell to his shoulders. And through it...pointed ears. He was no man.

He was Fae.

"What news do you bring, sweet Evaine?" he said with a dull, unamused tone. The low tenor rumbled in my gut.

I glanced to the middle of the room. And there she was. Evaine. The pure embodiment of death. She bowed to the Fae.

"Milord." Inky, black ribbons swirled up and around her. "I've found her."

His storm grey eyes flashed and widened as he shot up straight. "Are you certain?"

Evaine shrugged and began to pace the creaky castle floors with her rotten bare feet. "I've been following her for weeks. Ever since the bargain came to life." Black talons gripped her upper arms as she crossed them over her chest. "But I could always gut her and see."

He flew to Evaine in a flash. Gripped her neck before his chair hit the floor. Forcing her to her knees. *Evaine. On her knees.* Who was this man, this... fairy? To have such power. All I could do was stare. I was a lifeless form, intruding on a dream. Or was it real? Was this some sort of vision?

"Please, Milord!" she cowered. "I promise to bring her to you unscathed."

He loomed over her for a moment, stared down in thought. "No."

"No?"

"Not yet," he confirmed and released Evaine. She scrambled to her feet and glared daggers into his back as he sauntered back to his chair. "Follow her some more. Learn all that you can and report back to me."

"What do you want to know?" Evaine's black eyes dripped tar down over her pallor cheeks.

He grinned and folded an ankle over one knee as he leaned back. "Everything. I want to know what makes her tick." A tumbler of golden liquor appeared in his hand, and he sipped from it. "I want to know how to undo her, inside and out. It's time." The Fae took another sip and stared off in the distance with a cunning promise in his eye. "To claim what is mine."

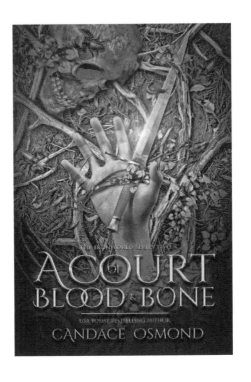

Continue Avery and Cillian's dark and epic love story in book two of The Ironworld Series, A Court of Blood & Bone!

Other Titles by Author Candace Osmond

Dark Tides Series

Kingdom of Sand & Stars Series

Silently Into the Night

A Touch of Darkness Series

About the Author

Candace Osmond is a **#1 International & USA TODAY Bestselling Author** and **Award-Winning Screenwriter**. She currently resides on the rocky East Coast of Canada with her husband, two kids, and bulldog.

Connect with Candace online! She LOVES to hear from readers!

www.AuthorCandaceOsmond.com

Check out all of Candace's book merch and signed paperbacks in her reader merch shoppe, Death by Reading on Etsy!